SABBAT MARTYR

A FIGURE STOOD upright in the Salamander's open-topped cabin.

The Beati looked down at Gaunt. She wore a suit of intricately-worked golden battle armour so fine and form-fitting that it had been clearly fashioned for her by master metallurgists. A halo of light surrounded her, so fierce and bright it made her seem almost translucent. Nine cyber-skull drones hovered around her in the radiant glow, forming a circle behind her head, their eyes lit, their miniature weapon pods armed. She was terrible to behold.

She smiled.

'I've been waiting for this, Ibram. Haven't you?'

'Yes,' was all he could say. He realised he was weeping, but he didn't care.

A WARHAMMER 40,000 NOVEL

Gaunt's Ghosts

SABBAT MARTYR

Dan Abnett

For John Ernest Vincent, regimental archivist.
Thanks to Gary Hughes and James Hewitt at
GW Maidstone.
Eleven willing volunteers from the Maryland HQ were
harmed during the making of this book. Let their sacrifice
not be forgotten.

A BLACK LIBRARY PUBLICATION

First published in Great Britain in 2003 by
BL Publishing,
Games Workshop Ltd.,
Willow Road, Nottingham,
NG7 2WS, UK

10 9 8 7 6 5 4 3 2 1

Cover illustration by Adrian Smith
Map by Nuala Kennedy

A CIP record for this book
is available from the British Library

ISBN 1 84416 012 2

Set in ITC Giovanni

Printed and bound in Great Britain by
Cox & Wyman Ltd, Reading, Berkshire, UK

See the Black Library on the Internet at
www.blacklibrary.com

Find out more about Games Workshop
and the world of Warhammer 40,000 at
www.games-workshop.com

IT IS THE 41st millennium. For more than a hundred centuries
the Emperor has sat immobile on the Golden Throne of Earth.
He is the master of mankind by the will of the gods, and
master of a million worlds by the might of his inexhaustible
armies. He is a rotting carcass writhing invisibly with power
from the Dark Age of Technology. He is the Carrion Lord of
the Imperium for whom a thousand souls are sacrificed every
day, so that he may never truly die.

YET EVEN IN his deathless state, the Emperor continues his
eternal vigilance. Mighty battlefleets cross the daemon-infested
miasma of the warp, the only route between distant stars, their
way lit by the Astronomican, the psychic manifestation of the
Emperor's will. Vast armies give battle in his name on uncounted
worlds. Greatest amongst his soldiers are the Adeptus Astartes,
the Space Marines, bio-engineered super-warriors. Their comrades
in arms are legion: the Imperial Guard and countless planetary
defence forces, the ever-vigilant Inquisition and the tech-priests
of the Adeptus Mechanicus to name only a few. But for all
their multitudes, they are barely enough to hold off the
ever-present threat from aliens, heretics, mutants – and worse.

TO BE A man in such times is to be one amongst untold
billions. It is to live in the cruellest and most bloody regime
imaginable. These are the tales of those times. Forget the power
of technology and science, for so much has been forgotten,
never to be re-learned. Forget the promise of progress and
understanding, for in the grim dark future there is only war.
There is no peace amongst the stars, only an eternity of carnage
and slaughter, and the laughter of thirsting gods.

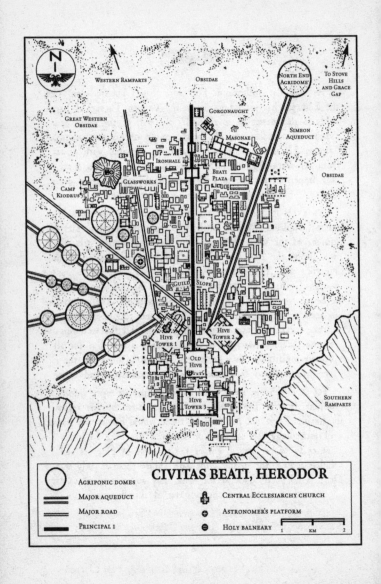

WESTERN RAMPARTS · OBSIDAE · NORTH END AGRIDOME · TO STOVE HILLS AND GRACE GAP

GREAT WESTERN OBSIDAE · GORGONAUGHT · SIMEON AQUEDUCT · OBSIDAE

MASONAE

IRONHALL · BEATI PLAZA

GLASSWORKS

CAMP KIODRUS

GUILD SLOPE

HIVE TOWER 1 · HIVE TOWER 2

OLD HIVE

HIVE TOWER 3

SOUTHERN RAMPARTS

CIVITAS BEATI, HERODOR

○ AGRIPONIC DOMES

▬ MAJOR AQUEDUCT

▬ MAJOR ROAD

▬ PRINCIPAL I

⚜ CENTRAL ECCLESIARCHY CHURCH

⊕ ASTRONOMER'S PLATFORM

⊕ HOLY BALNEARY

1   KM   2

'**B**Y 773.M41, the eighteenth year of the Sabbat Worlds Campaign, the Imperial crusade force under Warmaster Macaroth had yet failed to take the notorious fortress world Morlond. As long as Morlond stood, the thrust of the crusade was stalled, and Macaroth could not drive his forces onwards into a decisive war with the core military strengths of the archenemy overlord ("Archon"), Urlock Gaur, in the Carcaradon Cluster. More than ever, the crusade host seemed disastrously overstretched and increasingly vulnerable to flank attack. Already, Chaos hosts commanded by two of Gaur's most ruthless lieutenant warlords, Anakwanar Sek and Enok Innokenti, had enjoyed considerable success by counter-striking along the coreward portion of the Imperial thrust. If such successes continued, the crusade force risked being split in two, and the greater part of it, along with the Warmaster himself, becoming cut off, surrounded and annihilated.

'Macaroth was all too aware of the danger, and all too aware of the imponderable nature of the problem. He could not remain overstretched for fear of flank attack, but neither could he spare any forces from the Morlond front, as a weakening there would leave his vanguard vulnerable to Gaur. Either option seemed cursed with failure. Macaroth simply had to decide which one to risk. Famously, he showed one of his generals two identical cups of wine and asked him to pick one. "One is elixir, one is poison," he said. "How can I tell them apart?" the general asked. "By taking one up and tasting it," replied the Warmaster.

'Macaroth eventually decided to remain as he was, risking overstretch, and fight on to take Morlond with one last effort. In the third quarter of 773, Enok Innokenti began his murderous, catastrophic flank attack in the Khan Group. It was a time of disaster, looming failure.

'And miracles…'

— from *A History of the Later Imperial Crusades*

PROLOGUE

THE INTELLIGENCE, SUCH as it was, had been in their possession for a week. Yet two or three times a day, and more often during the watches of the night, He would review it, as if somehow He expected it to change.

Etrodai wasn't sure what that meant. He wasn't sure if it meant He was excited by the news, or disquieted. That troubled Etrodai enormously, for he prided himself on knowing His whims and moods like no other. Etrodai had been His life-ward for ninety-two years, had won that vaunted position by besting the previous holder of the office in a legal murder-fight. No one knew Him better than Etrodai.

Except now, Etrodai was no wiser than the rest.

All along the tarnished pillars and dusty alcoves of the Process, the cobwebs fluttered and the bones began to chatter. It meant He was restless again. Before the onyx door had even opened, Etrodai was on his feet, his changeling blade skinned and raised in front of his face.

Etrodai waited, attentive, apprehensive. The chatter became more urgent. The dry, beetle-clicks of the human skulls, most of them mottled brown with decay as if they had been varnished, were bearable enough. The sounds of the more alien skulls were harder to tolerate. They lisped and coughed, clucking like birds, ticking like clocks, disarticulated mouthparts twitching in the dust like dead leaves. Once, while He had been resting to heal a psi wound, Etrodai had idled the long hours attempting to count the skulls in the Process. He had given up around about ten thousand. They kept interrupting him and making him lose count.

A soft rumble, and the onyx door, tall as five men and as broad, slid back into the wet marrow of its hatch seal. Warm air exhaled through the gap. The bones fell silent.

He emerged from His inviolable chamber. The null field popped like surface tension around Him.

'Magister,' said Etrodai, keeping the blade raised but averting his gaze respectfully. 'What is your will?'

'I have made psyk-audience with the Archon, and now know his mind on this. He says that if the news is true, I must act according to my heart.' His voice was brittle, yet musical, like the notes of a bale-pipe or a sonoret, and always made Etrodai feel ashamed of his own ugly, mechanically-formed speech. 'And my heart tells me we must make this our first duty above all other concerns. Now, the instruments?'

'They're assembled, Magister. On the hinterdeck. All of those it was safe to assemble, that is.'

'I'll speak with them and charge them,' He said, then hesitated. 'But first… I will review this great truth one last time.'

Etrodai was not surprised. He turned and led the way down the Process, hearing each and every skull grate in its alcove as it turned to watch Him pass.

The Process, tomb-dark and lit only by ancient, crazed glow-spheres, was a kilometre long. At the far end, goat-headed slave-carls turned the iron keys and swung the towering brass doors open. The slave-carls looked at the walls and sobbed, terrified lest they should catch the slightest glimpse of Him.

Seven times thirteen men of the Retinue waited in the anteroom, under the gilt-arched ceiling and the flaking murals of the Five Atrocities. Their heavy boots slammed to attention in one perfect motion and they shouldered arms. Their flanged body-armour was blue-black like Etrodai's, and their heads were concealed under broad-tailed helmets and visors with bulbous, insectoid goggles.

With Etrodai leading, his sword pointing at the roof and skinned for so long now that beads of blood were welling up along its thorny edge, the Retinue fell in around them and marched in escort, right arms bent and locked around each shouldered weapon, left arms snapping free like pendulums at their sides. Two men ran ahead to open each set of doors in turn.

Access to the data crypt was sealed by a void shield that shimmered in the air like oil on water. It disengaged at His merest touch. Any other man would have lost his arm to the elbow if he had made contact. The Retinue waited outside as Etrodai stepped into the crypt with Him.

The data crypt was cold and dim, and ribbed with a porous tissue like calcified sinew. In the panels between the ribbing, the walls were etched with words from a pre-Imperial language. A foggy, hazy light billowed around their feet.

The secrets kept here whispered about them, hissing like steam or fat on a skillet. Their murmur was not as loud as the chatter of the countless skulls in the Process, but it was more insistent and far more repellent. Vile whispers settled around Etrodai, penetrating his armour, his skull and crawling into his brain, telling him things that he, even he, had no desire to know.

The intelligence had been placed on a pedestal near the centre of the crypt. It had been teased from the fused synapses of an expended seer gestalt and kept in its latent thought-form to preserve its accuracy. This glowing engram was a ribbon of light circling in a figure-of-eight path around a doughy lump of vat-farmed cerebral tissue, on which it had been anchored onto to give it focus.

Etrodai stood back as He stepped to the pedestal and ungloved His hands. The chrome gauntlets hung from the wrist straps of His vambraces as His long, quadruple-jointed fingers slid into the light and began to knead the tissue with lascivious strokes. The winding ribbon of light faltered and broke, and then the luminous strands of information began to flow up His outstretched arms, across His wide shoulders and into the base of His brain.

He sighed and His head rolled back. Light shone out of His mouth and illuminated a tiny spot on the crypt roof.

Etrodai waited...

The long fingers withdrew, and the engram streamed back into its orbit around the lump of tissue. He replaced His gloves.

'There's no mistake,' He said. 'I have examined this every way I know, testing for invention and falsehood. This is not a lie. This is a manifest truth from the sentiences of the imma-terium.'

The notion chilled Etrodai and He seemed to notice the look on the life-ward's face.

'Don't be troubled. While it might appear that this is a great blow to us, I believe this is rather our perfect moment of triumph, and the feeble godlings of human order have given it to us themselves.'

'Then my heart rejoices, Magister,' said Etrodai.

A respectful silence awaited them on the hinterdeck. The only sound was the gusty hiss of the air scrubbers and the sub-threshold harmonic thrum of the massive warp engines twenty decks above. The hinterdeck was a subsidiary landing platform, reserved for the Magister's personal use. It jutted out like a shelf high above the long, gothic vault, fifteen hectares square, that formed the primary flight deck for the colossal flagship's fighter screen. The squadrons had been ramped out to secure storage during the voyage. The echoing space below was empty now except for rows of energy bowsers, electric munition trains, and the launch cradles hanging like open crab claws from the high roof. Yellow lights winked in series along the runways scribed into the bat-tered floor.

There were eight beings assembled there in the middle of the empty metal platform. He had specifically requested nine for, according to Him, nine was a significant number. The ninth, too dangerous for direct intercourse, was suspended in a null field outside the hull, in the mouth of the main bay, connected by tele-audience relay to the proceedings on the high platform.

Etrodai ordered the Retinue to wait by the entry hatch, and then stood beside Him as He presented Himself to the assembled figures. Etrodai's skinned blade was so hungry by then that blood was dripping off his knuckles and his arms ached with it. But Etrodai would not reskin his blade until it was all done.

'I've a task for you,' He said. 'A task of significance. I charge you nine with it.'

They murmured. The triplets slithered and coiled their clammy grey hides around each other. The other trio bowed their heads. The two loners remained stiff and unmoving. An obscene rasp of digital filth crackled via the vox relay from the thing in the null field outside.

'A martyr. A martyr once, a martyr always. Our enemies think they have us, so we'll abuse them of that idea. We'll take this, their latest burst of vitality, and make it their last. One amongst you will perform this deed. I don't care who. You will break their renewed hopes and cast them into the dust. This trust I put in you.'

They murmured again, a vow of promise.

'Look at me,' He said.

They had all been standing with their backs to Him, fearful of gazing directly upon His form. Now, one by one and hesitantly, they turned. The triplets hissed at the sight of Him and regurgitated venom-soaked lumps of their last meal, which had been digesting in their throat sacks. The other trio turned, but only their leader, the tall one with the green silk robes and intricate body art, blanched to look on Him. The tattooed leader was as tall and thickly muscled as Etrodai, but his two companions were little base-formed things with the morbidly blind eyes of psykers. The two loners turned too. The figure in the crimson armour of the Blood Pact dropped to his knees and uttered a stifled prayer. The other, the cadaverously pale xenosbreed in glossy black, just stared.

'Good,' He sighed. He turned around and stared out of the main deck's mouth at the feral thing trapped in the forcesphere. 'And you, Karess? Are you ready?'

From the null field outside, a brutal curse rasped over the vox-link. It was as ingenious as it was anatomically horrific.

He smiled. That was the one thing Etrodai could not stand. His Magister's smile was the most terrible thing in creation. He shuddered and felt as though he were about to retch.

'Two rotations from now,' said Enok Innokenti, Magister and Warlord, 'the word will be given and my host will fall upon this cluster and quench the fires of its suns with blood. The crusade of the Imperium of Mankind will break and beg for a quick death.'

He paused. He was still smiling. 'Under cover of that great attack, the real work will begin.'

ONE
THE BRINK OF MIDNIGHT

'How many times have we stood here, you and I,
surveying the field before battle? How many times have we won?
How many times must we lose to have lost all those
victories and promises of victory? Once, old friend.
Once. Once. Once.'

— Warmaster Slaydo,
to an aide, before Balhaut

'Bad day coming!' the man cried aloud. 'Bad day coming! Bad day in the morning!'

He had clambered up onto an almsman's wagon, ignoring attempts to pull him down, and was now shouting, arms outstretched and fingers clawing, at both the sky and the gathering crowd.

'Bad day is coming down upon us all! On you! And you, sir! And you, madam! Nine more wounds! Nine times nine!'

Some in the crowd were booing him. Others made the sign of the aquila or the beati mark to ward off any evil luck he was bringing on with his words. Others, Anton Alphant noticed wryly, were listening quite intently.

15

There was nothing new in the man's rantings. He, and others like him throughout the camps, had been causing scenes like this regularly in recent days. It wasn't good for morale, and it certainly wasn't endearing the pilgrim mass to the city authorities.

Almsmen, their rank denoted by the blue ribbons that fluttered from their long dust-cloaks, were trying to coax the man down off the wagon. His feet had already knocked over several sacks of the corn-wafers and hardtack they had brought to distribute through the camp. An ayatani from one of the farworld congregations had elbowed his way through the crowd and was holding up a prayer-paddle as he shouted benedictions at the man. Two junior Ecclesiarchy adepts were clutching pewter cups and using their silver aspergillums to shake water at the improvising preacher. Holy water, Alphant was sure, that they had purchased at great expense from the stoups of the Holy Balneary.

Alphant closed his fingers around the ampulla of holy water in his own coat pocket. He'd come an awfully long way to get it, and it had cost him the last of his coins. He wasn't about to waste it so generously.

'Maybe we should stop him,' Karel said.

'We?' smiled Alphant. 'You mean me.'

'Everyone listens to you.'

'He's entitled to his opinion. Every last soul here came because it mattered to them more than anything else. You can't deny his passion.'

'He's scaring people,' said Karel, and a fair few of the other infardi grouped around the clock shrine with them agreed. 'Things could get ugly.'

They were right. Several penitents in the crowd had become so agitated by the man's preaching they had begun to scourge themselves. The row had even captured the attention of some of the nearest stylites. They turned round on their pillar tops to watch, and some shouted out over the heads of the crowd. Other pilgrim troupes had wheeled or carried their clock shrines up close to the wagon, pointing them at him as if the symbolism might deter him.

It seemed to make him worse.

'The brink of midnight, and then the bad day dawns! Fire from the heavens and the precious blood spilled!'

'Can't you make him stop, Alphant?' Valmont asked.

'I'm no priest,' said Alphant. How many times had he said that? Just an agri-worker from Khan II who had made the pilgrimage here when he'd heard the news because it seemed like the right thing to do. Along the way – and it had been a hard journey – he'd somehow become the nominal leader of those he'd travelled with. They looked to him for opinion and direction, more than ever since they'd reached the cold, austere reality of the camps. He'd never asked for the responsibility.

Then, of course, she'd never asked for hers.

Alphant had no idea where that sudden, sobering notion had sprung from. But it was enough to make him change his mind, hand his bowl and breviary to Karel, and walk towards the ruckus around the wagon.

He'd gone no more than three steps when someone in the angry crowd hurled a lump of quartz at the gibbering man. It missed, but others followed. One cracked against his forehead and he toppled back off the wagon top.

'Damn!' said Alphant.

The crowd went mad. Fighting broke out, and more missiles flew – rocks, ampullas, bless-bottles. The alms wagon overturned with a crash and people started shrieking.

Alphant put his head down and shouldered into the surging mob. The hapless preacher would be torn apart in this, and the last thing the camp needed was a death. Alphant was still a strong man, and he found he remembered some of the old moves, enough to tackle and dissuade the most boisterous rioters in his path anyway. Nothing too vicious, just a little deflection and the occasional squeeze of a nerve point.

He got round the upturned wagon, and paused to prevent three screaming infardi from throttling one of the almsmen. Then he looked for the preacher who had started it all.

And saw an amazing thing.

The preacher was sitting on the rough ground, both hands clamped to his forehead. Blood was pouring out through his fingers, staining his robes and making dark patches in the dust. He was in no state to protect himself.

But no one was touching him. A girl, a young girl no
more than eighteen, was standing over him. Her face, thin
and pale, was confident, the look in her green eyes soft. She
had one hand extended, palm out, to ward off the riot.
Every time a part of it spilled towards her, she moved her
hand in that direction and the people drew back. That simply, that quietly, she was maintaining a tiny circle of calm
around the preacher, keeping at bay a crowd lusting for his
blood.

He moved towards her. She looked at him, but did not turn
her palm towards him, as if recognising his peaceful inten-
tions.

'Do you need help?' Alphant asked.

'This man does,' she said. Her voice was tiny, but he heard
her clearly over the uproar. He bent down at her side, and
examined the preacher's injury. It was deep and dirty. He tore
a strip off his shirt, and wetted it with water from his ampulla
without even thinking of the cost. Wasn't it said to cure all
wounds?

'Bad day coming,' the man murmured as Alphant wiped
the blood away.

'Enough of that,' Alphant said. 'It's already here as far as
you're concerned.' He wondered how long the frail girl could
hold the commotion at bay. He wondered how she was
doing it.

'What's your name?' he asked, looking up at her.

'Sabbatine,' she said. He laughed at that. Saint names and
their diminutives were common enough in this part of the
Imperium, and there was, as might be expected, a dispropor-
tionately high number of Sabbats, Sabbatas, Sabbatines,
Sabbeens, Battendos and the like in the camps. But for her, it
seemed terribly appropriate.

'I think he's right,' she said.

'What?'

'I think something bad is about to happen.'

There was a quality to the way she said this that was more
alarming than the entirety of the preacher's manic declama-
tion.

'You mean like another attack? The raiders again?'

'Yes. Get to safety.'

Alphant didn't question her any further. He got his hands under the preacher's arms and hoisted him up. When he'd got the lolling man upright he realised that the girl had disappeared.

And the nature of the uproar around him had changed. It wasn't a riot any more. It was a panic. People were fleeing, screaming, falling over one another in their anxiety to leave. Something was burning. Smoke filled the low sky above the Ironhall camp.

'Bad day...' the blood-streaked man gurgled.

'Yeah,' said Alphant. He'd just heard a sound that he hadn't heard in twenty years, not since he'd handed back his standard issue mark IV, put his cap pins and badge away in a dresser drawer, and used his Guard-muster pay-out as deposit on a nice little parcel of cropland in the agri-collective west of the primary hive of Khan II.

The snap-crack of a lasrifle.

THE TAC LOGIS situation reports were urgently identifying a heretic raid in progress in the pilgrim encampment just west of the Ironhall Pylon, and true enough there was a furious plume of smoke rising from that quarter, a plume ominously undercut by the blink of weapons fire.

But as Udol rode a lurching carrier down the Guild Slope, through the deafening uproar of the panicked suburb, he caught sight of fat brown vapour clouds wallowing up heavily from the obsidae east of the Simeon Aqueduct.

'Is that the aqueduct?' he shouted.

'Fixing it now, major!' answered his signals officer, dropping back inside the carrier's rusty top hatch to man the tactical station.

'It is the aqueduct, sir!' the signalman called back a moment later.

'What?'

'The aqueduct, and the obsidae on the other side of it!'

Their helmet mics were turned up full, but it was still nigh on impossible to hear one another over the din. The engines of the APCs were revving, and the vast crowds packing the street were wailing and shouting. Gorgonaught, the great prayer horn at the northern end of Principal I, was booming

at the white sky from its ancient tower. Udol was sure he
could also hear the slap of distant detonations and the sizzling kiss of impacts against the outer fan of shield cover. It
was coming down again, fourth day in a row.

Udol slithered down inside the hull and cranked his bare-
metal rocker seat around so he could look over the
signalman's shoulder at the screen.

'What does tac logis have?'

'Nothing on that, major. They're directing us forward to the
Ironhall zone. Captain Lamm has engaged. Heretic raid coming in from the wastes. He–'

'They're in at the east door too,' Udol muttered. He
adjusted his vox set's channel. 'Pento? Udol here. Take the
front six with you and go look after Lamm's interests. Seven
and eight? Move off with me.'

Objections and several requests for clarification crackled
back, but Udol ignored them. He tapped his driver on the
arm and pointed.

The carrier obediently veered east, parting the rushing
crowds with blares from its warning sirens. Two other units
from the convoy turned with it. They got off the Guild Slope
and rumbled down a gravel linkway deeply shadowed by the
tall buildings on either side. At the end of the linkway, the
buildings framed an oblong of sky stained with clots of smoke.

They emerged onto Principal VI, flanked by low-rise habs,
and crossed the wide boulevard until they were facing the
towering lime-brick arches of the Simeon Aqueduct. Beyond
that massive arched structure lay the open reaches of a glass
field. Like so many vacant spaces at the city edges, the area
had become a pilgrim shanty over the last two months, a sea
of rough canvas tents, survival blisters and hastily raised
clock shrines. Another makeshift expansion of the city's limits to accommodate the massive influx of believers.

Filthy brown smoke billowed across the whole campsite
and washed out between the arches of the aqueduct. Dirty
pilgrims were pouring out with it, struggling with children
and belongings.

'Some damn infardi's knocked over a campstove in his
jubilation,' said the signalman. 'It happened the other week
over at Camp Kiodrus. Whole row of tents went up and–'

'I don't think that's what it is, Inkerz,' Udol snapped. 'Driver! Get us in through there!'

The driver dropped the gears down to the lowest ratio and began to roll the carrier through the nearest arch span onto the obsidae. Almost at once they were crushing tent structures and lean-tos under their heavy, solid wheels. Frantic pilgrims, flowing around the vehicle as they fled the area, hammered their fists on the armoured sides and implored them to stop.

'No go, major,' said the driver, hauling on the brake. 'Not unless you want to, you know, crush them.'

'Everybody out!' Udol ordered. 'Rove-team spread! Get on with it!'

The side hatches on all three troop carriers rattled open and the troops dismounted, fifteen from each. They lunged their way forward against the tide of the crowd, carrying their weapons upright. Udol paused long enough for Inkerz to strap the compact accelerant tank to his back and connect the hose, then he took off, pushing to the head of his men. He raised his armour-sleeved left arm, squeezed the stirrup built into the palm of the glove, and scorched off a little rippling halo of flame into the air so they could pick him out in the crush. Once he had their attention, he dispersed them left and right through the forest of tents and personal detritus.

Fifty paces into the shanty, the place was almost deserted. The smoke was thicker. Udol was appalled but unsurprised at the wretched conditions the pilgrims had been living in. Junk, rubbish and human waste covered the narrow tracks that wound between the pathetic tents. It was hard to see more than a few metres in any direction. Quite apart from the smoke and the shelters, there were clock shrines everywhere. No two were identical, but they all followed the same essential pattern: a timepiece of some sort – domestic clock, electric timer, digital chronometer, handsprung horolog – set in a home-made wooden box, the taller and more gaudily painted the better, it seemed. He looked at one nearby. As tall as a man, with reclaimed tin shutters open at the top to reveal the clock face, it was set on a wooden handcart and anchored in place with industrial rivets. The thing had been painted gold and silver and, in places, green, and skirts of plastic

sheeting had been wrapped around the towering body. Inside
that upright box, a stationary pendulum hung down, fes-
tooned with dried flowers, crystals, keepsakes, coins and a
hundred other votive offerings. At the top, inside the shutters,
the old clock face and the hands had been sprayed green and
then the dial and the tips of the hands picked out again in
gold. The hands were set at a heartbeat before midnight.

Major Udol knew precisely the significance of that.

He went around the shrine, waving the troopers behind
him close. The pilgrim shelters ahead of them were burning
freely. Dirty yellow flames licked away shelter cloth and canvas and leapt up into the morning air, swirling into dense,
dark smoke. Udol saw a clock shrine in the heart of the fire
succumb and topple.

The trooper beside him suddenly jumped back, as if in surprise. Then he did it again and fell on his back.

Shot through the torso, twice. Udol didn't even have to
look.

He barked a hasty warning into his vox. The men around
him scattered into cover. Two-thirds of them made it. The
bastards had been waiting.

Udol crouched down behind the relative shelter of an overturned flatbed as energy bolts spat and whistled overhead.
One of his men nearby got in behind the frame of a plastic
tent and then rolled over onto his side as a las-round came
through the fabric skin and into the back of his head.
Another man, caught in the open, was knocked over by a
laser bolt that broke both his legs. He fell hard, and started
crawling until another shot hit him in the face.

Udol felt his heart race. He glimpsed movement on the
pathway next to the fire, drew his laspistol, and fired a few
bright bars of energy down the narrow track. The troopers
around him began to open up with their carbines.

'Inkerz!' Udol voxed. 'Get tac logis. Tell them there's
another hot raid coming in right down here under the
aqueduct!'

'Acknowledged, sir.'

It was hot, all right, and getting hotter. Udol counted forty-
plus hostiles out there, in amongst the abandoned tents. He
glimpsed drab red body armour and dust-cloaks. They

matched the description of the hostiles that had been hitting and running all around the city skirts for the last four days. Heretic zealots, drawn to the city as surely as the pilgrims, as anxious to deny the truth occurring here as the pilgrims were to celebrate it. Marshal Biagi had told Udol personally that the hostiles were most probably militant cultists from a world in the local group. They'd made their way to the planet under cover of the mass pilgrim influx to stage terror attacks on the city.

The bastards could fight. Fight disciplined, and that was what made them really scary. Udol had tangled with warp scum many times before – had the scars to prove it – and Imperial military rigour had triumphed over zealot fanaticism every time.

Maybe it was the Imperium's turn to play the fanatic, Udol considered. According to every clock in sight, the hour was on them. They certainly had something to be fanatical about at last.

A sudden wind picked up, and began to drive the smoke cover hard north. A great part of the hostiles' position in amongst the tents was abruptly unveiled. Udol coordinated his shooters and began systematic counter-fire. His troop pounded rapid fire into the shamble of tents and bivouacs, and then pushed forward through the shanty, keeping their heads low.

A weapon cracked close to Udol, and the man to his left tumbled over onto the remains of a survival blister. Udol swung round and fired his sidearm, hitting the hostile square in the snarling iron visor he was wearing. Before the bastard's body had even folded up under him, another two came charging out of cover, firing wildly. Udol dropped to one knee, raised his left arm straight and clenched the stirrup grip. A long spear of incandescent flame leapt from the torch-vent behind the knuckles of his glove and broke around their torsos. Both staggered, ablaze, screaming. The flames cooked off the powercells in the nearest one's webbing and blew him apart, shredding his arms and torso right off his collapsing legs in a searing flash. The explosion felled his companion, who lay writhing and burning on the ground. Udol walked over to him and executed him with a single shot from his laspistol.

'Farenx. Beresi. Get forward on the double,' Udol told the men behind him. They were close to the edge of the shanty spread, and the hostiles were falling back fast. Just heretics, Udol thought. Maniac cultists testing the faith and resolve of the city with their cowardly terror-tactics. Exactly what the Regiment Civitas Beati had been formed to fight.

But when he reached the hem of the shanty, he realised he was wrong. It was more than that, far more. The open vista of the obsidae lay before him: a flat, cold waste of grey pumice and dust flecked by litters of black volcanic glass. It stretched away north for three kilometres towards Grace Gorge and the murky crags of the Stove Hills.

Three vehicles were approaching, striding in towards the shelter camp. Stalk-tanks. Behind them, at their plodding heels, came a fanned out line of over two hundred hostiles on foot, draped in dull red dust-capes. Since when did cult heretics have armour? Since when did they assault like a military force?

'Oh crap!' Udol heard himself say. 'Fall back! Fall back!'

The stalk-tanks came on, scuttling like arachnids. Each had six piston-geared legs that supported the low-slung body casings. Udol could see the drivers in the underslung bubbles beneath the tails. On each raised head section, dual mini-turrets rotated and began to fire.

The blistering shots came in constant, rippling waves as the barrels of the double pulse lasers in each mini-turret pumped, recoiled and fired again with brutal, mechanised rhythm. Udol saw Beresi cut in two, and three other troopers lifted off the ground by the overpressure of impact blasts. Detonations threw pumice and obsidian chips into the air. Twinkling scratches of light flickered along the advancing row of blood-red troopers as they began to fire their weapons too. Udol fell into cover. He heard men he'd known since childhood screaming their last words into their moulded rebreather masks.

He did the only thing he could think of. He prayed to the Saint.

FIFTEEN KILOMETRES SOUTH, at the crest levels of the inner city, the immortal choir was tuning up. Rampshel, the choir-master, was limping to and fro, waving his baton, and calling for the second vocids to 'pitch yourselves, for Terra's sake!' The children in the front rank, some no more than six years old standard, were fidgeting with their formal ruffs and vestments, and gazing into the distance. The fumes of incense burners filled the cool air, and the temple slaves were setting out the last of the golden reliquary boxes under direction of the High Ecclesiarch and his black-robed provosts.

'Almost there, first officiary,' assured Rampshel as he shuffled past, leaning on his silver-knobbed cane. 'Absolutely nearly almost there.'

'Very good, choir master. Carry on,' said Bruno Leger, elected first officiary of Beati City. He was a small man, with a cleanly shaved scalp and a neatly clipped goatee. He settled his mantle of office around his shoulders with a fastidious gesture, and double-checked that his amulet was hanging squarely on his chest. By his side, Marshal Biagi folded his huge arms and sighed.

'We're good, I think,' muttered the first officiary. 'Are we good?'

'We're good, sir,' replied Biagi.

'Are we? Fine. Excellent. I mean, is this... you know... sufficient?'

'It's fine, first officiary,' said Biagi. He smoothed his regimental sash. 'If the bloody choir can hit a note, we'll be laughing.'

'Are they off-key? Are they? Off-key?' First Officiary Leger craned his head and cupped a hand around his ear. 'They're off, aren't they? I'll have a word...'

'Sir, please,' said Ayatani Kilosh, extending a gnarled hand out of the folds of his long, blue silk robes and placing it reassuringly on Leger's arm. 'Everything is quite perfect.'

'Is it? Is it perfect? Good. Excellent. Why are those little boys wandering off? Shouldn't they be in the front rank of the choir?'

'Rampshel will see to it, sir,' said Biagi.

'Will he? I hope so. I want everything to be perfect. These are heroes we're welcoming today. Veterans. Their reputation precedes them.'

'Certainly it does, sir,' said Ayatani Kilosh.

A shadow flickered past overhead, momentarily blotting out the skylights of the ceremonial docking terrace. They all felt the thump of touch down.

'Well, they're here,' said Leger.

Rampshel raised his arms and the choir began to sing. He was conducting them strenuously when the first set of the terrace's inner hatches cycled open and steam hissed in.

First Officiary Leger wasn't quite sure what to expect, except something heroic. The choir, lungs bursting and antiphonals held open in front of them, voiced the Great Supplication of the Beati. They were bloody well almost in tune too.

Two figures sauntered down out of the steam. They came side by side. A louche male with a handsome face and the eyes of a joker, and a slender female with cropped bleached hair and an attitude. Both were dressed in matt-black fatigues and body armour; both had lasrifles slung casually over their shoulders. The man had an augmetic shoulder, and winked the moment he saw Leger. The woman was wearing a fur-trimmed bomber jacket, and carried her lasrifle yoked horizontally so that her right arm could hang near the trigger grip and her left folded casually over the top like it was a speeder's door.

They stalked down into the docking terrace, ignoring the efforts of the choir.

Leger stepped forward. 'On behalf of the people of–'

The man with the augmetic implant turned, smiled, and put a finger to his lips. Behind him, the female completed her sight check of the area and raised a hand to her headset.

'Site's clean,' Biagi heard her say. 'Come on out.'

A silhouette appeared in the hatchway, back lit at first by the vapour. An imposing figure in a long coat and a peaked cap. First Officiary Leger breathed in expectantly.

The figure walked into the light. He was a tall, lean man in the field dress of a commissar, but his epaulettes showed the rank of colonel. His face was as hard as a knife. He came down the ramp to face the trio of dignitaries, knelt before the first officiary and took his cap off.

'Ibram Gaunt, Tanith First, reporting as ordered,' he said.

So this was the famous Gaunt, thought Biagi. He wasn't especially impressed. Gaunt and his men, so the briefing files had said, were front-line grunts. They certainly had that mad dog smell about them. Not house-trained. Biagi had serious doubts they were suitable for the task they had been chosen to perform.

Gaunt rose.

'Welcome, welcome, colonel-commissar,' said Leger, taking Gaunt daintily by the shoulders and kissing him on the cheeks. He had to stand on tiptoe to do this. Gaunt seemed to tolerate the custom the way a guard dog tolerates the occasional brisk rub between the ears. Leger began to make a fuller and longer speech of welcome in High Gothic.

'You arrive cautious of your own safety,' Biagi cut in, nodding at the pair of troopers who had preceded Gaunt out of his lander. Gaunt narrowed his eyes and looked at Biagi questioningly.

'Marshal Timon Biagi, commanding the PDF and civic regiments.'

Gaunt saluted. 'My sergeants here insisted,' he said, indicating the waiting pair. 'During our descent, we were informed that a raid was underway.'

'In the city fringes, not here,' Biagi replied. 'My forces have it contained. We have a minor ongoing problem with heretic dissidents. There was no threat to your safety.'

'We prefer to check that sort of thing for ourselves,' said the female sergeant, addressing Biagi directly.

'Criid,' Gaunt scolded softly.

'My apologies,' she said. 'We prefer to check that sort of thing for ourselves, sir.'

Biagi grinned. Seemed this famous pack leader couldn't even keep his dogs in line. He looked the female – Criid, was it? – up and down and said, with a mocking tone, 'A woman?'

She fixed Biagi with an unblinking stare and then repeated his head-to-toe appraisal. 'A man?' she said. The male sergeant with the augmetic limb sniggered.

'Zip it, Varl,' said Gaunt. He faced Biagi. 'Let's not get off on the wrong foot, marshal,' he said. 'I won't reprimand my people for being dutiful.'

'What about for speaking out of turn?' Biagi said.

'Of course, the moment I hear one of them do so.'

'Well, it's quite wonderful to have you here!' the first officiary said with a rush of false enthusiasm, clearly desperate to brush over the awkwardness. 'Isn't it? Quite wonderful?'

'I'm here because I was ordered to be here by the Warmaster himself,' Gaunt said. 'It remains to be seen what else is wonderful about it.'

'May I say, colonel-commissar,' said Kilosh, speaking for the first time, 'that remark disturbs me.' Though tall, he was a very old man, yet his gaze had more strength and confidence in it than that of either the marshal or the first officiary. 'It might easily have been mistaken for heresy.'

Gaunt stiffened and said carefully 'No such offence was intended. I was not referring to the wonder that has taken place here, rather I meant the grave consequences that might be set off by such a thing.'

Kilosh nodded, as if appeased. 'We have met before,' he began.

'I remember, Ayatani Kilosh,' said Gaunt making him a small, formal bow. 'Three years ago, sidereal. In the Doctrinopolis of Hagia. A brief meeting, but it would be rude of me not to recall it. Your king, Infareem Infardus, was dead, and I was the bearer of that ill news.'

'That was a dark moment in the history of Hagia,' Kilosh agreed, rather flattered by Gaunt's precise recollection. 'And a bleak time for my holy order. But times have changed. The miracle has happened. The galaxy is a brighter place now, and you deserve thanks for your part in that.'

'My part?'

'The efforts of your regiment. You protected the Shrinehold and drove away the enemy. That's why you're here.'

'You requested it?'

'No, colonel-commissar,' Kilosh smiled. '*She* did.'

Gaunt hesitated, and stroked his fingers down one side of his lean chin thoughtfully. 'I look forward to talking with you more on this subject, ayatani-father,' he said. 'First, I would like the permission of the first officiary... and the honourable marshal... to dispose my men.'

Leger nodded eagerly, and made another little bow. Gaunt turned away and walked back towards the docking hatches.

'What do you make of him?' Kilosh whispered.

'Not enough to care about,' said Biagi.

'He seems like a decent fellow,' said Leger brightly. 'Doesn't he? Decent sort?'

'Oh, I think he is,' said Kilosh. 'Almost too decent. And that's where we might have a problem. It almost seems to me he doesn't believe.'

'Then he must be made to believe,' said Biagi. He paused as he saw a thick set man in the uniform of a line commissar emerge from one of the hatches. 'Excuse me,' he said, and walked away.

TANITH PERSONNEL POURED out onto the assembly floor. As he strode down the metal deckway, Biagi could see hatch after hatch opening along the ornamental terrace. Men and, in places, women, clad in the same dirty black and draped with camo-capes, were exiting the fleet of drop craft, lugging munition boxes, stow crates and kitbags. They had a smell to them. The smell of dirt and fyceline and jellied promethium that no amount of bathing could scrub out. The shadows of other landing ships flickered across the terrace skylights, and there was the thump and clank of landing clamps engaging. Steam vented through the floor grates.

The newcomers gave Biagi a courteous wide berth. He was a senior officer, and also an imposing figure. Shaven-headed, with dark olive skin and amber eyes, he wore the ceremonial battledress of the city regiment: gleaming brown leather embossed with gold-wire detailing. His left arm and chest were covered with polished, segmented armour plating and, on his back, under the fold of the scarlet sash, his accelerant tank was locked in place.

Biagi stopped as he came on three troopers hefting a pallet of promethium tanks out of a landing hatch.

'You. What is this?'

'Sir?' said the nearest, a bear-like oaf with a shaggy moustache.

'What are your names?' asked Biagi.

'Trooper Brostin, sir,' said the bear. He gestured to his fellows. 'This here's Lubba and Dremmond.' The other two men saluted quickly. Lubba was a short, heavy brute covered in the most barbaric tattoos. Dremmond was younger and more plainly made, his hair short and dark.

'You're flame troopers?'

'Sir, yes sir,' said Brostin. 'Emperor's own. He puts the fire in us and we put his fire into his enemies.'

'Well, you can put those tanks and those burner pumps back on the lander, trooper.'

'Sir?'

'City bye-laws. Only the officer class of the Regiment Civitas Beati is permitted flamers in battle.'

'Begging your pardon, your sir-ship... why?' asked Lubba.

'On this world, water is power, and the enemy of water – flame – is a privilege exercised only by the high-born warrior class. Do you require more of an explanation?'

'No, sir, we don't,' said Brostin.

Biagi moved on. 'Commissar Hark?'

The commissar turned, and quickly saluted.

'Biagi, Marshal Civitas Beati. Welcome to Herodor,' Biagi said, returning the salute and shaking Hark by the hand. 'I was asked to look out for you.'

'Really?'

'The general would like a word in private.'

'I thought he might,' said Viktor Hark.

GINGERLY LOWERING HIS aged frame, Ayatani Zweil prostrated himself and kissed the metal deck, murmuring prayers that he had known most of his days but which only now seemed to have meaning.

There were Ghosts all around him, off-loading from the landers. Many knelt down around him, producing their own green silk faith ribbons and kissing them the way he had taught them. They were faithful, these boys and girls, these soldiers. It was a glorious thing to see. He unwound his own beaded green ribbon from around his wizened knuckles and began to recite the litany.

Gaunt appeared beside him and gently raised him to his feet.

'I must finish–' Zweil began.

'I know. But you're in the middle of a landing deck and liable to be crushed underfoot if you stay there.'

Zweil huffed but allowed Gaunt to lead him out of the way as Obel and Garond manhandled a crate of rockets out onto the docking terrace with an anti-grav hoist.

'Are you all right?' Gaunt asked.

The imhava ayatani stared up at Gaunt with ferociously beady eyes. 'Of course I am! How could I not be?'

'You are over-tired, ayatani-father. The long voyage has drained you.'

Zweil snorted. If Gaunt had suggested such a thing back on Aexe, he might well have agreed. Back there, he'd tried to ignore the signs, but there had been no denying that his great age was catching up with him. He had honestly begun to wonder how much longer fate was going to give him.

Then, the news had come. And new vitality had filled his arthritic joints and dimming mind.

Zweil looked at Gaunt and regretted his sharpness. 'Ignore me. I'm old and wishful and I've spent the last few months on a Navy packet ship dreaming of what awaits us here. I expected...'

'What?'

Zweil shook his head.

'A smell of sweet, uncorrupted flesh permeating the entire planet? A scent of islumbine?'

Zweil chuckled. 'Yes, probably. All this long voyage from Aexe Cardinal, I've been wondering what to expect.'

'Me too,' said Gaunt.

'Ibram... I almost can't believe it's true.'

'Nor I, father.'

There was something in Gaunt's voice that made Zweil pause. He glanced at his friend the colonel-commissar and saw from the look on his face that Gaunt had let something slip in the tone of his reply.

Zweil stared at him and frowned. 'What's the matter?'

'Nothing. Skip it.'

'I will not. Gaunt? If I didn't know better, I'd take you to be a doubter. What aren't you telling me?'

'Nothing, like I said.'

'On Aexe, she spoke to you–'

Gaunt's voice dropped to a whisper. 'Please, ayatani-father. That must remain between us. It's a very private thing. All I meant was...'

'What?'

'Has anything ever seemed too good to be true to you?'

Zweil grinned. 'Of course. There was a rather limber girl on Frenghold, but that matter is even more privy than your incident on Aexe Cardinal. I understand doubts, Ibram. The Beati herself warned us against false idols in her epistles. But the divinations cannot lie. Every Ecclesiarchy church in the subsector has been sent signs and prophesies. And you... you have more reason to trust than any living being on this world.'

Gaunt breathed deeply. 'I trust in the ministry of the Saint, and the inscrutable workings of the God-Emperor. It's men I don't trust.'

Zweil was disconcerted, but he managed a smile and patted Gaunt on the arm. 'Forget the frailties of men, Ibram. On Herodor, there is emphatic wonder.'

'Good. If you see Ana... never mind, there she is.'

Gaunt left the old priest and edged through the press of disembarking Ghosts.

'Ana?'

Surgeon Ana Curth looked up from a shipment of sterilised theatre tools she had been itemising. She rose, tucking her data-slate under her arm and smoothing her short, bob-cut hair away from her heart-shaped face.

'Colonel-commissar?'

'The matter we spoke of during the voyage...'

She sighed. 'You know what? I was humouring you, Ibram. All those weeks stuck with you on a transport. It was easier to nod along than speak my mind. Well, we're here now, and I'm speaking my mind. You should be talking to Dorden about this.'

Gaunt winced. 'The chief medic and I aren't getting along at the moment.'

'Well, that's because you're both stubborn fools and I for one–'

'Shut up, Curth.'

'Shutting up, sir.'

'I want you to do this for me. Please. Privately. Quietly.'

'It's a matter of faith–'

'You may question me on anything, surgeon, except faith.'

She shrugged. 'Okay. You win. I'll get my kit, even though… even though, mind… I don't like it.'

She moved away, and then turned and called back: 'You understand I'm only doing this because you're so amazing in bed.'

The Ghosts around them came to a sudden halt. Several dropped their kitbags. Curth scowled at them all. 'A joke. It's a joke. Oh for feth's sake, you people…'

She disappeared into the press. Gaunt looked at the staring troopers around him. 'As you were,' he began and then sighed and made a dismissive gesture.

'Sir?'

It was Beltayn, Gaunt's adjutant. Gaunt didn't like the look on his face.

'Out with it.'

'Sir?'

Gaunt tipped his head down and looked at Beltayn. 'Something's awry. I can tell.'

Beltayn grimaced toothily and nodded. 'We're… we're missing a couple of landers.'

'A couple?'

'Three or so.'

'Three or so?'

'Well. Four actually.'

'Which ones?'

'Two, three, four and five.'

'Corbec, Rawne, Mkoll and Soric. I know I'm going to regret asking this, Beltayn, but do you have any idea why that might be?'

'They diverted during descent, sir.'

'Diverted? On whose authority? Let me guess… Corbec?'

'Yes sir.'

'And they are now where?'

'As I understand it, sir, they were alerted to the action at the city perimeter and Colonel Corbec – as it were – decided they should…'

'Should?'

'Muck in, sir.'

'Oh feth,' said Gaunt.

* * *

MAJOR UDOL ROLLED. Fire from the stalk-tanks was smashing up the terrain all around him. The high-pitched *whoop-whoop* of their pumping guns was all he could hear. He was bleeding from a scalp wound. The scorched remains of one of his men was hanging from a semi-collapsed tentframe in front of him.

A shadow passed overhead, and he saw from the dust the wind had changed again. It was blowing a gale suddenly. Grit pattered against him.

What the hell was *that*?

Udol looked up and froze. Thrusters flaring and sunlight glinting off its hull, a drop-ship was coming in right on top of them. A second was dropped down not five hundred metres away, and there were two more besides, falling like giant beetles out of the sky.

They were standard pattern Imperial Guard landers. Bug-nosed, bulk-made delivery ships. The Imperial Guard. He'd been praying to the Saint for deliverance. What kind of answer was this?

Udol felt the ground shake as the first drop-ship zeroed, bouncing hard on its hydraulic landing struts. Men leapt out of the drop-ship's opening hatches. Men in black fatigues and body armour. Men wrapped in camouflage capes. Guardsmen. They were spreading out into the barrens of the obsidae, laying down a fire pattern against the advancing hostiles, facing them down, and the damn stalk-tanks too. The dust-filled air was thick with rapid las-fire.

Udol got to his feet in time to see the closest stalk-tank re-aim and fire on the first drop-ship as it dusted off again. The impact slewed the nose round hard and made the engines wail with protest, but it lifted clear, right over his head, gear still down and hatches still wide open.

There was a puff of smoke from the newcomers' hasty file and a rocket spat at the first stalk-tank. Another followed it. A fireball bloomed around the tank's forebody, and it came to a standstill, its leg frame rocking back and forth. It hesitated, took another step, and another rocket smacked it in the snout. A blast-flash lit the glass field for a moment, and when it was gone, so had the stalk-tank, and hot fragments of Chaos-fashioned engineering were raining down out of the smoke.

Udol tried to raise his men on the vox, but an alien signal washed through the channel. He only caught snatches of it. Something like '...fething waiting for?' followed by '...live forever!'

He ran forward, rousing his men. The Guard had the phalanx of raiders on the turn. Another fireball briefly lit the sky, bright like a rising sun. A second stalk-tank had gone up.

The air was full of ashy debris. Through it, the soldiers in black poured forward, guns crackling, only half-visible in the haze.

They were like ghosts, Udol thought.

WHOEVER THEY WERE, they seemed insufferably pleased with themselves. As Udol approached, the black-clad troopers were whooping congratulatory exchanges as they jogged back to recover the heavy packs and bergens they'd ditched in haste as they'd come out of the landers. The hostiles, those few that had survived, had fled away into the dusty distance of the obsidae. The third and last stalk-tank was a burning mass on the glass field. Corpses in red uniforms littered the ground.

Udol tried to identify an officer amongst the Guardsmen. These men seemed to have no disclosing marks except a dagger-thrust skull pin and the aquila of the Imperial Guard. Their faces were hidden by crude, bulk-issue rebreather masks.

'Are your boys okay?' asked a deep voice from behind him.

Udol turned. The man addressing him was big and broad, the unruly tufts of a thick black beard emerging around the edges of his mask. His accent was strange.

'What did you say?' Udol asked.

'Your boys. I was asking after them. You were in a bit of a spot there.'

'We–' Udol began. He didn't quite know what to say. 'You came in on drop-ships,' was all he could come up with.

The big stranger jerked a thumb at the sky. 'We've been stacked orbital for the last sixteen hours, then we got the word to go to landers, for which everyone gave thanks. So, we're on the way down and the word comes up there's an attack and we gotta abort the drop. Feth that, I say, 'sides it

was too late for going back, if you know what I mean. We
spied the LZ from way up, then we spied the feth-storm–'

'The what?'

'The shooty-shooty. Friends in trouble, says I, so we wriggle
out of the pattern and fall in where, as it might be, we could
be most advantageous.'

'You… you dropped into the firefight rather than the LZ?'
asked Udol.

'Yes, we did. I see it as an economy of effort, myself. If we
were going to drop anyways, we might as well drop for a purpose. And so we did. Fething good thing too. By the way, who
are you?'

Udol gazed at the gloved hand held out to him. 'Major Erik
Udol, Third Company, Regiment Civitas Beati.'

'Clearly pleased and all that, Udol. Pardon me but this
old wardog's still riding the combat high. Got my boys
here boisterous too. Too many months in a belly hold, too
little killing. This is Herodor, eh? Heard so fething much
about it.'

'Do you know…' Udol began. 'Do you know how counter-
regs it is to drop troop landers into the path of an assault?'

The big stranger paused, as if thinking about this. 'Fairly
sure the answer to that is "yes". Do you know how effective it
is to drop-assault an ongoing ground attack? Or would you
rather not live forever?'

'I–'

'See for yourself,' the stranger said, extending a big arm in
a wide gesture. 'Observe the debris, the pleasant lack of
incoming fire, and the arses of many enemies fleeing for
safety. Was there something else, major?'

'Who *are* you?'

'Colonel Corbec, Tanith First-and-Only.'

'Oh,' said Udol, understanding at last. 'The Tanith. You're
the ones. The ones she's been waiting for.'

CORBEC'S IMPROMPTU RELIEF force, four platoons strong,
assembled itself into vaguely ordered groups at the edge of
the fight zone. Word was the officer in charge of the local
force had voxed tactical logistical command to request transports to take them into the city proper.

Major Rawne of the Tanith Ghosts, ranking third officer beneath Gaunt and commander of third platoon, wandered away from the makeshift assembly point and stood alone, slowly turning in a circle to take in the scene. This was his first look at Herodor, a world that had taken them months of monotonous travel to reach. A world, so he understood, that contained a great miracle.

It was not a pretty place, and didn't look at all miraculous, but it had a sort of cold beauty, Rawne conceded. The sky was a flat, bright white, with the merest smudges of grey-blue along the horizon, particularly in the north, where dirty crusts of rock pushed up into the air. The ground around them – an obsidae, the locals called it – was a bare field of blue dust, littered with black volcanic glass. The thin air was cold, and abrasively dry. Rawne had been told most of Herodor was an arctic desert: a dry, sub-zero waste of dust fields, glass crags and crumbling escarpments. It reminded him, unpleasantly, of death, of the cold, desiccated, brittle truth contained in all tombs. The Ghosts had yet to go to a world that did not cost them life and blood. What price was Herodor going to demand? Whose last sight would be these forlorn wastes?

Any of us, he thought. *All of us. Death is never choosy, never selective.* On Aexe Cardinal, he'd come to within touching distance of death himself. He sensed that cold grasp was still on him, reluctant to let him go again.

Or maybe that was just the chill wind gusting in across the obsidae.

Rawne's slow circle of contemplation brought him up at last looking south at the city itself. The Civitas Beati, the city of the saint, a minor shrine, just another of the many places and many worlds touched by Sabbat thousands of years earlier and made holy. It was a sprawling place, the main population centre on Herodor. Three slab-like hive towers of white ashlar stood like bodyguards around a higher, older, darker central steeple, encircled by sloping skirts of lower level habs, manufactories, transitways and brick viaducts. To the west lay the tinted domes of the many agriponic farms that fed the city, farms that were themselves kept alive by the hot mineral springs on which the city had been founded.

That's what made it a special place, Rawne thought pragmatically. It wasn't who might have been here or what they might have done. This city was here only by the grace of the thermal water that gushed up through the cold crust of the world in this one place.

Rawne heard someone shout his name. The shout was muffled by a rebreather mask. He turned and saw Mkoll, the regiment's chief scout, jogging over to him.

'Mkoll?'

'Transport's here, sir.'

There was an aqueduct at the edge of the obsidae, and a string of battered carriers was rolling out from under the arches.

'Let's get everybody moving,' Rawne told the chief scout.

By the time the two of them rejoined the main group, the Ghosts were boarding the waiting transports. Mkoll checked his own platoon had their equipment stowed. He looked over and saw Sergeant Soric of five platoon, who seemed to be taking his time getting settled with his men. Mkoll ran across to him. The last of five were finding their places in the carrier's rear payload bay. Soric, the old rogue, was studying a piece of paper.

'Everything all right?' Mkoll asked him.

Soric looked up, as if Mkoll had made him jump. He balled up the piece of paper, a scrap of blue tissue, and tossed it away. 'Everything's fine!' he told Mkoll, and then reached up to the tailgate so the nearest men could help haul his bulk up into the truck.

Mkoll thumped twice on the rear bodywork and the carrier started away in a splutter of exhaust and over-revved engine. He turned back towards his own transport.

The ball of blue paper blew across his path, carried by the wasteland wind across the flinty shards of the glass field. Mkoll stooped and caught it. It was torn from a despatch pack, one of the flimsy blank forms for written messages if the vox was down. Soric's vox was fine, wasn't it?

Mkoll unfolded the paper. A single line was handwritten there: *Trouble before you even reach the ground.*

What in the name of Terra, Mkoll wondered, did that mean?

TWO
THE GIRL FROM
THE HILLS

'That which was will be.
That which dieth will live. That which falleth will rise up.
This, I say to you, is the nature of things,
if you but once believe.'

— Saint Sabbat, Epistles

HE STOOD ON one of the highest decks of the inner hive and looked down over the sprawl of Beati City, across the ceramite and white-ashlar slopes of the hive towers, the mosaic of brick-tile rooftops lower down, crosscut by the lines of boulevards and viaducts, the mouldering stone of the old districts, the stained metal sides of the processors and agriponic domes, the maze of alleys and slums, the warrens of low-rise habs.

Not a secure town. Not secure or securable. There were no curtain walls or encircling fortifications, except the natural bowl of rocky headlands around the valley site. There was a shield system, generated by pylon stations around the city limits which, along with main sequence masts on the roofs of the hive towers, could raise a coherent energy field like a

39

carnival marquee above the city. But the shield system had
been designed to ward off dust storms and glass blizzards,
not munitions.

And that was what was coming. Full-scale war, drawn
inexorably towards Herodor as surely as the pilgrim flocks
had been drawn. The Civitas Beati would not survive. It
hadn't been constructed for war, and he didn't know how
he would begin to defend it. He thought of Vervunhive –
great, solid Vervunhive – and how hard that had been to
hold on to. Vervunhive had been designed by military plan-
ners with principles of defence uppermost in their minds.
Its Main Spine and curtain walls had formed a solid fortress
within which the entire hive population could shelter during times of attack and siege. Beati City, in contrast, had
simply grown, spilling low-rent, low-rise habs out further
and further from its more modest and overcrowded hive
towers.

God-Emperor, but this was going to be fething bloody.

Gaunt turned from the tinted observation window and
scribbled some more notes down on the data-slate he'd kept
at his side since arriving, every last idea he had to make the
city as proof against assault as possible. Stronger shield generators, for a start. Mobile artillery batteries, and some real
armour. Reinforcements, naturally. The damnably wide
boulevards would have to be blocked, and the aqua system
managed. Food and power and munitions had to be stock-
piled. According to the last Navy report, the Munitorum fleet
was two days out, and a three regiment force, including
armour, was inbound from Khan. Herodor needed battlefleet
cover too, and he'd put in a request, through channels, for
assistance from the Adeptus Mechanicus, though no answer
had yet come.

He heard the door to the wood-panelled deck open and
presumed it was Beltayn, returning at long last with caffeine
and a snack. It wasn't.

'Nice of you to decide to join me,' Gaunt said. Corbec
grinned and nodded. He was munching on a cut of bread
filled with salt-meat, and carried a hot cup of caffeine in his
other hand. Rawne, coming in behind him, carried two more
cups and handed one to Gaunt.

'We intercepted Beltayn on the way in,' Rawne said.

'There was supposed to be food too,' said Gaunt. Corbec stopped chewing immediately and looked down at the cut in his hand guiltily. 'Sorry,' he said.

Gaunt shook his head dismissively. 'Take seats. You've had a busy day, as I understand it.'

'Couldn't just leave 'em to fry out there. It was a pretty major assault, worst they've had, so I'm told,' said Corbec. Both he and Rawne had dust adhering to their uniforms, and Corbec's face still displayed the ruddy pressure marks where his rebreather mask had cut into his skin.

'Armour?'

'Three stalk-tanks. Light stuff, but even so. Caff and Feygor messed them up good with a brace of tread-fethers. More particularly, we got a positive ID.'

He reached into his musette bag and pulled out a snarling iron visor. There was a las-hole in the middle of the mask's forehead.

'Feth,' said Gaunt.

'The Blood Pact are here. In big numbers.'

Gaunt gestured to the iron visor Corbec was holding. 'It could just be–'

'I'd know the fethers anywhere,' said Rawne.

Gaunt nodded. 'The local military seems to think the raids are down to some heretic-dissident cells. They've been hitting the city for the last four days.' He took the mask from Corbec's hand. 'They have no idea, have they?'

'About time they did,' said Corbec.

Gaunt put the mask down. 'I think we're dealing with an advanced unit ordered to keep us busy until the main force arrives.'

'And you think that main force is inbound?'

Gaunt laughed darkly at Rawne's question. 'Find me someone in this sector who doesn't know what's happening here! If you were the enemy–'

'If?' smiled Rawne.

'If you were the enemy,' Gaunt continued, passing over the jibe, 'wouldn't you consider this world a primary target?'

Rawne looked at Corbec, who simply shrugged. 'So... any sign of this impending doom?'

Gaunt shook his head again. 'Fleet has nothing. Too many pilgrim ships confusing the picture.'

'Forget what might be. What about an operational base for the ones already here?' asked Rawne.

'Orbital surveys found what might be some landers in a deep glass desert a thousand kilometres west of here, but there were no life readings. The active hostiles here on Herodor are well hidden. Probably in the range of volcanic uplands called the Stove Hills, but that's just conjecture.'

'I say we–' Rawne started.

'We haven't got the manpower, Rawne. It'd take us weeks to find them, even with our skills. This is a big, bleak world with a lot of corners and holes to hide in.'

'But not an important world,' said Rawne darkly.

'No, major,' agreed Gaunt. 'Not an important world at all.'

'Then why–' Rawne began, and stopped dead when he saw the look in Gaunt's eyes.

'Have you… seen her?' Rawne said instead.

'Not yet.'

'You said the pilgrim ships were confusing things,' Corbec said. 'There are plenty of pilgrims here already. Hundreds of thousands. Orbital space is thick with them.'

'More ships arriving all the time,' Gaunt said. 'Some have come from beyond the subsector.'

'Probably should stop them,' Corbec ventured. 'I mean, we have to get this place locked tight. Can't just have anyone wandering in, even if they are harmless happy-clappies. Remember on Hagia, the way they came in with the pilgrim traffic?'

'I remember, Colm. I just don't know how we stop it. Some of these ships are old, barely serviceable and woefully unsupplied. If we try to form a picket and turn them away, we'll be consigning Imperial citizens to their deaths. Tac logis here tells me that ninety per cent of the pilgrim ships would not survive the return voyage. In most cases, they've spent their last savings on a one-way trip here. A trip to salvation.'

Corbec set down his empty cup and brushed crumbs off his tunic. 'The poor, sorry bastards,' he said bitterly.

Gaunt shrugged. 'The whole cluster and beyond knows what's happening here on Herodor, so you can bet the enemy does too. I can't begin to imagine why the information was released publicly.'

'Because she insisted,' said a voice behind him. Rawne had left the door open and no one had heard the newcomer walk in. They leapt to their feet and saluted.

'At ease,' said Lord General Lugo.

'I was told to report to you at 1700, sir,' said Gaunt.

'I know. I finished up earlier than expected and thought I'd move things along. Welcome to Herodor, Gaunt.'

'Thank you, lord general.'

Lugo glanced at Corbec and Rawne. 'Perhaps a moment alone…?' he suggested.

'Of course.' Gaunt turned to the others and waved them out. 'Dismissed, you two. Get the regiment settled.'

Corbec and Rawne hastened from the room and closed the door behind them.

'Feth,' whispered Corbec as soon as he was outside. 'I had hoped we'd never see that bastard again.'

'Not as much as Gaunt had, I'll be bound,' said Rawne.

'I SUGGEST, if I may, man to man,' said Lugo, 'that we put all previous unpleasantness behind us.' Lugo was a tall, bony individual with thin, greasy skin that clung like parchment to the curves of his shaved skull. He wore a stark white dress uniform, the chest covered in medals.

'That might be advantageous, sir,' said Gaunt.

'Things were said on Hagia, Gaunt. Deeds were done. You redeemed your reputation and abilities in my eyes with that little excursion to the Shrinehold. So… say no more about it, that's my motto.'

Gaunt nodded. He found it difficult to answer. Lord General Lugo was, in his opinion, one of the most inept and self-aggrandising officers in the Crusade's upper command echelon, a political animal rather than a military leader. In 770, he had negotiated for himself command of the liberation of the shrineworld Hagia, believing it to be a simple task that would win him much glory and bolster his political ambitions. When the liberation effort went disastrously wrong, he had blamed Gaunt and tried to make the Tanith First's commander carry the can. In doing so, he nearly lost

the entire shrineworld to Chaos, a calamity only averted by
the Tanith during the peculiar happenings at the Shrinehold
itself. After Hagia, his slate clean, Gaunt had been transferred
with his forces to the Phantine theatre. Lugo, though not
actually disgraced, had remained on Hagia as Imperial Gov-
ernor, his ambitions in tatters.

Sadly, that meant he had been in exactly the right place to
benefit from the extraordinary events that then took place
there. His star was now in the ascendant again. He was, by
default, in control of what might prove to be the most influ-
ential part of the entire Imperial interest in the Sabbat
Worlds. Rumours were already spreading that Lugo could be
looking to replace Macaroth as Warmaster if the current stag-
nation continued. He was very much the coming man.

Gaunt could almost smell that confidence and ambition
on the lord general. It was actually the smell of hair tonic and
cologne, but to Gaunt such pampering scents were the same
thing. Lugo had his sights on power. Real power. It gave him
an appetite so great you could almost hear his stomach
growling.

And it was absolutely obvious that the last thing Lugo
wanted in his path was Ibram Gaunt, who had shamed him
so on Hagia.

'Why is there a smile on your face, Gaunt?'

Gaunt shrugged. 'No reason, my lord. Just pleased that
things can be square between us.' No reason indeed. Gaunt
was smiling because, for the first time since he'd received his
orders on Aexe Cardinal, he was pleased to be on Herodor.

As he understood it, he was only here because she had
requested it. Lugo would never have sent for Gaunt. Whoever
– whatever – she was, she had clout. She was in charge here,
really in charge, and Lugo was forced to obey her will. Lugo
and his tacticians were taking her seriously. Either that, or
Lugo's capacity for intrigue was so great Gaunt couldn't even
begin to see its devious mechanisms.

'You say she insisted that word of her return be broadcast?'
Gaunt asked.

Lugo nodded. He had stalked over to the window and was
staring out at the city as the first shrouds of evening began to
fall across the scene. 'She would not have it kept secret, no

matter how strenuously my advisors objected. She cannot…
as I understand it… see why her return should be kept from
common knowledge. She calls herself an instrument, Gaunt.
An instrument of the Golden Throne. She embodies a power
and a purpose for the good of Mankind. Kept secret, she has
no power or purpose at all. It makes a certain sense.'

'It makes her vulnerable. It makes this world and this… forgive my candor… feeble city vulnerable.'

Lugo watched the city lights as they came on in the covering darkness. A wind from the wastes had picked up and
pattered glass flecks against the thick window pane. 'It does.
It does indeed.'

'Then why here, sir? Why this backwater? Surely her power
and purpose could be put to better use at the vanguard of the
crusade. With the Warmaster on Morlond, for example?'

Lugo turned from the window. He was smiling now. 'It
pleases me no end to hear you speak this way, Gaunt. It
agrees entirely with my thinking. She should not be here. We
must persuade her to… relocate.'

'Of course,' said Gaunt, 'though this all presumes she is
what she says she is.'

Lugo's expression suddenly darkened. 'You don't believe?'

'I–' Gaunt began.

Lugo took a step forward. 'If you don't believe, I can
scarcely see the point of you being here.'

'I remain to be convinced, lord general.'

'You what? You're talking like a damned heretic, Gaunt.'

'No, sir. I–'

'Saint Sabbat has been reincarnated. She is made flesh so
that she might lead us to victory here in the worlds that bear
her name. This is a moment undreamt of in human history!
A moment of sacred wonder! And you *remain to be convinced?*'

Gaunt opened his mouth and then closed it again. He met
the lord general's hard stare.

'I think it's high time you met her,' said Lugo. 'Either that,
or it's high time I had you burned at the stake.'

ON A COLD, forlorn night just like the one presently bearing
down on the Civitas Beati, but six thousand years earlier, the
Saint had left her mark on Herodor. The Civitas Beati hadn't

been called that then. It was but a single colony tower, the basis of what would one day become Old Hive, the central hive steeple, and back then it was called Habitat Alpha (colonial). The Saint, at the head of her flotsam cavalcade of an army, a host made up of colonial regiments, armed pilgrim retinues, a commandery of the Sisters Militant later to form the Order of Our Martyred Lady, and an echelon of the now extinct Astartes Chapter the Brazen Skulls, had bested and driven off a Chaos force at Grace Gorge, and she had come to Habitat Alpha to cleanse her wounds. She and her chosen bathed in the thermal springs and made them blessed for all time. The next morning, the Saint's host arose, refreshed, and annihilated the renewed thrust of the Chaos force in the Battle of the Shard Valley where, it was said, she alone disposed of eighteen hundred enemy warriors, including their Archon, Marak Vore.

It was all in the annals, and the storybooks. Gaunt had known them since childhood. Under Slaydo, he had committed them to memory.

The Balneary Shrine where Sabbat had washed her wounds lay in the lowest depths of Old Hive. It was constructed from black basalt and lit only by electro-candles and biolumin globes. Attendants and shrine priests hurried out as Lugo, with his chief staffers and life company troopers, approached down the long stone corridor. The air was hot and damp, and smelled of sulphur and iron.

They reached the doorway. 'We will wait here,' Lugo said. 'All of us,' he added, looking pointedly at Surgeon Curth, whom Gaunt had summoned to join him before following the lord general into the depths of the hive tower. Curth caught Gaunt's eye and he nodded.

'Stay here. I'll call if I want you.'

Gaunt stepped through the heavy doors, and they closed behind him. It was dim and quiet, and the close air was clogged with steam rising from the deep-cut bathing pools. A narrow staircase of a hundred steps cut from gleaming white limestone led down from the doorway, thousands of electro-candles lining the edges of the flight. The candlelight reflected off the slowly lapping water below. To the east lay the Chapel of the Emperor, to the west the votive chapel of the Saint. Gaunt went down the pale, polished steps, and took off his cap. He was sweating already. He walked to the side of the main bath, and stared down at his chopped reflection in the rust-stained water. The water rose from an aquifer deep beneath the city, broiled and heated by the volcanic vents in the crust. It was said to heal all wounds. Along the edge of the bath, Gaunt could see hundreds of brass spoons, cups and ladles that were used by the faithful to drink or baptise or cleanse themselves. Deep in the pool, shimmering, he saw millions of coins and blades, badges, medals and other offerings.

He knelt down at the poolside, plucked off a glove, and ran his bare fingers through the warm water.

There was a splash on the far side of the bathing pool, and ripples circled across towards him. He looked up in time to see a pale figure rising from the water, its back to him. It was a woman, clad in a simple white shift. She came up the bath's side steps, dripping, the wet linen sticking to her body, and he averted his gaze. Two shrine adepts emerged from the steam and draped her in a long, grey robe. She pulled it close, and brought the hood up over her head.

Then she turned, facing Gaunt across the water of the sacred balneary.

'Ibram.'

He looked up. 'You know my name?'

'Of course.' Her voice was soft and breathy. He longed to see her face. A sweet scent reached his nostrils as if the departing adepts had thrown incense on the lamp flames. Islumbine, that was it. The smell of islumbine, sacred flower of the Saint.

'I'm glad you're here,' she said.

'I came because I was told to come,' Gaunt said. 'I was ordered.'

She folded her arms, facing him across the steaming pool.

'You can stand up, if you like. You don't have to bow.'

He rose, slowly.

'I requested you. I requested the Tanith Ghosts. It pleases me that Gaunt's Ghosts are here with me on Herodor.'

The voice was so sweet. So penetrating. It was almost as if he already knew it.

'Why us?' Gaunt asked.

'Because of what you did on Hagia. You and your men put up their lives to vouchsafe my remains against the archenemy. You defended the Shrinehold to the last. It is only right I ask for you here, now, to protect me as you did before. I want the Ghosts to be my inner circle. My honour guard.'

'We will not shrink from that task,' Gaunt said. He took a few steps and began to move around the side of the pool. 'I had a… well, I don't know what it was. I had a vision on Aexe Cardinal that this would come to pass. A woman six millennia dead told me to find you here.'

'Really?' she said, as if thinking for a moment. 'That is good. That is as I intended it to be.'

'Did you?'

'Of course.'

He took another step closer. 'You intended that? That vision of the sororitas? You created that chapel in the woods out of nothing?'

'Of course, Ibram.'

'I believed that. It was real. Beltayn and I, we were totally convinced by it. We felt… touched by a strangeness beyond our power to explain.' He took a step closer. She began to back away slightly.

'Not like now,' he added.

'Ibram, you alarm me. What is this agitation in you? Why do you approach me?'

'Because I want to see your face.'

'No.'

'Why not?'

'Because–'

'I want to see your face because I know your voice!'

He lunged at her and grabbed her. She thrust out a hand and pushed his face aside, but he shook it off and yanked back her hood.

'I know your voice,' he said again, as she fought to break free.

'Sanian.'

Sanian pulled away from him and dragged her robe tight. She stared at him with eyes he couldn't fathom.

'You don't believe.'

Gaunt took a step back and shook his head, laughing out loud. 'I wanted to. Oh, believe me, I wanted to. Five months in a transit ship, waiting to see the truth? I've longed for this moment since Slaydo first explained the mysteries of Sabbat to me. I expected all sorts of things… truth, lies, fantasies. But not *you*, Sanian.'

She glared at him. Her black hair fell in wet ringlets around her beautiful face. It had grown long since he'd last seen her, a far cry from the shaved scalp and braid she'd worn as an esholi student. 'Understand this, Ibram. I'm not Sanian.'

'You are. I know you. You were the esholi who guided my men to the Shrinehold. Milo still talks about you.'

The look in her eyes changed suddenly and unnerved him. 'Oh, Ibram. Of course I am Sanian. My flesh is, at least. I needed a vessel, and she was the right one. She was a sweet girl and she gave her flesh to me. I look like Sanian. I sound like her. But I am not her. I am Sabbat. The girl from the hills of Hagia, reborn into this fragile body.'

'No…'

'Answer me this, Ibram. How else might I come back? How else might I find flesh to clothe me?'

He shook his head. 'This is a trick. Lugo is using you. You're not my Saint.'

GAUNT STRODE OUT into the corridor outside the balneary and Lugo's party stood back to let him pass.

'Well?' asked Lugo.

Gaunt stared at Lugo for a moment. 'It doesn't matter what I believe, does it?'

'Why?'

'Because as far as the Imperium is concerned, as far as hundreds of thousands of pilgrims are concerned… and as far as the archenemy is concerned… we have a reincarnated saint here on Herodor. And that's all that matters.'

Lugo grinned. 'At last, Gaunt, you're grasping the idea.'

GAUNT MARCHED AWAY from the balneary and the lord general's retinue, and headed down the long, stone colonnade that led to the nearest elevator bank. The attendants from the balneary, the hierarchs and adepts who had withdrawn from the

place at Lugo's approach, were waiting quietly in the colonnade, silent robed figures in the gloom. He pushed through
their huddled groups, knowing they were all watching him.

'Gaunt! Gaunt!' Curth called as she ran after him. He
didn't break stride. When she finally caught up with him, he
was waiting outside the iron cage door of the elevator for a
lift car to arrive.

'You want to tell me what's going on?' she snapped.

He looked at her, his eyes in shadow. 'Ever have a secret,
Curth? One that will hurt as many by telling it as it will by
keeping it?'

'Yes,' she said honestly, the thought of Gol Kolea flashing
through her mind.

He seemed surprised at her reply, as if he'd been expecting
her to say no. 'How did you decide?'

'I didn't. It was decided for me.'

'That's what I'm afraid will happen here.' The mechanically
wound elevator car clanked and moaned to a halt, and he
wrenched open the collapsible cage door. Curth had to leap
in after him to stop him closing the cage in her face. For a
moment, she thought he was going to pull the cage open
again and order her out. Instead, he walked to the wall panel
and pulled on the brass lever. The elevator began to rise, gears
whirring in the blackness of the shaft.

'Did you see her?' she asked, watching the lights of passing
floors slide down his face.

'I saw her.'

'And it's put you in this mood?'

He let out a slow, dangerous breath and looked like he
might punch something.

'You asked me to help you, Gaunt. You said you needed
proof to put your mind at rest.' She patted the equipment
satchel slung over her shoulder. 'I brought the bio-scanner.
Did you not need proof after all?'

'Apparently not,' he said.

'It's not her, is it?' Curth asked. Gaunt said nothing. With a
sigh, she leaned over and pulled the brass lever down to sus-
pend motion. The elevator clanked to a halt between floors.
Somewhere, a buzzer rang. An amber light began to flash on
the control panel.

'Talk to me,' she said.

'Let it alone, please, surgeon.'

Curth shook her head. 'I've watched you, Ibram. All the way from Aexe Cardinal, ever since the news broke. Part of you wants it to be her, part of you is afraid it won't be. Know what I thought? I thought the moment you saw her, you'd be sure. Just like that. No need for me to do a gene procedure to get the answer for you. I knew you'd know. And you do.'

'I do.'

'It's not her.'

'It's not.'

'Throne!' she gasped, then recovered her train of thought. 'So what is this? Disappointment? Anger? You came here needing proof one way or the other, and you've got it. That at least should satisfy you.'

'Do you remember Sanian?'

She shrugged. 'No, I… oh, wait. Hagian girl, a student… esholi, that's what they were called, wasn't it? She went along with Corbec's mob.'

'That's her.' He stared at her.

Her eyes widened. 'You are fething kidding me, Gaunt! Her? She's the Saint?'

'Far as I can tell, Sanian believes she is the reincarnation of Sabbat. She's quite lucid, and convincing, I would imagine, to someone who didn't know her already. She needs psychiatric treatment in an Imperial asylum. But her potential value has been recognised. Her value as propaganda.'

'By Lugo?'

'You can see how delighted he is his career's back on track. He doesn't care if she's real or not. All he cares about is the fact that she's convincing. The crusade needs a miracle right now… and he's the one who's going to be remembered forever as the man who made that miracle happen.'

She reached out tentatively and chaffed his shoulder reassuringly. 'So, tell the truth. As a servant of the God-Emperor, you've always been honest to a fault.'

'It's not that simple. She is strategically valuable, there's no getting away from that. As an icon, a rallying point, she could win this war for us. Her presence could bolster our morale and destroy the enemy's resolve. If she continues to

play the part, and we all go along with it and say we
believe, we could liberate the entire cluster. But I don't
think I can lie about something like this. Not to Zweil...
not to Corbec and Dorden and Daur and the others who
were touched by the Saint on Hagia. They believed in a
truth there, a truth that I felt too. I can't ask them to believe
this lie instead.'

'Let them make their own minds up,' she said.

'Ah, there you are,' said Corbec, looking up from the data-
slate he had been fiddling with. 'You'll be pleased to know
we're settling in. Billets are fine. I've got a list of their locations here, if you want.'

Gaunt ignored the slate Corbec held out to him.

'Or maybe you don't. Anyway, we're getting the lie of the
land. Rawne and Mkoll are out there right now, deploying
platoons around the city perimeter. We got about nineteen in
the field, setting up waystations in cooperation with the local
militia. It won't be much, but by dawn we should have a
basic defence established around the north and east flanks of
the city. The locals add about twelve thousand to the numbers, along with medium armour, and the lord general's
landing force has about a thousand more, plus light armour
and some special weapons units.'

'Where's Milo?'

'Milo?' Corbec furrowed his brow and scrolled down the
disposition lists on his slate. 'Right now, I'd say he was out
with his platoon at the Glassworks. That's... ah... up in the
north-west sector.'

Gaunt nodded. 'Get on the vox and get him back here.'

'Well, they're due for return rotation to the billets at ten
tomorrow and–'

'Now please, colonel.'

'Right. Yes, sir.'

Gaunt walked past him into the wide, vaulted chamber on
the eightieth level of the third hive tower where the Tanith
First had set up their operations post. The wide room, with
shuttered windows on two sides, was busy with regiment personnel, working with members of the Regiment Civitas Beati
and tech-adepts from the regular Herodian PDF to set up

main-caster vox stations, tactical superimpositionals and relay nodes. Power cables and data-flexes snaked across the floor. Technicians were wiring up the portable comm-desks and holo-chart tables.

'Is he all right?' Corbec asked Curth, who had followed Gaunt into the room.

'Not really,' she said.

Gaunt turned and looked back at Corbec. 'What's through here?' he asked, gesturing to a side arch into another room.

Corbec hastened over to join him. 'Just an annexe. Daur thought it might do as a briefing room. The Munitorum's bringing chairs up, and a few tables. Beltayn's organised some food too. Down the hall on the left, plenty of grub for–'

Gaunt cut him off. 'Two minutes. I want you, Dorden, Zweil and Daur in the annexe for a privy briefing. Hark too, if he's around.'

Corbec shrugged and nodded. 'As you ask, sir.'

THEY TOOK THEIR seats. Corbec; the old ayatani priest Zweil; Captain Ban Daur, the Verghastite third officer; Dorden, the chief medic and Viktor Hark, the regiment's commissar. Curth slipped in and sat at the back. Before he sat down, Daur configured and activated the portable confidence screen that would generate electroference patterns to keep the meeting private.

'What I've got to say doesn't leave this room,' said Gaunt.

The men nodded. Curth, at the back, folded her arms and hunched her shoulders.

'I've met the Saint,' said Gaunt.

'Praise be!' Zweil murmured.

Hark had a sick look on his face that indicated he knew what must be coming next.

'She isn't real.'

There was a long silence. Corbec stared blankly at the wall opposite him. Daur groaned and put his head in his hands, fingers wrapped with a green silk faith ribbon. Dorden closed his eyes and folded one hand around the other. Zweil blinked.

'She... I'm sorry, what?' Zweil said.

'She is a fake. An invention. A subterfuge.'

'Oh, feth...' sighed Corbec.

'Seriously?' Daur asked. His eyes were welling up.

'More particularly,' Gaunt said, 'she is known to us. To you, Colm, and you Dorden, and Daur too. As far as I can tell, she truly believes she is Sabbat incarnate. But when I met her, face to face, I realised it was the poor girl we'd met on Hagia: Sanian.'

'Sanian?' Corbec started.

'No, no... this... no, this isn't right,' Zweil said, agitated. 'The Saint has come back, the Beati. This is what we were told. She is here...'

'She isn't. It's... a scam,' said Gaunt.

'Absolutely not!' Zweil cried, and got up.

'Father... father, please. I understand this is hard for you to hear.'

'It is her! It has to be!' Zweil had become so upset that Dorden and Curth had both risen to their feet. 'This is the Saint returned, not some esholi child with her head all messed up!'

'I believe,' said Hark, slowly pulling on his black leather gloves, 'that Zweil ought to know. He is an ayatani of the Beati Cult, after all.'

Gaunt shot a dangerous look in Hark's direction. 'She isn't real,' he repeated.

'She was on Hagia,' said Dorden, his arm around Zweil's shoulders. He was staring at Gaunt. 'She spoke to me.'

'I know she did, Tolin,' said Gaunt.

'She spoke to me too,' said Daur.

'And me, boss,' said Corbec.

'I know, Colm. I fully believe that on Hagia you and Ban and Tolin... and others too... had a communication from the Saint that drove you to do what you did. All I'm saying is... this isn't the Saint. Not here. Not now.'

'But–' Daur began.

'Has she spoken to you since?' Gaunt asked.

The men were silent.

'Heretic! She spoke to you,' Zweil cried suddenly.

'What?'

'You... and Beltayn. On Aexe Cardinal. Through her servant.'

Gaunt closed his eyes, trying to master the anger that boiled inside him. 'Ayatani Zweil… I told you that in strictest confidence. It was meant to remain between just us. An act of confession, sacrosanct. I trusted you would keep it to yourself.'

'Well, this is too important!' snapped Zweil. The bone-thin old priest swayed, and for a moment Gaunt was afraid he was about to keel over. 'Devil take my vows, you're lying about this and I won't have it!'

'What's he talking about, Gaunt?' asked Dorden.

'He's speaking out of turn, doctor,' said Gaunt.

'He knows!' Zweil cried.

'I think you should tell us, sir,' said Corbec.

'This is hardly the time or–'

'Tell them!' Zweil screamed. 'Tell them what you told me! Tell them what made me believe!'

Gaunt looked from one face to the next slowly. He realised that, right then, he didn't have a friend in the room.

'All right. On Aexe, I took a trip from the frontline to Meiseq to meet with Van Voytz. Beltayn was with me. Our train was delayed and we went on foot for a while, and we found this chapel in the woods. There was an old woman there. She seemed to know us, and she warned me about Herodor, long before the orders came through. Later, Beltayn and I tried to find the chapel again. We… couldn't, and I can't explain that.'

'Tell them the rest,' said Zweil.

'It's not pertinent,' Gaunt said.

'It is! It speaks volumes! The woman they met identified herself, and later they discovered she had died here on Herodor six thousand years ago!'

'That's enough,' snarled Gaunt.

'Yes, it is,' said Zweil. 'It's enough. Enough proof by anyone's standards. The Saint told you to come here and serve her! How dare you deny her now!'

Gaunt took off his cap and sat down. Everyone was staring at him.

'I don't know what happened in the woods on Aexe. It has been with me ever since. I'm sorry I never told any of you about it. But it doesn't change the facts. The Saint here is not the Saint. She is a pretender.'

'And for the record,' Gaunt added, looking at Zweil, 'I'm appalled by your lack of confidence, father.'

'Oh, get over it!' Zweil spat. He shook Dorden's arm off him. 'Tell me this, Ibram Gaunt... if this Saint is such an obvious fake, why did she request you here? You, the one man who could expose her?'

Gaunt shrugged. 'I don't know the answer to that.'

'And if Lugo is really calling the shots,' added Corbec, 'why would he let that happen?'

'I don't know,' said Gaunt.

'I know this,' said Hark, rising to his feet. 'It doesn't matter if she's the Saint or not. As far as millions, maybe billions, of Imperial citizens are concerned, she is Sabbat reborn. Truth or lie, we have to uphold that, or Imperial morale will collapse overnight.'

'I was getting to that part, Hark,' said Gaunt. 'We have a duty here, whether we like it or not...'

'To lie?' asked Dorden coldly.

'Even that,' said Gaunt.

Zweil let out a low moan and shuffled towards the door. He paused there and looked back at Gaunt. 'Why here?' he asked. 'If it's a lie, why the hell here?'

Gaunt couldn't answer him. Zweil paced out of the room, and Curth and Dorden followed him in concern.

'Dismissed,' said Gaunt. Corbec and Daur both left, uneasily.

Gaunt looked at Hark. 'I see your old master has been working on you.'

Hark shook his head. 'Lugo? He's not my–'

'Shut up, Viktor. Lugo placed you with the Tanith on Hagia. You were meant to be my replacement. He–'

'No, Ibram. I was meant to be your judge and executioner. That was what Lugo wanted of me. I'd like to think that I have proved myself to you and the Ghosts since then. Yes, Lugo spoke to me when we arrived. I won't lie. He asked me to work on you. He thought you could persuade Sabbat to relocate to Morlond. That would really do his cause no end of good.'

'I see. And?'

Hark smiled. 'I told him you'd make your own mind up.'

Gaunt nodded.

'Zweil will calm down,' said Hark. 'It's in his nature to blow hot and cold. What interests me is how right he was.'

'What do you mean, Viktor?'

'If this Saint Sabbat is a fake... why us... and why here?'

THREE
UNHOLY NIGHT

'Everyone has a choice. Me, I choose to not make a choice.
What? What? Why is that funny?'

— Hlaine Larkin, Ghost

IF HE'D LEARNED anything about Herodor so far, it was that the nights were fething cold. The city shield was lit, and for that they might be somewhat thankful, but the wasteland wind, with a cutting edge like a chainsword, slid in under the canopy of energy and bit them to the bone.

If Larkin had understood his sergeant's pre-brief right, the area the carriers had dropped them off in was called the Glassworks, a ramshackle, two thousand hectare arrangement of dingy workshops, storebarns and manufactories in the northwest of the city. It seemed a long, long way from anywhere nice. The main bulk of the Civitas, well-lit and cosy-looking, was a good distance behind them. Here, the light of drumfires and phospha lamps combined with the gauzy glow of the shield overhead to produce a blue, submarine halflight.

Above, in the night sky, stars twinkled that were not stars. Those indistinct pinpricks of light were the hundreds

– possibly thousands – of pilgrim ships that had swarmed
to Herodor.

Larkin's platoon, number eleven, had been sent to the
Glassworks with ten and twelve to secure that section of
perimeter. Easy job, to say it. In practice, it was hard to even
find the perimeter in the first place. The whole area had been
overrun by pilgrims, and their tent towns had grown like forest fungus between the empty buildings – inside some of
them, in fact – and out into the edges of the wasteland itself,
beyond the limits of the crackling shield. There was no defin-
able edge to the city at all.

Weapons slung, uneasy, the Ghosts moved through the twilight world of the camp. The pilgrim contingent was huddled
around feeble fires, cooking late meals or forming prayer circles. Infardi worshippers in green silk were performing rituals
around their clock shrines, or moving through the camp
passing out pamphlets. Many were tonsured or had their
napes shaved, others hugged placards or emblems of the
Saint. The most extreme had pierced themselves with the stig-
mata of the nine wounds, or inscribed holy tracts on their
skin. Some had whips or sticks to scourge themselves with.
Every single one displayed his or her pilgrim badge proudly,
and every one looked pinched and painfully cold.

'Keep it tight, Larks,' Sergeant Obel called. Larkin hurried to
catch up. Just for the hell of it, he shouldered his long-las and
panned the scope around. Through the enhanced and magni-
fying viewfinder, he spot-picked locations in the fuzzy cold of
the obsidae beyond the camp. For one brief second, he
thought he glimpsed movement in the distance. Just wind
blowing the dust up. That's all, he told himself. Not the enemy.

As far as Hlaine Larkin – the regiment's finest marksman –
was concerned, the enemy wasn't really out there anywhere.
He was already inside the city, inside with them.

And his name was Lijah Cuu.

JUST FIVE HUNDRED metres from where Larkin was standing, in
another part of the straggled-out camp, Trooper Cuu raised
his standard pattern lasrifle to fire.

'Not another step, gak-head,' he hissed. 'Or I'll ventilate
your torso, sure as sure.'

'Put that up,' Sergeant Criid snapped, pushing past Cuu and jerking his gun-muzzle skywards with an off-hand gesture. 'Sir? Mister? I need you to identify yourself.'

Anton Alphant turned and looked at her. He raised his arms so she could see his hands were empty.

'I don't mean any trouble, trooper,' he said.

'Sergeant,' she corrected, and moved forward to face him as her platoon – the tenth – closed in behind her.

'My apologies, sergeant. It's been a few years.'

'Since what?' she asked. Alphant liked her already. Sharp to the point of brittle, fast-eyed, confident. A looker too, if you liked hard, thin girls. A little beyond an old man like himself, of course.

'I was Guard. Years back. Sorry, that's not important, is it?'

Criid shrugged. 'We've been told to secure this area, sir. It's okay if the pilgrims keep to their camp areas, but we can't have them moving around after dark.'

'Because of the raiders?' he said.

She nodded. 'You are a pilgrim, I suppose? You've got papers?'

Alphant affirmed with another quick nod, and then gently opened his robe so she could see what his hands were doing at all times. He pulled out his sheaf of certificates.

DaFelbe, Criid's number two, a tall, thin, earnest young man, hurried forward and examined Alphant's papers with a handheld verity-reader.

'Anton Alphant,' DaFelbe called back. 'Registered infardi pilgrim. Place of origin, Khan II, place of birth–'

'Enough,' said Criid. She took the papers and walked over to face Alphant. 'Says here you were assigned camp space in the Ironhall district. You've roamed a little too far.

'I… I was looking for someone,' said Alphant.

'Who?'

'It's not important now. I got sidetracked, I'm afraid. I was just going to see if the doors on that manufactory were open. There are a lot young children in this part of the camp and I was hoping to get them into shelter.'

'Why? Are you some kind of elected leader?'

'No, not at all. It's just… the nights are cold.'

'Aren't they just?' said Criid. 'Hwlan?'

The tenth platoon scout hurried up.

Criid nodded to the empty building nearby. 'Get that place open, please. Some kids here who could do with shelter tonight.'

'On it,' Hwlan said.

'Nessa… watch his back,' Criid added, signing to the platoon sniper. Nessa Bourah scooped up her long-las and hurried after the scout.

There was movement behind them, but it was just Sergeant 'Shoggy' Domor and twelfth platoon closing up.

'See much?' asked Domor.

Criid chuckled at the unintended irony of his question. 'You tell me.' His bulbous, augmetic eyes were clicking and whirring as they scanned the horizon.

'Not enough to spit on, Tona,' he said.

'Be thankful for that,' she said.

Back down the file of Ghosts, Brin Milo chaffed his cold hands and looked into the distance.

'What the feth are those people doing?' he asked.

'Them there?' Nehn replied. 'Keeping their fething balance, I'd say.'

Throughout the fire-lit sprawl of the pilgrim camp, as ubiquitous as the bizarre clock shrines, thin towers rose up into space. Wood, mostly, some steel, some stone on wheeled trolleys. On top of each one stood a pilgrim, poised vulnerably on the summit of his or her thin pillar.

'Stylites,' said Corporal Chiria, as if she knew. She was a heavy-made Verghastite, her plain face badly scarred by the last campaign they had gone through. 'Stylites, you know? They stand on top of plinths and pillars, Milo.'

'Uh… why?'

'Well,' considered Chiria, 'I don't exactly know.'

'Brings them closer to the Saint,' said a voice from behind them. 'Proves their faith.'

'Really, Gol?' asked Milo.

Gol Kolea set his lasrifle down and thought hard. It was painful to watch. Gol Kolea had once been leader of tenth platoon, with a fine war record behind him. Some said he was senior officer material. But on Phantine, two years before, the spray'ng fragments of a loxatl flechette round had

ripped into his head and torn away his wits and his personality. It was a crying shame, a real tragedy. Kolea seldom said
more than a few words. His last comment was a downright
magnum opus.

'How do you know that, Gol?' asked Milo.

'Dunno,' said Kolea. He scratched at the side of his head.
'Just is a thing.'

'Oh, you know the sergeant,' said Cuu, sauntering up. He
was the only man who still referred to Kolea by his former
rank. 'Talks a lot of gak, don't you, gak-head? Eh? Eh? Sure as
sure.'

'One day, Lijah,' said Chiria, venomously, 'someone's
gonna plant a las-round straight between your eyes.'

'Uh huh. Who'd that be? You?' giggled Cuu. 'You haven't
got the balls, Chiria. Sure as sure.'

Milo turned to face Cuu and stared into his deep set, scar-
cut face. 'You don't stop mocking Kolea and I'll do it myself,
you understand?' Milo said.

Cuu grinned. 'Whoo, careful, mascot. You'll bust a seam!'

Milo dropped his lasrifle and balled his fists.

'Enough! That's enough!' said Bonin, the twelfth platoon
scout. He put himself in between Milo and Cuu. 'Milo… signals is asking after you.'

'Me?'

'Yes, you. Cuu. Go and be busy elsewhere.'

Cuu sniggered and wandered off.

'NOT EXACTLY HOMELY,' Hwlan sniffed, looking around. The
manufactory interior was dark and empty, and smelled of
woodrot, motor oil and ozone. Nessa moved past him, scoping around with her long-las. DaFelbe advanced with her,
shining his lamp pack into the darker corners. There were
holes in the roof over their heads, and through them, they
could see the shifting luminescence of the city shield.

'It's out of the wind, that's the important thing,' said
Alphant. 'A few drum fires in here and it'll be almost cosy.'

'I guess,' said Hwlan.

'All right if I bring some of the families in?' Alphant asked
Criid.

She nodded. 'As many as there's room for.'

In less than fifteen minutes, the place was teeming. The pilgrims dragged belongings with them on barrows and litters, and some manhandled clock shrines in through the doorway. Fires were laid. The pilgrims were singing a slow, pastoral hymn as they settled themselves. Alphant moved amongst them, helping them get comfortable. Criid watched him for a while. The man might not claim to be a leader, but he had a natural, reassuring air of command that the pilgrims all responded to. He was, however, clearly preoccupied, and kept looking at the door as newcomers entered. Who was he hoping to find in the Ironhall camp?

Criid was helping an elderly man find a corner to sit in. The old man had a handcart loaded with crudely painted plaster busts of the Saint, undoubtedly copied cheaply and in bulk using a fabric replicator, which he sold to the faithful to keep himself in soup money. Once Criid got him bedded down on his ragged mattress roll in a corner of the manufactory, he pressed one into Criid's hand.

'No, that's all right.'

'Please.'

'Honestly, I have no money.'

'No, no,' the old man shook his head. 'Not for money. It is my thanks for your kindness.'

'Oh,' Criid looked at the plaster effigy. It was hideous. The paint had been applied so badly and so clumsily that Saint Sabbat looked like a pre-teen clangirl wannabe from Vervunhive who had just that morning discovered cosmetics and applied them enthusiastically.

'Thank you,' Criid said, tucking the plaster bust into her jacket pocket. It was a non-uniform garment, a fur-trimmed Shadik army field jacket that she'd appropriated on Aexe Cardinal. She'd slit the insignia off. So far, no one had brought her up for wearing it, and she was glad of the warmth.

'May the Saint bless you,' the old man said.

'Thanks for that too,' she added, but her attention wasn't really on him. She could hear raised voices coming from the factory entrance.

In the doorway, DaFelbe and Lubba were having an altercation with a tall man dressed in the ornate demi-armour of the local military.

'…just have to get them out of here, then,' she heard the man say as she walked up.

'Problem?' she asked.

The local turned to look at her. He was clad in brown synth-leather and his torso and left arm were cased with segmented steel. Behind him were over a dozen Herodian city troopers with bullnose carbines.

'Are you in charge?' he asked.

'Sergeant Criid, Tanith First,' she answered smoothly. With a flick of her head, she signalled DaFelbe and Lubba to back off. Lubba seemed curiously naked without his trademark flamer pack. Gakking city ordinances.

'Captain Lamm, Civitas Beati. This is an unauthorised use of civil property. Get these lowlifes out of here.'

'No,' said Criid.

The captain bristled. 'No?' he said.

'These *people*,' Criid emphasized the word, 'needed shelter. This building was not in use. Derelict in fact. This isn't unauthorised because I authorised it.'

'Use of property is a matter for the city council to decide. Did you break the lock?'

'Not personally, but I take responsibility. Let's be nice about this, Captain Lamm. There's no need for unpleasantness. We're on the same side.'

From the look on Lamm's face, he didn't quite agree. His men shuffled, edgy.

'Get these vagrants out of this building,' Lamm said, slowly and deliberately.

Criid had one of the choicest and most vulgar replies of her life ready to throw back at him, but a sound from beyond the factory interrupted her.

It was the sound of gunfire. The first shots of the night.

And it was swiftly followed by the sound of screaming.

'FIND A POSITION!' Obel yelled. 'Find a position and hold it!' The Ghosts in eleven platoon had started moving the moment they heard the first shots, but they were met by a surge of panicking pilgrims rushing out of the camp area. Two or three guardsmen were knocked off their feet by the moving crush.

The initial bursts of enemy fire had appeared only as flashes of light in the distance behind the press of bodies, but now actual laser bolts were visible, bright and hard, searing over the heads of the crowd. Hot red or hotter white, the lines of shots walked and bent like tracer rounds through the gloom. A series of them struck the warehouse wall behind Obel's location and blew out thick chunks of plaster and brick. Two loose rounds hit a stylite in the middle distance and knocked him, flailing, off his pillar. Other shots arced down mercilessly into the terrified masses.

'Oh feth!' Obel cursed, down in cover behind a handcart with his vox-officer. The vox-man was shouting to be heard as he relayed the situation in.

'Estimates?' Obel yelled.

'I can't see a bloody thing, sarge!' Brehenden barked back, trying to push through the disorder.

Larkin had managed to reach a doorway on the other side of the thoroughfare. He narrowed his eyes and watched the light show for a few seconds.

'At least a dozen shooters. Light or standard las,' he called out once he'd assessed the pattern. 'But they've got something heavier. A grunt cannon or even some kind of plasma cooker.'

That was what was doing the real harm. Potent firepower, auto-cycle, indiscriminate. Dozens of pilgrims were already dead. The heavy had so much kick, it brought down another of the hapless stylites by chopping clean through the pillar he was standing on. Larkin observed with astonishment that the other pillar-dwellers didn't try to flee or climb down. They simply sank to their knees on the precarious perches and started to pray.

'Can you knock it out?' Obel yelled.

Larkin studied the play of las-bolts in the air, watching for the fat, dull red ones. About two hundred metres north and east.

'I can try,' he said, without enthusiasm.

Obel waved Jajjo and Unkin forward to partner Larkin. Jajjo, dark-skinned and handsome, was eleven's new scout and the first Vervunhiver to achieve promotion to that elite speciality. Larkin knew Mkoll had high hopes of Jajjo's abilities.

'Call it, Larks,' Jajjo said. Ordinarily, the scout would take point, but this was now the sniper's play.

'Left, down there,' Larkin said. The trio pushed across the flow of the screaming crowd and hurried down a short flight of flagstone steps onto an arched walkway that ran along the back of a factory blockhouse. Several dozen pilgrims had elected to hide along here, and cowered into the walls as the three guardsmen ran past.

The walkway reached a corner where it split, continuing on over a stone footbridge into the side of a fabrication mill or descending to the lower service street by a wooden staircase. Pilgrims flooded along the street below. Larkin stood at the top of the steps for a moment and cocked his head. The gunfire sounds had altered slightly, relative to his location.

'Down,' he said and the three of them thumped down the wooden steps and began following the street by hugging the wall as civilians ran past the other way.

They reached a cross street. The flow of pilgrims had ebbed. Bodies sprawled all around on the rutted roadway. A clock shrine lay overturned at the junction.

Larkin darted out and got in cover behind the clock shrine. Immediately, the street lit up; light las-fire, hissing like quenched steel, and the heavy, diaphragm-vibrating belch of the cannon. Peppered, the carcass of the clock shrine shook and pieces of wood and plastic splintered off into the air. Shots chopped into the street paving too, or thudded dully into the draped and hunched corpses.

Larkin kept his head down. The fusillade he'd stirred up was so intense there wasn't a chance of Jajjo or Unkin making it across to join him. They were still pinned around the corner.

Several cannon rounds came right through the twisted clock that sheltered him and missed his head by a short margin. Larkin rolled and pulled his long-las up to his shoulder. Prone, he had a very limited field of view under the shrine's cart base, but it was enough for him to slide his long-las through and clear the sights.

The street beyond resolved in the cold, green shimmer of his night scope. He had to tweak the visual gain down because the las-flashes swooping his way were testing the limits of the radiance contrast.

Better. A hot spot. Very hot. A superheated muzzle, something big. He looked again, identifying three shadows working a heavy cannon on a tripod behind a parked motor truck forty metres away. More hot spots, smaller, cooler. Men with lasrifles. One in a doorway, another behind a row of fuel drums, another low against a side wall. All of them pumping fire at him.

He reached back and opened his musette bag, pulling a handful of powerclips out and selecting a standard low volt cell. He did it all by touch, reading the difference between the upright and diagonal crosses of tape he'd marked the sides with. He'd have preferred to go with a hot-shot for maximum power, but there were too many targets. A hot-shot was a one-use cell and he didn't have the time to keep changing between hits.

Larkin popped the hot-shot clip out of the long-las and replaced it with a low volt. He made sure he had a green 'armed' tell-tale showing on the back-sight, and then snuggled in. Feth, but they weren't letting up. Another minute, no more, and the clock shrine would start falling apart and he might as well be naked in the middle of the street with a target painted on his face and a feather up his arse.

The cannon was the obvious initial target, but the noise it was whooping out would cover him as he picked off the others first. He set on the shooter in the doorway, waited for him to blaze away again to pick him out of the shadows properly, and then fired. The enemy probably didn't even see his muzzle flash in the confusion.

The one by the side wall now. *That's it, keep shooting. Show me right where you are…*

The long-las kicked. The figure by the wall flopped over.

The shooter by the drums suddenly realised that his cronies were down. He started to run back towards the cannon. That was when Larkin put his third shot through the man's spine.

The cannon started to crank up and fire right at him instead of hosing the street. No time for chances. Larkin ejected the low volt and slammed a hot-shot home. Each blast of the cannon had many times more power than the long-las, even with a hot-shot in the pipe, and it was cycling

them out at a rate of five a second. The clock part of the toppled shrine disintegrated and a wheel went spinning off the
cart, dismembered and shedding spokes.

'Yeah, yeah,' said Larkin and fired.

The hot-shot made a growling howl and the stock banged
back against the permanent bruise on Larkin's right shoulder.
It hurt. It always did. He liked the pain because he always
associated it with a kill-shot.

The gunner's head vaporised and he pitched forward over
the cannon. Sudden silence. Larkin could see the gunner's
two teammates scrambling to pull him aside as the Tanith
sniper locked another hot-shot in place.

*Power-cell pack, one metre left of the tripod stand, feed cable
attached...*

Shoulder smack.

The cell pack exploded with the force of several grenades
and tossed the whole cannon, tripod and all, into the air,
along with all three figures, lifting balletically in a bright
bloom of fire.

The tripod carriage bounced twice, making hard, metal
clangs. The bodies didn't bounce.

'Clear!' Larkin yelled, reloading and getting up. Jajjo and
Unkin swept out of cover and started running past him, snapping off semi-auto bursts to wash the street. Larkin ran after
them, keeping close to the wall.

'Feth me, Larks!' said Unkin, surveying the sniper's
handiwork as he got into a covering position at the next
corner, near to where the destruction of the cannon had
made a burning crater in the roadway. 'You don't mess
about!'

'Pat him on the back later,' said Jajjo. He was crouching
beside the truck and had begun firing down the left hand
street.

More assaulters were moving up towards them. Lots of
them. And Jajjo recognised their blood-red uniforms at once.

BLOOD PACT. So it was true, Tona Criid thought to herself.
Up to a point, at least. The 'heretic dissidents' raiding Beati
City were actually trained, drilled and seasoned infantry
from the archenemy's elite field corps. What Corbec's

briefing had omitted was the scale. This wasn't a skirmish raid. This was a full-on assault.

The enemy was pouring out of the wasteland into the Glassworks sector in force, heavily serviced by infantry support weapons and portable shields. By her own estimate, fifty or more pilgrims had been slaughtered in the opening phase, caught between the ruthless shock-fire of the attackers and the virtually helpless Imperials. Now the pilgrims had mostly fled into cover nearby, or en masse up into the inner city, and the battle had opened up, a ferocious streetfight running up through the obsidae, the camps and into the manufactories in the zone. Criid's platoon, supported by Domor's, held a three block area, with Obel's unit not far away to their west. She was reinforced fifteen minutes into the fight by three more platoons transitting in from the east, and by the column of local warriors voxed up by Captain Lamm.

It was ugly, as ugly as anything she'd ever known, and that was saying something. It felt a little like the street war she'd been caught up in back at Vervunhive, but there the enemy had been the well-equipped but drone-like Zoicans. The Blood Pact were a different thing altogether. They knew how to fight the streets. They were as skilled as the Ghosts and more disciplined than any Chaos force she'd ever encountered. It also compared unfavorably with the trench war on Aexe Cardinal that they'd only recently left behind. At the time, she'd believed that to be the benchmark of bad in terms of combat. Trapped – like rats and with rats – in narrow, filthy dugouts, sometimes fighting hand to hand.

But this was a gakking nightmare. The Glassworks was too open, too meandering. Every corner and twist of walkway, every sub-alley and back run, was a death trap. In a trench, you at least knew the enemy was in front of you.

Laughing, she burst off a spray of las-shots and slammed a Blood Pacter backwards through an archway. Two more appeared, and she felled them both as well.

'What the feth is funny?' Lubba shouted at her, blasting with his newly issued lasrifle. It seemed too small for his meaty, tattooed hands. She knew he dearly missed his flamer. Gak, but how useful would a flamer have been right then?

'I caught myself longing for trenches,' she said, re-celling her weapon. 'Struck me as laugh-your-brains-out funny.'

'Left! Left!' Subeno was yelling suddenly. A torrent of las-fire whickered down a side street and Criid and Lubba had to dive to find cover. Domor ran past her, with Nehn, Bonin and Milo. They closed down the fresh angle of attack with a heavy sheet of rapid fire. Several more Ghosts, led by Chiria and Ezlan, pushed through the gap and drove the fight back down the street. One of the Ghosts lurched and dropped. Criid couldn't see who it was. But she could see for sure they were dead.

Lamm's men had the cross street down from them locked up. Every few seconds, Criid could hear the hiss-burp of his sanctioned flamer. Behind them, in the next street block, Herodian PDF were engaged in a running battle with the enemy inside a row of iron-framed tithe barns.

'How's our back looking?' she called to Lubba. He was covered in plaster dust and looked like he'd been rolled in flour.

'Like I have the remotest fething idea,' he replied.

She got up and ran back down the narrow street, picking her way between the bodies of slaughtered pilgrims. DaFelbe, with nine troops in a good location, had the back end of the street sealed, but was coming under increasingly heavy fire. She saw Posetine and Vulli dragging Mkhef back out of the firing line. He'd been shot through the neck and chest. She doubted he'd see sunrise.

Rounding the corner, she ran right into Captain Daur leading his platoon up through the smoke.

'Report!' he yelled over the shooting.

Criid made a vague gesture around her. 'They're fething well all over us!' she began. 'Get back!'

'Cover!' he yelled, and his platoon broke towards the doorways and shattered windows of the barn opposite.

Criid moved the other way into a rubble strewn alley and straight into three Blood Pact troopers coming the other way.

Criid yelped and dropped. A las-round burned across her scalp.

It knocked the sense out of her. She lay face down in the rubble, unable to move, to see…

Something came down off the roof behind the Blood Pacters. A single Ghost, laspistol in one hand, straight silver in the other. In less than two seconds, all three enemy troopers were dead, two shot point-blank, the other slit open.

Breathing hard, Lijah Cuu lowered his hands. He was dripping with blood. He walked over to Criid and crouched down beside her. Figures ran past the end of the alley. Shots whined.

He holstered his pistol, and twitched the combat knife over so it was point-down from his bloody fist. Then he rested the tip of it against the nape of her neck. A drop of dark blood welled up around the razor-sharp point.

With his other hand, he stroked her hair, matted with blood, and then dragged a dirty finger down the slope of her exposed cheek.

'Sure as sure,' he muttered hoarsely. He raised the blade to slam it down.

A big hand closed around his rising wrist and held it dead. Cuu gasped in pain and glanced up.

'Don' you hurt nobody,' Kolea said.

'Get off me!' Cuu said.

'Don' you hurt nobody, Lijah-Cuu,' Kolea repeated, rising. Cuu was forced to come up with him, his wrist viced in Kolea's monumentally strong grasp.

'I was trying to help her! She needs help! Look at her!' Cuu squealed. 'Her gas-hood is twisted around her throat! Look! Look, gak it! I was gonna cut it off!'

'You go 'way,' Kolea said. 'Go 'way now.'

He released Cuu's wrist. Cuu backed off, staring at Kolea. Kolea returned the gaze, placid.

'You help her then,' Cuu said, 'you stupid gak-head.' He raised the war knife slightly, then wiped the blood off it on his trouser leg and sheathed it.

'Go 'way!' Kolea said. Cuu vanished into the shadows.

Kolea bent down and rolled Criid over, stripping off her constricting gas-hood. Then he gathered her up in his arms and started to walk.

Out on the street, Lubba saw him coming and felt his heart freeze. He'd been there, on Phantine two years before, and seen this exact thing. Kolea carrying the injured Criid to safety. Seconds later, Kolea had been hit and the man they all knew and loved had disappeared.

Lubba leapt up before it could happen again and pulled Kolea into cover. 'Medic!' he shouted. 'Medic here now!'

TWO STREETS AWAY, mortar rounds were falling on the sheds and factory spaces. Seething sheets of flame rushed out of doorways and windows, spraying glass into the air and shaking the earth. A roof caved in. Two long assembly shops were ablaze.

Milo cowered in the cover of a half-fallen wall. His ears rang with overpressure. Blood from a shrapnel wound dribbled down his cheek. Bonin lay beside him, trying to tug a sliver of glass out of his palm.

'Well, this is fething nice, isn't it,' he said over the roar of detonations.

'Indeed,' Milo answered. He was rattled and dazed by the explosions but, beyond that, he had the oddest feeling. Like…

Like on Hagia.

He never had found out what signals had wanted him for.

'Wise up!' Bonin suddenly hissed, and rolled over, bringing his lasrifle up. He cracked off a couple of rounds and Milo joined his efforts. Red-clad figures had just emerged from the bombed-out buildings ahead of them.

They fired with care and precision. Bonin, a hugely able scout, had been trained in warfare by Mkoll, and knew how to shoot and how to wait to shoot. Milo had learned his battle-craft from a variety of sources… Colonel Corbec, Gaunt himself and, most especially, Hlaine Larkin. Milo picked his targets with a huntsman's expertise.

Between them, they shot down nine Blood Pact attackers as they emerged from the ruins and tried to push down the street.

They huddled in the rubble for a few minutes, and when the mortars started up again, they slid back in the direction of the main force.

'Help me!' someone was shouting. Flames were licking up around the buildings nearby and spitting sparks up at the fluttering shield.

Milo broke into a run, Bonin alongside him. They saw a man up ahead, a well-built man in late middle age wearing the robes of an infardi pilgrim. He was trying to drag an elderly man out of a burning manufactory.

'There are more inside!' Alphant yelled at the two Ghosts as they reached him. 'By the Saint, the place is on fire!'

The abandoned barn Criid had opened for Alphant's faithful just a short while before was now riven with flames. Many of those inside were too old or infirm to save themselves. Or they were children, helplessly lost and terrified.

Milo and Bonin went back in with Alphant and shooed the screaming children out. Rafters came down in scuds of flame. Bonin and Alphant grabbed an old woman in a litter seat and struggled out with her, patting out the flames which had caught on her dress.

Milo grabbed up two small children and scrambled them through into the night air.

Outside, they were met by a rain of las-fire and hard rounds. The Blood Pact had caught up with them. The old woman Bonin and Alphant had carried to safety died in her chair. Milo couldn't bear to look at the other casualties.

He and Bonin dragged their lasrifles off their shoulders and began returning fire, using the masonry of a disintegrated store front as a barricade.

'Give me something! Anything!' Alphant yelled from cover in a doorway, children huddled around him.

'You know what to do with it?' Milo shouted back.

'I was Guard! I know!'

Milo fetched out his laspistol and threw it to Alphant. Then he chucked over some spare clips from his musette bag. The three of them began to fire down the street.

Ducking in and out and shooting, Alphant suddenly saw the girl, Sabbatine. He'd been looking for her all night... ever since their encounter in the Ironhall camp, in fact. There was something about the girl, something remarkable, something that had driven him to seek her out.

She came out of a lathe shop down the street, rushing a group of child pilgrims from a block where flames were leaping up. They ran in line, holding hands. She looked like a scholam teacher on an outing.

'Get back! Get back!' Alphant shouted out to her.

She turned, saw him, and began hurrying the children towards the cover position where Alphant and the two Ghosts lay.

'For feth's sake!' Milo exclaimed, seeing them come. Las-fire whipped around the heads of the little, urgent procession. How was it missing? How were they not dead?

Bonin and Milo rose up a little, and fired to give them cover, then began dragging the wailing children down behind the barricade as they reached them.

'Come on!' Alphant yelled at the girl. She seemed to be making no effort to duck or keep low. He risked his own skin and ran out of cover to grab her and the last of the children. A shot grazed his thigh. Somehow, the tiny girl kept him upright until they tumbled back into shelter.

'I was looking for you,' he said.

Sabbatine smiled. 'I know.'

Milo crawled over to them, urging the sobbing children to stay low, trying to make it sound like a game.

'That was a very brave thing you did,' he said to the girl. She looked over at him and Milo was lost for words. He'd never seen her before in his life, but he knew her. As if he'd always known her.

Milo shook himself to clear the distraction from his mind. 'We have to get these children out of here,' he said. 'Bonin?'

'No go!' Bonin yelled from nearby, in amongst the cowering kids and other pilgrims himself. 'The fire's choked off the back end of the street. We can't get through that way.'

Milo slithered forward and dared a look out down the street ahead. Spark-filled coils of smoke washed across the trashed, shot-up accessway. He saw men moving up through it, men with rifles and chilling iron masks. Every few seconds, one or more raised his weapon and fired in their direction. Far too many for just the three of them to repel.

Then even that became academic. The advancing Blood Pact infantry were drawing aside into the edges of the ruined street. Something was approaching from behind them.

'Oh feth...' groaned Milo as the assault tank, painted crimson and defiled with abhorrent symbols, rolled into view.

* * *

'THIS IS NOT an appropriate time for an audience,' said the Civitas Beati staff officer. 'The city is under attack.'

'Really? Make a list of more appropriate occasions then, feth you!' Zweil snarled. The soldier, in his heavy battle-dress and polished armour segments, towered over the aged ayatani, and in the candlelight of the atrium it was impossible to read the expression on his hard-set face. Behind him, the massive bronze doors of the city's chief Ecclesiarchy cathedral, situated near the summit of hive tower one, were engraved with images of Kiodrus holding up the bowl for the Saint to cleanse her wounds. The doors were shut resolutely.

'Father, please,' the staff officer began.

'I've come a long way to see her,' Zweil told him.

'So have very many people.'

Zweil waggled his bony hands in frustration. 'Do you know who I am?'

'You are Imhava Ayatani Zweil, and only an old rogue like you would see fit to make a ruckus like this.'

The voice came from behind him. Zweil glanced round and found himself facing another old man in priestly robes.

'Kilosh,' he said, bowing. Kilosh returned the gesture. 'You're a long way from home for a tempelum ayatani, brother,' said Zweil.

'The circumstances of our devotion change, brother.' Kilosh smiled. 'It's surprisingly good to see you again, you cantankerous old troublemaker.'

'And you, though you seem as starchy and straight-laced as ever. I need to see her, brother.'

'That much is evident to everyone in shouting distance. I might see what I can arrange, except...'

'Except what?' Zweil scowled.

'There is enough trouble for us all tonight. I'll not have you causing more.'

Zweil drew Kilosh to one side and lowered his voice. 'I know what you think. Not only do I have a less than pristine reputation, I've been consorting with these Tanith heathens for longer than might have done me good.'

'Brother, I do not regard Gaunt and his men as heathens.'

Zweil paused. 'Neither do I, as it goes. But you're afraid I'll go in there and denounce her to her face. Disbelieve as Gaunt disbelieves.'

'His lack of faith indeed pains me, brother.'

'Not half so much as it does me. He is a good man, and honest, and I've hitched myself to his regiment this last while because he seemed a true devotee of the Saint. I do not know what has occurred to break his faith, but it saddens me.'

Kilosh nodded. 'So you haven't come as his emissary, to unmask the false idol?'

'Rather the reverse. Brother, I need to seek audience so I can go back and affirm the truth to him. Make him see. Make him believe.'

'You entertain no doubts of your own?'

Zweil shook his head. 'There have been signs, portents, omens, enough to mass an exodus of pilgrims, enough to turn this part of the Imperium on its head. The divination of a dozen temples of a dozen worlds has foretold, emphatically, that the Saint is reborn and come here to Herodor. The evidence is unequivocal. I believe she is here. I believe full stop. I will do everything in my power to make Gaunt believe too. For without his faith, we are doomed.'

Kilosh studied Zweil's face for a long moment, then beckoned him to follow.

The Civitas Beati regimentals drew back the bronze doors, and the two old priests hobbled into the vast chancel of the great church. The marble walls and pillars were laced with gilt, and obsidian mosaics had been chased into the stone facings. Clock shrines had been clustered inside the entrance, along with glacial heaps of islumbine garlands. A massive, sculptural eagle wrought from black iron, thirty metres from wingtip to wingtip, was suspended from the domed roof. The deep rows of pews, arranged in a semi-circle fan, were made of a dark, varnished wood and, at the high altar, great candlesticks worked from gleaming chelon shell fluttered with yellow flame. The altar itself was a large, rectangular basin of stone, filled with holy water from the balneary. The water was smooth and unrippled, like a brown mirror.

Zweil knelt and made devotion for a moment facing the altar. Then Kilosh helped him back to his feet and led him through to the inner chapel. Esholi handmaids, robed in violet albs and white bicorn headdresses, waited outside the gilded screen of the iconostasis. Kilosh opened the old screen door and the pair descended the few, worn steps into the tiny crypt.

It was dark, save for phospha lamps and a shaft of faint exterior light, swirling with the glow of the city shield, that fell through a narrow slit high up the wall above the simple shrine altar. A woman was kneeling there, in prayer, the window light dipping onto her.

She heard them and rose, turning. She wore long, blue robes and a white stole, and her glossy black hair was tied up away from her face. Kilosh bowed at once. Zweil stared at her, unable to express himself. He felt his heart pound as if it was about to rupture, as if he had come this far and this long only for his ancient body to fail him now.

'Ayatani Zweil,' said the Saint, her voice like silk. Islumbine. He could smell islumbine strongly on the air.

He gasped and fell to his knees. Words would not come.

'I–'

'Shhhh, loyal father,' she said, and reached out a hand. He took it between his own.

Something thrilled through his skin, like an electric charge. Like needles. He broke the grip sharply and looked up at her, confused.

'Sanian…' he said.

Her smile had not faded. 'You know the vessel I am in, Ayatani Zweil. You recognise it, but–'

'No!' he said, struggling to his feet. He was blinking hard, as if trying not to cry. 'Oh, God-Emperor, he was right. You're Sanian…'

She backed from him. Kilosh rose, grunting with effort. 'Damn you, Zweil!' he hissed. 'You said you would not do this! You tricked me!'

'No, no…' Zweil said, still staring at her. 'With all my heart, Kilosh, I meant what I said back there. But now I see the truth. It is not the truth I wanted to see, but it is the truth nevertheless.'

Kilosh angrily pulled at Zweil's sleeve to drag him back.
The imhava ayatani pushed him away. 'The Saint is here. I feel
her in every stone and every breath of air. But this is not her!'

THE TANK FIRED again, burying a shell in the facade of the
burning manufactory behind them. Rock and glass was
hurled into the air. The children and the pilgrims were
screaming.

'Tube-charge!' Bonin yelled.

'You'll never get close enough!' Milo bawled back, shield-
ing his head from the fluttering debris. He scrambled over to
Bonin and pushed the tube-charges from his satchel into
Bonin's hands. 'Not unless it's distracted! On three!'

Another shell howled over their heads. The tank was just
twenty metres off now. Its hardpoint stubber started chattering, raking the rubble barricade.

The two Ghosts started to run in opposite directions, heads
down. Bonin hurtled down the left side of the roadway, tight
to the wall, trying to strap the tube-charges together as he ran.
Milo crossed to the right side, went on hands and knees until
he reached a doorway, and then flopped round. Through the
smoke, he could see Alphant and the other adult pilgrims trying to squeeze the children into what little cover remained.

'Ready?' Bonin's voice crackled over the micro-bead.

'Go!' Milo said. He swung up out of hiding and let rip with
his lasrifle on full auto. The shots pinged and flashed against
the bruised metal hull of the war machine. It lurched to a
stop and then the stubber came round to aim at him.

He barely got down in time. The hefty, solid-slug weapon
blew the wall and doorway over his curled up body into fragments. It wasn't enough. He hadn't distracted it for anything
like long enough for Bonin to get close.

Milo started to crawl again as more flurries of shrieking
stub rounds went over him. If only he could–

He heard Alphant shouting and looked up.

The girl was running from cover. Running into the middle
of the war-wounded street, right out in front of the tank.

'Feth, no!' Milo yelled, and started to dash after her.

She was right in front of the tank, both hands raised like an
arbites officer controlling road traffic. The tank stopped as if

puzzled. The main turret turned, lowering the massive cannon, like a cyclops eye-stalk, to stare at her.

Bonin came out of the smoke alongside the tank and hurled the tube-charges. They bounced along the hind-part of the hull, and came to rest under the lip of the turret's aft cowling.

Milo dived headlong and brought the girl down hard, smashing her aside just as the main tank weapon fired.

And the tube-charges detonated.

AT THAT MOMENT, on a sliproad leading down between manufactory sites into the Ironhall sector, Captain Daur fell down so hard and so suddenly the troopers around him thought he'd been hit.

'Captain!' Brennan yelled, running to him. A few sparkling las-shots from the raiders down the slope drifted past like fireflies. Trooper Solia was yelling for a medic.

'I'm allright,' Daur said. His teeth were chattering, like he was cold. 'I mean, I'm not hit.'

'Why did you fall down, captain?' Solia asked, fierce concern on her dust-smudged face.

'I just had… the most awful feeling,' Daur said, and then laughed at how stupid it sounded.

There was nothing stupid about the expression on his face.

IN THE BACK of the transport, in the rancid, recycled air, Curth stepped back from the Herodian trooper she'd been trying to sew back together and shook her head with a sigh. Many more injured, most of them infardi, were gathered around the entry ramp of the heavy vehicle. Every now and then, it vibrated as the ground shook from nearby shell-falls.

Curth heard a clatter and looked round. Chief Medic Dorden, working at a gurney beside her, had just knocked an entire tray of surgical instruments over.

'Dorden?'

He swayed. His face, behind his plastic mask, was grey and unhealthy.

'Dorden!' Curth cried, hurrying to him.

'Ana? What just happened?'

'What do you mean?'

'Didn't you see that flash? It was so bright...'

'No... nothing more than the barrage we're already getting.'

'So bright...' he whispered.

THE TANITH REINFORCEMENTS leapt out of their transports the moment the column of trucks pulled up. They'd reached a crossroads on Principal I, facing north on the Guild Slope, where the southern boundary of the Ironhall and Glassworks sectors began. One by one, light tanks and self-propelled guns of the Regiment Civitas Beati powered past, moving up to the front line, along with Salamanders and light cannon-platforms from Lugo's landing force.

Gaunt checked his bolt-pistol clip and walked the length of one of the stationary troop carriers to where Corbec was briefing squad leaders.

'I know these babies have nice, thick armour,' Corbec was saying, slapping the hull of the carrier, 'but they're also big fat targets. We've got close-engage street fights up ahead, and you'll be more use – and safer – on foot. Get ready to disperse by squad.'

He glanced round at Gaunt. 'Anything you want to add, sir?'

Gaunt was about to answer when Corbec suddenly put a hand to his head and swayed.

'Colonel?'

'Oh my God-Emperor...' said Corbec, looking up into Gaunt's eyes. 'Did you not just feel that? *Did you not just feel that?*'

'AYATANI ZWEIL! AYATANI Zweil, withdraw yourself now!' Kilosh was shouting.

'Don't you understand, Kilosh? Can't you unbend enough to see it?' Zweil pointed across the chapel at the Saint, who watched him with reproachful silence.

'I will summon the temple guards and have you ejected if you do not cease and depart now!' Kilosh stormed.

Zweil, his head pulsing, was about to reply when he felt a smoky, rusty tang in his mouth.

He looked at Kilosh and coughed. Blood spattered into his raised hand.

'Zweil? What's the matter with you?'

Oh my dear lord Emperor, Zweil thought. *This is it. I'm having a stroke and—*

And that was all he thought. Soundlessly, he pitched forward and cracked his head on the flagstones.

'Zweil?' Kilosh said, more mystified than anything else. He stooped beside his elderly colleague, felt for a pulse and started to call for help. There was a shriek from behind him.

He turned to see that the Saint had fallen to her knees. In the light of the phospha lamps, he saw a frightened, horrified look on her face. Her shaking hands were dabbing at the blood streaming from her nose.

'Help me!' Kilosh screamed. 'Help me here!'

THERE WAS NOTHING left of the tank apart from a heap of blackened metal shreds. Dense blue smoke filled the narrow street, making it hard to breathe, Bonin was coughing and choking as he ran back. His ears were still ringing.

'Milo! Milo!'

The boy was face down in a ditch, covered in ash and pebbles. Bonin reached him about the same time as Alphant did. Milo came to as they rolled him over. He was miraculously alive and intact.

But the girl, nearby, curled up by a broken kerb, was not. The blast of the tank round, which had dug the ground up beneath both of them and hurled them into the air, had landed her hard. Her neck was broken and she was dead.

Alphant cried out in despair.

Milo hadn't seen any of this, but at the sound of the cry, his guts tightened.

He got up and knew, long before he actually saw her body, that something awful had just happened. Something huge, something dark, something more than all the waste and death and slaughter around them.

Something unholy.

FOUR
MAGNIFICAT

'I know what I saw then. And I know what I see now.'

— Zweil, ayatani

FROM THE STREETS of the Guild Slope in mid-city, a nimbus of russet-pink and yellow could be seen suffusing the darkness over the north-west skirts of the metropolitan area. Individual sparks of light flickered in that blanket glow like grounded lightning. Dull booms and roars, pent in by the acoustic lid formed by the city shield, rolled back to their ears, and smoke, similarly trapped by the shield, collected into a wispy roof like low cloud. According to the now frenetic reports of Civitas tac logis, over a thousand hostiles, with supporting armour, were assaulting the city.

And the city was falling. Partly under the fury of the attack, and partly beneath the weight of an inexplicable sense of defeat and loss that had settled over the population during the hours of the night.

Viktor Hark could not account for it, but he could feel it. An ache, a feeling of disillusion, a sapping misery. Perhaps it was the unexpected speed and ferocity of the chaos onslaught. Perhaps it was a general realisation of how fragile the Imperial position really was.

Even in his worst-case contemplations of disaster, Gaunt had never expected things to go so badly wrong so rapidly. Hark knew that as a certainty. He'd spent considerable time with Gaunt, risk-assessing the woeful defensive opportunities afforded by the Civitas Beati, the far from adequate numerical strengths at their disposal, the complete lack of preparation time. It was a bleak picture, and Gaunt had made no secret of his fear that once the archenemy's main force arrived, the fight for Herodor would be as good as done.

But that main force had still to reach Herodor, and yet the city already seemed close to collapsing in one night.

Tac logis was still referring to the invaders as 'heretic dissidents'. Hark sighed when he heard this and tugged the micro-bead from his ear. He didn't want to listen any more.

The streets were clogged, by people and by lamentation. That was it. This was not the sound of terror and alarm rising from the crowds. This was the sound of woe.

Hark was riding in a heavy-fendered troop transporter near the front of a reinforcement column. There were twelve transporters, all identical grey, long-bodied Munitorum vehicles, and they were only making any headway through the crowds at all because of the three Chimera heavies from the lord general's life company that were leading them through. The sight of tracked armour made the distressed crowds part sharply.

Colonel Kaldenbach, Lugo's field commander, had command of the column, and the Tanith and Herodian PDF squads in the troop carriers answered to him. Hark knew Kaldenbach fairly well from his time on the lord general's staff, an uncompromising but gifted officer who had crowned a good career in the Ardelean Colonials with elevation to Lugo's personal life company.

The column turned west off Principal II, under the broad aqueducts that serviced the agriponic district, and rolled into the wide plaza of Astronomer's Circle in the shadow of the great volcanic plug on which sat the Astronomer's Platform, that bastion of Herodian science and learning. It was up there, in the ancient observatories that had been operating permanently for over two thousand years, that Cazalon had devised and written his treatise on non-baryonic matter and Hazmun Zeng, three centuries later, had doggedly completed his Theory of Gravitation in the face of fierce Inquisitorial displeasure. Hark had been told that it was possible to visit Zeng's workshop study, which had been preserved, by order of the first officiary, exactly as the great man had left it. The idea appealed to Hark immensely. To climb the steps rough-hewn in the side of the rock plug up into that quiet little island of observatories, macroscope towers, sidereal calculators and libraries high above the murmur of the city and spend a few quiet moments in the dusty room where Zeng had made such a staggering contribution to Imperial science, filling notebooks with mirror-script to fool the watching eyes of the Inquisition.

But war, as ever, anchored Hark to the ground. In twenty years, he had travelled to and served on over forty worlds, many of them rich with cultural treasures and sites of significance. He had never enjoyed the indulgence of visiting any of them. There was always fighting to be done, or battle orders to review and, when that was over, a troop-ship waiting to convey him to the next theatre.

The column drew up in the Circle and the units disembarked. Kaldenbach, sturdy in his long green coat and cap, marched the line of assembly, issuing orders. There were fifty troopers from Lugo's life company in the support force, all of them clad in heavy green fatigues and camo-helms. A major called Pento from the Regiment Civitas Beati was in charge of the Herodian portion, two platoons of Civitas Beati elite and five of regular Herodian PDF. Sergeant Varl drew up the Ghost element of five platoons: his own, Haller's, Arcuda's, Raglon's and Ewler's.

Putting his commissar's cap on brim first – 'Gaunt-style', the Ghosts called it – Hark felt somewhat surplus to requirements. Kaldenbach even had his own commissars, an inseparable pair of identical twins called Keetle. They were thin, bony redheads with fair skin and thyroid eyes, dressed in black, patent leather stormcoats that creaked as they strode along, singing out incendiary and fortifying mottoes in stereo. Bad form, in Hark's book. The assembling soldiers were clearly spooked. They were on the doorstep of a savage urban fight zone and about to go in head first, and around them lay a city that seemed to have already given up.

'Soldiers of the Imperium!' yelled Keetle One.

'You see that up there?' bawled his brother, pointing up at the Astronomer's Platform.

'The seat of Herodian learning! From there, astronomers maintain a permanent study of the enfolding majesty of the heavens, comprehending their secrets and discerning their truths!'

'But even their vigilance,' yelled Keetle Two, 'is but a brief glance compared to the eternal vigilance of the holy God-Emperor!'

'Praise be the God-Emperor!'

'Praise be the God-Emperor, who watches over us all, at all times, and in all things!'

'His eyes are on you all now,' declared Keetle One. 'They do not stray, they judge and consider your every action!'

'So do not disappoint him! Do not fail in this great hour of warfare!'

They rattled on for a good while like this. Hark could kindle a rousing speech like the best of them when necessary, but this seemed like overkill. Just as Gaunt sometimes allowed himself to play genial soft fiddle to Hark's brimstone, so now Hark felt it was his time to be more sympathetic.

He started with Sergeants Arcuda and Raglon. Both were newly lifted to squad command. They were still finding their feet, and on Aexe Cardinal, Raglon's first taste of combat leadership had been cursed by massive bad luck and heavy losses.

They tensed as he walked up, so he smiled, and that seemed so unusual to them they both sniggered.

'Ready to go?'

'Sir,' they both affirmed. He looked at their platoons, drawn up in triple lines, sparing a particular moment to study Trooper Costin in Raglon's outfit. It had been Costin's drunken errors that had proved so expensive to Raglon's unit on Aexe. Gaunt should have shot him by rights, and would have done too, but for the passionate intervention of Dorden. Dorden had put his neck on the line to spare Costin,

and had undermined Gaunt's authority in the process. The
once-warm friendship between the colonel-commissar and
his chief medic had been seriously strained ever since. Hark
had his eye on Costin, but the man seemed to have cleaned
up his act in a real effort to redeem himself.

'Let me tell you something,' Hark said quietly to Raglon
and Arcuda. 'I know what's in your heads right now. Fear.
Fear of pain and death, fear of failure. The weight of your new
responsibilities. That sick feeling you'll feth up and let the
side down. And those two are not helping your nerves with
their pompous yakking.'

He thumbed sidelong at the Keetles, who were now leading the reluctant Herodians in a declaration of the Imperial
creed. Raglon and Arcuda both laughed nervously.

'Forget about them,' Hark said. 'Think about this. The men
out there, our friends and comrades, our fellow Ghosts,
down there in the battle zone, up to their necks in the worst
kind of feth. Think about them and think about this... it's
you they most want to see. Not just reinforcements, Ghosts.
The fething best field troops it's ever been my honour to
know. There is nothing they are hoping for more than the
sight of these five platoons storming in, guns blazing and
hearts afire, to ease their heavy burden. To them, you'll be a
dream come true. Think about what it'll mean to them, and
I promise you, all your worries will seem insignificant by
comparison.'

They both nodded, firm and resolved. Hark clapped them
both on the shoulders. 'You'll be fine, sergeants. Spread the
word amongst your men, get them set.'

Hark walked on to Haller, a Verghast vet, and Ewler, a griz-
zled old Tanith career soldier. They needed no soft soap, and
his chat with them was a more workmanlike discussion of
tactics and deployment. He answered their queries, compli-
mented them on their squad turn-out, and told them a joke
about an Ecclesiarchy convent and a curiously shaped fruit
that made them laugh so loud it drew disapproving stares
from the Keetles.

Finally, he strolled towards Varl. To the Ghosts, Varl was
the soldier's soldier, smart-mouthed, cock-sure, roguish but
utterly cool under fire. He'd slogged up through the ranks

from common dog-grunt to get squad command, earning it
on sheer merit, and was loved by all. He'd lost a shoulder
on Fortis Binary, and had a hefty augmetic inbuild to
replace it. If there was a hot centre to any fight, Varl would
most likely be in it. If there was a scam or practical joke in
the barracks, Varl would be in the thick of that too. The joke
about the nuns and the fruit was one of his. Hark had overheard it just thirty minutes earlier, during Varl's platoon
warm-up.

'Ready?' Hark asked.

'I was born ready, sir,' Varl replied, then paused. 'That's a lie.
I was born horny. I got ready during my early teens.'

Hark laughed, but he could tell from Varl's manner something was bothering him. 'What's up, Ceg?'

Varl looked uncomfortable. He tapped a finger to the
micro-bead plug in his left ear. 'I've been tuned to the local
channel, the tac logis, monitoring the chatter,' he said quietly.
'It sounds like shit in a nalnut is going on down there. And
the mood on the street tonight is like we've already lost.'

'Yes, I feel it. I won't lie, I think this is going to be bad.'

'It's not just that, sir,' said Varl. 'Report came in, five minutes back. Said the Tanith second officer was down.'

'Down?'

'Dead or hit real bad, they weren't sure. And then no confirmation.'

'Do they mean Corbec or Rawne?'

Varl shrugged. 'Could be either, both are in there. Then
again, before the first wave of reinforcement went in, Captain
Daur was the second officer on the ground.'

Corbec, Rawne or Daur dead. Any of those things would be
a critical blow to the Tanith morale.

'You've not said anything to the men?' Hark asked.

'I'm not stupid,' Varl replied acidly, and Hark knew he'd
deserved the rebuke.

'Of course not.'

'I just wish we could move. Get on in there and find out,'
Varl said. He looked over at Kaldenbach who, with the ubiquitous Keetles, was now addressing the lord general's life
company troopers. 'I mean, we're here. All this fannying
around, what are we waiting for?'

'We're waiting,' said Hark, 'for Lugo to vox us the word to advance.' He thought for a moment. 'Come with me,' he said.

They walked over to the colonel's side. 'What is it, Hark?' Kaldenbach asked.

'Shall we advance, colonel? We are deposed and ready, and the night isn't getting any younger.'

'We await word to go,' said Kaldenbach, a pale, handsome man in his fifties with clean-cut features and wiry grey hair. Given that, from the sounds of it, tac logis was having difficulty differentiating its arse from its elbow, that word could be a long time coming in Hark's opinion.

'Well, sir,' said Hark gently, 'my troopers are famous for their scout specialisation. We should be going in already, preparing the way for your force.'

Kaldenbach frowned. 'I wasn't aware they were *your* troopers, Hark. Last time I checked, you were commissar, not… a ranking colonel as well.' This, an unwelcome reference to Gaunt's unusual and unpopular dual status, was a thinly veiled dig.

'My troopers are famous for their scout specialisation, sir,' said Varl quickly, beautifully timing his interjection, 'and last time I checked, I was ranking Tanith officer. I'm sure Commissar Hark will agree.'

Hark smiled and nodded.

Kaldenbach looked coldly at Varl, and the Keetles whispered darkly to each other.

'Anxious to die, sergeant?' Kaldenbach asked.

'Anxious to serve the God-Emperor… and you, sir.'

'Very well,' Kaldenbach snapped. 'Move in. We will stand to until word is given. Pave the way for us, if you're so damn good at it. And stay in constant vox-contact.'

Varl saluted and hurried away with Hark beside him. 'Ghosts of Tanith!' he shouted. 'Let's get wriggling! Game's on!'

The Ghost units massed forward to join him.

'Nicely done, Ceg,' Hark whispered.

'You set him up, sir. I was just there to finish him off.'

The Ghost force surged forward across the paved Circle, dressing their camo-cloaks, and melted into the narrow streets beyond.

Pento, the Herodian officer, watched them disappear. The last thing he or any of his men wanted to do was rush prematurely into combat.

Not, it seemed, like the off-worlders in black.

THE SCRIVENER'S OFFICE ruptured and collapsed, all eight storeys of it. Dust and fire flushed out from the avalanche of masonry, and the men of five platoon ran for cover.

Squat, robust, one-eyed and nothing like as mobile as his younger troopers, Agun Soric threw himself flat and the dust flow rushed over him like a breaker. The air was full of smouldering paper scraps, millions of pages of notation physically liberated by the explosion.

'Chief! Chief!' Vivvo's voice rang through the billowing smoke. Soric pulled himself up.

'Hold your gakking water, Vivvo. I'm not so much as half dead yet.' Even so, Soric didn't object as Vivvo steadied him.

'We have got to find that gakking tank,' Soric said.

'Round up! Round up!' Vivvo yelled, and the scattered elements of five platoon came out of cover. The street was a mess. White rubble covered the cobbles and most of the buildings on the west side of the road were ablaze. Soric hobbled forward, sending hand signals to fan his beleaguered troopers out. Then he sat his wide rump down on a slab of alabaster, took off his mask and spat.

Kazel, Mallor and Venar suddenly switched round, rifles aimed, as they picked up movement south of them.

'Twenty, seventeen! Hold your fire!'

'Safeties, boys!' Soric urged, as Sergeant Meryn's platoon ran up to join them out of the drifting smoke.

Meryn was a young, slickly handsome Tanith with more front than the entire fething crusade. It was said Rawne was grooming him, and that, Soric believed, explained why the previously amiable Meryn had become such a hardboiled bastard of late. He was openly ambitious in all the wrong ways, and there were dirty rumours that during the insurgency mission on Phantine, he'd exposed a cruel, almost psychotic side to his character. It was said he'd murdered civilians. Soric didn't know about that, and didn't want to, and there was no arguing with the pretty boy's combat record. But of all the squads he could have meshed with, Meryn's was about last on the list, save Rawne's platoon, of course.

And then there was the matter of that ridiculously sinister moustache Meryn had been cultivating.

'Taking a breather, chief?' Meryn suggested as he approached the seated Soric.

Soric didn't rise to the bait. 'Just waiting for you to win the gakking war single-handed, lad,' he said, replacing his rebreather. 'There's a tank somewhere in the streets yonder. It's making a gakking mess.'

Meryn turned and yelled: 'Guheen?'

Trooper Guheen hurried up, a compact missile tube slung over one shoulder. Coreas came with him lugging the satchel of long-snouted rockets.

'Treads to feth,' Meryn told him. He turned to Soric. 'So where's this tank?'

Soric rose to his feet. He was a head shorter than Meryn and as ugly as Meryn was handsome. 'If I knew that,' he said, 'I'd have fethed the bastard myself.'

'Sure you would,' said Meryn, dubiously. He waved his platoon forward into the maze of side alleys behind the ruin of the scrivener's. 'Keep low!' he shouted. 'Find this armour for me!'

Meryn's platoon, fourteen, was tight and well-drilled, Soric had to give the pretty bastard that much.

He was about to yell at Vivvo to drag five platoon to order and show Meryn's lot how it should be done when a scrap of paper landed at his feet. It was just one from the blizzard that had been blown up and out of the office collapse. Drifts of them, many burning, were settling over the ruins. But where all the others were white, Munitorum grade sheets, this was blue and lightweight.

He looked down at it, sighed deeply, then scooped it up.

On it, written in his own handwriting, were the words: *Guheen's going to get himself pulped if he goes that way. The tank is behind the cabinet maker's shop.*

Just like that. Bold as gak.

Soric shivered, tossed the scrap aside and yelled at the top of his voice: 'Guheen! Hit the bricks!'

Guheen and Coreas both heard him, halted and looked back.

'Get down, you gakkers!' Soric bellowed, running forward. He slammed into Hefron from his own squad, and wrenched the tread fether out of his bemused hands.

'What the feth is–' Meryn yelled.

Guheen and Coreas dropped flat about a half-second before a tank shell slammed through the side wall of the laundry they were passing. The wall blew out and showered bricks in all directions. The shell, shrieking and leaving an eddying vapour-trail in the still settling white dust, went over their heads and hit the corner of a shuttered café. The blast deafened them all and collapsed the café frontage in a welter of flame and flying stone chips.

Everyone was down, dazed and bewildered.

Except Soric. Panting, he ran through the rubble until he had a clear view down the side of what had to be the cabinet maker's shop. There was the tank, a hefty mid-sized model painted crimson and daubed with markings that flopped Soric's stomach. A flayed human hide was stapled across the front of its hull. Its fat turret was traversing. Soric could hear the clank of the chain drive.

With his trick leg there would be no kneeling down to soften the recoil... or hide. He stood his ground as the heavy-gauge barrel tracked round towards him and sat the missile tube he had wrenched from Hefron's grip onto his broad shoulder.

'Hello, gakkers,' he hissed and squeezed the trigger-spoon. The rocket banged away, kicking smoke out of the tube's back end with such fury it threw Soric over. The missile flamed across the rubble and hit the tank just under the edge of the waist plating. There was a loud explosion, and pieces of shrapnel zinged through the air, hot and hard as las-rounds.

When Soric looked up, the tank was gutted with fire.

He got to his feet and turned to his men, arms raised and brandishing the launcher. 'Who's the chief? Who's the gakking chief?'

They cheered him vigorously.

Meryn crossed to him, pausing to check on Guheen and Coreas, who were temporarily deaf but otherwise unhurt.

'How the feth did you know?' he asked Soric.

'Lucky guess,' Soric replied.

The vox clicked, and another Ghost platoon closed in on them out of the dust. It was two platoon, Corbec's mob, or at least what was left of it. Mkvenner was in charge, with Rerval at his side.

The tall, lean scout had still not properly recovered from the serious wounding he had taken on Aexe Cardinal. Mkvenner's long face was gripped by swallowed pain.

'Ven!' cried Soric. 'Where are the rest of your boys?'

Mkvenner shrugged. 'We came under fire. Tank fire. Three or four units. Got out all I could. I think–'

'What?'

'I think Corbec might have bought it. We can't find him anywhere.'

Soric looked away, blinking hard. 'Gak, that's... that's not good.' He looked at Rerval. The young signals officer was trying hard not to cry.

'You tried the channels?' Soric asked.

Rerval nodded.

'Try 'em again,' Soric said.

Two closed up with five and fourteen. Vivvo hurried over to Soric and handed him a brass shell.

'What's this?'

'Found it in the rubble, sir,' Vivvo said.

Soric took it. He didn't even have to check now. It was his message shell. Like a bad penny...

He unscrewed the cap and knocked out the fold of flimsy blue paper inside.

It read: *Colm's alive, but he's pinned down by cannon fire. Ven will be dead in two days unless you get him help. Two stalk-tanks south of you, well hidden. Be wary... a lot more Blood Pact are about to hit.*

Soric breathed out hard. 'Corbec's alive,' he told Mkvenner.

'How the feth do you know that?'

'Call it a hunch. Let's fan west. Rockets to the front. There are a couple of stalk-tanks out there, hulls down, if I know anything. But we can do this.'

Mkvenner nodded and wiped blood away from the corner of his mouth with his cuff. Why in the name of the

God-Emperor hadn't he sat back and let himself heal? What sort of internal damage was he doing to his body?

'Get to a field hospital, Ven,' Soric said.

'I'm fine.'

Soric faced him, brows furrowed. Tall and lean and deadly, Mkvenner was about the most frightening man in the Ghosts, and that was before you knew anything about him. No one ever chose to confront him. Life wasn't worth that much hurt. But Soric persisted.

'That's an order, Mkvenner. Find Dorden or Curth and find them now,' said Soric.

Mkvenner stared at the thick-set, older man and finally nodded. 'Sure,' he said, and shambled away through the enclosing smoke.

'Move it up! You heard me!' Soric yelled. 'Two platoon, you answer to me now!'

'Jumped up runt,' Meryn said, watching Soric rally the troops around him. They loved him, the fools.

'Sir?' said Fargher, approaching Meryn. He held out a crumpled ball of flimsy blue paper.

'What's this?' Meryn demanded.

'Chief Soric was looking at it before… before he took out the tank, sir. I thought you'd like to see it.'

Meryn unballed the paper and read it: *Guheen's going to get himself pulped if he goes that way. The tank is behind the cabinet maker's shop.*

'What is this… warpcraft?' he whispered.

'Sir?' asked Fargher.

'Never mind, Fargher,' Meryn said as he folded the paper carefully and tucked it into his jacket pocket. 'Just thinking out loud…'

For the fourth time in twenty minutes, third platoon attempted to get around the same street corner without dying. They were bunched up in a little access terrace behind an oil and gas separation plant in the Ironhall district. The terrace joined the main street at right angles, and something down that thoroughfare had them pinned with heavy fire.

With the bulk of his unit huddled low in the terrace way behind him, Rawne cautiously approached the junction with his platoon scout, Leyr, and Troopers Caffran and Feygor. If they stayed put much longer, they'd be swamped by the advancing enemy ground troops, and the terrace was no place for a firefight.

Most of the Tanith scouts had their own signature trick for looking round blind corners. Leyr's was a sweet little pocket periscope, a precision brass instrument that he'd picked up on Aexe Cardinal. 'I got it from an Aexegarian colonel,' Leyr told anyone who asked, 'who stood when he should have ducked. He had no use for it any more. Likewise, he had no use for his spectacles, his moustache comb or his hat.' The periscope was powerful but small enough to slip into the chart-pocket of his fatigues. He slid the business end round the fractured brick corner and took a squint. Fifty metres down the rubble-strewn main street, a stalk-tank sat in the centre of the roadway, its weapon pods pointing in their direction.

'You were right,' Leyr whispered. 'Scuttle-armour.'

Rawne curled his lip in annoyance. 'Any AT rockets left?' he asked, already knowing the likely answer.

'No, sir,' said Caffran. 'We're out. The tread fethers are dry.'

'Suggestions?'

'How far down is it?' Feygor asked Leyr.

'Forty, maybe fifty,' Leyr replied, looking again. Too far for even the strongest of them to throw a tube-charge. 'We better think of something quick,' he added. 'There are troops moving up.'

'I don't think we've got much choice,' Rawne said. 'We'll have to pull back, maybe reform a position a few streets that way.'

The men nodded. No one liked giving ground, but no one liked dying needlessly either.

Feygor relayed the orders with a series of quick, clear gestures, and the platoon began pulling back down the terrace.

The terrace led along to an iron walkway over a chemical drain trench, and then down into a wide, paved concourse from the centre of which rose the aluminium tubes and flanges of an atmosphere processor. Units like it, fed by ducts from the main hive structures, were dotted throughout the outer city, pumping air to maintain the thin, local atmosphere of the Civitas.

The platoon came to a sudden halt. Rawne hurried up to the front, keeping low. Banda, the platoon's sniper, had brought them to a standstill. She was huddled in beside a low wall, long-las raised. Rawne, a spectacularly unreconstructed Imperial male, had been dead against the admission of women troopers from the outset, and Banda – oozing self-confidence and physical appeal – had long been a particular thorn in his side. But in the trench hell of Aexe they had been wounded together, and had helped each other through, and in the process had reached an understanding. Rawne relied on Banda's good counsel now as much as he did that of Feygor or Caffran. Some even rumoured that Rawne and Banda were lovers, but no one dared ask either of them to confirm it.

'Movement,' she reported.

'Identity?'

'Can't tell.'

Rawne hand-signalled 'ready to engage' back down the file. 'Head shot as soon as you see a head,' he told the girl.

She took aim, and waited until something bobbed into sight in her scope. At the last moment, she relaxed her finger from the trigger.

'Friendlies,' she said.

A ramshackle squad of Civitas Beati guards was moving warily into the concourse. Rawne got on the vox and hailed them. Their leader was Udol, the major he had met during their unorthodox arrival on Herodor just the day before.

'No going that way,' Udol said, gesturing in the direction he and his men had approached from. 'They're pasting the area with mortars mounted on tractor units.' Rawne had already heard the distant, persistent *whoop-crump* echoing in their direction.

'It's as bad behind us,' he said simply. 'Blood Pact ground troops advancing, with at least one stalk-tank. They've got the up-street locked.'

'Blood Pact?' Udol asked. 'We weren't told anything about Blood Pact. Tac logis says its heretic raiders.'

'With respect,' Rawne replied, clearly expressing none at all, 'your tac logis is voxing out of its arse. It's Blood Pact all right. Trained, tight, well-supported and systematic. Their handiwork identifies them. Besides, I've met them before.'

'What do we do?' Udol asked, hoping the tremble in his voice wasn't too obvious.

'Do?' sneered Rawne. 'I don't think we've a great many options.'

The words were scarcely out of his mouth when their meagre options fizzled away dramatically. The peeling energy rounds of a stalk-tank's cannons splashed across the concourse area, blasting sections of paving up into the air. Several more punched through the metal duct-work of the processor and it began emitting an eerie, wounded moan as air escaped from the holes.

The troops – Tanith and Civitas alike – scattered for cover. Several troopers fell, cut down.

The options had been reduced to two.

Fight, or die.

A KILOMETRE-LONG stretch of the wide Principal I, from the tower of the prayer horn Gorgonaught back through Hazgul Square towards Beati Plaza, was then the scene of a major armour battle. Twenty-nine vehicles of the archenemy's main force were driving south, countered by twelve Civitas Beati light tanks, and six Vanquishers from Lugo's life company.

The broad, and once majestic, boulevard was littered with burning wrecks and dimpled with shell-craters. Most of the Chaos armour was stalk-tanks or light standards, but they had at least one super-heavy, a crimson monster that annihilated all before it.

Gaunt's platoon held position in the ground floor of a glassblower's fabricatory on the west side of Hazgul Square. They had exhausted their anti-tank munitions long since, and could do precious little about the armour. They concentrated their efforts on the enemy ground troops instead. But it wouldn't be long before their continued harassment of the infantry drew the attention of a Chaos battle tank.

Keeping low to avoid the occasional stray shot that whined in through the holes in the brickwork, Gaunt moved along his platoon's position, distributing encouraging remarks and quiet comments. In a fight-zone like this, he would have normally gone up a gear or two, maybe resorting to one of his favourite quotations or an ad hoc speech to rally the mood.

But this mood was flatter than any he'd known. Had he become so transparent that his men instantly saw in him the looming prospect of failure? Now he knew the painful truth about the 'Saint', Gaunt could hardly swallow the rage and disappointment he felt. Without that one spark of light and hope, the fight here on Herodor seemed no better than suicide.

Strangely, it was as if the whole city sensed that too. As if its heart had been torn out, as if it felt as lost and despairing as he did himself. Gaunt couldn't forget the look on Colm Corbec's face just before they'd deployed an hour before. 'Did you not just feel that? *Did you not just feel that?*'

Corbec hadn't been able to explain it, but Gaunt had seen other troopers in the vicinity similarly upset for no apparent reason at the very same moment. And the vox traffic had been abruptly flooded with anguished calls of dismay. That had been the moment the mood had truly crashed.

Corbec had pulled himself together, and they'd pressed into the zone. The last time Gaunt had seen his number two, Corbec was shaken and uneasy, leading his platoon off down a smoke-hazed sidestreet.

Everything shook as two tank rounds hit home nearby. The fabricatory rocked and dust spattered down from the ceiling. Gaunt checked the box-mag of his bolt pistol, and clambered across the rubble to where troopers Lyse and Derin were guarding a doorway. They were both pinking the occasional shot out of the broken entrance with their lasrifles.

'How are you holding?' Gaunt whispered, crouching behind them.

Lyse raised a dusty hand and indicated some features of the fire-lit battlefield outside for her commander's benefit. 'They've got foot units moving up behind that wall there, and behind the dead truck,' she said. 'We can't get a clear shot.'

'But you'd have 'em finished by now with your torch, right?' he asked. Lyse nodded. On Phantine, she'd become the first female trooper to become squad flamer, and was proud of that role. A tough, broad-shouldered Verghastite in her late thirties, Lyse preferred to wear her black vest top to show off arms that were as well muscled as any male's. Like all the Tanith flame-troopers, she missed her speciality weapon, and so did Gaunt. A few spurts of an Imperial standard man-portable flamer Mk.VIII would have cooked the Blood Pact now edging up to their position in the blindside of the building.

Beside them, Derin started firing more urgently. A few figures in red-brown battledress had emerged from behind the burning vehicle wreck outside and were attempting to rush the side wall. Lyse began shooting too, and Gaunt scrunched forward on his knees and added his own firepower to the repulse. Lasrifle shots and bolt rounds rattled out from the doorway. One of the figures simply fell over and vanished in the rubble. Another jerked back dramatically in mid-stride. The rest ran back for cover.

'Right,' said Gaunt, about to move on. 'Keep sharp and do that every time they try something.'

'It's like she's abandoned us, sir,' said Derin suddenly. Gaunt stopped. For a second, he assumed Derin was talking about Lyse, which made no sense. Then he looked into Derin's face and realised that wasn't what he'd meant at all.

'The Saint, sir. It feels like we've come all this way for her and now she's abandoned us.'

Gaunt remembered that Derin had been one of the misfit band Corbec had led on his private mission back on Hagia. Derin had not shown the same signs of beatific inspiration at the time as the likes of Corbec and Daur and Dorden – he'd simply joined Corbec's endeavour out of loyalty to the old man – but the experience had clearly affected him.

'She hasn't,' Gaunt said simply. 'She's here with us. She always is.'

'H-have you met her?' Derin asked.

'Yes, soldier, I have,' Gaunt said, trying not to say anything that was an outright lie.

'It doesn't feel like she's here. Not any more. It did when we first got here. It was like there was something in the air. But it's gone now. Just gone.'

'The Beati Sabbat is right here still, Derin. She will not abandon the defenders of her shrine. And never forget... the Emperor protects.'

Derin was comforted slightly, but the troubled look didn't completely leave his face.

Gaunt was called to the rear of the hab, where his platoon scout Caober had just slipped back inside from a run down through the shelled street to their left.

'We're gonna have to start moving, sir,' he said. 'Three or four of the enemy tanks have turned west, and they're coming round the back. We're gonna get pinned if we stay in here.'

'Where do you suggest?' Gaunt asked.

Caober shrugged. 'I linked up with Sergeant Mkoll's platoon and Captain Daur's, sir. They've both already been forced back across the intersection into those habs there.'

'Retreat, in other words?'

'Sir, back is the only operative direction. There's no forward any more.'

Gaunt nodded. 'Any sign of Corbec?'

'No, sir.'

'Let's peel out, odds then evens, through those blast holes in the back. Caober, find us a hab to take position in and show the Ghosts the way as they come through. Beltayn?'

His adjutant hurried over.

'Odds and evens, out that way. Caober has point. Spread the word and let's make it snappy.'

Beltayn turned to distribute instructions when the hab was struck squarely by a shell that blew a section of wall in on them and killed two members of first platoon. A shrieking *whoop*, a blitzing, gritty fireburst and then everyone still alive was picking themselves up in the choking smoke.

Gaunt could hear heavy assault fire from outside. Over the micro-bead he heard Derin.

'They're coming in! They're charging us! They're coming in!'

Gaunt knew there'd be no retreating now. He drew his power sword and ignited it. 'Ghosts of Tanith!' he shouted. 'In the name of the God-Emperor of Mankind... give them hell!'

'WHAT ARE YOU doing here, chief?' asked Domor in surprise. Corbec, his fatigues and pack layered with grey dust, had just scrambled into the manufactory basement where Domor's platoon was guarding the wounded. Above ground, the district was ablaze for the most part, and artillery was pounding it. There was no hope of carrying injured troopers out.

'I got lost,' Corbec said. 'In all the confusion. It's hairier than me out there. Any of my lads show up here?'

Domor shook his head. 'We've got people from ten, eleven and thirteen here, but no sign of anyone from your unit.'

'Vox?'

'You're joking, in this?' The ground above them shook with the heavy shelling. Even short-range micro-beads were only barely making it. Corbec saw Criid lying on a pile of sacking nearby. Kolea and Lubba were with her.

'How is she?'

'Okay,' said Domor. 'Head wound. Nothing too bad. Others are worse.'

Corbec could see that for himself. It was ugly and going to get a lot uglier before daylight. There were civilians down here too. In one corner, Corbec saw several adults trying to comfort a group of terrified children. Everyone was black with ash-soot. He wandered over. The adults with the kids were all civvies, pilgrims by the look of them. Bonin was standing nearby, leaning his tired body against a wall and sipping from his water bottle.

'Taking a personal interest?' Corbec asked him.

'Me and Milo had to fight like bastards to get those kids out. We were all penned in a few streets away. It was close.'

'Armour?'

Bonin nodded. 'You might want to have a word with Milo,' he said softly.

'Milo? Why?'

Bonin just shrugged and said nothing.

Corbec found Milo in the furthest, darkest corner of the basement space. He was hunched over, bruised and exhausted. A small shape lay under a dirty sack beside him.

'Brinny boy?'

Milo looked up. The grief on his face took Corbec's breath away.

'You look like I feel,' he tried to joke, but Milo was too burdened by emotion to even respond.

Corbec sat down next to him.

'What happened?'

'There was a girl,' he said. He spoke so quietly, Corbec had to lean forward to hear him above the bombardment.

'A girl?'

'Yes…' Milo looked at the crumpled form under the sack. Corbec put the rest together.

'It's always hard, that. Take your eye, did she? You'll just have to–'

'You don't understand, sir. She was… I don't know. There was something about her. Something amazing.'

'Well, y–'

'I thought she was the Saint.'

Corbec paused. 'What?'

'I knew the Saint was with us. I could feel it. Like on Hagia, you know?'

Corbec nodded. He knew the feeling. It had got into his soul on Hagia and never really left.

'I knew she was with us, really with us. Not just on this planet like we've been told, but right there on the street, in the middle of everything.'

'She watches over us,' Corbec murmured.

'She was there. I saw this girl and I just knew.'

'And?'

'She died. She saved the children and then she died. It wasn't meant to happen. I can feel it wasn't. It wasn't meant to happen like that. What will we do without her?'

Corbec didn't reply. He lifted the corner of the sacking. The girl was very peaceful and very dead. Just a young girl, another victim of the endless war. He laid the sacking back.

'It wasn't meant to happen,' Milo repeated.

'None of this was,' Corbec growled.

From outside came the rattle of small-arms close by. Domor, Bonin and the other able-bodied troops in the basement shelter grabbed up their weapons and headed for the exit.

'Come on,' said Corbec, getting up and checking his rifle's power cell. 'Come on, Milo. It's a long way from over yet.'

THE FIRST BLOOD Pact warrior who made it into the shattered hab was a massive brute, even bigger than the late, lamented

Trooper Bragg. He came through a gap in the east wall that
Trooper Loff had, until a moment before, been defending.

The heretic warrior was clad in heavy fatigue battledress
coloured a dark, patchy russet, with steel-plated boots and
iron armour strapped around his thighs, shoulders and belly.
His face, under the red bowl-helmet, was visored by a black
metal mask, an iron grotesque shaped into a snarling, hook-
nosed, feral face. His hands, thick with the scar tissue of the
heinous Pact ritual, clutched a laser pistol and a wickedly
curved bill-hook.

Loff lay dead on his face in the gap where a blow from the
bill-hook had dropped him. The Blood Pact warrior howled
out an obscene war-cry and ploughed into the hab, firing
wildly. There were others behind him.

Gaunt met him head on. His scything, energised blade, the
power sword of Heironymo Sondar, glowed like a sliver of ice
as it deflected two of the storm-warrior's laser bolts up into
the blackened roof. Then he brought it sidelong and the murderous bill-hook – along with several scarred fingers – spun
into the air in a puff of blood. Borne forward by his own
momentum, Gaunt slammed the blunt nose of his bolt pistol up against the howling grotesque and fired. The brute, his
head demolished, crashed backwards. Gaunt began firing
over his collapsing corpse into the weight of enemy troopers
scrambling through the gap at his heels.

Beltayn and Neith jumped forward beside him, shooting
point blank with their lasrifles and thrusting with the Tanith
warknives they had fitted as bayonets. 'Straight silver! Straight
silver!' Beltayn was yelling.

It wasn't the only breach. The hab reverberated with the
clash of hand-to-hand combat as Blood Pact storm-squads
burst in through window lights, doorways and shell holes,
driving first platoon backwards into the ruins. It was a killing
frenzy, the malevolent, red-hot heart of pure war. The smoke-
filled chamber, murky and firelit like daemon hell, was thick
with screams, blows, spraying shots and thrashing figures.
They were enveloped in chaos.

Gaunt's bolt pistol was spent. There were spare mags in his
belt-pouches, but absolutely no chance of reloading in the
turmoil. He let it go and wrenched out his Tanith warknife,

plunging into the nearest enemy trooper with both blades. Blood soaked his jacket and his cloak so much the cloth slapped heavily around him. He realised he was screaming wordless sounds of rage at the swarming enemy.

They stank. They brought their abattoir reek with them: foul breath, sour sweat, dried blood and the noxious aroma of the oils and paints with which they anointed their bodies.

The sword of Sondar split a black-iron visor in two. Blood sizzled off the charged blade. Gaunt's warknife hacked into a throat. Something knocked his cap off. A Blood Pact trooper crashed sideways into him and staggered him, but the wretch was already dead. Then a laser round clipped the top of Gaunt's left shoulder and knocked him to his knees. He put the power sword through the armoured thighs in front of him, and was flattened as the severed bodyweight toppled forward onto him.

Beltayn had lost his lasgun. He snatched up a fallen billhook and slammed it with both hands into the nearest enemy sternum, then leapt forward and grabbed Gaunt by the shoulders, trying to drag him to his feet. Vanette and Starck charged in to support him, firing full auto into the scrum of Blood Pact all around.

'Back! Get back!' Beltayn yelled in Gaunt's face. The colonel-commissar didn't even seem to recognise him. He was dripping with gore. 'We have to get back!' Beltayn repeated, his throat raw from the smoke. Gaunt shoved him out of the way and butchered another Blood Pacter who was surging at them. The power sword cut him in two and cracked stone chips out of the pillar beside him.

An explosion knocked them all off their feet. Masonry rubble rained down from the roof and the end wall of the hab fell like a stack of child's play-bricks. Cold air washed in, thick with the smell of fyceline, and contorted the dense smoke around them into weird eddies and gusting coils.

Sword still clamped in one blood-smeared hand, Gaunt grabbed Beltayn by the arm and dragged him towards the caved section of wall. Vanette and Starck followed them, backing their way, emptying the last of their power cells from the hip as they went. There was no sign of any other member of first, just dark red figures scrambling through the smoke at their heels.

The four men fell out down the mound of rubble into the open. Las-shots sizzled out of the hab building after them.

They were in the wide concourse of Hazgul Square itself. The whole area was on fire. Buildings, reduced to hollow shells by the firestorm, spurting flames and sparks from their blind windows. Three tanks – one Imperial light and two enemy models – were burning where they had died. Bodies littered the ground, half-covered by the ash falling like snow from the boiling smoke. The heat was so fierce it felt like a summer noon on Caligula.

There was no way of telling where anything or anyone was. It was as if they had washed up in the middle of the apocalypse.

Gaunt recovered his wits enough for his hands to start to tremble. His heart was banging like an autoloader. Limping from a wound he couldn't remember receiving, he hurried the other three across the twenty metres of open square to the nearest cover. It was a burned-out RCB troop carrier. They cowered down, scanning the nightmare around them.

'One! This is one!' Gaunt cried, and then realised the lack of response was because his micro-bead was no longer in his ear. Its snapped flex dangled from his collar clip.

He looked at the other three. All of them were covered in dirt and blood and multiple minor wounds. Vanette's jacket was shredded and blood streamed down his right forearm from a wound at his elbow. Starck had his head in his hands, shaking with nervous energy and adrenaline. Both still had their lasrifles. Beltayn's grazed, cut hands were empty. He sat with his back against the troop carrier wreck, staring out at the firestorms with the blank look of a man who had reached his limits.

'Vox?' Gaunt said, shaking him.

'Sir?'

'Vox?'

Beltayn shook his head. A las-round had blown the vox-caster off his back during the melee in the hab.

Melee, Beltayn thought. How inadequately did that stupid fething word describe what they'd just come from.

'Micro-bead, then? Beltayn? Beltayn!'

The signalman snapped out of it. He fumbled to his ear and started to call into his intercom.

Gaunt heard the clanking even before Starck called him. Two hundred metres north of them, across the shattered square, an Imperial light tank was reversing hard, smashing debris and ruined vehicles out of its way. As Gaunt watched, an AP shell hit the pavement beside it, showering it with dirt and stone, and then another blew its turret in half. It veered wildly, trailing thick smoke, and came to a halt. Gaunt saw the driver struggle clear. The man started to run, then fell as small-arms fire cut him down.

Two Blood Pact battle tanks, with a stalk-tank clattering up on their left flank, advanced into the square. The tanks rocked as they fired, sending shells screaming over Gaunt and his comrades and into the buildings on the south face of the plaza. Loose formations of Blood Pact fire-teams were hurrying forward with the armour. Whilst Gaunt and his platoon had been caught up in the hell of the fabricatory fight, the battle outside had been lost. The enemy had broken the Imperial resistance, crushed the armour, and was storming down Principal I.

Las-fire began to hit the bodywork of the troop carrier. It was coming sidelong, from the ruined hab. The Blood Pact unit that had driven first platoon from its position – and most likely slaughtered them all – was now spilling out of the hab over the shelled wall the way Gaunt and his men had come. They were shooting across the open ground towards the huddled Imperials.

The four of them scrambled around into cover at the rear of the carrier, but even that offered precious little protection from the crossfire. To their right, the main advance and the rolling armour; to their left, the flank push of the infantry.

Vanette and Starck returned fire with their lasrifles, concentrating on the enemy unit advancing from the hab. Gaunt wished he had something more than his sword left. Beltayn gave up with the micro-bead and took out his service pistol, squeezing off shots around the end of the truck. The wrecked vehicle shuddered as incoming fire struck it, denting the metal and spalling off the scorched paintwork.

'Starck! Vanette! A pistol, either of you!'

Starck had lost his – lost the entire holster, in fact – but Vanette unshipped his laspistol and slid it across the rock-crete to Gaunt. Gaunt sheathed his sword and ducked down by the buckled rear wheel, taking shots at the main advance. By the counter display on the pistol's butt, he had about thirty shots left before the cell expired.

Thirty shots. That was the measure of life left to him.

'Munitions?' he shouted over the crackle of enemy fire.

'One cell left!' replied Vanette.

'Half a cell!' reported Starck.

'Two clips!' Beltayn stammered.

'Make them count,' said Gaunt.

The fire they were receiving was getting heavier. Both infantry fronts were targetting the troop carrier, and the stalk-tank had begun to spit cyclic pulses at them. The wreck rattled and shook, and actually moved more than once under the impacts. Bodywork casing fragmented off into the air. Beltayn howled out as a piece of shrapnel tore into his arm. Vanette's cheek was scorched by spall bursting from a hull-strike. Any moment now, Gaunt knew, a tank round or a rocket grenade would finish them off.

Ten shots left.

'Sabbat Martyr,' Gaunt began to murmur, 'in the name of the hallowed Emperor of Terra, deliverer of the Imperium of Man, I commend my soul and my dying deeds, and the souls of these three brave soldiers, into your hands that you–'

Fire sheeted across the square from the south, cones of flame, white hot and hungry, spraying like water from pressure hoses, it gushed across the archenemy troops emerging from the hab and turned those that didn't break and flee into jerking, stumbling torches.

'Something...' Beltayn gasped. 'Something's...'

Not awry. Not by any stretch of the imagination.

Four Chimeras, displaying the insignia of the lord general's life company, stormed into the square, crashing through burning buildings with their toothed dozer blades. They were moving fast, their hulls rocking back on their treads as they accelerated out of the rubble. In their top turrets, troopers manned the autocannons, blazing tracer fire into the air. Behind the fast, armoured carriers, lumbering tanks emerged. Civitas Beati armour, PDF lights and two life company Vanquishers. They began firing as soon as they had visual target on the enemy vanguard. Flooding in around the vehicle charge were troopers, many carrying company banners, flags and aquila standards on long poles. Leading the ground troops with a standard clenched in one hand, Gaunt could see Marshal Biagi. He was striding forward at the head of a dozen officers of the Regiment Civitas. They were razing the ground before them with their flamer packs.

The four Ghosts crawled under the wreck for safety as shells and heavy cannon fire whipped over their heads in both directions. The noise and concussion were physically painful. From where he lay, Gaunt could see Biagi directing the ground forces forward. Someone, Lugo himself most probably, had mobilised all the reserves into this counter-push. The damn fool! If this failed, there would be nothing, absolutely nothing, left to defend the inner hives with.

Gaunt knew Lugo was hardly the most gifted tactician ever to emerge from officer candidate scholam, but this was an act of madness even by his dismal standards. Already this night they had been surprised at the sheer scale of the advance force the archenemy had managed to land on Herodor. Who was to say that another force of equal size wasn't now waiting to strike at the southern agriponic zone, or another poised in the Eastern Obsidae? What would Lugo do then, if his entire military strength was committed here?

It was madness. It was…

…it *was* madness, but not the kind Gaunt supposed.

He blinked.

Something odd was happening. Every sound was dulling, everything in sight beginning to shimmer. Shards of glass on the floor under his bloodied hands twinkled like diamonds. The scabby metal of the tailgate above his head looked like mother of pearl. Tank shells slid overhead in perfect clarity, leaving slow billows in their wake, the smoke turning and spiralling into perfect double-helix trails.

Everything seemed
to slow
down.
Feth!

For a moment, Ibram Gaunt thought he'd been shot. He felt no pain, no impact, but he'd heard invalided veterans describe the way really bad wounds happened without you knowing it, turning the world into a slow motion wonderland as your failing senses registered the simple, profound splendour in everything.

There was a light in his eyes. A golden light. A life company Salamander, squat and heavy on its tracks, rolled up into his view, coming to a halt just a few metres from where he lay under the wrecked carrier. A figure stood upright in its open-topped cabin.

She was beautiful.

She wore a suit of intricately-worked golden battle armour so fine and form-fitting that it had been clearly fashioned for her by master metallurgists. Pieces of polished chelon shell had been set into the bodice and wide pauldrons. Imperial eagles formed the couters at the elbows and the poleyns at the knees, and the same symbol was also etched in repeated ribbons down the thigh plates and along the vambraces. Her left hand was covered with a gilded glove that had silver eagle claws extending from the fingertips. Her right hand was bare. Beneath the dazzling golden plate, she wore a suit of tightly-wound black mail, each link formed in the shape of an islumbine bloom. A white skirt, long and flowing and fixed with purity seals and prayer streamers, billowed from her waist. The heavy golden gorget rose up high to her chin, but her head was uncovered. She'd cut her hair short, sheared it off crudely in fact, so it fell in a glossy black bowl over her pale head. Her eyes were green, as green as an infardi's silk, as green as the rainwoods of Hagia.

The Beati looked down at Gaunt. A halo of light surrounded her, so fierce and bright it made her seem almost translucent. Nine cyber-skull drones hovered around her in the radiant glow, forming a circle behind her head, their eyes lit, their miniature weapon pods armed. She was terrible to behold.

She smiled.

'I've been waiting for this, Ibram. Haven't you?'

'Yes,' was all he could say. He realised he was weeping, but he didn't care.

She raised her arms wide. A green cloak unfurled from her back and became wings. A perfect aquila form spread out around her, five metres on either side, not silk but shimmering green light. Behind her head, the double-heads of the Imperial eagle clacked and hissed, encircled by the skull drones.

Gaunt got to his feet. He was so intent on her he knocked his head against the rear fender of the carrier, but his eyes didn't waver from the vision before him.

He drew his sword and held it out to her, grip first.

'You'll need that, Ibram,' she admonished quietly, and drew her own blade. It was slender, silver and well over a metre long. Islumbine garlands were looped around the hilt and jewelled pendants dangled from the pommel. She activated it and the blade thrummed into life.

'Let us educate the archenemy of mankind,' she said.

'What lesson do we teach?' Gaunt asked.

'The Emperor protects,' she said.

She raised the sword and pointed it at the enemy. The unseen driver slammed the Salamander forward but she didn't even stir. On either side, Imperial warriors surged forward towards the recoiling foe. Flamers hissed, cannons barked, lasguns cracked and the heavy tank guns roared. The Imperial banners fluttered.

Sword in hand, Gaunt ran after her.

FIVE
TRIUMPHS AND MIRACLES

'Where there is an enemy, rage!
Where there is a victory, rejoice!'

— Saint Sabbat, Epistles

THERE WERE CROWDS everywhere.

It was barely daybreak, but the streets were packed. Teeming masses of chanting pilgrims, celebrating soldiers and rejoicing citizens clogged the transitways and boulevards of the Civitas Beati, united in a raucous and unstinting expression of triumph. The wounded city had woken up to find it was, miraculously, still alive.

Wide slicks of black smoke stained the early daylight, wiping deep smudges across the flat, cold whiteness of the sky. Outlying northern sectors of the city were still-burning ruins littered with wrecked war machines and the uncounted bodies of the dead.

An early estimate suggested hundreds of military personnel and citizens had perished. The pilgrim community had suffered the most. Thousands had not made it through the gruelling night.

But the body count and the serious destruction inflicted on the Civitas seemed to bother no one in the crowd. They were as abnormally excited now as they had been inexplicably deflated in the small hours of the night. Easy to explain perhaps, for humans are simple things: they were alive, they had won, and they were rejoicing in that fact.

The greatest concentration of people was mobbing in around Beati Plaza, hundreds of thousands of exhilarated human beings, all of them chanting and whooping and dancing and cheering. Banners were flapping in the dawn air, white petals swirling like confetti from the garlands the people wore. Soldiers, their grinning teeth white against the caked dirt on their faces, were hugged and kissed, and lifted up on shoulders. Drums pounded. The ancient prayer horns of the city boomed. Fabricatory sirens wailed.

People had got up on roofs and balconies, or waved eagerly from upper floor windows. Streamers and fireworks flashed in the sky. On several street corners approaching the plaza, infardi preachers had climbed up onto the carts of their clock shrines and were leading prayers and hymn singing. Ecclesiarchy processions, led by choirs, carried reliquaries from the hive shrines through the streets. Ministorum workers scattered petals and flower heads harvested at random from the agriponic farms.

By the time Gaunt reached the heaviest crowds in the plaza area, he had garlands of islumbine and irridox around his neck, and had been kissed and hugged more times than he could count. His clothes were ragged and torn and he was covered in cuts and bruises. He still carried the aquila standard that he'd picked up from a fallen RCB trooper in the thick of the fighting before daybreak.

He felt strange, dazed, dislocated. The noise of the jubilation around him seemed louder and more oppressive than the bitter warfare of the night. Everything felt like a dream, but that was just his fatigue, he was sure.

On the cold, flinty plain of the Great Western Obsidae, as dawn came up, he had helped undertake the extinction of the enemy forces. There had been no quarter, and that was all right, for the Blood Pact were devoted and sworn servants of the archenemy of mankind.

But they had slaughtered them. All of them.

The glass fields beyond the city's north-western perimeter were scattered with corpses and with the smouldering hulls of fighting vehicles. Faced with the Beati, and with the renewed vigour she had inspired in the warriors of the Imperium, the Blood Pact had snapped and run. Biagi and Kaldenbach, the acknowledged victors of the fight, had led the pursuit and annihilated the enemy in the obsidae. Now the winds of the ice-desert, gusting in over the Western Ramparts, would shrivel the Blood Pact bodies, and the ground frost freeze-dry their flesh, and they would remain as fragile mummies amidst the litter of their ruined armour, a testimony to the brutal zeal of an Imperial army inspired by faith.

Gaunt reached the plaza. The crowds were packed fifty deep, but they parted to let him through. Pilgrims and citizens reached out to touch him or to clap him on the shoulders. He was limping and using the banner for support.

She was at the centre of the plaza, standing on top of a Chimera, raising her hands to the exulting crowds.

'Sir! Sir!' Gaunt glanced around and was almost knocked over by Raglon's enthusiastic hug of a greeting.

'We feared you were dead, sir!' Raglon cried.

'I'm not, Rags.'

'I see that, sir. God-Emperor, it's good to see you! What a day this is! What a moment!'

Gaunt smiled a tired smile. Raglon's excitement was contagious. Too seldom had he seen his men filled with the simple joy of victory.

'How's your platoon, Rags?'

'In fine shape, sir.'

'You came through it all right?'

Raglon nodded eagerly. 'We came through. No losses. But we gave them hell. I'll be filing a report… recommendations…'

'I look forward to it.'

Raglon turned and looked towards the centre of the plaza. 'I can't believe this, sir,' he said. 'I mean… she's here. Really here.'

'Yes, she is, Rags,' he said. 'She really is. Enjoy this moment. They don't come often in our walk of life.'

Gaunt looked at the Saint as Raglon pulled away, laughing. She seemed to be staring directly at him.

'I'M HAPPY AND all, but I wish she'd stop doing that.'

'Doing what?' asked Feygor, raising his voice to be heard over the din.

'Looking at me like that,' replied Rawne. Third platoon were in the crowd on the far side of the plaza from Gaunt. 'She won't stop looking at me.'

'It's me she's looking at,' Feygor said. 'Not you. Why would she look at you?'

'Well, I don't know…' Rawne said, rolling his eyes.

'I do,' said Banda. 'The major's sex on legs, real catnip for us womenfolk.'

Feygor laughed. Rawne looked at Banda with disdain.

'But I hate to disappoint you,' Banda continued. 'Her holiness the Beati is actually looking at me.'

'IT IS A good day,' said Gol Kolea quietly.

'Yes, Gol, it is,' Criid replied. She patted him on the arm. Around them, the crowd was going mad with chants. The Beati was a distant figure at the heart of the packed square.

'A good day,' Kolea repeated. 'She looks at me and sees me and sees I'm happy that it's a good day.'

'Who does, Gol?'

'The sainty-woman.'

'Uh huh.'

'Hey, sarge.' Criid looked round and saw Jajjo shouldering his way through the press. 'Found him,' he said, with a grin.

Caffran appeared behind Jajjo and grabbed Criid in a tight embrace.

'Thought I'd lost you!' he breathed, kissing her cheek and neck. He raised a hand and gently touched the bandage around her head.

'You're hurt.'

'Nothing that won't mend. Kolea got me to a medic.'

'I din't think I'd ever see you again, Tona,' Caffran said.

'It'll take more'n a few Blood Pact to keep me from you,' she replied and met his mouth with hers.

'Yeah, yeah… not in front of the troops,' said Lijah Cuu as he wandered past.

'SEE HER?'

'Of course I do.'

'Then be thankful,' said Colm Corbec, 'your little nightmare was just that… a little nightmare. There she is. Alive and well and… saintly.'

Milo nodded. 'Yes, I suppose so. She's amazing. She seems to be looking right at me.'

'At you? At me, more like. Right at me.'

Milo smiled. 'Believe what you want, colonel.'

'I believe I will.'

'That she's looking at you?' scoffed Mkoll dryly. 'I think she's certainly looking at me.'

The vast crowd around them suddenly sent up a booming cheer and the Ghosts in their midst joined in.

'Me, definitely,' murmured Mkoll.

LARKIN STARED. IT was like he had her in his crosshairs and she had him the same. If it had been a kill-sight, it would have been tough. Ninety metres, with a crosswind and hundreds of cheering bodies between him and her. But he'd have made it. Larkin was sure.

And even more sure that she'd have made it too. The way she looked at him. Like a marksman.

HARK PUSHED THROUGH the crowd. He almost fell over Daur, who was sobbing his heart out, and then bumped into Meryn, who was just staring.

'Meryn?'

'She's real.'

'I think that's the idea, sergeant.'

Beside them, Sergeant Varl had climbed up on a clock shrine cart and started to dance, putting on a beret plumed with struthid feathers and pulling it down comically over his ears.

Hark laughed despite himself.

* * *

'CHIEF?' VIVVO HANDED Soric the brass message shell.

'Thank you,' Soric said, and nodded Vivvo away. The crowd around them was going crazy. The cheering was so loud it was making him twitchy.

Soric undid the shell's cap and used his fingers as tweezers to fish the note out.

It said: *It's you she's looking at. She knows.*

Soric dropped the paper scrap and pushed the message shell into his pocket.

A moment later and Vivvo re-emerged from the bustling crowd.

He held out a message shell.

'This yours, chief?' he asked.

Soric patted his pant pockets. They were empty.

'Must be,' he said.

Vivvo handed him the shell and turned away. He glanced back over his shoulder. Soric knew Vivvo was catching on.

Soric opened the shell. This one said: *Tell Gaunt. Nine are coming. Nine are coming.*

The handwriting was hasty. Really rushed and badly formed, like he'd been writing in a hurry.

Despite the celebration around him, Soric felt his heart sink.

THE LITTLE GLADE was quiet. It was a spring morning, early, the first rays of sunlight gleaming through the leaves. A vague mist covered the path to the chapel door.

Each step he took sounded too loud in the cool silence. There were no birds singing. That seemed odd. His boots crunched on the stone pavers.

His pulse was racing. There was nothing to be afraid of, but he was afraid anyway. Why was that? He wanted to be here. He wanted to go inside, but his heart was thumping.

He reached the door. Dew glittered on the iron handle. He reached out to take hold of it, but the door began to open of its own accord. It began to open and behind it he saw–

GAUNT WOKE WITH a start. He had to fight to catch his breath. The room around him was dark and over-warm. He had no idea what time it was.

He got up off the bed and started to walk towards the windows to open the shutters. Only then did he feel the terrible aches of his tired body. Every step was painful.

He opened a shutter, and white light shafted into the small chamber. Outside it was late afternoon, and the sweep of the city-scape below showed that the celebration was still going on. He could see banners, the occasional spark of a firework, and crowds still streaming along the narrow streets.

He fiddled with the climate control vents built into the window sill, but no amount of jiggling eased the oppressive heat. He wished he could open the chamber window, but it was a hermetically sealed unit. This level of hive tower three was too high above the city shield and the Civitas's atmosphere envelope.

Gaunt tried to remember the dream he'd been having. It had been so vivid, but it had melted away the moment he woke. Aexe Cardinal. He had been back on Aexe Cardinal, at the chapel. More than that, he couldn't say.

He caught sight of his own reflection in the heavy dressing mirror in the corner of the room. He was dressed only in his under shorts, and his lean, muscled flesh looked unnaturally pale and white. The dark furrows of old scars looked like relief features on the surface of a chalky moon, especially the long, ugly rip across his belly that Dercius had left him with so many years before.

The newer wounds, the ones Herodor had given him, were more livid. So many abrasions and scratches he didn't care to count, scabbing black with blood. Bruises too, dark black and sickly yellow. The most serious were the las-burn across the top of his left shoulder and the gash in his right calf. Lesp had cleaned him up pretty well, dressed the worst, and sutured a few of the deepest cuts.

He limped out of the bedchamber into the outer room. His personal effects had been set out on the dresser and his spare uniform was laid out over the back of the chair.

'Beltayn?' he called out. There was no sign of his adjutant.

He was dressing when the door opened and Rerval came in.

'Sorry, sir. I should have knocked. Thought you were asleep.'

'As you were.'

Rerval, Corbec's signalman and adjutant, entered and closed the door. He was carrying a musette bag.

'Where's Beltayn?' Gaunt asked.

'He was bushed, sir. Corbec ordered him to billets and asked me to cover. I hope that's all right.'

Gaunt nodded, buttoning up his dress jacket.

'How long have I been asleep?'

'About four hours, sir. Everything's calming down a bit. Captain Daur's running things in operations.'

'Have we got any numbers yet?'

'Not for me to say, sir. Lugo's throwing a banquet tonight, which you're expected to attend.'

'Do you mean Lord General Lugo, Rerval?'

Rerval blushed. His cheeks went red apart from the white puckering of the long scar he'd taken across the face on Aexe. 'I do, sir.'

'I don't honestly care what you call him... except a bad habit might get you into trouble.'

'I'll remember that, sir.'

Gaunt finished buttoning his jacket and started to look around for his cap. Rerval reached into the musette bag he was carrying.

'Looking for this, sir?'

The cap was a little dusty and the worse for wear, though Rerval had done his best to clean it up.

'Colonel Corbec sent a scout back to the hab to find it, sir. No sign of your bolt pistol though, I'm afraid, so I requisitioned you this for the time being.' Rerval produced a brand new laspistol in a black leather holster.

'Thank you, Rerval,' said Gaunt, strapping it on. He buckled on his sheathed sword and warknife too and then put on his cap. Then he paused. 'I... I must have lost my cape somewhere along the way,' he said ruefully. He felt ashamed to admit it.

Rerval took off his own camo-cape. 'Take mine, sir. Please, it'd be an honour. I'll get myself another.'

Gaunt took the trademark Tanith garment and nodded his thanks. Rerval's gift was astonishingly generous, given how fiercely the Tanith protected their knives and capes.

'How do I look?' Gaunt asked.

'Like a conqueror of worlds, sir.'

'Very kind. How do I look really?'

'Tired, sir.'

THE OPERATIONS CENTRE was quiet. Only half the console positions were manned, and in most cases it was Munitorum
clerics who were on duty. Daur was sitting in the side annexe,
working his way through a stack of data-slates.

He started to get up when he saw Gaunt enter, but Gaunt
waved him back into his seat.

'Long night, Ban. How're you holding up?'

Daur smiled reassuringly. 'I came through pretty much
intact. Feel like a million credits now. You?'

'Weary, but a victory is a victory. Puts fire into even the
most exhausted bones.'

'Not just that, though. Not just victory. I mean... after
everything you said to us in here yesterday. You were wrong,
weren't you?'

Gaunt sat down beside him. 'About the Beati?'

Daur nodded. 'I saw her. We all did. In the fight, and after-
wards, down at the triumph. That was no fraud.'

Gaunt sighed. 'No. No, I can't think it could have been. The
moment I saw her I was sure... as sure as I had been yesterday she wasn't real.'

'You must have been mistaken yesterday, sir,' Daur said.

'Do me a favour, Ban? Keep an open mind. The girl I met
yesterday was not the Martyr. I know that in my heart as well
as I know anything. For all her passion and conviction and
self-belief, she was not the real thing. The woman who
appeared last night... well, she was everything the other had
not been. I don't know what happened... but something very
strange took place as the battle was raging.'

'Thank the God-Emperor for that!'

'Indeed, the Emperor protects. But keep an open mind.'

'Because what can change one way might change back?'

'Quite so. Now why don't you bring me up to speed on the
situation?'

Daur handed Gaunt a data-slate imprinted with the general
operations report. 'I've rotated every Ghost who saw action

last night off active to rest and resupply. Marshal Biagi wanted some bodies to add to his perimeter patrols, but Lord General Lugo seems to think we've got nothing to worry about now, so he went easy. Everyone's in billets, either standing ready or sleeping. Except those in the infirmary.'

'How many?'

'Thirty-nine. Eleven serious, including Mkhef, Sapes and Bewl. And Mkvenner.'

'Not again, not after Aexe.'

'Indeed no. He still hasn't recovered from the pasting he took on Aexe. Soric encountered him in the field last night and saw he was ailing, so he sent him back to the field hospital. Dorden reckons Ven's been pushing himself too hard and started bleeding internally from some of the old injuries. In a bad way, apparently.'

'How bad?'

Daur shrugged. 'I'm not the chief medic.'

'Is Ven going to die?'

'Probably.'

'Feth,' Gaunt took off his cap and set it on the desk beside him. 'I'll go and see him.'

'Make it fast. The Lord General's summoned all the senior staff to a banquet tonight.'

'I thought it was customary to *invite* officers to a banquet, not summon them.'

'I don't believe this is optional, sir.'

Gaunt shook his head. He didn't feel much like hobnobbing with Lugo's officer cadre. He looked across at Daur. 'I might as well get the rest of the bad news over with now. How many fates?'

'Thirty-two,' said Daur. He passed another data-slate to Gaunt. 'That's pending, of course. We've still got about twenty unaccounted for.'

The Tanith dead were listed by squad. The first six were from Gaunt's own platoon, number one. Reading each name gave him a twinge of pain, but he was relieved. The storm-fight in the hab had been so vile, so brutal, he'd been expecting to see many more names there. He knew Beltayn, Vanette and Starck had made it because they'd come out with him. It turned out that Caober, Wersun, Myska, Derin,

Neith, Lyse, Bool, Mkan and another eight had made it out alive too.

'Mkoll says it was Caober, Derin and Lyse who led them out safe. A real fighting retreat, well ordered despite the vicious hand-to-hand. They got them far enough back for Mkoll's platoon to cover them. He's recommending honours for the three of them. I spoke to Derin myself. It sounds like it was hell in there.'

'It was hell everywhere, wasn't it?'

Daur sighed. 'I think so. But I get the feeling your stand in the hab there was the worst bout of close-quarters.'

'It shouldn't have happened. If we'd had flamers, they'd never have got within spitting distance of staging a storm.'

'You know the rules here, sir.'

'Know 'em, loathe 'em, gonna fight to change 'em. I won't get us caught like that again. When the next wave comes, we're going to be ready, and that means flamers to the front.'

Daur picked up his caffeine and sipped it, grimacing when he realised it had gone cold. 'Next wave? You think we're honestly going to get more?'

'I have no doubt, Ban,' said Gaunt, getting to his feet. 'We had a tough few hours there, and I'd not want to relive them, but we'd be fools to think that was anything except an unexpectedly heavy advance. The main force is coming. And they'll be loaded for behj.'

'There may also be a bright side, Gaunt.'

They looked up as Viktor Hark entered the annexe. He paused to sign off some slates a Munitorum scribe was holding for him, exchanged a few words with the robed, implanted functionary, and then strode in to join them.

'Are you rested, sir?' Hark asked, sweeping up his coattail and seating himself facing them.

'Well enough, thank you, Viktor. See much action?'

'In the closing stages. Enough to keep my hand in. Not enough to merit honours. Many did though; I have a list.'

'I look forward to reading it.'

'The lord general has a list too,' said Hark. 'You're on it.'

'Me?' said Gaunt.

'Both of you. Kaldenbach and Biagi are being given the credit for winning the fight, but Lugo wants to cite you and all the other senior officers – Tanith and Civitas alike – who were out in the thick of the first phase. But for your actions, the lord general says, there would have been no fight left to win. He's called the banquet to issue the citation pins.'

Gaunt was about to retort, but he saw how pleased and excited Daur looked and bit it back instead. He had no wish to be decorated by Lugo, but men like Daur, Rawne and Corbec deserved the recognition. It was about fething time.

'What did you mean when you said there was a bright side?' he asked.

'Astropathic signals from the reinforcement fleet, just received. I took the liberty of signing them off and passing them on to Lugo. Our replenishment will be here tomorrow at dawn, warp permitting. Nine Munitorum packets laden with munitions and medical supplies, three regiments of Khan Heavy Ground, and an Ardelean tank company out of San Velabo. Word is there's a Fleet Mechanicus pioneer ship inbound too, carrying a batch of mid-range plasma reactors to beef up the city shield. Plus five warships and a fighter carrier from the Segmentum battlefleet. Two days from now, Herodor's going to be a much tougher nut to crack.'

'Bright side indeed. What about enemy movements?'

Hark shrugged. 'Nothing. The balloon went up on Khan VI last night, according to transmits. Their far-listening stations thought they'd locked up an incoming warfleet heading our way. Turned out to be a flotilla of pilgrim ships from the Hagia system.'

Gaunt picked up his cap and put it on. 'Consider me a great deal happier than I was five minutes ago. I'll be in the infirmary if anyone needs me.'

'The function starts at 20.00, sir,' Hark reminded him.

'I won't be late.'

Gaunt left Daur and Hark talking and limped out through the quiet operations centre. At the door, he met Sergeant Meryn on his way in. Meryn saluted sharply.

'Problem, Meryn?'

'I was looking for Commissar Hark, actually, sir.'

'Nothing I can help you with?'

'I wouldn't want to trouble you, sir,' said Meryn.

* * *

THE PRIMARY TANITH billet was in a scholam on the thirtieth level of hive tower three. The double-bunked dorms had been cleaned out to accommodate the off-world troopers. The shutters were closed and the phospha lamps turned down, and smoke from lho-sticks filled the dim air.

Soric limped down the aisle between the bunks in dorm five, exchanging quiet greetings with those men that weren't asleep. Many were just unconscious, sprawled out on their cots, still wearing their battledress and the dirt and dried blood of the night before.

Soric himself was tired, but he was edgy too and he couldn't sleep. His lost eye ached like a bastard.

'You all right there, chief?' Corbec called to him. Soric stopped and stomped over to Corbec's cot.

'Fine, Colm. Fine and dandy. You know me.'

'Indeed I do,' said Corbec. He'd been stretched back in his undershirt on his cot, but now he sat up and pulled out a hip flask.

He offered it to Soric, who took it and sat down on the edge of the bunk.

'Good stuff,' he said, smacking his lips and handing it back. 'Surely that's not the sacra?'

That's what the Ghosts had begun to call it: *the* sacra. Several of the men, and many of the sutlers and traders accompanying the regiment, had become very handy at distilling the Tanith's beloved liquor. But none of them had quite the same knack as the lamented Bragg. His stuff had always been the best. A few flasks of it were rumoured to remain. And that stuff, like some mythical relic, was called *the* sacra.

'Indeed not,' smiled Corbec. 'But I commend your palate. Not many Verghasts can tell the difference.'

Soric shrugged. 'We're getting the taste for it. I've heard rumours that Trooper Lillo is close to perfecting the first Verghast distilled brand. He's calling it Gak Me Number One.'

Corbec chuckled. 'I know. With respect to Lillo – and let me confide in you that he's had me, Domor and Varl in for intensive taste tests – Gak Me Number One will get you blind pissed and clean brushes. It is not, however, sacra. This little job, which has, I'm sure you will agree, a fine nose, an agreeable undertaste, and a soft hint of ploins, vanilla and antifreeze, is the product of dear old Brostin who, let's face it, knows how to boil things. It's about the best there is in these dreary, post-Bragg days.'

Soric took another swig. 'He's got a bright future in illegal intoxication head of him, that Brostin.'

'So… what's got you wandering around at this hour?'

'Can't sleep.'

'Me neither. Got the itch.'

'The itch?' Soric blinked his one good eye at Corbec.

'Not something I picked up from one of Aleksa's girls, I assure you. The combat itch. Seems like I've been out of it for too long. Too, too long. Oh, I saw some shooty-shooty on Aexe, but it wasn't after much. I feel like I need to get back in the game.'

Soric nodded. On Phantine, both he and Corbec had been badly wounded. It had been the latest in a long series of injuries the colonel had suffered. He'd almost died on his medi-bed, but for Soric.

Because that had been where it had started.

Injured, Soric had suffered some kind of transformation. He couldn't say what exactly, and he'd kept it quiet. But it was like something inside him had woken up. Something he knew he had to keep secret from his friends and comrades. There had been twitches of craft in his family line, though never enough of anything to cause trouble. He'd believed the trait had passed him by, until the wounding on Phantine.

There, he'd known – simply known – that Corbec had been dying of a nosocomial infection. His warning had saved Corbec's life. And that had just been the start. Since then, the messages had been coming more and more frequently.

Gak, but he wanted them to stop.

Still, he knew what Corbec meant. Corbec wasn't a young man any more – neither of them were – and one injury too many would spell the end of their careers. Neither of them wanted that. But still…

'Don't push it,' he said.

'What do you mean?'

'You want to prove you're young still, young and fit. But don't push it. The shooty-shooty isn't known for its mercy.'

Corbec smiled at him. 'I'm first officer of the finest regiment in the Imperium, Agun... and it's a place I want to be for a long time. Don't worry about me. Me, I'm gonna live forever.'

'Make sure you do,' Soric said and got to his feet. 'Milo around?'

'Down yonder,' Corbec said with a flip of his thumb.

Soric shuffled his squat bulk down the aisle. He saw Larkin fast asleep on a lower bunk, his long-las wrapped in his arms like a favourite girl.

Soric stopped dead and slowly looked around. Something... something nagged him. Something he didn't even have to open his damn message shell to know.

Two bunk rows away, he saw Lijah Cuu. Cuu was flat on his belly on a top bunk, appearing to all around him to be asleep. But Soric could see Cuu's feline eyes were open, open and staring at Larkin.

He shuddered. Cuu was a piece of work. If he had it in for Larks, Soric pitied the poor bastard sniper. Maybe he should tell someone about–

He stopped himself. Cuu was looking at him now, returning the stare. Soric looked away and walked on. What would he tell anyone anyway? That he'd got a feeling? A bad feeling? A hand-written note from himself saying Cuu was a mad feth who needed to be watched at all times?

'What's up, chief?' Soric had come to a halt next to Milo's bunk. The youngest Ghost had spread his Tanith pipes out on his bedroll and was cleaning the chanters with a wire brush.

'Hello, Brinny. Got a moment?'

'Sure.'

Milo moved the chanter pipes so that Soric could sit down. The old Verghastite pulled a scrap of blue paper from his pocket.

'I need your help. It's a delicate matter. Can you promise me you'll be discreet?'

'Of course,' whispered Milo, sitting up, wondering what the hell Soric was going to tell him. Instead of speaking, Soric handed the scrap of paper to him.

'What's this?'

'Read it.'

Milo did. Hand-written on the sheet was the line: *Ask Milo. Trust Milo. He'll know.*

'What does that mean?' Milo asked.

Soric shrugged.

'Well, who wrote it?'

'I did.'

'When?'

'I have absolutely no idea,' said Soric.

GAUNT HATED COMBAT hospitals. They reminded him too much of the consequences of his profession.

The Civitas Beati had assigned a public health clinic on the tenth floor of hive tower three as the Tanith infirmary. It was a spartan hall of metal tiles and plastic screens. As he limped through the entranceway, he was assailed by the reek of antiseptic, which was so sharp and strong it almost but not quite masked the underlying aroma of blood and human waste.

A hand bell was ringing. Infardi volunteers and local medicae staff moved between the beds in the dim light, and in one corner an Ecclesiarchy provost was delivering the last rites. Candles flickered under their glass hoods. Someone was crying out with pain. Through a partly-drawn screen, Gaunt saw Curth and Lesp fighting with a thrashing body. Blood was pooling on the floor under the gurney.

He took off his cap and limped further into the chamber. Looking left and right, he finally located Mkvenner, lying in a cot at the far western end under the windows. Night was falling outside, and Mkvenner's bed was bathed in bars of cold, blue light. Gaunt saw Kolea sitting by Ven's side in silent vigil. Though his mind was ruined, Kolea seemed to know things, sense things. Gaunt was glad that Mkvenner wasn't alone at this time.

He started to walk towards Ven's bed when Dorden appeared from a side room.

'Ibram,' he said, as if surprised to see Gaunt.

'Doctor. I came to check on the wounded. Ven in particular.'

Dorden nodded. There was tension between them. Both of them hated how awkward things had become. 'Look, if you've got a moment,' Dorden said. 'I'd like you to look in on Zweil.'

'Zweil? He was wounded?'

Dorden shook his head. 'He collapsed from a stroke in the cathedral last night.'

'Feth, why wasn't I told?'

'I didn't know you hadn't been.'

'What's the prognosis?'

'He's stable. It's hard to say at this early stage.'

'Any idea what caused it?'

Dorden looked at him. 'Stress. Upset. I'm sure you remember that the ayatani was fairly worked up last night.'

'Are you blaming me?'

'No, of course not!' Dorden snapped. 'Not everything is about you, Gaunt.'

Trying not to rise to this, Gaunt walked past Dorden and into the side room. Zweil lay on his cot, as white as the sheets wrapped around him.

'Ayatani father,' Gaunt whispered, sitting down beside the bed.

'Oh, it's you,' said Zweil. The words came out slurred. The left half of his face seemed reluctant to move.

'How are you?'

'The feth you care!'

'I care a great deal. Stop it with the hostility, Zweil. You'll only make things worse.'

Zweil closed his eyes, as if in regret. 'You were right,' he hissed. 'I went to see her. I met her. She's just a lie, a fething lie. Just that silly girl Sanian. You were right.'

'I wasn't,' said Gaunt.

Zweil turned his head slowly and looked at Gaunt.

'What?' he gasped.

'Last night she was a lie. Today, she isn't.'

'Don't torture him, Gaunt,' said Dorden from the shadows of the doorway behind him.

Gaunt looked round at Dorden sharply. 'Have you not seen what's been happening today, doctor?'

Dorden shrugged. 'I've been busy. I understand we won.'

'The Saint is here,' Gaunt said. 'She led us to that victory. I don't understand it at all, but it's true.'

Dorden stepped into the room and into the light cast by the electro candles around the old priest's bed. 'Is this another of your games?'

'You know me. I don't play games.'

'I thought I knew you, Ibram. Aexe Cardinal proved me wrong. But... I guess you wouldn't.'

'Doctor, you went through hell on Hagia because you believed. I only said what I said last night to protect your faith. Last night there was no Saint Sabbat on Herodor, at least not one I had seen. This morning, there is.'

'I want to see her,' Zweil said suddenly.

'He's too sick to–' Dorden began.

'I want to see her!'

'He wants to see her, and I think he should,' said Gaunt. 'You too, Tolin.'

Dorden shrugged. 'I don't know...'

'Get a wheelchair. And get some orderlies to lift Zweil.' Gaunt checked his pocket watch. It was a quarter after seven and he wasn't even changed. 'Do it!' he insisted. He turned back and squeezed Zweil's hand. 'I'll take you to see her. Let me check on Ven first.'

Zweil nodded.

Gaunt limped out into the main infirmary hall and started down to Mkvenner's bed. Then he stopped.

Mkvenner and Kolea were gone.

THE HOLY BALNEARY was empty. There was no sound except the gentle slap of the water in the main pool. The dim air was wreathed with steam and the tangy smell of iron.

By the light of the fluttering candles that lined the long, limestone staircase, Kolea helped Mkvenner plod his way down. Biolumin globes shone on the steam below, their light picked out on the ripples of the sacred pool.

Mkvenner coughed violently, and his hand was wet with blood as he took it from his mouth. Kolea held on to him tightly to stop him falling.

'Take me back, Gol,' Mkvenner said, his voice husky with rattling fluid.

Kolea shook his head. 'Make you better. This will, it will. It will make you all better. It heals all the wounds. That's what they said. You'll see.'

'I'm tired. Too tired. I can't...'

'Don' you stop now, Ven. Don' you stop. Hold me tight and I'll get you there. You won' fall.'

'Gol, please. Let me die in my bed. Let me–'

He started coughing again. The wracks hit him so hard that he bent over and blood spattered on the gleaming limestone stairs. Mkvenner sank to his knees.

'This is madness,' Mkvenner gasped.

Kolea shook his head. 'She'll fix you better,' he said. He reached into the pocket of his jacket and produced a truly awful plaster effigy of the Saint, a pilgrim nick-nack. Kolea displayed it with huge pride. 'Found this. Lucky charm. Lucky lucky. Was Tona's. In her pocket.'

'Criid?'

Kolea nodded and smiled encouragingly. 'Found her hurt. Found it on her. Lucky lucky. It kept her safe. Real safe. Keep you safe too. Make you better.'

'Just take me back, Gol.'

'Saint make you better. Water make you better. You'll see.'

Kolea put the effigy back into his coat. Mkvenner started coughing again. More blood came up and Mkvenner's wracks became so violent, he passed out.

Kolea bent over and picked the big Tanith up. Grunting with effort, his legs shaking, he continued on down the steps, carrying Mkvenner in his arms.

He reached the bottom, and crossed the pool side towards the deep steps that ran down into the fuming water.

'Make you all better,' he repeated, over and over. Mkvenner didn't answer. His head hung limply.

Carrying the dying scout, Kolea descended into the water, up to his shins, his knees, his thighs, his waist. The buoyancy of the water collected Mkvenner's limp form up and floated him. Kolea pushed out, the water up to his throat, keeping Mkvenner on the surface.

Blood stained out in a wide fan around them.

'Be better! Be better now!' Kolea cried out.

He looked up suddenly. On the far side of the pool, a figure had appeared, indistinct in the smoking steam.

'Make him better!' Kolea demanded, trying to keep Mkvenner's limp body above the water level.

'Make him better!'

* * *

'WHAT NOW? You want me to walk?' Zweil leaned forward in the bathchair Lesp was pushing and stared at the candlelit flight of white steps below them. They could smell the sulphurous water.

Zweil made an effort to turn his head to look up at Gaunt. 'Do you expect me to get up and walk down that?' he snarled.

'No,' said Gaunt. 'Lesp? Help me.'

Between them, the Tanith commander and the slender orderly gathered Zweil up in a chair-lift between them and started to edge down the stairs. It was hard. Gaunt realised how unreliable his wounded leg was. If he fell now…

Behind them, Dorden shook his head wearily and pushed the empty bathchair to one side. Then he began to follow the others down the steps into the humid chamber of the Holy Balneary.

'Could you stop fidgeting?' Lesp grunted.

'I'm not!' Zweil complained.

'I think you are. This isn't easy,' said Gaunt. Sweat was beading on his forehead from the effort, and Lesp was panting. Moisture coated every smooth limestone stair, and every step they took was a disaster waiting to happen.

'What… what the feth is happening down there?' Dorden said suddenly from behind them.

Gaunt nearly fell. They were halfway down the white staircase. 'Put him down! Lesp, put him down!'

They eased Zweil's paralysed body onto a step and let go. Lesp had to crouch and hold on to Zweil to stop him slithering away down the stairs. Gaunt rose and looked at what Dorden was pointing at. Below them, in the pool, three figures were standing in the water.

'Wait here,' Gaunt said. Dorden bent down beside Lesp and helped to keep Zweil stable. The three of them watched Gaunt stagger his way down to the pool.

Gaunt limped from the foot of the staircase to the edge of the balneary pool. The three bodies in the water were now submerged, one of them pressing hands down on the backs of the others' heads to dunk them.

Or drown them. Or baptise them.

Gaunt couldn't tell. He thumped down the bath steps into the water himself.

The figures surfaced in a rush of bubbles and spray. Kolea. Mkvenner.

And her.

'What the hell is this?' Gaunt cried.

The Beati, clad only in a white shift, smiled at him, wiping away the water that dripped down her face from the fringes of her bowl-cut hair.

'The water heals, Ibram,' she said.

Just the sight of her stilled his fears. He stopped where he was, the warm water rocking against his legs.

Mkvenner turned and splashed his way towards him.

'Ven?'

Mkvenner got up on the steps and sat down, soaked through. He started to laugh.

'Ven? Are you all right?'

Mkvenner was laughing heartily, as if at some enormous cosmic joke. A man in his condition surely shouldn't be able to laugh so violently. Unless...

'I told you,' said Kolea, splashing up to the foot of the steps and clambering up beside Mkvenner. 'Didn't I tell you? Heals everything. That's the thing about this place, it–'

Kolea paused, and looked around, blinking in the wet air. His gaze finally found Gaunt's face.

'I–' he said. 'Sir, I think I may have missed something. How did I get here?'

SIX
PERTURBATION

'Bad day coming!'

— Unidentified preacher, Herodor

'SAY THAT... AGAIN, if you please.'

Lord General Lugo exuded power and authority in his white, high-collared dress uniform, but his tone didn't match his appearance at all. He sounded positively nervous.

'I said, lord, that I apologise for attending this function late, but I was delayed by an extraordinary event in the Holy Balneary. Before my eyes, the Beati performed a sacred miracle. Two, in fact. Sacred miracles of healing.'

Gaunt paused and allowed the silence to last. The room, a high-tier ballroom in Old Hive that Lugo's staff had requisitioned for the banquet, was full of formally attired officers – Herodian PDF, life company, Regiment Civitas and Tanith – who were all staring at Gaunt and the lord general. They'd been standing around, sipping preprandial amasecs and chatting, when Gaunt entered, and they'd heard every word.

'A miracle? What miracle?' Lugo asked, edgily. Biagi and Kaldenbach were nearby, and Gaunt could see Rawne, Mkoll,

131

Daur and Hark in amongst the gathering. Behind the huddle of officers, servitors and household staff putting the finishing touches to the long table ceased their activity, as if realising something was in the air.

'Two of my troopers went to the Holy Balneary tonight. One, Mkvenner by name, was at death's door. He was wounded on Aexe, and had never made a full recovery. The other, Sergeant Kolea, had been left a mental cripple during action on Phantine. It was a chronic condition that no amount of surgery could fix. As I understand it, Kolea had taken Mkvenner down the balneary. It was an act of comradeship. I think Kolea's simple mind had seized on what he had been told about the holy waters and so he believed he was doing the right thing.'

Lugo's eyes narrowed as he listened.

'When I arrived,' Gaunt went on, 'they were in the main pool, and the Saint was present. She was with them, in the water, almost as if she was…'

'…baptising them?' murmured Biagi.

'Just so, marshal,' said Gaunt. 'When it was done, both men were healed. Completely healed.'

'You must be mistaken, sir,' said Kaldenbach.

Gaunt shook his head. 'I admit, truth and falsehood seem to keep switching places with each other here on Herodor, but I know what I saw.'

'Were you alone in witnessing this, Gaunt?' Lugo asked.

'No, sir. It was also witnessed by my chief medic, an orderly named Lesp, and by Ayatani Zweil.'

Lugo and Biagi exchanged quick glances. Gaunt could see the disguised unease on both their faces.

'When did this happen?' asked Lugo.

'An hour ago, sir.'

'And only now do you come here and tell me?'

Gaunt paused. 'Ayatani Zweil made me conversant with the etiquette concerning such events. I made haste to summon the senior ayatani, the provosts of the Ecclesiarchy, and the first officiary, so that the miracles could be corroborated and documented, and entered into the holy record.'

'You informed church and state before you informed me?'

Gaunt nodded. 'I wasn't aware miracles were a military matter, lord. Ayatani Zweil told me that being a site of proven miracles would greatly increase Herodor's significance as a sacred place. This made it a matter for the Imperial Church. All Imperial subjects are legally obliged to inform the Ecclesiarchy of wonders and portents. And of course, it adds provenance to the authenticity of the Beati herself.'

'She needs no provenance!' Lugo snapped.

'Sir, I don't understand,' said Gaunt. 'The Saint is reborn here on Herodor and she has proved her divinity by performing genuine miracles. That surely is a cause for universal rejoicing. Why do you seem angry?'

Lugo stiffened and looked around, suddenly aware of the image he was projecting. He forced a smile. 'You misunderstand me, my dear colonel-commissar. I am just... astonished. Miracles, as you say, are beyond our understanding, beyond the remit of normal life, and I confess I am alarmed by anything that does not fit into the pragmatic, physical world of soldiering. I'm sure my brothers here will agree?'

There was a general murmur of assent from around the room.

Lugo looked at Gaunt. 'I'm not ashamed to admit that the notion of miracles terrifies me, Gaunt. The unseen universe exerting its power over our material lives. That sort of... magic is so often the stock in trade of our archenemy. So, please forgive my tone just then. Of course it is a cause for joyful thanks.'

It was an excellent recovery, Gaunt had to give him that much.

'I will go to the first officiary at once, and consult with him about how we should proceed.'

The assembly saluted as Lugo strode out, Biagi at his side. Then the chatter renewed, urgent.

'Is this true?' Hark asked softly, as he reached Gaunt's side.

Gaunt nodded.

'But Kolea was...'

'Permanently crippled, I know. Dorden doesn't know what happened. It's quite scared him.'

'And Lugo too.'

'That's different,' Gaunt said. 'I think Lugo's scared because he was in control of his game here until five minutes ago and now he most definitely isn't.'

THE SCARS WERE still there: old, pink, smooth, knotted across the back of the head from the base of the neck up to the crown. The hair had never properly grown back through the crumpled tissue, and Kolea had kept his head shaved.

'Let me see it once more,' he said. Ana Curth paused and then lifted the hand mirror again. Kolea craned his eyes sideways to study the marks on the back of his skull.

'A real mess.'

'Yes, it was,' she said. She put the mirror down because her hands were trembling and she didn't want to drop it. 'Just a few more tests,' she said, hoping she sounded breezy.

'Haven't you done enough?' he asked. She met his eyes and swallowed. There was a light there, a human spark back in them that hadn't been around since that day on Phantine two years earlier. It was like he'd risen from the dead, and though she was overjoyed to have him back, it terrified her. It was beyond her professional expertise to explain it.

'Why don't you sit down?' he suggested. 'You look like you've seen a ghost.'

She laughed, stupidly delighted by the awful joke, and sat on a wooden stool facing the bedside where he was perched. The infirmary was quiet, though those patients still awake had heard what was going on and were whispering from cot to cot. From nearby came the soft whir of a medicae resonancer as Dorden ran the machine over Mkvenner's torso for the umpteenth time. Dorden glanced up from his work, saw Curth looking at him, and shrugged. They were both spooked. They'd seen plenty in their days with the regiment, but nothing like this.

'How much do you remember, Gol?' she asked.

He frowned, his lips pursed, for a brief second resembling the brain-damaged Gol Kolea, struggling to remember someone's name or what he was supposed to be doing.

'With any clarity, I remember a street in Ouranberg, in the habs of the Alpha Dome. Criid was down. Hurt. Enemy fire. Those damn loxatl freaks. I remember the impacts of their flechette blasters. That distinctive sound… the hiss, the rattle of the shrapnel barbs. I went to get Tona. She was with Allo and Jenk, and they were dead. She'd caught shrap in the arm and the side. It looked bad. I picked her up and started to run. I…'

'What?'

'I don't remember anything after that. It's just a blur from there. You know how when you're swimming and you dive down, and sounds from above you become all muffled and hollow? It feels like my memories since then are like that. Vague, out of focus. When my head came back up out of the water in that pool all the sounds flooded back and I remembered who I was.'

'It's been two years.'

'Two years?' he gasped. 'Tell me.'

'Tell you what?'

'Tell me where I've been. Tell me what happened.'

She breathed out and looked at the floor. 'It was a loxatl round. It hit you in the back of the head and… and there was nothing we could do. You nearly died. You have to understand, Gol…'

'I understand you did your best.'

'No, I mean… this isn't normal. You'd lost a considerable percentage of brain tissue. Your personality was destroyed. You could barely answer to your own name. You were just a shadow. An empty body.'

'And now I'm not.'

She stared at him. 'Gol, I've scanned your skull with the infra-ometer and the mag resonator. There's no change. Your brain is still as damaged as before. There's been no real reconstruction, just basic tissue healing. There is absolutely no way you should be… cogent again like this.'

Kolea reached up and ran his fingers over the mess of scartissue.

'You said it was a miracle.'

'It is. In the strictest, most literal sense of the word. You and Ven both.'

'That scares you.'

'Yes, it does.' He blinked at this and looked away. Curth jumped to her feet.

'Oh, Gol! no! Don't misunderstand me! I'm only scared of the unknown. Dorden's the same... God-Emperor, everyone is!'

She reached out and hugged him tightly, pecking a quick kiss on his cheek before pulling away again.

'But we're fething glad to have you back.'

He smiled. The old smile. The one she'd once been rather keen on.

'Tell me the rest,' he said. 'Where is this place again?'

'Herodor,' she said.

'And before that we were where?'

'On Aexe Cardinal. Trench war.'

He nodded slowly. 'I have a vague, muffled recollection of mud and water. And bombardment. Huge bombardment. Who's been leading the squad?'

'Criid,' Curth said and laughed when he opened his mouth in surprise. 'First female sergeant. Things have moved along a bit in two years. Jajjo made scout.'

'Our first Verghast scout? Oh Holy Terra...' Kolea murmured, genuinely moved and proud. 'About gakking time.'

'Muril almost made the grade too. She was in the program, and Ven says he would have recommended her to the specialty.' Curth's face darkened. 'But she died on Aexe.'

'Who else?' he asked quietly. 'Get it over with. Who else have we lost while I was in the dark?'

'So... CAN I go?' asked Mkvenner.

Dorden was packing up the instruments and glanced over at him. 'You seem astonishingly unmoved by this, Ven,' he said. He was trying to disconnect the power lead from the base of the resonator paddle, but his mind was everywhere and he couldn't remember how the lead-lock worked. He had to put the device down quickly so Mkvenner wouldn't notice his distraction.

Mkvenner shrugged. 'You say I'm fit?'

'Rudely healthy. There's no trace of any internal bleeding. There's not even a residue of blood pooled in your abdomen.'

Mkvenner started to pull on his black vest. 'So I can go?'

'Do you know what just happened?'

'Yes,' said Mkvenner.

'Well, I fething don't! Explain it to me.'

Mkvenner shrugged again. 'It is my honour to serve the Imperium of Man, and in so doing the God-Emperor who protects us all. Tonight, in his infinite wisdom, he spared me, and he did so through the instrument of his chosen one. I'm not going to argue with that. I'm not going to be scared by that, either.'

'Yes, but–'

'There are no "buts", Dorden. We fight the archenemy because we believe in the Holy Truths. Terrible things happen, unnatural things, warp-magic things, and we accept them because we believe. Now a good thing happens and you think we should question it?'

Dorden frowned. 'No, put like that.'

Mkvenner looked up. There were sounds coming from outside. Voices.

'Stay here,' Dorden said, and walked towards the infirmary exit.

A crowd was gathering in the torch-lit hall outside the hospital facility. Dorden saw huddles of ayatani and esholi, groups of ecclesiarchs and adepts, even a few infardi. Most of them had prayer beads, pilgrim badges, ampullas of holy water or placard boards with pictures of the Saint pasted onto them. Some were incanting, or swinging incense burners. Many carried votive candles.

'What is this?' he asked.

'We want to see the Miraculous,' said one ecclesiarch.

'That's not possible. This is a hospital, and there are sick men here who need rest.'

'The Saint has touched men here!' an ayatani declared. 'We must have audience with these men and test them for faith and truth.'

'Go away,' said Dorden.

Ayatani Kilosh moved towards him through the gathering crowd.

'Show me the men,' he said to the old doctor.

'Can't this wait?'

Kilosh shook his head. 'Corroboration must be had and witnessed, and testimony recorded so that these miracles may be written into the holy record.'

'Why?'

'Why? Doctor, if a plague breaks out do you not try to contain it, identify it and document it for the good of the Imperium?'

Dorden blinked. 'Of course.'

'Well, a wonder has happened here that has profound significance for the Church of Man. We must investigate it and document it so we can understand fully what it means. The God-Emperor has spoken to us, and we need to find out what it is He has said.'

Dorden sighed. 'Just you then, Ayatani Kilosh. You and your scribes. I will not have the other patients discomforted.'

THE AIR WAS heavy with the hot smell of baking bread. Down the promenade from the scholam where the Tanith were billeted there was an arcade of merchant shops – a weaver, a milliner, a measure-arbitrator, a meat-packer and a bakery. It was nearly dawn, and a civic light-keeper, a long-bodied servitor, was clunking down the arcade, adjusting the wall-mounted phospha lamps to the day setting. The bakery was the only business up at that hour. The ovens were running in the back of the store, and the lamps were lit in the windows. In less than an hour, the hive's morning function pattern would begin, and the area would be busy with workers walking from their habs to the main-hive elevator banks to get to work. The bakery, which did a busy trade every morning in breakfast rolls and sugar-loaves, was preparing for the morning rush.

This early, it was still eerily empty. The antique speaker horns along the promenade were playing the same soft music they had been broadcasting throughout the night cycle, and the public address screens were scrolling random, soothing texts from the Imperial creed.

It reminded Soric of Vervunhive. He felt sadly nostalgic. He'd always loved this time, the early calm at the start of a day in the hive, the brief hiatus between night shift and day shift. He remembered rising at this time, walking to work, purchasing caffeine and a sosal from the food-house on his hab-block, seeing the open gates of the smeltery as he approached.

He'd knocked on the door of the bakery and got the bleary assistant to sell him some soft dough-twists, still warm from the ovens. Not sosals, but still… Now he and Milo sat under the gantries of the upper walkway, munching the food. A pair of arbites wandered past, but they didn't spare them a second glance. Two off-duty soldiers, heading home after a night in the taverns.

'So… you think you're a psyker?'

Soric's mouth turned into a firm, upside-down U. 'That's not what I said, Brin.'

'But you're worried about these… these happenings?'

'Of course I am! Worried… terrified.'

Milo ate the last of his dough-twist and wiped his mouth on his sleeve.

'You know what happens, chief.'

'I know. I know, gak it.'

'Seriously, I don't know why you're talking to me.'

'Because–'

'Because this said so?' Milo produced the crumpled blue paper from his pocket.

'I don't want to die, Milo,' Soric said.

'No one said anything about d–'

Soric shook his head. 'A bullet in the head. That's what I'll get. They don't even have to prove anything. If anyone thinks, or even thinks they think, that I'm touched by the warp, I'll be executed. No hesitation.'

'Gaunt wouldn't–'

'Wouldn't he? It's his job. It's the duty of every one of us. If I found out one of my boys was touched, I'd do them myself. No question. I'm not an idiot. You don't take chances with gak like that.'

Milo thought for a moment. 'By rights, then, I should shoot you. Or report you at least. Why have you trusted me?'

'I heard things.'

'Heard what?'

'Things. Things about you. I thought you might be sympathetic. I thought you might know what to do.'

'Why?'

'Because you're still here. Gaunt never shot you.'

Milo widened his eyes. 'Chief, I'd be lying if I said you don't scare me. The feth you've told me tonight… I should be running away and screaming for you to be gunned down.'

'But you're not.'

'No. I was interrogated. By an inquisitor. Did you know that?'

Soric blanched. 'No!'

'Back on Monthax. It was before your time. Before Verghast. Right from the Founding, I was regarded as a bit of a lucky charm. You know the story.'

'Corbec told me a little. You were the only civilian to get off the world alive.'

'Right.'

'Because of Gaunt.'

'Right. He saved my life. I was the only non-com to make it off Tanith. And the youngest. All the men looked at me like I was special. Like I was a little piece of Tanith, saved and preserved.'

'But you were special, weren't you?'

Milo sniggered. 'Oh, yes. A kid, surrounded by grown-up soldiers that I so desperately wanted to impress. Corbec, Cluggan, Rawne – I guess. Gaunt himself, certainly. I loved the fact they paid attention to me, took me seriously. I think I milked it a bit.'

'Milked it?' Soric sat back.

'I had a knack of knowing things. Well, that's what they all thought. I was the mascot, the lucky charm. If I had a funny feeling, they all took notice of it. Believe me, chief, it was child's play.'

'You faked it? Gak!'

Milo shook his head. 'No, no… nothing like that. I did get a feeling every now and then. A sense of premonition. But look at it this way. I was a kid, following men round into war zones. Shit was likely to happen at any moment. Bombardments. Raids. Sneak attacks. I mean, probability law alone means I got it right a lot of the time. I was scared and jumpy. When I jumped, the men listened. When I jumped and they listened and something happened… well, bingo. As far as they were concerned, I was a lucky charm who had a sixth sense for danger. You know troopers, chief. They're a superstitious lot.'

'Gak me,' said Soric, deflated. 'So it was all a turn. Little Brinny-boy doing his thing so the troops would love him.'

'Not quite,' said Milo. 'Are you going to finish that?' he asked, nodding at the half-eaten twist in Soric's hand.

Soric shook his head and passed it to Milo.

'There were times,' Milo said, through a mouthful, 'there were times when it seemed real. I know Gaunt was worried. He didn't know what to do. If I did have a touch about me, he knew he'd have no choice but to execute me. But he didn't dare.'

'Because?'

'Come on, chief! I was the kid, the lucky mascot, the last living civilian from Tanith. What the feth would it have done to the Ghosts' morale if he'd shot me?'

'I see your point…'

'Anyway, this inquisitor got wind of it. Varl had been playing on my rep to stage a few "entertainments" on the troop transport and some of the other regiments got nervous. I was reported. Next thing I know, I was in front of this inquisitor.'

'I've never had the pleasure. Was he a bastard? I've heard they are.'

'He was a she. Lilith. But yes, she was a bastard. Put me through the wringer. Gaunt was there. Tried his best to keep me out of the crap.'

'And?'

'And… she did her job, Agun. She got to the truth and uncovered it. She found out I was a fake and exposed me. And that's why I'm still alive.'

Soric breathed heavily and rubbed his dry hands together. 'You were a fake…'

'Not deliberately. I had been starting to believe myself. But she got the truth out. And I realised I'd been playing with fire. If that's all this is, chief, stop now.'

'It isn't,' said Soric. He reached into the thigh pocket of his fatigue pants and fished out a crumpled packet of lho-sticks.

'I thought you'd given those up.'

'So did I,' Soric said, lighting one. 'They help with the headaches. I get this pain across my skull, and in my dead eye.' He reached up with his left hand and splayed the fingers across his scarred head. 'It hurts, a lot.'

'You should tell Gaunt,' said Milo.

'About my headaches?'

'About everything. Tell him. If I know anything about Gaunt it's that he's no bastard. He'll protect you. He'll do what is necessary to keep you safe without breaking Imperial law.'

'The black ships…' Soric murmured.

'Maybe. I don't know. All I know is, I'm not touched. Never was. I'm not in any way special. But I know how hard it can get if they suspect you. So tell Gaunt. Maybe that's why the message told you to speak to me. Sound advice.'

Soric exhaled a plume of fragrant smoke. 'I need to do something. The messages are getting…'

'What?'

'More urgent. I've had a warning. I don't know what it means, but it's gonna be bad. I have to tell someone… Gaunt, who knows? But if I tell, that's the end for me. Goodbye, Agun, nice to have known you. I don't know, Brinny. Should I be looking after myself or looking to the greater good?'

Milo got up, dusting crumbs from his lap. 'I think you know the answer to that, chief.'

Milo walked away down the promenade.

Soric sat for a moment in silence. 'All right, already!' he hissed, reaching into his leg pouch. The brass shell had been wriggling like a rat.

He unscrewed it and routinely tipped out the note.

Nine are coming. Stop gakking around and be a man. Milo can be trusted, but he's lying. He IS special. Don't tell him. Don't scare him. The clock's reached midnight.

'I PRESUME YOU have a pass, trooper?'

Milo stopped in his tracks in the scholam entrance.

'Sir?'

Hark stepped out of the shadows. 'An exeunt pass, permitting you to stray from quarters.'

'I haven't, sir.'

Hark nodded. 'Who were you with?'

'No one, sir. I was just taking a walk.'

'With Sergeant Soric. I saw you.'

'It's nothing, sir.'

Hark raised a gloved hand and beckoned Milo over to him with one crooked finger.

'I will judge what is something and what is nothing. I have my eye on Soric.'

'Why, sir?'

Hark's eyes were hooded. 'Reports. I don't intend to divulge my sources to a common trooper.'

'Of course not, sir.'

'You lead a charmed life, Brin Milo. The Tanith dote on you. Gaunt dotes on you. All I care about is the well being of this regiment. Its health... spiritual, physical... mental. I believe that you, like any of the Ghosts, would tell me if there was something – wrong – going on. It would be your duty.'

'It would, sir.'

'Tell me about Soric.'

'The chief is upset, sir.'

'Upset?'

'He is suffering from headaches.'

'And?'

Milo shook his head. 'And nothing. Headaches.'

Milo stiffened as Hark produced a scrumpled piece of blue paper from his storm-coat pocket and opened it out, holding it so that Milo could see.

It read: *Guheen's going to get himself pulped if he goes that way. The tank is behind the cabinet maker's shop.*

'I have no idea what that means, sir,' said Milo.

'Soric is warp-touched, isn't he?'

'Not that I know, sir.'

'If I find out he is, and that you've been covering for him, I'll have your neck as well as his. Clear, trooper?'

'Crystal, sir.'

'Get to your billet!' snapped Hark.

Milo hurried away and Hark turned and stared up at the massive window lights that ran along the promenade bay. Up in the deep blue, stars were shining.

SOME OF THE stars were ships.

On the wide bridge of the frigate *Navarre*, Executive Officer Kreff leaned forward in his padded seat and said, 'Authorise.'

The bridge crew nodded, touching console switches. There was a low hum as the gravitic assemblies in the massive ship's

underbelly cycled and flat-banded mag waves to compensate
for the ship's orbital drift.

A proximity horn started to wail.

Kreff tutted and got up, sauntering over to the main
pilot well where the helm servitors sat in recessed floor
sockets. The demi-human crew sat hunched forward, their
plug-crusted skulls looping hoses behind them like
braids.

'Station keeping,' he ordered.

'Maximal one oh one,' the nearest servitor croaked from its
augmetic voice-box.

With a press of his hand on the imprint reader, Kreff cancelled the siren. Orbital space above Herodor was thick with
ships, most of them informally registered pilgrim tubs. Every
few minutes, as the elegant frigate reclined in orbit, tracking
sensors would fire off, warning of another near miss. It had
become routine.

Kreff walked into the actuality sphere in the centre of the
bridge space, and looked around at the speckle of glowing
ship-phantoms that appeared in 3D in the light-impressed
sphere around him. Tactical readouts glowed beside the various images, blinking as the images slowly tracked. There was
a mass conveyance called the *Troubadour*, part of a newly
arrived pilgrim caravan, that kept wandering into the
Navarre's collision cone.

The vox beeped. It was the captain.

'Alarms woke me, Kreff.'

'Nothing to worry about, captain. Just routine.'

Captain Wysmark signed off.

'Bloody hulk is wandering again...' Kreff said.

'*Troubadour* is signaling, sir,' said one of the deck officers.
'They have a fire on board. Major fire, in the hold space.
Requesting urgent assist.'

'Check it.'

'*Navarre* is reading massive heat build in the hold section.
They're burning alive.'

Kreff nodded. 'Fire suppression teams to standby.
Board teams to ready. Move us in, helm, and tell the
Troubadour to stand by for immediate docking. Let's
hustle.'

'Should I have the troops stand by, sir?' asked Colonel Zebbs, the ship's senior armsman, standing to attention behind Kreff.

'It's a bloody pilgrim ship, not a hostile,' said Kreff.

ENSIGN VALDEEMER TOOK the data-slate from the waiting deck servitor, reviewed it quickly, and then began to stride purposefully across the steel deck of the *Omnia Vincit* towards the fleet captain's pulpit. To his left, where the edge of the bridge deck dropped away, the dozens of helm servitors, tech-priests and astropath navigators were arranged in descending tiers, like the upper circle of a great theatre. It took a massive crew to control a battleship the size of the *Omnia Vincit*, a massive bridge crew alone. The bridge space was vast and vaulted like a gigantic basilica, its high domed roof painted with beautiful frescos of the actes sanctorum.

Valdeemer was just a small part of that crew, and a recent part too. He'd joined the ship just eighteen months before, but already he was a junior deck officer. He knew he had a bright future. One day, it would be him sitting up there in that magnificent throne, bio-linked to the ship's systems, commanding the power of a god in the Emperor's name.

To get there, he had to shine. To excel. To do his job in exemplary fashion and be seen to be doing it too. He could have voxed the report for the fleet captain's attention, but it was important, and suited personal delivery. Besides, it brought him to the fleet captain's attention.

He hurried up the alabaster steps of the pulpit, pausing briefly at the top as the Navy armsmen guards scanned him and then stood aside.

Fleet Captain Esquine terrified every member of the great ship's crew. Even Valdeemer, for all his confidence, was cowed by him. It was hard to tell where the fleet captain's gilded throne ended and his own body began. He was encased in golden armour, intricately wrought and etched, and his armour engaged directly with the throne so he formed a solid, engraved structure. His hands and arms were fused into the arms of the seat, and the back of his head, in its skullcap of gold, was locked against the throne's high back.

Esquine's hands were set palm-down on the arms of the throne, and only his gold-jacketed fingers moved, dancing like a pianist's. At their bidding, multi-jointed servo arms raised and lowered in front of the fleet captain's eyes, presenting pict-plates, larger actuality screens, and data-slates. The fleet captain held them up, sometimes four or more at a time, overlaying, comparing, transferring data from one to another with a blink, interlocking and compressing information into tight holographic spheres that floated around the throne.

Esquine's face was long-browed and noble. His blade of a nose had a slight hook to it, and his pale eyes were lashed with nearly invisible white hairs. The gold tracery of circuitry was woven into his ears, his cheekbones and the skin of his forehead from the edges of the skullcap, giving his flesh a jaundiced tinge. His mouth was invisible behind the grille of a vox-caster that rose from his gilded chest plate like a breathing mask.

Valdeemer smoothed the crisp front of his uniform jacket, shook out his braided cuffs, adjusted the sit of his emerald sash, and stood to attention.

'You have a report for me, ensign?' Esquine asked. His voice was soft and fluid, each word sounding like a rounded stone dropped into a deep pool.

'Sir,' Valdeemer nodded, and held out the data-slate. Esquine's fingers flickered, and a servo arm extended out from the throne's side and took the slate, swinging it back before the fleet captain's eyes.

'From the astropathicae,' Valdeemer went on. 'They have detected an advance perturbation in the Empyrean, warp modulus eleven two nine nine seven, at a point–'

'Nine AU out from Herodor. I can read, ensign. A standard Imperial arrival vector.'

'I thought I should bring it to you at once, sir.'

Locked in place, Esquine's head could not turn, but his pallid eyes glanced sidelong at Valdeemer for a moment.

'Of course.' Esquine's gaze returned to the slate, and a servo-arm moved in to offer up another for comparison. 'The reinforcement fleet is approaching. That worm Lugo will be pleased, no doubt. Let us prepare. Ensign, step onto the throne plate.'

Valdeemer blinked and looked down. He was standing on the outer decking of the command pulpit. The throne itself was set on a raised disc of polished plasteel in the centre. He quickly stepped up onto the edge of this inner platform.

There was a slight vibration. The disc began to move, sliding backwards. The adamantine bulkhead wall behind the throne parted with a hiss of disengaging magnetic locks, and the entire throne platform – and Valdeemer along with it – retracted through the opening space.

As the shadow of the bulkhead passed over him, Valdeemer felt the retracting throne-platform begin to rotate too. It turned them through one hundred and eighty degrees until Esquine's throne was now facing into the secret, armoured chamber behind his pulpit. The strategium.

The bulkhead shutters closed, sealing them in. Valdeemer felt a rush of excitement. This was the first time he had been invited into the inner sanctum of command.

The dim, heavily buttressed chamber was ovoid. Techpriests and senior deck officers stood or sat at console stations built into the walls between the buttress stanchions, and seven more perched at high podium consoles facing inwards around the actuality sphere that flickered and glowed in the centre of the room. There was a constant background murmur of vox chatter, cursor chimes and machine language.

Commander Velosade was in charge here. He snapped to attention as the throne rotated in and called out, 'Captain on the strategium.' Everyone made formal salute.

'At ease and continue,' said Esquine. 'Display the warp perturbation, if you will.'

Velosade cracked his fingers, and a dimple of mauve light appeared in the lower hemisphere of the actuality globe.

'Reduce scale and give me tactical,' said Esquine.

The actuality sphere flickered, dissolved and reformed, slightly wider and sparer in detail. Valdeemer recognised immediately they were looking at a 3D verisim of the entire inner system. There, the bright fuzz of the local star, there Herodor, and the other four inner planets, the bright band of the asteroid belt. The mauve dimple lay outside this inner group, as far from Herodor as Herodor was from its star.

'Overlay tactical!' Velosade ordered.

A geometric grid graphic flowed into the sphere, graphing its dimensions, and the disposition of Esquine's vessels – along with the myriad pilgrim and merchant ships – appeared as slowly drifting, numbered light-points.

'Astropathicae report parameters verified. Perturbation reads at warp modulus eleven two nine nine seven, nine AU out. Tracking cogents. Concordance estimated at ninety-three minutes. Awaiting confirmation.'

Velosade turned and looked at the fleet captain. 'Orders, sir?'

'Remain as they were, commander. Warmaster Macaroth has charged us to exercise extreme caution. Move a frigate up in front of the modulus point, fighter screens up. They can greet arriving friends… or deny arriving enemies. The remainder of the fleet stays as vanguard.'

A flutter of Esquine's fingers made cursor points appear on the glowing sphere. Valdeemer knew the commander was using the word 'fleet' ironically. An officer of Esquine's rank – and a ship like the *Omnia Vincit* – could normally expect to have a considerable attendant fleet in support. However, Esquine's battleship, with only two frigates in attendance, had been sent to carry Lord General Lugo to Herodor by the Warmaster as a mark of special respect, and the recently arrived Tanith had brought only one frigate and one heavy cruiser as escort vessels. Three frigates, a cruiser, a ship of the line, and fleet tender vessels – not too shabby as far as a flotilla detail went, but badly under strength in terms of fleet engagements.

'Inform the surface,' Esquine continued, 'and alert the civilian traffic that there is a manoeuvre, code magenta, and that we expect their cooperation and their careful station-keeping for its duration.'

Velosade nodded, and started growling orders. All the strategium crew began working, many of them suddenly speaking loudly and urgently into their vox-links.

'Your choice of frigate, sir?' called Velosade.

'The *Navarre*,' replied Esquine without hesitation.

'The *Navarre* is occupied, sir,' Veldeemer said suddenly and winced at the sharp look the commander gave him for speaking out of turn.

'Let him talk, Velosade,' said the fleet captain. 'Occupied how, ensign?'

'A mercantile mass conveyance in difficulties, sir. The *Navarre* signaled it was moving to assist.'

'Let them carry on,' said the fleet captain. 'Charge the *Berengaria* instead.'

'Sir,' affirmed Velosade.

'Well appreciated, ensign,' said the fleet captain softly to Valdeemer. 'A slight diversion I hadn't accounted. You read sphere tactics well.'

'I like to stay on top of things, sir.'

'Keep it up,' said Esquine.

Valdeemer felt a flush of pride run through him.

ITS VAST ENGINES cycling up to one tenth power, the frigate *Berengaria* moved away from Herodor, prowling forward into the interplanetary gulf. Though only classified as a light cruiser, it was massive by any standards of measure: a long, fortified, angular vessel, its barbed hull dull green. Frigates of the *Berengaria's* pattern were fast and well-armed, the blade-edge of any serious Navy group.

'We have broken orbit and are advancing to the advised modulus,' Captain Sodak said quietly, standing in the actuality sphere of the *Berengaria's* bridge.

'Signal sent and noted by fleet command, sir,' an ensign replied.

'Flight decks?'

'Fighter screen reports ready aye.'

'So noted. Cycle up the launch ramps.'

'Aye, captain.'

Sodak looked at the warp dimple in the depths of the impressed-light sphere in front of him. It was getting larger and darker.

'Order is launch.'

'Order is launch, aye!'

TINY SPECKS OF LIGHT darted from the flanks of the *Berengaria*. The specks raced ahead of the massive warship, catching the backscattered light of the distant sun as they fanned out into a cloud like dust-flies at twilight.

They were Lightning-pattern fighters, swift and deadly one-man craft, spat out of the frigate's launch decks by mag-catapult. In wide formation, they spread out before their mighty parent craft.

Squadron Leader Shumlen, a thrice-decorated ace and flight commander of the *Berengaria's* fighter wing, dropped his heads-up scope into place and gunned his Lightning forward into the apex point of the fighter screen. Despite the physical rush of launch and the metabolic rush of the prospect of combat, Shumlen's vitals-reader showed that his cardiac rate was astonishingly level and calm.

'Keep it spread,' he said unhurriedly over his vox-comm.

'Concordance in forty-two minutes and counting,' vox-link from the frigate reported.

THE NAVARRE SHIVERED as its docking clamps secured the mass conveyance *Troubadour*. On the frigate's bridge, alert sirens rang and hazard lights flashed.

Kreff cancelled them with a wave of his wand. He took the vox-horn from a waiting servitor.

'Open the hatches. Boarding parties to ready. Transfer the wounded out. Medicae, stand by to receive injured.'

'Sir?'

'What is it?' Kreff snapped impatiently.

'That heat source sir, on the *Troubadour*...' The aide looked confused. 'It's gone.'

'Gone?'

'Faded, sir. I guess they could have got the fire under control...'

Kreff looked at Zebbs.

'Go!' he said, and the soldier was running to the bridge exit.

'Shall I alert the captain?' asked the aide.

'No!' Kreff halted. 'Yes, yes. Wake him.'

A DETAIL OF Navy armsmen was waiting for Zebbs in the prep-chamber of the mid-starboard air-gate. The colonel was pulling on his armour-jacket as he entered. The detail stood to attention, bulky in their emerald green armour suits, their combat shotcannons held ready, their faces hidden behind tinted visors.

'Safeties, but let's go careful!' he said, taking his own shot-gun from his number two.

He racked the grip of his powerful weapon and stepped to the gate.

'Open up mid-two!' he shouted.

The hatch ground open. There was no one on the other side. No sirens, no alarms, no smell of fire or scenes of panic.

Zebbs stepped through. His armsmen hurried in after him, spreading out.

The hallway was dark, and it smelled of stale air as if the scrubbers were malfunctioning. Zebbs wasn't surprised. This was an old ship, poorly maintained. It was a wonder it had ever made a warp-transition.

'Floor's wet, sir,' popped one of his men over the inert vox.

'Coolant leak,' said another, his voice punctuated by the crackle of the link.

'You think?' said Zebbs, looking down. The deck was awash, about two centimetres deep in dark liquid. It looked for all the world like–

There was a little splash as something landed in the liquid and rolled towards them. It ended up between Zebbs and his point man. They both looked down at it.

It was a grenade.

'Shit,' was all Zebbs had time to say.

'Zebbs? Zebbs? Colonel, report!' Kreff yelled into the vox horn. He'd just heard a loud and suddenly cut-off roar over the channel that had wiped signals out. Now there was only a dull murmur of static.

'Clean it up!' Kreff shouted at his aides. 'I want Zebbs on the link now!'

They rushed to obey. A second later, from a different vox source, they tuned in the sounds of shouting. Confused, demented shouting. And the smack of gunfire.

Kreff lowered the vox-horn in dismay.

'Sever the dock-clamps! Break us off!'

'Clamps are locked out, sir!'

'What? What?'

'Docking clamps one through nine are locked out, sir,' said his aide.

'Holy Throne, no!'

'Is there a problem, Kreff?'

Kreff turned to see Captain Wysmark striding towards him across the bridge.

'We've… we've been boarded, sir,' he said.

Wysmark, tall and saturnine in his green dress uniform, seemed unflustered. He took the vox-horn from Kreff's trembling hands and spoke into it.

'Armsmen to all active airgates. On the double. Repel boarders. Repeat, repel boarders.'

SPACE BUCKLED. SPACE shimmered, and tore. Out of the splitting dark fabric, the inscrutable light of warp space flashed and seared.

Out of the breach, ships thundered into view.

They came fast at first, as if flung out of the Chaotic reality, and then slid down to a more dignified drift. Imperial ships. Three Munitorum conveyances, then a Navy frigate, then four more heavy transporters.

'Open formation,' Shumlen ordered. 'They're friendlies. Repeat, they are friendlies.'

The fighter screen broke around him, spreading wide and zipping like tiny silver reef fish along the lengths of the ponderous new arrivals. The vox-channels were suddenly busy with hailing signals.

'Request permission to return to carrier decks,' Shumlen voxed.

'THE FRIGATE *Glory of Cadia* sends greetings and compliments,' Sodak's ensign reported.

'Respond as per form, ensign.'

'The perturbation is not dissipating, captain,' called a tech-priest.

Sodak would have been surprised if it had. According to the watch briefing, they were expecting something in the order of sixteen ships, and the actuality sphere showed only eight newcomer vessels. A fleet disposition emerging from warp space often came through in several waves.

'Instruct the *Glory of Cadia* to escort its charges into Herodor high anchor. Inform fleet command that we will remain on station to await the next wave.'

'Yes sir.'

'Fighter screen, captain?' asked the flight controller from his raised, glasteel-bubbled console station.

'Keep them aloft,' replied Sodak. He was a cautious man. Without that caution, he'd never have lived long enough to become a warship's commander.

A CREW-SERVITOR, short and broad with circuitry glinting across its black metalwork, turned from its station and handed Valdeemer a data-slate. The ensign immediately hurried it across to the fleet captain's throne. Esquine was watching the fleet arrivals at the concordance point.

'Distress report, sir,' said Valdeemer anxiously. 'The *Navarre*.'

'Show me,' said Esquine softly.

'They are under internal attack,' said Valdeemer, handing the slate to one of the fleet captain's grasping servo limbs. 'Captain Wysmark reports intruder hostiles attempting to board from the merchant ship.'

'Signal Wysmark. Ask him if he requires assistance.'

HARD ROUNDS WHINED down the companionway and rattled off the metal partitioning, causing the armsmen in Sublieu-tenant Epsin's team to duck for cover. Something was wrong with the deck lights. Only the frosty green auxilary lighting panels were illuminated and, from the smell of the air, the circulators were out or dying too.

There was a buzzing noise too, very faint, that came and went. Cabling fritzing out, Epsin thought.

Another volley of shots. Epsin saw the deformed slugs bounce onto the deck plating and roll. They looked like the crushed butts of lho-sticks.

It was sweep-fire. Random auto-bursts fired around corners and down blind halls to clear a path.

'Hold fire,' Epsin whispered. 'Let 'em think the way's clean…'

Hunched down along the companionway behind bulk-head stanchions, his men shifted uneasily, their shotcannons raised ready.

The enemy appeared. Three... then four, five... man-shadows hefting short-pattern autoguns, hurrying down the hallway ahead.

'Repel,' Epsin whispered.

His cannon boomed, barking out a bright white flash in the dim green light. Other shotcannons around him did the same. The shadows ahead collapsed, hurled back violently by the heavy firepower. Acrid smoke filled the air and, without the circulators in operation, stayed there.

'Forward!' Epsin ordered. The armsmen party hurried ahead, hugging the metal walls of the companionway. Almost immediately, more hostiles appeared around the junction turn ahead, rattling auto-fire in their direction. Epsin's pointman let out a cry and slumped sideways against the wall. The man behind him recoiled, bent double and collapsed on his face.

'Bastards!' Epsin yelled. 'For the Emperor! For the *Navarre*!' The shotcannon bucked in his hands as he blasted with it. His team had almost fought its way to the intersection leading down to the nearest airgate.

It was just then, above the roaring gunfire, Epsin heard the buzzing again.

'THE FLEET CAPTAIN enquires if we require assistance, sir,' said Kreff.

Captain Wysmark looked up from the situations monitor at his exec. 'What do you think, Kreff?'

'I think we're in for a hell of a dirty fight along the airgates, sir. But I hardly think the fleet captain wants to lose another fifth of his flotilla to a boarding action when we're at magenta stand-by awaiting arrivals. We can manage. The *Navarre's* armsmen are the best in the fleet.'

Wysmark smiled slightly. 'My reading exactly. Signal the *Omnia Vincit* so. We'll have this contained in another fifteen minutes.'

Kreff turned smartly and instructed the signals officer. He turned back to his captain's side.

'What was that?' Wysmark asked.

'Sir?'

'That buzzing. Did you not hear it, Kreff?'

'No sir.'

Wysmark shook his head and returned his attention to the monitor. 'This is the price we pay for wet-nursing the pilgrim craft.'

'Sir?'

'A mass of unregistered, unregulated traffic, filling orbit, packed with citizens it's our duty to protect. The odds were high there'd be infiltrators and heretics amongst them. We're obliged to help a ship in distress, even if it turns out to be a trap. All part of the job, Kreff.'

'I was wondering, sir…'

'What?'

'Why now, sir? If there are heretics aboard the *Troubadour*, then they've been here in orbit for three days. Why choose this moment to act?'

'I was thinking that myself. Coincidence that we're at magenta standby and thus stretched?'

'There's no such think as coincidence, captain.'

Wysmark nodded. 'Get me a verisim link to the fleet captain.'

'INCOMING VERISIM!' VELOSADE called. 'Captain Wysmark of the *Navarre*.'

'Display,' said Esquine.

A half-size holoform image of Wysmark appeared like a pale red phantom in front of the fleet captain's throne, projected up from the holo-emitters in the strategium's decking.

'Wysmark?'

'I wanted to advise extreme caution, fleet captain,' Wysmark's voice crackled over the vox-relay. 'The boarding action we are enduring would seem pointless unless it is part of a larger scheme.'

'The enemies of mankind are not famed for their tactical brilliance,' said Esquine.

There was a slight time-lag delay before Wysmark's image nodded and smiled at the fleet captain's remark. 'Agreed, sir. But I fear this is a strategy to take the *Navarre* out of useful disposition.'

'I see.'

'I simply wished to advise caution.'

'So noted. Thank you, Wysmark.'

The holoform faded. Esquine fixed Velosade with his hard, pale eyes. 'Wysmark is a sound commander not given to over reaction. Arm the main batteries, captain.'

EPSIN PLUNGED THROUGH the thick smoke pluming down the air-gate's entry deck. The walls were marred with shot damage, and several bodies lay on the deck. Rough, dirty men in drab red armour, their faces covered in black iron masks.

More than simple heretics, Epsin thought.

He waved his men up. Along the side hallway that led to the other gate entries, he heard sporadic gunfire.

And the buzzing again, that damn buzzing. Like an insect in a jar.

Epsin saw a figure in front of him, through the smoke. A tall figure…

No, three figures. One tall man, cloaked in pilgrim green and hooded, clutching two smaller figures to his sides with thick, powerful arms that were laced with tattoos. The smaller figures were dressed in rags, shivering and clinging to the man in green like frightened children. They turned their faces towards him, and Epsin gasped as he beheld their twisted, runtish, eyeless visages.

In unison, they opened their mouths, and the buzzing grew much louder, as if the lid had come off the jar and freed the insect. Epsin coughed and staggered, shaking his head frantically to get rid of the buzz.

He knew what this was. He tried to adjust his headset to send a warning to the captain.

The armsman beside him, a stalwart ship-trooper who had been in Epsin's team for nine years, turned slowly. His mouth was slack, and blood ran copiously from his nose and tearducts.

He brought his shotcannon up and blew Epsin's head off.

'CONCORDANCE NOW IN two minutes,' the vox-link rasped.

'Thank you, *Berengaria*,' responded Shumlen, tilting slightly in the tight embrace of his grav-seat as he brought the Lightning round in a tight turn. 'Flight leader to screen elements, form on me for a second pass. More traffic inbound.'

The pilots of the squadron chattered back in confirmation and the Lightning flight, like a flock of racing birds, turned as one and made course towards the calculated real-space entry point about seven hundred and fifty kilometres ahead.

There was nothing to see. The starfield at this speed was a striated blur, and the warp perturbation that preceded a re-entry was visible only on instruments.

Shumlen checked his scope, and saw the swirling dimple of colour on the low-res screen swell and flutter. 'Arm weapons,' he said.

His pulse was barely idling.

FOR THE SECOND time in less than an hour, space tore open. The reality fissure leapt and crackled like a luminous cephalopod, lashing tendrils of warp energy into real space that twisted out, fizzled and faded. Non-baryonic light flared brilliantly through the tear, backlighting the arriving ships. Monumental silhouettes, they were shot forward into real space.

They did not slow down. They were moving at cruise speed. Attack speed.

Shumlen blinked. The arriving ships were just dots against the glare-spot ahead of his squadron, but his pattern recognition systems began to hoot and warble.

'Hostiles, hostiles, hostiles,' he said, matter-of-factly. 'We have hostile vessels in system and advancing. Flight leader to screen elements... accelerate to attack velocity.'

'HOSTILES REPORTED!' THE ensign sang out, a tremor in his voice.

'Battle stations,' said Sodak. The sirens began to wail. 'Shields up. Arm batteries. Power to main lances.'

'Shields aye!'

'Fighters are engaging,' said the flight controller.

Sodak gazed at the flickering images on the actuality sphere. 'Increase magnification. Get me a clearer picture.' At the current resolution, the holographic display was overlaying tag cursors and disposition icons. Code numbers were jumping and blinking.

'Tenfold mag aye!' said the ensign.

The tactical image enlarged rapidly. It looked like three enemy ships, possibly four, but the overlay icon of the fighter screen was making it hard to read the details.

'Take out the fighter icon,' snapped Sodak, and an aide cancelled the overlay image of the *Berengaria's* attack squadron.

Four ships. One of them very large. And they were moving. Point seven five light at least, cutting straight towards Herodor.

'Enginarium,' said Sodak. 'Flank speed, please. Reactor output to ninety per cent. Last ready call for weapons.'

'Weapons aye. All green.'

'Firing solutions, all batteries and lances. Target the big one.'

'Aye sir.'

'HOSTILES, SIR,' SAID Velosade. 'Four marks. We believe three cruisers and a capital ship.'

'Hold position.'

'*Berengaria* is engaging.'

'Hold position,' Esquine repeated.

'Signal from the *Glory of Cadia*, sir,' Valdeemer called out. 'Requesting permission to come about in support of the *Berengaria*.'

'Denied. I want them here, in line with us. Get that order confirmed.'

'Yes, fleet captain.'

'Status?' Esquine asked.

'*Solstice* is standing by. *Laudate Divinitus* is standing by. They both report battle readiness.'

'The *Navarre*?'

'Still locked in the boarding fight, sir.'

Esquine fell silent. Around him, above the machine-code chatter of the strategium, he could hear the ship's priesthood chanting their blessings to secure victory in combat. The Imperial creed was being broadcast over the intercom system.

'Battle stations,' said Esquine softly. Bright red lamps began to cycle and flash and a moaning alarm siren started to sound. Esquine felt a shiver run through him as the neuro-plugs linking him to the ship's systems delivered the multiple responses of an Imperial battleship rising to full combat mode. Esquine's heart pounded as the reactors came to full power, his fingers twitched as the weapon batteries made ready to fire, his flesh tingled as the shields rose. He closed his eyes and experienced a rushing sense of expanded vision as power was diverted from non-essential systems to boost the main sensor cone.

He looked, and saw the enemy bearing down.

THE VOID WAS incandescent with rippling fireballs and traceries of light. Shumlen gunned in under the rake of the enemy's forward anti-ship batteries and headed under the belly of the main vessel.

It was huge, easily the size of the *Omnia Vincit*, a Chaos battleship, its black hull so covered with turret clusters and shield pods it looked diseased and blistered. Three Chaos cruisers ran with it, fearsomely lithe warships with serrated hulls. Two were decked in red and gold, the third black with its ribbed superstructure painted white.

The *Berengaria's* fighter screen had met the ships head on, so as to minimise the angles of fire available to the enemy gunners, but even so Shumlen had already lost about thirty ships to the massive anti-fighter barrage. Every pilot knew the drill. Once they were on the enemy, it was individual action. There was no hope of formation tactics in a fight zone this confused.

Shumlen hugged the enemy hull as close as he dared. He loosed one underwing missile, but was already well past by the time it detonated and he was unable to tell what surface damage he might have inflicted.

A Lightning tumbled past in front of him, causing him to veer as his collision warning system blared briefly. The Lightning was coming apart, shredding as it fell like a comet towards the hulking surface of the battleship's hull.

Pulse lasers chased Shumlen, stitching the darkness with phosphorescent bolts. He banked hard left, saw a raised missile turret ahead, and fired his second missile. The blast dazzled him and his whole ship shook violently as he flew out of the blastwash.

A Lightning slid close to him, almost in formation, and then exploded as pulse fire from the hull found it. Another two shot over the top of him and began strafing runs along the underhull. Shumlen lost sight of them in the vivid firestorm.

Shumlen half-heard a transmission on the vox.

'Repeat, repeat,' he said. His pulse was just beginning to lift.

'Bats, bats, bats!' one of his wingmen repeated.

The enemy had got its fighter screen launched.

FLICKERING WITH TWINKLING flashes of light from the small-ship fight racing around their hulls, the Chaos vessels bore on.

'Archive sweep results, captain,' said Persson, Sodak's tactical officer.

Sodak looked over the data. Two of the enemy cruisers were positively identified: the *Cicatrice*, with its white-ribbed superstructure, and the *Revenant*, its red hull laced with gold. The third cruiser was either the *Harm's Way* or the *Suture*. The identity of the main battleship was vague, for such giants were much more seldom seen, but Persson's pattern recognition program suggested the monster was the *Incarnadine*, an ancient, infamous craft.

'Master of ordnance? Have we firing solutions?'

'Solutions and range, captain,' replied Adept Yarden.

'Fire!' snarled Sodak.

The deck rocked beneath him slightly. Streaks of light from the lances and main batteries spat into the darkness.

'Main batteries have fired. Lances have fired. Torpedoes are running.'

On the augur-scope, blips of light crackled around the dark bulk of the approaching *Incarnadine*.

'Damage?'

'Their shields have held, captain,' said the master of ordnance.

'Second cycle, fire!'

Berengaria trembled again.

'Third cycle, fire!'

'Torpedoes have reached target, captain.'

'Damage... give me something, Yarden!'

The master of ordnance glanced over at the captain from his position at the fire control station.

'I'm sorry, sir. Nothing.'

'The *Revenant* is breaking formation, captain!'

Sodak turned his attention to the actuality sphere. One of the enemy cruisers was accelerating away from the battle group and advancing ahead of it.

'Engaging us?' asked an ensign.

'No,' said Sodak. 'They're going for the convoy.' The *Revenant's* course was vectoring it in after the slow moving Munitorum ships that had come out of the warp.

'Maintain course. All forward batteries and lances to sustain firing cycles at the primary target. Torpedoes too, if you please. As the *Revenant* passes us and presents, I want sustained fire on it from the flank batteries.'

'Aye, captain,' replied Yarden, swiftly moving to task his gunnery officers and their servitor crews.

The *Revenant*, swooping in like an interstellar predator, seemed to fine-tune its path as it passed the *Berengaria* as if to taunt Sodak. Its main weapons blasting forward, the *Berengaria* lit up its port side with fierce fire from its flank batteries. The *Revenant* made a desultory return of fire from its own side armaments as it thundered past.

'We hit them sir. Minor hull damage. Not enough to slow them.'

'Us?'

'Shields held.'

'Signal the fleet captain and verify his instructions. Does he want us to maintain assault?'

The bridge suddenly lurched hard, and damage klaxons beeped wildly.

'The *Incarnadine* has begun firing on us, sir. Minor shield damage.'

The ensign had barely finished when the ship shook again. Several crewmen were thrown off their feet, and the wail of the klaxons got louder. Sodak could see from the main console that they'd been hit hard on the upper hull. Moderate damage, hull punctures, interdeck fires…

'Auxiliary power to the shields!' he cried.

The *Berengaria* yawed as it was struck again. And again.

* * *

AT THE HIGH anchor point above Herodor, the *Glory of Cadia* rumbled in well ahead of the reinforcement convoy it had been escorting. As per Esquine's firm orders, it came about in a wide arc and took up station in battle formation with the massive *Omnia Vincit* and its smaller sisters the *Solstice* and the heavy cruiser *Laudate Divinitus*. Behind and below them, the mass of pilgrim ships formed a wide scatter of small, vulnerable targets, huddled close to the upper atmospheric reaches of the cold planet. Despite Esquine's command edicts, some of this motley host had begun to break orbit and flee, a few directly out into interplanetary space, chasing off towards Herodor's star and the further reaches of the system. Others were moving to geo-sync orbits behind Herodor, hoping to keep the planet between them and the terrifying attackers.

At a twitch of Esquine's fingers, an aft lance battery on the mighty *Omnia Vincit* fired, and crippled the merchantman *Somnambulist* as it attempted to break anchor.

That was all the time and firepower the fleet captain intended to waste. 'Signal the civilian fleet again, Velosade. We will punish any further infringement of the edict in a similar fashion. I will not have non-military vessels confusing the issue with unauthorised movement. Tell them any such action will force us to suspect they harbour heretic agents and that we will fire on them accordingly.'

'Sir!'

'The *Berengaria's* in trouble, sir,' whispered Valdeemer.

'I see that plainly, ensign. We will hold position. If we move to assist them, we will lose our formation initiative. Sodak knows when to fight and when to break and run.'

Valdeemer frowned. He knew Sodak's orders had been an unequivocal instruction to engage. There had been no discretionary option for flight.

'Should I inform him of such, sir?' asked Valdeemer.

'No,' said the fleet captain.

HE HAD FIRE on nine decks, a reactor crippled and shields close to failure. There was no longer enough power for the lances.

'Torpedoes!' Sodak ordered.

'Torpedoes aye!' cried Yarden.

'Cancel some of these damn alarms,' Sodak added. The air was ringing with overlapping klaxons. He could smell acrid smoke. Smoke gathering in the circulator system, too thick and dense to be expunged by the air scrubbers.

The massive enemy warship was right on them now, so close Sodak could actually see it as a dot through the glasteel windows of the bridge.

'Keep us true! Keep us face on!' he shouted at the helm officers. The frigate's strongest hull armour was concentrated around the prow. He didn't want to expose the flanks. Moreover, he wanted to maintain as small a target as possible.

'Aye, sir!'

'We're yawing, helm!'

'Attitude control is damaged, captain. We're trying to compensate…'

The *Incarnadine* fired on them again. Sodak didn't have time to even register the salvo on the augur scope.

The *Berengaria* pitched wildly. Parts of the upper hull splintered away in a spray of micro-fragments. Power failed for a few seconds on the bridge as an explosion tore across the forward helm position, incinerating three helm officers, five servitors and Tactical Officer Persson.

Yarden was still at his post, blood gushing from a shrapnel wound in his chest. Blood bubbled at his lips as he tried to call out a situation report, his dripping hands fumbling with the fire control console.

Sodak knew the situation, even though Yarden couldn't report, even though the actuality sphere had failed and the augur-scopes were dead. They were mortally wounded and helm-less, drifting now under the momentum of impact to present their starboard side to the archenemy monsters.

'Signal the *Omnia Vincit*,' Sodak cried. 'Signal begins… The Emperor protects–'

A salvo of torpedoes from the *Harm's Way* hit the *Berengaria* amidships, followed a scant moment later by a lance strike from the *Incarnadine*. The *Berengaria* seemed to blink and twitch for a second as plasma fire coiled and rippled like lava along its broken flank.

And then it vaporised in a shockwave of expanding white light.

IN THE OMNIA VINCIT'S strategium, Valdeemer almost didn't notice the death flare of the *Berengaria*. He was staring at the actuality sphere with horrid fascination as the enemy frigate the *Revenant* powered in after the desperate relief convoy. The indicator icons of two mass transports flickered and died. The others tried to break and evade, but the archenemy killer was directly astern.

'Commence formation advance,' Esquine called. 'Battle engagement pattern. Signal Wysmark and tell him to stop wasting time. We need the *Navarre* now.'

In a wide, firm line, the four Imperial warships prowled forward from high anchor, shields raised, to meet and deny the enemy assault.

SEVEN
PLANET FALL

'Nine are coming.'

— message written in Soric's hand

GAUNT HAD ARRIVED half asleep at the hastily called meeting just before dawn. After the night's curious events, he'd tried to nap for a few hours, only to be woken by Beltayn in the middle of the afternoon.

'The lord general wants to see you, sir,' Beltayn said.

Lugo and his house staff had occupied a mansion on the ninety-seventh level of Old Hive. It was a place of faded grandeur. The walls and high ceilings were cased in shiny black ebonite inlaid with matt detailing in arthrocite, and the floor was paved with pink, earth-fired tiles throughout. On every fourth wall panel in the entry hall, an electrolamp was set in a brass wall sconce, and long webs of glinting steel-lace hung as drapes at each arched doorway.

It wasn't made clear to Gaunt whose palace-home this was, or where they had gone to make way for Lugo.

To be honest, he wasn't thinking much of that. He was bleary headed as the postern sentries let him in and showed

165

him the way down two long hallways and up a flight of brick steps to the room where Lugo was waiting.

Gaunt had been expecting some kind of formal staff summit, and was surprised to find Lugo alone except for Kaldenbach.

The room was cold – the whole mansion was cold – as if the ancient heating pipes and hypercausts of the crumbling Old Hive were weak and inefficient at this high level. Lugo sat in a suspensor chair, dressed in a thick houserobe over his uniform shirt and breeches. His jacket and cap lay on a tall wooden dressing stand beside him.

He was sipping caffeine from a porcelain cup. A portable thermal heater was standing on the floor, warming his booted feet.

The room had tall, lancet windows of touched, coloured glass in two walls, and a set of ornate glass doors in the third that appeared, through the veil of a steel-lace drape, to give access out onto some kind of balcony or roof terrace. Kaldenbach stood beside these doors, arms folded, looking either stubborn or threatening. Gaunt wasn't quite sure what the man was shooting for. Threatening, he guessed.

'Sir.'

'Come in, Gaunt. A hot drink?'

'Thank you, no, sir.'

Kaldenbach, who had started to move at Lugo's offer, continued anyway even when it was refused, and helped himself to a cup from a silver vacuum-jug that stood on a dresser against the wall.

'I apologise for the early call,' Lugo said, almost cordially. 'I wish to speak with you about the Beati.'

'About the Beati...'

'About what we should do.'

'In what respect, sir?'

Lugo cleared his throat delicately and took another sip. 'I have so far made myself and my resources available to the Beati. To, shall I say, the whim of the Beati. Her sanctified mind perceives the cosmos in a way ours do not, so I trust her judgment, even if it might seem... wayward.'

Gaunt smiled slightly.

'At her urgings, we decamped here to this... place of insignificance. I suggested that her person might be of greater use alongside the Warmaster at the front, but no. She was very polite, as you might expect, but she refused the idea. Herodor was what she insisted on, and to Herodor I escorted her.'

'We have spoken of this before, sir,' said Gaunt. 'You hoped to enlist my aid in convincing her to change her mind. Indeed, you applied pressure on my commissar to get me to do just that.'

Lugo shrugged as if this was trifling. 'We are past such shadow play now, Gaunt. The Beati must go to Morlond. She must quit this place and go directly to Morlond. I'm not asking for your help. I'm ordering that you give it.'

'I see,' said Gaunt.

'Come, come,' said Lugo, smiling. 'We're all friends here, Ibram. Tell me your thoughts.'

'You want to know what I think?' Gaunt asked.

'The lord general was quite clear,' said Kaldenbach sharply.

Gaunt glanced at him, and Kaldenbach looked down. 'Very well,' said Gaunt. 'I think you knew the truth all along. From the moment on Hagia when Sanian first became known to you. You were completely aware that she was a fake... a troubled, delusional girl who believed she was the incarnation of Sabbat and played the part reasonably well. You saw the currency in this, and backed her claim, for the good of Imperial morale... and to advance your own interests.'

'You insult the lord general with such slander–' Kaldenbach started. Lugo held up a hand smartly.

'Allow Gaunt to talk or leave the room, colonel.'

'I'm sorry if I'm too honest, sir,' said Gaunt. 'You did say the time for shadow play was over.'

Lugo nodded, and gestured for Gaunt to continue.

'You saw the best way to control her was to let her have her way for a while. Let her make decisions, grow into the role with confidence. A pilgrimage here... well, that sounds like the sort of inexplicable but lofty thing a reincarnated saint would do. To cleanse herself before the coming war. You'd indulge her for a few months, working on her all the while, and then make the journey to the front seem like her own idea. You'd join the Warmaster, no doubt inspiring his forces to a conclusive victory, and your eminence would be assured. What were you hoping for? A sector governorship? Host command? Higher than that?'

Lugo retained his smile, but there was a glaze of bitter ice in it. Gaunt knew he had hit the mark.

'And everything was going so well… apart from a few unpredicted inconveniences like the fact she requested the Tanith as bodyguards. That must have rankled, having me arrive and get in the way. But nothing you couldn't handle. Your plan was still intact. Until last night.'

'Last night?' echoed Lugo.

'Last night, lord general. When your little pawn did something you weren't expecting. When Sanian – and don't ask me to explain this, for it defies rational explanation – when Sanian became the real thing after all. She is the Beati, she is truly everything she believed herself to be, everything you pretended she was. A miraculous being in the strictest sense of the term. And that changed things. You have no idea what to do. You can't manipulate her any more. She is suddenly beyond your powers of reason and control, beyond your basic understanding. You're afraid. You're out of your depth. And your plan is coming apart at the seams.'

Lugo sucked his teeth thoughtfully, then got to his feet, shed his houserobe and started to put on his dress jacket. Kaldenbach started forward like a valet to hold the garment for him.

'A gripping piece of speculation, Ibram,' said the lord general, 'and quite convincing in its own way. Thank you for being so open.'

He turned to Gaunt, buttoning up the jacket's frogging. 'Utterly specious, of course. I have known the Saint to be genuine from the very start, and have supported her in that light. Nothing has changed. She has always been a miraculous figure to me. I bless the God-Emperor of mankind for placing me in this role of trust.'

'Just so,' said Kaldenbach.

'Just so indeed,' said Gaunt with a light shrug. 'As I said before, it doesn't matter what I think anyway. The important thing is that you realise I agree with you. Fake or real, the

Beati should be with the Warmaster on Morlond. For the good of the Imperium, the Sabbat Worlds, the entire Crusade. I'm not going to fight you over that. I'll do everything I can to help persuade her. I don't, of course, know if I have any influence over her at all. But I will try.'

Lugo put on his cap, looked Gaunt in the eyes, and then stretched out his hand. Gaunt, surprised, shook it.

'Thank you, Ibram,' Lugo said. 'I knew you were a team player.'

'One last thing you should know, sir,' Gaunt added as their hands parted.

'What?'

'I am pretty sure this event we are part of, this incarnation, this manifestation… I'm pretty sure it is more significant than we realise. Space and time and… fate, if you will… are all coming together, and synchronising. Even before Sanian truly manifested as the Beati last night, the ripples of that happening were spreading through this sector and beyond. Signs, portents, auguries. You've heard them all, and put them down to hysteria amongst the faithful, I'm sure. But they are more than that. Every psyker in the sector – ours and theirs – must have felt as much. The cosmos is turning for a purpose, lord general, and this is one of those rare occasions when we can hear its machinery whirring and see its handiwork.'

'You speak like a prophet, Gaunt!'

'No prophet me… but still. I knew about Herodor long before I was summoned here. I was told to expect the Saint. My troopers have told me numberless stories from the pilgrim camps of men and women who share that supernatural inkling. Not the fanatics, not the stylites and the flagellants and the mystics who jump at any rumour. You'd be amazed how many normal, regular people there are out there. People who have thrown their lives and homes away to make the journey here because they simply, indelibly knew something.'

'Are you trying to scare me, Gaunt?' Lugo said with a falsely hearty chuckle.

'No, sir. But a healthy sense of fear would not be amiss. We stand in a time of wonder, sir. There is no telling what it might bring, but it will be momentous.'

Gaunt heard voices and footsteps in the hallway outside the room, but ignored them. 'Let us hope,' he said directly, 'that we are witnessing the end of the Crusade. Victory in the Sabbat Worlds, the archenemy put to fire and flight. With the Beati at Morlond–'

'I will not go to Morlond,' said a voice from behind him.

Gaunt turned. Sabbat stood in the doorway of the chamber, one hand raised to hold back the steel-lace drapes. She was wearing simple, grey combat fatigues and heavy black troop boots. Her skin was deathly pale and her eyes showed signs of upset and reproach.

'Beati,' said Gaunt, bowing his head. Lugo and Kaldenbach did likewise.

'I will not go to Morlond,' she repeated, stepping into the room and letting the steel-lace fall back into place. Through its patterned folds, Gaunt could see the household troopers hovering outside, too scared to come in after her.

'There is work to be accomplished here,' she said. 'Vital work. That is my purpose. Morlond can wait, or be tamed without me.'

'Lady, we–' Gaunt began.

Sabbat placed a hand gently on his arm and he fell silent, unable to speak.

'Herodor is the key, Ibram. The warp has shown this. I will not leave until this work is done.'

'How…' Lugo began. 'How can we serve you, lady?'

'I was looking for Ibram. It's time. They're coming, and I am afraid. I was looking for my protector. My honour guard.'

'The Tanith?' Gaunt whispered.

'You and the Tanith. I need you now.'

'What do you mean, "it's time"?' Gaunt asked.

She took him by the hand and led him over to the glass doors, which she opened with a press of her fingers. They went through, out onto the roof terrace. Lugo and Kaldenbach followed.

The terrace was a semi-circle of rockcrete jutting like a shelf from the steep roof levels of the Old Hive spire. A glasteel dome shielded them from the arctic atmosphere. The great sprawl of the Civitas Beati spread out below them, far below, a brown maze of angular shadows. The massive shape of the second hive tower rose up nearby, almost to their level, a slabby silhouette against the just rising sun.

Around the edge of the terrace were terracotta planters. The roses and sambluscus planted in them had withered and died into gnarled twigs, untended, but they reminded Gaunt of Lord Chass's roof garden in the upper Spine of Vervunhive.

Gaunt felt a twinge of fear and melancholy. But for a metal flower from that garden, he would have died on Verghast.

There were no flowers here.

Sabbat pointed up at the sky. It was thin blue, creased by bars of lustrous yellow and furrows of cloud in the east. The last stars were still visible.

'They are coming,' she said again. 'They are here. That's why I will not go to Morlond. I can't go anywhere now.'

Gaunt stared up at the part of the sky her slender fingers had indicated.

'What do you–'

A flash. For a moment. A little spark high up among the stars. Then another. Like impossible lightning, up in space.

'What does she mean?' Lugo hissed to Gaunt, shivering in the unheated air of the high garden.

'Ship to ship fire. The fleet has engaged. A planetary assault has begun.'

'Surely not,' said Kaldenbach. 'We would have heard…'

'It's only just started,' said Gaunt. 'Circulate orders, sir. Prepare for ground assault.'

'Oh, premature!' Kaldenbach scoffed. 'Fleet Captain Esquine has our interests protected. Four ships of the line… the *Omnia Vincit* alone could–'

Gaunt ignored him. 'Lady?'

'They're here, Ibram. Now I need you. You will protect me, won't you? You and your Ghosts? You will protect me until the work is done here?'

'You have my word, lady.'

A junior officer in the uniform of Lugo's life company hurried onto the terrace behind them, clutching a data-slate.

'Lord general! A signal from the fleet captain, sir. He's engaged with an incoming hostile battle group, sir and–'

Lugo took the slate from him abruptly. 'I know already. Dismissed.' As the junior backed off, bemused, Lugo read the slate data and handed it to Kaldenbach.

'Four archenemy ships. Potent, but Esquine should be able to hold them.'

'He won't.' Her voice was soft, almost a whisper.

Gaunt looked straight at Lugo. 'Prepare for ground assault,' he repeated firmly.

Lugo held his gaze for several seconds. Gaunt could almost see his mind working through possibilities, necessities and maybes. Lugo closed his eyes and sighed deeply.

'Do as he says,' he told the life company colonel.

'Lord General, I–'

'Now!' barked Lugo, and Kaldenbach turned and ran.

Now THAT WAS interesting.

Shumlen's vitals-reader had just shown his pulse rate spike the highest it had been in seventeen years. One for the log-book, he thought.

He'd just pulled a turn so tight the G-force had all but crushed him and blinded him for about fifteen seconds. He blinked hard to get his squeezed eyeballs to refocus.

Where the hell was that bat?

He hit the thrusters and spun his bird down into a wide evade. Blitz fire and enemy cannonades fluttered brightly in the darkness outside his canopy. He saw a Lightning far to his left, two bats on its back. Twenty-seven? Was that Liebholtz?

Las-fire chattered and pinked, studding the blackness, brilliant, then gone. The Lightning dogged, banked and came around, but the bats were still on him.

'Twenty-seven, twenty-seven, rake-turn to port,' Shumlen said over his vox as he soared down through the AF fire. A bat he hadn't even seen, wings hooked, chin-cannon flashing, went by and over him, away. Damage alerts beeped from his instrumentation and he cancelled them out.

His heads-up display swam and shifted, crosshairs drifting as he turned again.

'They're all over me! All over me!' Liebholtz's voice squealed over the link.

'Turn one-eight-one and come around hard,' Shumlen said.

His thumb trembled over the fire-stud in the top of his stick.

He was head on. He kicked the burners to full, crossing the Lightning coming the other way. The nearest bat, right on its tail, slammed into his display and the finders locked it up. The crosshairs went bright and hard and started to flash. The lock-tone sounded, a rising shrill.

He depressed his thumb and fell into a roll. He felt the shudder of his cannon pumping, the rhythmic grind of the autoloaders.

The bat flamed out in a bright fireball. Winnowing pieces of debris clattered off his hull and canopy.

Liebholtz wasn't clear yet. He was trying to climb out of the horizontal vector.

Typical air-boy, Shumlen thought. Liebholtz was a great pilot, truly gifted, but he'd come out of planetary airforce, like so many pilots. He still thought in terms of up and down, right and left.

No such things. Any true void-fighter knew that. And Shumlen was a true void-fighter. Oh yeah, this close to a planet or super-massive ships there was a marginal grav-element to allow for, but that was just part of the game. To void-fight, you had to think in three dimensions at once.

Shumlen flipped his bird up and over. Liebholtz was trying to cut up, but the bat was sticking with him.

Shumlen's heads-up hunted, washing left and right.

He saw the bat. A Locust-pattern interceptor, painted in tiger stripes. Long nosed, twin-boomed, spiky. Its chin-gun was already spelling out Liebholtz's doom.

Liebholtz's inarticulate last words spluttered out of the vox. His bird was consumed in a bright yellow flare.

Shumlen had the bat. The killer. It jinked back and forth, but he kept it in field. God-Emperor, but this jockey was good.

Shumlen tried a shot and missed.

He snatched his thumb off to conserve ammo. Thirty-seven per cent munitions left. One missile. Twenty-two per cent fuel remaining.

The Locust rolled back and over, coming down facing the other way and spiralling.

Neat… but not neat enough. Shumlen powered past him, and began to dive down towards the vast hull landscape of the archenemy battleship as it slid by, taunting the gun batteries.

They didn't let him down. Neither did the bat.

The batteries started pounding the moment Shumlen went over them, but he was too fast for them to make a kill.

They were still pounding when the bat chased after him, hungry for Shumlen's bird.

The bat went up in a messy spray of burning gases and hull debris.

Shumlen switched back up, got a lock almost immediately, and killed another bat on the turn with a drumming salvo from his cannon.

A cannon shell from somewhere punched through his port wing and he turned hard again, right into the backwash of an AF blitz.

Shumlen slunk away, circling in a deep, open turn. The bat zipped past him and he locked it tight. His cannon shuddered.

It blew out like a flower, the fuselage peeling away into silver shreds. He saw the pilot vaporise as he tried to eject.

A dismal toll rang from his instruments. He looked at his ammo counter and saw the worst.

Count zero. And the fuel load wasn't much better.

He flipped back. One missile left. Time to make it count.

Sweeping in and out of the bursting patterns of AF, he powered towards the bow of the archenemy battleship. The forward launch decks, open like mouths in the front snout of the beast. A missile there…

Bats passed in front of him, chasing Lightnings. More AF, incandescent. Then a bat with a bird on its tail, spraying rounds.

The bow of the super-massive craft dropped away under him, and Shumlen turned tightly, thrusters burning away the last dregs of his fuel as he came in for the final run of his career.

* * *

'SIGNAL FROM THE *Omnia Vincit*, sir!' Kreff yelled. Captain Wysmark didn't seem to hear him. The captain was standing by the master console, adjusting settings.

'Sir?'

That buzzing. Kreff could hear it. What the hell was it? It made his ears ache.

'Sir!'

Wysmark glanced up at him. 'Kreff?'

'*Omnia Vincit* is ordering us to join formation. The fleet captain says we should seal internals and blow the *Troubadour* off us.'

'Does he, indeed?'

Wysmark's hands danced over the master console.

'Sir?' said Kreff, alarmed. 'We should issue an emergency brace warning and clear the gates before we–'

There was an almighty thump. It shook the bridge of the *Navarre* so hard that Kreff was thrown over. Wysmark remained on his feet.

In a blizzard cloud of fragments, the *Navarre* had blown locks and torn away from the *Troubadour*. In the process, it had opened three of its skin-level decks to hard vacuum, but Wysmark had sealed the internal hatches and prevented a total breach.

Even so, ninety-six armsmen, who had spent the last half hour fighting for the very life of the *Navarre*, were locked out and voided to their deaths by the drastic manoeuvre.

The *Troubadour* slumped away from the frigate, spilling material and debris. It dropped away towards the glinting shoals of pilgrim ships in the high atmosphere.

As its engines ignited, the *Navarre* came nose up, and turned away from the bright planet below it.

Wysmark co-opted fire control to his console, and tasked the *Navarre's* batteries. When the actuality sphere gave him solution, he fired.

The *Navarre* blew the tumbling *Troubadour* into a billion glittering fragments.

'Sir! We need to get into the fleet formation!' Kreff stammered, getting up. He was astonished at the captain's brutality. Crewmen had just died, unnecessarily. Wysmark ignored him, but the *Navarre* was coming around nevertheless.

Kreff joined his captain at the master console, reading the display. Enginarium to full motive, shields up, weapons to power…

And a red light Kreff didn't recognise.

Kreff flinched back as he realised it was a drop of blood on the console, underlit by an enginarium rune.

Another drip fell next to it.

Blood was running out of the captain's left tear duct.

The buzzing was back, so loud, so very loud–

'Captain?'

'Firing solution, please, exec.'

'Firing solution?' Kreff recoiled in dismay. The *Solstice*, the *Navarre's* sister ship, was rolling into view ahead, side on as it faced the incoming enemy.

'Now, if you please, Kreff!'

'Sir, it's one of ours!'

The knuckles crushed his nose and made him bite through his lip. Crying out in pain and spitting blood, Kreff fell sideways.

'Captain!'

Buzzing, buzzing, buzzing…

The *Navarre* lurched as its main lances fired. The beams, on full load, cut through the *Solstice's* flank plating and opened its inner decks to space. All two thousand metres of it crumpled like metal foil and tore apart. A moment later, its reactors went up. Where the *Solstice* had been, only a white hot blast radius remained.

The expanding shockwave hit the *Navarre* bow-on. The ship bucked and threw like an unbroken steed. Kreff hit the deck for a third time.

Prone, he looked up at Wysmark. He had been with the captain for ten years, ten years of loyalty and love. Blood was dribbling from Wysmark's nose and eyes, and his expression was oddly slack.

He was no longer the officer Kreff had followed into the mouth of death and back too many times to count.

Kreff fumbled with his uniform's holster and pulled out his service pistol.

Wysmark, without looking, had already produced the compact auto-mag anchored under the master console. He pointed it down at Kreff and fired, his attention on the main screen all the while.

The first shot smashed Kreff's pelvis. The second broke three ribs and ruptured a lung. The third pulped Kreff's right ear and spanked off the deck plating.

Gasping in pain, sobbing in ragged breaths, Kreff lay on his back in a widening pool of his own blood. He raised his service pistol in a shaking hand and shot Wysmark in the side of the head.

Wymark swayed. The impact of the round rocked him. The left side of his skull burst outwards, and bloody tissue dripped onto his braided collar.

He fell over to his left, hard.

'Help me! Help me!' Kreff gasped. Ensigns and servitors ran over to him, picking him up.

'*Navarre* to *Omnia Vincit*! *Navarre* to *Omnia Vincit*!' Kreff yelled into the vox.

'THE SOLSTICE... is gone...' Valdeemer stammered.

'Gone? How?' Esquine demanded.

'The *Navarre*... it fired on her. Direct, sustained hit to midships.'

'Heretics have taken the *Navarre*. Emperor protect us!'

'What are your orders, sir?' Velosade asked.

'Cleanse my ship,' said Esquine. There were furious tears in his inlaid eyes.

'Firing solutions! The *Navarre*!' Velosade bellowed.

THE SIDE BATTERIES of the *Omnia Vincit* lit up and stayed lit. The *Navarre's* shields soaked up the merciless bombardment for several seconds, swirling and coruscating like molten glass. Then they began to buckle and fail. The *Navarre* heeled over, its hull shredding and burning. Its gravitic assemblies shut down and it started to fall, stern-first, into the gravity well of the planet. A vast internal explosion disintegrated it before it hit the atmosphere.

On the *Navarre's* bridge, Executive Officer Kreff was still trying to raise the *Omnia Vincit* on the fleet channel as he died.

The debris from the *Navarre* rained down towards the surface of Herodor, becoming meteors in the upper atmosphere.

* * *

ONE OF THOSE meteors was a standard pattern escape pod. It rocked and tumbled violently, rattling and vibrating as it plunged.

The two runt psykers were wailing in terror, flinching at every lurch. The big man in green silk robes murmured soothing words of reassurance and comfort to them as if they were his children, his massive tattooed arms holding them tight.

'Almost there,' said Pater Sin. 'Almost there...'

'YOU READY FOR this?' Mkvenner asked lightly.

Gol Kolea straightened the front of his fatigue jacket and nodded. Side by side, they walked in through the entrance of the Tanith billet.

The dawn call had sounded some minutes before, and the troops were rousing. Water pots were clattering onto stove rings, and men were dressing.

It was exactly the same as every morning in the Guard, simple routine. Only the place – a scholam by the look of it, Kolea thought – was different.

It made him smile.

'Morning, Gol,' said Obel, wandering past. Kolea nodded. No one gave him a second look. News hadn't reached here yet.

He wandered down the rows of bunks, looking around, hungry for the sight of familiar faces. There was a little ache in the back of his heart that some faces wouldn't be there. Muril... Piet Gutes... Try Again Bragg...

'This one's yours,' said Mkvenner.

Kolea stopped, and sat down on an unmade bunk. His pack was there.

He looked up at Mkvenner. The lean Tanith gazed down at him and shook his head. 'A night I won't forget. A favour I intend to repay.'

'No need, Ven.'

'You saved my life,' said Mkvenner. 'You're going to have to make it up to me.'

Kolea smiled.

'I'll see you later, Kolea,' said Mkvenner, and moved off through the dorm.

Kolea sat for a moment as the bustle went on around him. Then he took off his jacket and undervest and opened his pack to find a fresh shirt. The weight of the plaster effigy in his jacket pocket made him remember it was there. He took it out, looked at it for a moment, and stuffed it down inside his pack for safety.

He found a folded vest and shook it out to put it on.

'Know how to dress yourself, do you, gak-head?'

Kolea looked up. Cuu had been walking by, dressed in his undershorts, fresh from the shower block. He had a towel over his shoulder. The painfully white, unhealthy skin of his scrawny, corded torso was covered in crude tattoos. He sneered at Kolea.

'Want me to help, gak-head? Want me to help you dress, you pathetic gak-head?' Cuu's voice was low but sharp. 'Want me to wipe your arse for you too? Sure as sure you do.'

He laughed.

'You must have got away with murder while I was absent,' said Kolea softly.

'Huh?'

'You always were a little shit, Cuu, but bullying a brain-damaged vet? Where the gak is your sense of regimental honour, you insidious pus-ball?'

Cuu's eyes and mouth opened very wide. He took a step back. The area immediately around them had fallen very quiet.

Kolea rose to his feet. He towered over the trooper, and his naked torso and arms were massive, especially next to Cuu's bony frame.

'You... you...' Cuu stammered.

'Yeah, me. I'm back. Now run away before I break your rodent neck.'

Cuu ran.

'Sarge?' Lubba said, getting up off his bunk. He was staring at Gol, blinking fast. 'Sarge?'

'Morning, Lubba. So, how's it going?' Kolea said lightly, sitting back down.

Whispers were spreading, voices talking fast.

'Gol?' Corbec said, appearing from the row end and walking towards him. Mkvenner was with him.

'Hello, sir.'

Corbec shook his shaggy head. 'Gaunt told me about what went on, but I was keeping it to myself until… until… feth! What happened?'

'Well, it's a funny thing…' Kolea began. The rest of his sentence was lost beneath the crushing pressure of Corbec's bearhug.

'I GET THE impression his return has been popular,' said Dorden. Zweil made a chuckling sound and nodded. The doctor pushed Zweil's chair down the aisles between the rows of vacated bunks towards the mobbing, clamouring concentration of troopers in the centre of the billet chamber. Kolea was at the heart of it, laughing and chatting, answering the barrage of excited questions as best he could.

Everyone was there, morning drill forgotten. Somebody had ordered in boxes of hot loaves from a nearby bakery, and sutlers had arrived with wheeled barrows laden with heated caffeine urns.

No, not everyone, Dorden noted. Away through the rows of bunks, he saw Lijah Cuu, getting dressed. Every now and then Cuu looked up as laughter rose from the throng.

'So tell it again…' Varl called. 'You did what?'

Kolea shrugged. 'I don't really remember. I was worried about Ven, and someone had said the baths healed all wounds.'

'That's what they say,' Lubba nodded, solemnly.

'And she healed you?' asked Soric.

'I guess so. Actually, I think she healed Ven. I was just in the way.'

The Ghosts laughed.

'Do you hear me complaining?' asked Mkvenner.

'Will she heal me?' Varl asked, tapping his augmetic shoulder.

'Not a chance, Ceg. She only cures the deserving.'

More gales of laughter.

'What about me?' asked Domor.

'You're as bad as Varl, Shoggy,' said Kolea. 'And besides, you wouldn't be without that enhanced vision now, would you?'

Domor shrugged. 'The Emperor protects,' he admitted.

'What about me?' cried Larkin from the back.

'I dunno, Larks. What's wrong with you?'

'Where do we start?' blurted Bonin. The crowd broke up in guffaws again.

'Will she cure me?' Chiria asked quietly.

Kolea looked down at her scarred face. She'd never been pretty, but he knew the scars on her face were the worst thing that had ever happened to her. He sighed.

'Who knows? I'll ask her.'

Chiria smiled. Nessa put her arm around her.

'I guess you'll be wanting your platoon back, Gol,' Criid said.

Kolea shook his head. 'I see you've been doing a fine job, sergeant. It'll be an honour to serve.'

There were cheers and whoops of affirmation. Criid blushed, and Caffran looked at her with a proud smile.

'I need to thank you, though,' Kolea said as the noise died down.

'Me?' asked Criid. 'Should be the other way around. You've saved me twice now, and the first time got you... hurt.'

'Maybe. But the second time got me cured.'

'What?'

'I don't remember much about it, as you will no doubt appreciate, but when I picked you up in that street, you had this... this effigy thing in your pocket. A plaster bust. Fething awful thing, it was.'

Criid nodded. 'An old guy gave it to me. A pilgrim. It was out in the Glassworks. He was trying to thank me for looking after him.'

'I found it. It reminded me... reminded my thick head, as was. Made me think about the Saint and how she cured people. I think that's what made me take Ven to the balneary.'

'You kept going on about the fething thing,' Mkvenner confirmed.

'It's yours anyway,' said Kolea, looking at Criid. 'I was just looking after it.'

She shrugged. 'I don't want it. Gakking eyesore. Just glad it had a use.'

'I would like to see it, if I may,' Zweil slurred. The mob parted politely to admit the doctor and the old man he was pushing in the chair. Zweil sat at a strange angle, half his face curiously limp.

'Of course, father,' said Kolea.

'I normally wouldn't bother over such trinkets,' Zweil said, carefully enunciating every word, 'but my brethren demand that every last detail surrounding a palpable miracle be scrutinised. It is the holy order of things.'

'It's in my pack,' Kolea said. He looked round at the troopers.

'I'll get it, sarge,' said Criid. She disengaged herself from Caffran's firm embrace and pushed away through the crowd.

'So, what did it feel like?' called Feygor through his throaty, monotone vox-box. 'Did it hurt?'

'What?'

'The miracle, you feth.'

'Yes,' said Zweil, nodding. 'What did it feel like, Gol?'

'I was wondering that myself,' added Dorden.

'Well…' Kolea began.

BEHIND HER, THEY were laughing and shouting out. Criid moved down through the rows of empty cots. She could feel the smile on her face. It wouldn't go. Kolea was back. *Kolea was back!* This had to be about the best day of her life, ever. Right up there along with the day she made sergeant and the day Caff told her he loved her.

She'd missed Kolea so much she hadn't realised, and she knew all too well she owed him everything. She'd have been dead on the streets of Ouranberg but for him.

She found Kolea's bunk and was digging through his pack. Everything was so neat and precise, everything folded and pressed. Kolea would gakking hate her for the mess she was making.

There was no sign of the effigy. She up-ended the pack and spilled its contents out onto the mattress. Clothes, ammo packs, a shaving kit, a boot-blacker, a pack of cards, a clutch of hololithic prints stuffed into a yellowing envelope.

And the effigy. Ugly gakking thing. The garish paint job was worse than she remembered.

She put it to one side, and began to repack Kolea's kitbag. The photo-prints fell out of the old envelope as she picked it up.

She looked at them.

A man. A woman. A young boy. A baby. Group shots, individuals. A father holding his newborn. A mother and her kids.

The man was Gol Kolea. Younger, true. Cleaner. One of him dressed as an ore-face worker.

She stopped dead.

Though they were years younger, she recognised the faces of the children. Dalin and Yoncy. And the mother. She'd only known the mother for a few brief minutes. In carriage station C4/a, Vervunhive. Criid had tried to help her with her toddler and her baby-cart. Then the shells had started to fall.

Gak! She'd seen this woman die, this woman in the pictures. The mother of the children Criid now counted as hers.

What the hell were the pictures doing in Gol Kolea's p–

'No,' she said. 'Holy Emperor, no!'

She got up and fell over, pulling the open pack down off the bunk. Kolea's stuff fell out onto the floor. She started to scrabble around, collecting them up and pushing them back into the bag.

An alarm started to sound, so loud, it made her jump.

'SORRY TO BREAK things up, ladies,' Rawne cried, sounding anything but sorry. He pushed his way through the throng of Ghosts around Kolea. Klaxons were bleating.

'Time for work. The archenemy is orbital and inbound, and we're expecting mass ground assault in the next hour. Get dressed, get kitted, get ready and get moving. If you're of a faithful disposition, ask the God-Emperor for his blessing. If you're a layman, put your head between your legs and kiss your fething ass goodbye. This is it. The real thing.'

The crowd of Ghosts broke up immediately, troopers running to their bunks, struggling into clothes, prepping weapons.

'Bad as that?' Corbec asked, coming up alongside Rawne.

'Worse than you can possibly imagine,' replied the major.

ON THEY CAME. The *Incarnadine*, the *Cicatrice*, the *Harm's Way*. Running side by side like hunting dogs, angling in at twenty degrees to the plane of the ecliptic. And the *Revenant*? Where was that?

Flanking in from sunward, obliterating pilgrim ships. It had already incinerated all the transports in the relief convoy.

Esquine tensed. This was still manageable. This was still a tactical possibility. He had three ships. The *Omnia Vincit* was a vastly powerful flagship. The *Laudate Divinitus* was also capable. The frigate *Glory of Cadia* ought to be up to the mark.

Their commanders appeared before him on the deck of the strategium, red-shot holoforms.

Captain Cask of the *Glory*.

Captain Massinga of the *Laudate*.

'The Emperor who gives us life also trials us now,' said Esquine.

Both holoforms nodded.

'The odds are not impossible, though they are against us. Massinga, the *Revenant* is yours. Take it to hell with all hands.'

'I will, fleet captain.'

'Cask, with me. We take this fight to the heart.'

'The Emperor protects,' crackled Cask's holoform over the vox.

'Attack speed!' Esquine commanded.

'Attack speed!' Velosade relayed across the strategium.

Valdeemer leaned back against a bulkhead. His heart was thumping.

THE GIGANTIC CAPITAL ship *Omnia Vincit*, flanked by its much smaller sister the frigate *Glory of Cadia*, powered away from the chilly light of Herodor towards the trio of archenemy warships.

Beside them for a while, the heavy cruiser *Laudate Divinitus* turned away to port, and lit up its thrusters as it burned down towards the *Revenant*.

The *Revenant* was picking off pilgrim ships, exploding them like paper targets on a circus showman's stall. Some started to run. That just gave the *Revenant* moving solutions. Its guns raked through the translucent skein of the upper atmosphere. Ships exploded and burned.

A flurry of torpedoes from the closing heavy cruiser unsettled the *Revenant's* shields, and it swung up to meet the Imperial warship.

The heavy cruiser was a third again as big as the gold-laced enemy ship. Its fighter screen puffed out from it like a cloud of dust, and was met immediately by the rival's own screen. As the massive vessels closed, spitting beams of light and sprays of plasma, the tiny fighters billowed around each other, cloud into cloud, dust particles whirling away to infinity.

The *Laudate Divinitus* fired a full volley of lances and torpedoes. The *Revenant* gunned away, shields flaring flat white. It fired its own cannonade broadside as it fled across the *Laudate's* bows.

The Imperial heavy cruiser shook. One of its shields ruptured. It fired back.

The *Revenant* brought its hind part in tight, turning in a forty-five degree angle on its prow. It came up facing the *Laudate,* facing the failed shield.

It fired its main lances.

The *Laudate Divinitus* didn't explode. It came apart in a series of coughing, jerking seizures. The final shudder kicked off the enginarium, and sent out a shockwave that destroyed nine pilgrim ships at anchor.

The *Revenant* dipped low into the thin reaches of the upper atmosphere, and began to disgorge drop-pods and landing craft.

Hundreds of them.

THE GLORY OF CADIA hit the *Cicatrice* so hard and with such sustain it began to burn. Esquine was savouring the victory when he saw the enemy ship turn.

The *Cicatrice,* immolating, spent the last of its reactor power pushing itself forward. It rammed the *Glory* amidships and the two vessels locked together, burning like a small star in close orbit space.

The *Harm's Way* and the massive *Incarnadine* were pummeling the *Omnia Vincit* with their batteries. Esquine felt the pain from the shields.

'Target the main ship, Velosade,' he gasped.

SHUMLEN HIT THRUST and came in at the open and lit port of the *Incarnadine's* starboard launch deck. He felt himself pressed back in the grav seat as the thrusters kicked in. His heads-up locked in at the hangar bay mouth.

One missile left.

Something flew out at him.

A bat, yes. But really like a bat. A dark, hooked shape. Small, fast; not a Locust-pattern ship, he was certain. Something xenos. Very xenos.

He banked, hunting. The bat zipped around and was behind him. Shumlen tried to turn, tried to get an angle so he could loose his last missile. The bat wouldn't let him be.

Shumlen turned hard again, and again. He couldn't lose it.

He turned for one last time and the stall siren howled.

Fuel out. He was drifting.

The bat zipped past him and then turned back, sliding up and coasting up alongside him.

Shumlen looked at it. His pattern recognition systems bleeped out confirmation.

A Raven.

A dark eldar Raven attack ship.

It hovered beside him for a second, and then flitted away.

There was no power left in his Lightning. Shumlen looked round, dead in space. The vast superstructure of the *Incarnadine* ploughed towards him.

And met him like a cliff face. His tiny craft burst and flared for a second as it was run down against the massive prow of the battleship. The *Incarnadine* didn't even feel it.

The Raven, circling nearby, dipped its barbed wings once to acknowledge the fall of a fine pilot, and then turned and burned towards the pallid glow of Herodor.

The control console of the sleek Raven reflected yellow light up across the features of Skarwael. He was grinning, a rictus of bared fangs and tight white flesh.

The bloody game was on.

EVERY ALARM AND klaxon in the Civitas Beati was blaring. Even the great prayer horns at the city quarter-points were wailing terrible rising notes. Storm shields began to close on all the windows, decks and apertures in the hive towers, and through the inner precinct of the Civitas. Segmented plating slid up to protect the glass domes of the agriponic farms.

There was uproar on the streets. Citizens fled en masse to the sub-level bunkers, to the storm cellars, to the lower levels of the hive towers. Technically, there were appointed shelters for all, but the protocols were old and hadn't been used for generations. Citizens ignored them, or had never known them, and fled hysterically to the nearest shelter.

The highways and principals of the mid-city and skirt districts were choked with road traffic. A lot of it had already been mobile at dawn, and it was swelled by private vehicles heading across town towards imagined places of safety. The traffic jammed up the routes, solid and nose-to-tail in places, and transports were quickly abandoned. In some outer streets, the roads were deserted but for rows of immobile vehicles, some with the engines still running, most with doors and hatches open.

THE MAIN BARRACKS of the Regiment Civitas Beati was an imposing keep that overlooked Principal I in the high town area, between the gigantic stacks of hive towers one and two. In the main yard inside the walls, the regiment was assembling and breaking up into troop elements. Columns of APCs and light armour units were grumbling up the ramps from the garages under the keep, directed by marshals to embarkation points where in theory they would pick up their assigned squads. There was no time for briefing. Instructions would be delivered en route via tac logis. All anyone knew was that they were following GAR3 – Ground Assault Response 3 – one of Biagi's pre-formed emergency strategies.

Timon Biagi himself stood in the open top of an armoured command vehicle, listening to the tac logis flow in his earpiece, watching the disposition. Troopers, some still buckling up armour, poured out of the keep and into the yard, filing past the armourers' platforms to collect munitions and combat supplies. Biagi was the two hundred and fifth marshal of the Civitas. From this hour forward it would be his name, and his name alone, that historians would think of when considering the Regiment Civitas. For he would be the marshal that stood alongside Sabbat at her Returning. Would they think of him like they thought of Kiodrus, he wondered? A second Kiodrus. He liked the feel of that idea.

Biagi looked up at the sky. It was unseasonably clear, and the violet dawn was turning into a cool white haze. In a corner of the sky, the future was making itself visible. Flashes and strobes of light, a thicket of twinkling stripes just visible in the growing glare, identified the monumental war now underway in orbital space. A war between gods, Biagi thought.

From down here where he stood, it looked like firecrackers.

THE GHOST AND life company elements moved out of the hive towers in rows of troop trucks and transporters, heading out into the skirt fan of the city. Life company tanks and tracked armour led the way, smashing rows of stationary, abandoned vehicles out of their path where they blocked thoroughfares and junctions.

Gaunt rode in a Salamander with Corbec and Hark. Hydra gun platforms travelled alongside them for a few streets, and then turned off to left and right to occupy good firing positions in open squares and plazas in the hilly inner reaches of the Civitas.

'This is Lugo's plan?' Hark asked.

Gaunt shook his head. 'He'll take the credit, but it's actually Kaldenbach's.'

'I thought it was too smart for that feth-wipe,' said Corbec, and then glanced at Hark's disapproving look.

'Did I say that out loud?' he smiled.

The plan was to assemble the main troop strengths in the city's geographical centre, towards the bottom of the Guild Slope, and wait. Even combined, the Tanith, life company, Regiment Civitas and Herodian PDF had nothing like enough numbers to cordon the entire perimeter of the sprawling city. First Officiary Leger had even seconded the city arbites and the local civic militia forces to bolster the military presence, and still that left them lacking in numerical resources.

The Imperial forces would loiter in the city centre, from which point any part of the city extent was as near as any other, and wait to see what direction the ground assault came from. Then they would respond fast, using transports, and channel their efforts in that particular area.

It was impossible to tell where the first wave of assault would come from. Gaunt had been through too many assaults from orbit – as assaulter and assaulted both – to think otherwise. There were so many variables.

From the data, Gaunt had seen, there were at least four archenemy warships up above them. Unopposed, their combined firepower could raze the Civitas down to the bedrock: streets, habs, hive-towers, even the armoured shelters underground. If the enemy decided not to bother with the complexity and effort of a ground assault, and simply went for the kill, this war would be over before it started.

There was one saving grace Gaunt was counting on–

'Sir!' Gaunt looked round as Corbec called out. The big Tanith was pointing up at the northern sky.

High up, streaks of orange fire were slashing across the pale sky. A few dozen at first, and then more. Hundreds more. Like a shower of meteorites, they rained down from high orbit overhead, diving north, leaving long, perfectly straight, perfectly parallel trails of flame and vapour in the sky behind them.

They weren't meteorites.

Gaunt saw distant flashes light up the northern horizon as the first hit. A second later, a distant sound like continuous thunder rolled in from the Great Western Obsidae.

drop-pods. For a half-second, Gaunt felt relieved. The archenemy was going for ground assault after all. Then he reconsidered. Death was not going to be swift and total. It was going to be slow and painful and hard.

But at least, if that was the case, he and his men had a chance to make it mutual.

'Ensign! Ensign!'

There was a voice in Valdeemer's dream, calling his name, and it wouldn't go away.

He blinked and found himself lying on his back in the strategium of the *Omnia Vincit*.

'Ensign Valdeemer! Are you alive?'

Valdeemer sat up and looked around. The air was full of smoke and flashing alarm lights and the baleful screech of klaxons and damage alarms.

'Ensign!'

He got up. The deck shook hard, and he steadied himself against a console. The crew servitor at the console was still working furiously, augmetic hands rippling over the display. The mechanical was totally oblivious to the chaos around them.

Valdeemer shook his head, trying to lose the swollen muzziness. Blood spattered on the deck. He raised his hand and felt a deep gash across his forehead.

They'd been hit.

He'd been at Esquine's side when the torpedo had struck them under the bridge tower. He remembered the numbing concussion, bodies flying. Yes, that's right. He'd been thrown to the deck.

How long had he been out?

'Ensign!'

He lurched forward towards Fleet Captain Esquine's throne.

'Sir?'

'I need you to man the main station. Can you do that?' Esquine looked like he was in pain, struggling, but there wasn't a mark on him.

'Sir? That's the commander's post.'

'Do it!'

Valdeemer turned and hurried through the smoke towards the main station. The deck was littered with smouldering debris and fallen panelling. He had to step over several bodies. Crewmen, deck aides, servitors, ripped apart by blast force or killed by flying debris.

One of them was Velosade. A piece of deck plating the size of a dinner plate had almost, but not quite, decapitated him.

Swallowing hard, Valdeemer got to the station and reviewed the board. Three shield failures. Two hull breaches. Fires on decks seven through eighteen and also in carrier bay four. Lances were out. Structural integrity was down to forty-seven per cent.

'Help me, Valdeemer,' Esquine whispered, his fingers flexing.

Valdeemer tried to assemble a plan in his mind. His fingers flew across the console, activating and deactivating runes as they lit up, calling up displays – enginarium, structural, shielding, deck-to-deck – and then cancelling them. He routed power away from the huge firestorm on deck eight. He bypassed two cogitator nodes damaged on deck eleven and brought lance number three back on line. He sealed the deck hatches that had not closed automatically and shut off the oxygen supply fuelling the lower deck fires. He shut down reactor two, which was red-lining and clearly damaged, and kicked in auxiliary power from the redundant reactor in the *Omnia Vincit's* belly.

Why hadn't Esquine already done these things? They were obvious, standard. The great capital ship was bleeding and burning to death, and Esquine hadn't even begun to apply emergency procedures.

'Report?'

'Damage is contained. I've got a lance back on line. We're painfully weak, but I'd like to divert all power from the engines to the shields.'

'Do it, Valdeemer!'

'I… I need the command override, sir. I'm not rank authorised!'

'The code is Vesta 1123!'

Valdeemer's bloody hands shook as they entered the code. He diverted power, ignoring the protesting howls of the tech-priests.

'Fighter screen?' Esquine urged.

'All but gone. Their small ships are all over us.'

'Where is the enemy?' Esquine asked.

Valdeemer looked round at the fleet captain. 'The *Incarnadine* is flanking us to port, sir, and returning full and sustained broadsides. Shields at thirty-five per cent. The *Harm's Way* is off the starboard bow, training main lances. Sir… can't you see this?'

'No,' said Esquine, his voice barely audible above the alarms and vox chatter.

The torpedo strike had vaporised the fleet captain's mind-impulse link, severing his connection to the massive ship. He was blind and deaf and lacking in all telepresent or hardwired connection to the *Omnia Vincit*, except for the waves of pain that washed through the ship into him as it took damage.

'Oh Holy Terra…' breathed Valdeemer, realising this. That meant he was in command. He, a junior ensign, was actually in control of the Imperial battleship *Omnia Vincit*.

How many times had he dreamed of command? How many hours had he spent longing for such a role?

Not like this. Gods of Terra, not at *all* like this…

'Orders, fleet captain?' he shouted over the din.

Esquine's answer was just a whisper. 'Kill them all… and if you can't do that, make the price of our lives a dear one.'

THE INCARNADINE USED its attitude thrusters to push in closer to the stricken *Omnia Vincit*. Its port batteries maintained their savage bombardment. The *Incarnadine's* constant scan-sweeps of the *Omnia Vincit* showed that it was dead in the water, its combined reactor power channelled from engines to shields. Massively protected, it was still a sitting target.

The *Harm's Way*, sitting off to bow-starboard of the Imperial warship, began to concentrate its lance blasts at the weak points of shielding, at the hasty overlap that barely covered the torpedo wound which had blown the fifth dorsal shield away and crippled the fleet captain.

The *Omnia Vincit* shook as the *Harm's Way* got a good, solid hit in. A huge section of upper hull splintered and peeled away.

The *Omnia Vincit* fired its reactivated lance and struck the *Harm's Way's* shields so hard it was forced to back off. The Imperial gunnery crews, sweating and half dead, cheered.

The combined fighter fleets of the *Incarnadine* and the *Harm's Way*, which had already obliterated the *Omnia Vincit's* fighter screen, concentrated their efforts around carrier bay three on the starboard side. The last of the Lightnings were atomised by the waves of Locusts – 'bats', as the Imperial Navy slang called them – gunning in, cannons flashing.

Three Locusts managed to enter the deck mouth. One was destroyed by AF turret emplacements inside the deckway. The second was also hit by AF fire, but managed to fire all six of its missiles into the belly of the carrier hold before it went up.

The third, accelerating to hypersonic, made it in down the main launch deck, strafing as it went, and banked right into the munitions loading bay. There, just before it catastrophically ran out of flying space, it dumped its payload into the sub-deck autoloader shafts that lifted munitions up to the carrier deck from the armoured heart of the *Omnia Vincit*.

The chain reaction blew the side off the noble Imperial ship in a vast flurry of underdeck explosions and fragmenting hull plates. Gored, its guts exposed, the *Omnia Vincit* yawed. In the strategium, Valdeemer desperately converted three per cent of shield power back to the engines and pushed the battleship out from between the vicing archenemy ships.

The *Omnia Vincit* slid forward out of the *Incarnadine's* firefield. A three per cent drop on shield power wasn't much, but the *Harm's Way*, waiting at the bow like a jackal on a kill, didn't hesitate. It cycled up full load power from its main reactors and fired its lances at the overlay weakness.

Valdeemer turned from his post to look at Esquine. The fleet captain was shaking with rage and sorrow, impotent and agonised.

'I'm sorry, sir,' said Valdeemer, 'but I'm afraid—'

He was incinerated before he could speak another word. Esquine was incinerated too, his golden throne melting around his combusting body. Blaze-fire swept through the strategium and out across the bridge, burning crewmen where they stood and vaporising control stations. The deep, glasteel ports fronting the bridge shattered and blew outwards under the superheated overpressure. The remaining shields failed.

The *Incarnadine* flurried off one final broadside to put the *Omnia Vincit* out of its death throes. Blown open, twisted, ruptured, its hull crackling with diffusing electric discharges, the *Omnia Vincit* rolled over.

The archenemy ships, satisfied, depowered their weapon systems, cancelled shields, and coasted away into high anchor station.

The burned-out ruin of the *Omnia Vincit* remained in orbit around Herodor for nine hundred and three years, until slowly decaying, unadjusted orbit rates finally sank it down through the gravity well into the atmosphere, where it burned up. The parts of it that survived atmosphere-kiss and heat-shear filled the skies of the southern continent like shooting stars, and hailed down onto the Lesser Southern

Dry Sea, creating impact scars and craters that later became radioactive lakes in that distant wilderness.

But that, of course, took place a long time after every person in this account was many centuries dead.

THE MIGHTY INCARNADINE and the frigate *Harm's Way* drew in tight alongside the *Revenant*, and began to disgorge the drop-pods and landers of the assault force. What had been hundreds became thousands. Troop pods banged down like tracer bullets. Drop-ships swam away from the carrier decks and began to bank down towards the surface. Heavy landers uncoupled and entered descent mode.

At the rear end of the *Incarnadine's* belly, an armoured iris valve slunked open and a small object fired out. Tiny, it had its own integral void shield, and shot like a missile down through the Herodian atmosphere. It left a smoking contrail behind it.

Its solitary occupant had set the trajectory. Now he rode, numb, down towards the planet surface. He had no other awareness except the hunger for blood.

Her blood.

The tumult and concussion of the steep, fast fall was nothing to him.

He dropped like a rocket just beyond the Glassworks quarter of the Civitas. His impact cratered the obsidae for five hundred metres in all directions and kicked out a shockwave flash so hard and bright the Imperials thought for a moment that the archenemy had decided to fire from orbit after all.

He had been very precise about his landing site. The force of his landing drove him down through the planet's crust and into the deep-seated darkness of the aquifer itself.

His pod splintered through sediment, rolled and came to rest, steaming.

He fired the explosive bolts and got out slowly. He was in a subterranean cavern, steaming with thermal waters.

He got to his feet and shambled forward. His every step shook the ground. His feet were massive, hydraulic limbs. His augmetic sensors began to chase and hunt, reflecting off the glossy limestone walls of the cave.

He set off, hunting his quarry.

His name was Karess.

OUT ON THE Great Western Obsidae, the drop-pods were raining in. A thick wave of dust was kicking out from their impacts. Drop-ships were circling down too, landing claws extended as they settled in.

The lander's hatch dropped open and fifty Blood Pact troopers hurled themselves out into the cold waste. Ahead, through the dust walls, they could see the rising terraces and towers of the Civitas Beati.

Following the troopers out, the Marksman looked at the city. His brethren were fanning off in a wide formation.

The Marksman took off his pack and set it on the dusty ground. He pulled out the sections of his long-las and fitted it together. He kept the scope in his pocket, away from the dust. He was dressed in the dull red uniform of the Blood Pact, and had the iron visor and palm-scars to prove his association.

His name was Saul. He was, by any standards of measure, the finest sniper currently attached to the Blood Pact coterie.

Resting the long-las across his shoulder, he began to jog towards the city.

THE TROOP LANDER settled down in a halo of dust but, unlike its companions, it did not lift off again. It sat there on the obsidae, its turbofan engines dying.

They'd got bored. It had only been a twenty minute ride down from the *Incarnadine's* carrier bays to the surface, but they'd got bored and hungry.

The co-pilot had been a fine plaything for a few minutes, but he had ultimately disappointed: heart failure through terror before they'd got to the kill. The pilot himself had been better sport. They'd pinned him and forced him to execute a safe landing, peeling off his scalp with their talons all the while.

The moment they had set down safely, they had cracked his bared skull and fed on his brains.

Now there was work to be done. That meant they had to go to the human mass living-structure in the distance. The idea was distasteful, but Chto, who had brood command, reminded the other two about the rewards on offer. Their memories were short. Once they were reminded, they got excited.

The triplets slipped away from the dormant lander, their wet grey bodies sliding together as they coursed through the obsidae on their bellies.

Their flechette cannons were loaded and armed.

HE SETTLED HIS Raven in to land on an outcrop of the Stove Hills. The Civitas looked far away.

Skarwael popped his canopy and climbed out of his tiny craft. Between him and the city, assault landers and drop-pods were falling like torrential rain.

If he didn't get started, it would all be over. And he didn't want that.

Hellfire take the sniper, and the Pater with his runt-psykers, and the loxatl filth, and the death-machine too.

This was his kill. His kill. The martyr would be his, and he would wear her screams like precious stones.

He was a mandrake, after all. Nothing in creation understood the art of secret murder better than him.

EIGHT
GAR 3

*'If you are the last man standing,
you're not fighting hard enough.'*

— attr. Kaldenbach's commissars

MKOLL CRIED 'DOWN!' His voice, seldom heard so forcefully, echoed over the vox link and everyone, even Gaunt and Rawne, obeyed.

Casting a brief, blurred shadow and visible only for a second, something hook-winged swept low across the hab-block streets. A moment later, blasts tore through the buildings to their left.

The Locust had come in against the wind, its jet-whine inaudible until the last minute. Gaunt had no idea how Mkoll had spotted it.

'The city-shield must be down already,' Rawne muttered, getting up. Ash and brick dust from the blasts were drifting across them.

'Not necessarily,' Gaunt replied. 'It's only a climate shield. A surface bomber like that, with its forward screens maxed up...'

As if demonstrating the colonel-commissar's point, two more Locusts, in fore and aft formation, whooshed east-west across the city limits about half a kilometre ahead of them. The one-man assault craft, black bodies glinting in the sun, were travelling at rooftop height. They banked up and away into the sunlight, one rolling. In their wake, fireballs rippled and flared along the surface. The Ghosts could hear the popping, banging reports.

There were other sounds too. The constant *thump* and *slam* of artillery and armour guns from all along the city's northern skirt. Occasionally, when the wind was in the right direction, they could hear the fierce crackle of small-arms exchanges.

Lugo and his staff strategae had taken over the Civitas tac logis, and were overseeing, literally, the Imperial efforts from the high levels of the hive towers. From there, they were able to despatch remarkably accurate and current assessments of the archenemy invasion. All of it was bad news.

Four strike columns had assembled in the Great Western and Northern Obsidaes within fifty minutes of set down, mobilising fast and spearing into the northern city limits. One was driving into the Glassworks from the north-west, two directly south into Ironhall, and the fourth from the north-east into the Masonae district. Most of this seemed to be light assault armour from landers and storm-troop brigades from the first wave of drop-pods. In total, close to three hundred vehicle elements and eight thousand men, well supported by air cover and the artillery sections setting up in the obsidaes.

That, under any circumstances, would have been bad enough. Imperial numbers in the Civitas Beati hovered just under the seventeen thousand mark, provided militia and arbites units were figured in. But the Imperials had only something in the order of one hundred and eighty armoured machines, of which seventy were unarmed carriers. No air cover. No artillery apart from some light Regiment Civitas field pieces.

This lop-sided equation became a joke when the rest of the picture was factored in. Out in the drop zone, behind the initial, fast mobilising enemy spearhead, a vast force was

assembling. It was taking its time, ferrying armour and
squads down in wave after wave of drop-ships and heavy
lander-transports. It would let the spearhead forces take the
brunt and crack the city open. Then it would move in to con-
solidate. Out on the obsidiae, tac logis calculated, over half
a million men and a hundred thousand fighting machines
waited to mount the second wave. And the count was rising
with every incoming wave.

Well commanded, and with a feth-load of luck on their
side, Gaunt estimated, the Imperial resistance would last five,
maybe six days before annihilation. With Lugo in the chair,
they probably had about two. It was death either way. The
only variable was time.

Supported by sections of the Regiment Civitas Beati, the
Ghosts advanced through the Masonae district, over which
Gaunt had defence command. Kaldenbach was leading the
Ironhall resistance, and a Herodian PDF colonel called
Vibreson headed the Glassworks line. Biagi, and a life
company officer, Major Landfreed, held most of the
remaining four thousand troop strengths in the middle
city, ready for short-notice deployment. Five hundred men
of the Regiment Civitas garrisoned the hive quarter,
mainly, Gaunt believed, to buy enough time in the final,
inevitable phase of the invasion for Lugo to flee via shuttle from the crest level platforms. Flee to where, only the
God-Emperor knew.

The Ghosts and their allies moved up through the narrow
streets east of Beati Plaza. This district was largely untouched
by war, apart from the strafing damage of the enemy air cover.
The thoroughfares were ominously empty. The citizenry had
fled. Homes and commercial properties stood empty and
lifeless, and discarded possessions littered the roads.

As they prowled forward, bounding cover by squad from
block corner to block corner, Gaunt considered they had,
despite everything, a kind of luck on their side. Unopposed
as they now were, the archenemy warships far above them
could have ended the war quickly with aerial bombardment.
Instead, the enemy had opted for the gross effort and huge
cost of a ground assault. He knew what that meant.

They wanted the Beati.

Poorly protected and underdefended as it was, the Civitas Beati was still large, and taking it a street at a time would be a bloody, painfully expensive task for any army. The archenemy was only undertaking it because of the prize. Indeed, the archenemy had only come to Herodor, only bothered with the place at all, because of that prize. The enemy commander wanted the Saint. A body, at least... but a prisoner, that would be the greatest trophy. So an annihilating orbital bombardment was out of the question. No tangible proof of the Beati's presence would be left.

This was all about Sabbat. Everything they did, everything the enemy did. It was all about Sabbat.

Tac logis crackled in Gaunt's ear. Kaldenbach's forces had engaged.

Gaunt was about to relay this to his officers when Mkoll voxed again.

'Contact!'

INITIALLY UNOPPOSED, THE invaders rolled into the northern edges of the Masonae district. To the west of them, smoke and low-level flashes above the roofs showed where their associated columns were lancing through the Ironhall.

Phalanxes of Blood Pact led the way, backed by files of stalk-armour, STeG 4 lights and AT70 Reaver-pattern tanks. Their way was unhindered. Two AT70s peeled off to destroy the prayer horn Gorgonaught in a hail of close range fire, and a trio of stalk-tanks assisted Blood Pact sappers in blowing and cutting the ancient arches of the Simeon Aqueduct. Water, the city's precious life-blood, poured from the shattered aqueduct and flooded several low-lying street blocks. Locust dive bombing had already ruined the North End Agridome. Burning crop produce was billowing yellow-grey smoke into the sky through the ruptured dome seals.

Without seeing a trace of the vaunted Imperial forces, the archenemy crossed Brigat Street into Actes Hill, and began to spread out into the Masonae.

The troopers, moving ahead of the armour, were singing. The song made Mkoll's stomach heave.

'We'll have to put a stop to that at least,' he murmured. He took aim.

'Ease!' he warned.

Mkoll squeezed the tube's trigger spoon and an AT rocket roared down the street, neatly killing the third STeG 4 in the approaching file.

The AT70 behind it started to rev, and spattered fire from its coaxial cannon, but it was pretty much blinded by the black smoke ripping out of the dead STeG.

The two STeGs in front of the kill spurred forward on their heavy, solid wheels, their compact turrets traversing as they hunted for the source of the ambush. The Blood Pact stopped singing and raced for cover positions.

They didn't get very far. Surch and Loell were set up on the west side of the street, Melyr and Caill on the east. The two .50 cannons had a tight, interlocking field of fire, and preyed on the scattering ground troops mercilessly. Red-armoured bodies tumbled, sprawled, flew backwards, flew apart.

The two STeGs up front wheeled round, now firing, raking the lines of the street and blowing out windows and plaster facades. In another few seconds they would lock on to one of the .50 positions.

But they didn't have anything like a few seconds.

Caffran's tread fether bucked and banged, and a smoking rocket slammed down from his upper storey position, blowing one of the STeGs in half.

'Ease,' Mkoll said again, reloaded by Harjeon. He hit the remaining STeG's munitions locker. The shockwave brought the front of a nearby house down.

The AT70 lurched forward, grinding up and over the blazing wreckage of the first kill. As it came over, it fired its main gun. The roar was loud and impressive, but the shot was premature and whined away into the empty end of the street.

Caffran put his second rocket through the big, red tank's port tracks and crippled it. It slewed around, broken wheel bearings shrieking raw on the rockcrete.

Ghosts slipped from cover and leapt up onto its superstructure: Bonin, Domor and Dremmond. Bonin nailed the top hatch with a tube-charge, and left the rest to Dremmond. Gleefully reunited with his flamer, Dremmond pushed the hose muzzle down into the smoking hatch-hole and gutted the tank with combusting promethium.

Bonin dropped down, grabbing the dead 70's pintle mount – a twin-linked bolter – and swung back to face down the street. He started to fire at the Blood Pact infantry squads pressing up to meet the ambush.

'Duck or dance, choice is yours,' he chuckled grimly as the heavy weapon mount shuddered in his hands.

'That's enough! Off and out!' Mkoll called over the link.

Bonin, Domor and Dremmond quit the top of the tank and disappeared into the alleys off the street. At the same moment, the .50 teams dismantled their support weapons and hastened out of their positions.

Pushing forward rather more tentatively now, the Blood Pact advance reached the dead AT70. There was no sign of enemy resistance.

But there was a pack of three tube-charges strapped to the AT70's shell magazine, courtesy of Shoggy Domor.

THREE STREETS AWAY, the lead stalk-tank was hit simultaneously by two tread fether rounds. Wrapped in a brilliant fireball, it spun around, some of its legs thrashing out slackly like a carousel's arms. One leg severed entirely, and flew off, crashing through the front of a habitat unit.

Unfazed, the two stalk-tanks behind it scuttled forward over the burning debris, weapons pods tracking and firing, and each one was greeted by a rocket that blew its main hull to pieces. One collapsed, the other remained on its feet, limb segments dead and locked out, central body ablaze.

'That's the way to do it,' Colm Corbec grinned, lowering his empty rocket tube. He was up on the low roof of a hab building, behind the parapet. Varl's platoon was dashing forward, along the line of the wall beneath him, in single file, firing into the bewildered Blood Pact troopers who suddenly found themselves without armour support.

Brostin's flamer gushed. Corbec could hear the enemy screaming.

'Now!' ORDERED MERYN, stone-faced.

Guheen pulled the trip wire and the tube-charges fourteen platoon had laid across the roadway ignited in geysers of fire and rockcrete. The AT70 almost flipped, its tracks blown away. It came down hard on its nose, the long snout of its main gun biting into the roadway before it came up.

It made the mistake of trying to fire. Either its barrel was deformed by the impact or clogged. Whichever, the hi-ex shell choked, and blew back so hard the rear portion of the turret vented out like a burst paper bag.

Blood Pact infantry flooded up around the burning beast and began firing. One, an officer, had a missile tube on his shoulder, and he dropped to one knee, aiming it at the store front where Meryn and Guheen were down in cover.

He never got to fire it. At least, not alive. A hot-shot round from Nessa Bourah, up on a nearby roof, tore out his throat. He fell sideways and his dead hand spasmed on the spoon.

The rocket winnowed away across the ground, spewing sparks and white flames. One Blood Pact trooper actually managed to leap up over it. He then died, along with the other dozen around him, when the rocket met the kerb and detonated.

THE ARCHENEMY FORCES penetrating the Masonae suddenly realised they were in for a fight after all. They pushed on, resolved now.

In Latinate Road, a slender, picturesque street of tailors' shops and leatherworkers' habs, Daur, Raglon and Ewler brought their platoons in tight to meet the Blood Pact storm-thrust. A ferocious small-arms battle began.

Nearby, Arcuda's platoon – twenty-three – met a flanking push from another five Blood Pact fire-teams. Criid pulled her platoon back from Meryn's position and joined with Curral's, Haller's and Rask's at the junction of Toborio Street and Mason Yard, where a vicious, mid-range infantry duel was developing.

Grell and Theiss scurried their platoons in across the Lanxlyn Road and Principal III, smoking two STeGs and a stalk-tank before meeting the infantry rush head on.

In Skye Alley, Soric's platoon was pinned down by a pair of stalk-tanks that wouldn't go away. They cowered under the deluge of laser fire, stone chips and debris fluttering around them.

'Gak!' Soric coughed. 'Gak this!'

'Support fire! Support fire needed now!' Commissar Hark, crouching nearby, snarled into his vox. 'Support to grid two-six, five-nine! Respond!'

'Ask it for help, chief,' Vivvo yelled over the gunfire. 'For gak's sake!'

'Ask what?' Soric replied, ducking down.

'The thing in your pocket!' Vivvo bawled.

'The what?'

'The thing, chief! The thing that knows!'

'What thing?' asked Hark, looking round at them.

'The kid's just being funny,' Soric said.

'Trooper Vivvo?'

'I… I was just being funny, commissar, sir…' stammered Vivvo, realising the implications of his words. He was loyal to Soric above all things.

Another salvo rained in.

Soric scurried away head down. Once he was behind a door frame, and out of Hark's sight, he scooped the twitching message shell out of his pocket and opened it.

Kazel has the angle, but he can't see it. Tell him to go for the window. He'll know.

What about the rest, Agun? She's going to die and her blood will be on your hands.

'Shut up!' Soric yelled aloud, tearing the paper into scraps. He got on the micro-bead link.

'Kazel? Go for the window. Go for the window.'

'Chief?'

'Go for the gakking window, Kazel!'

Up in a fourth storey room, Kazel turned and fired his tread fether out of the window. It was a hasty, automatic response to Soric's command. The back-blast, contained in the room, almost killed him.

The rocket spat out of the window, deflected sideways off a lamp-bracket and dropped down, entering one of the stalk-tanks through the roof hatch.

As it died, it went into death throes, destroying its companion with insensible, random weapon-pod bursts.

'Shit…' said Kazel, looking down out of the window, his ears still ringing. 'Did I do that?'

* * *

As HIS GHOSTS engaged, Gaunt conceeded he had to hand it to Biagi. Biagi had drawn up GAR 3 – Ground Assault Response 3 – and it was on the money. Rather than wasting time attempting to hold badly provisioned outer streets, Biagi's plan had identified and described the various junctions and street-meets where ambush and defence would work most effectively. It was pragmatic in that it gave ground to an invading enemy until good advantage could be had in defence, but it was thorough. Biagi had analysed every street – not by slate-chart but by eye, by methodical observation – and worked out the strengths and weaknesses. He had read the city well. The Ghosts' initial successes were as much down to Biagi's tactical intelligence as they were the Tanith battle skills.

Gaunt carried GAR 3 on him in a data-slate file, encrypted in case the device fell into enemy hands. Each time he read it, adjusting the fluid disposition of his force, he admired Biagi's work. He regretted the fact that the next time he and the marshal met up, it would no doubt be to clash. It was inevitable. Biagi had yet to find out that Gaunt had deployed flamers.

Even with GAR 3, it was down to the wire. The battle for the Masonae district had become focused on Latinate Road and Mason Yard, with minor skirmishes along Principal III and the atmosphere processor in Tesk Hill Square.

Gaunt waved Beltayn over and got on the vox, moving Daur's platoon and three PDF sections right up Principal III to a sub-access lane that let out into the east side of Mason Yard. Within fifteen minutes, Daur's force had the enemy's Mason Yard action in flank assault.

Gaunt's own trick to complement GAR 3, based on years of experience, was to keep his forces tightly engaged with the leading edge of the enemy advance. The invasive force was like an arm reaching blindly around an obstacle. Every time it came forward, the Ghosts grabbed it by the fingers and severed it at the wrist. By staying close to that leading edge, they discouraged air-cover attacks. The Locust pilots, even on low passes, even with the aid of smoke canisters and ident transponders, could not differentiate between friend or foe in the narrow, clustered streets.

Just before noon, stymied across a nine-block front, the invaders pulled back sharply and tried to redirect along Principal III itself. They led off this new phase with an armour charge – nine AT70s and four stalk-tanks, advancing at cruise speed behind a pair of AT83 Brigand-pattern giants. Corbec and Domor had their platoons in cover in a side-street off the Principal highway, and heard the revving turbines and clattering tracks before anyone else.

'Treads! Treads! On the highway!' Corbec voxed urgently. The Ghosts had to stay low. As they spurred on, the enemy AFVs were raking the sides of the wide boulevard with their pintle-mounts and coaxial cannons. Gaunt had pretty much anticipated this push. Domor's squad had already laced the Principal with tube-charges, the detonation of which took out one AT70 and slowed the entire charge right down as the AT83s lowered their dozer blades and began to clear the way.

Slowed down was good enough for Gaunt. His next signal brought three life company Vanquishers out of hiding in the warehouses beside Mason Yard. The *Wild One*, the *Demands With Menaces* and the *Access Denied*, all Gryphonne IV-pattern Leman Russ battle tanks with the trademark long guns.

Hurling specialist AT shells, the three Imperial tanks got down to business, their first three or four salvoes turning the Blood Pact's well-ordered chase advance into a bloody riot. The *Wild One* crippled one of the big AT83s with its first shot and killed it with its second. The AT83 Brigands, larger than their more primitive cousins the 70s, were, on paper, the Urdeshi forge world's equivalent of the Leman Russ. They had auspex guidance, weapon stabilisers and torsion bar suspension. They were the Blood Pact's best battle machines, not counting the very few ancient super-heavies they had inherited from defeated Guard units.

But there was just something about the Leman Russ. Its pedigree and reputation was second to none. When a Vanquisher or Conqueror appeared, the very sight of it filled Imperial hearts with pride and enemy hearts with fear. This, Corbec thought as he watched the engagement from a sheltered doorway, seemed to be the case now. Apparently numbed at the sight of three Vanquishers powering up in formation, the remaining 83 began to reverse hard. So hard, it ran into and over a stalk-tank, splintering its comparatively fragile frame.

An AT70 blew out under fire from the *Demands With Menaces*, and two more were rendered into scrap by the *Wild One*. One of the stalk-tanks strutted forward past the burning carcass of the first Brigand, its metal hooves chipping at the rockcrete roadway, and trained its weapon pods on the *Access Denied*. Twin double-pulse lasers flickered and chattered, and blast flashes blossomed across the Vanquisher's upper hull and turret. The *Access Denied*, seemingly oblivious, rolled forward, trailing smoke from burning ablative plates and scorched paintwork, and fired a single shell that disintegrated the stalk-tank's body segment so completely the port and starboard limb structures collapsed outwards, bisected.

An AT70 lobbed a shell at the *Wild One* that tore away its sponson and part of its track skirt. Another hit the *Demands With Menaces* on the turret, destroying its vox-mast, pintle mount and laser range-finder, and killing the assistant gunner with explosive spalling.

Wounded but not down, the *Demands With Menaces* plunged forward, laying its guns at the Reaver responsible. Corbec saw the top-hatch pop and the commander emerge, oblivious to the danger, to verify aim with a handscope now his range-finder was junked.

He knew his job. The *Demands* rolled to a halt and jolted hard as it fired, jerking plumes of accumulated white dust off its surfaces and hull grooves like sifted flour. The sound of the hypervelocity AT shell was just a crisp, flat clap in the augmented air. The AT70 made a much fuller and more satisfying sound as it exploded.

'Sir!' Corbec looked away from the show the life company tankers were putting on, and glanced at Domor.

'What's up, Shoggy?'

Domor pointed, looking across the street into the shadowed alleys that came up through a hab compound onto the highway. Corbec glimpsed movement behind the roadway's rockcrete revetment.

Enemy infantry. Fanning forward under the cover of the tank duel.

No, more than that. There were two or maybe three fire-teams over there, lugging tube launchers and long-stemmed rocket grenade bulbs.

They were going for the Vanquishers while they were occupied.

'Smart eyes, Shoggy,' Corbec called, stating the fething obvious. 'Five men… with me now!' he added, not caring who responded but knowing at least five would. Milo, Nehn, Bonin, Chiria and Guthrie were the first up, scrambling after him, heads down.

Corbec followed the enemy's example, and moved back down the side of the Principal behind the high revetment. He came to a break about fifteen metres south of the *Wild One's* rumbling hindquarters, and dropped down, adjusting his micro-bead.

'Shoggy, this is two, come back to me.'

'Two, clear.'

'Gonna rush across, mate. On a count of five–'

'Across the highway, chief?'

'Don't interrupt a man in the grip of a suicidal urge, Shogs. The count will be five. Draw up your unit and the rest of mine and hose that far side. Don't worry about hitting anything, just keep 'em ducking.'

'Understood is not quite the right word, but okay.'

'Good. Five, four, three, two–'

The rapidly assembled guns of twelve and two platoons started to rip and crackle, firing across the wide, sunlit roadway in front of the Imperial tanks. The las-rounds, and the solid slugs from the .50 teams, mottled the rockcrete revetment furiously until it looked like waxy cheese or the surface of a particularly unlucky moon.

Corbec started to run. The others went with him, Milo and Bonin overtaking him. They came up hard, backs to the outer side of the revetment, and waited. Corbec checked his rifle's load and then shot them all a wink.

'You want to live forever?' he asked.

They all nodded. Milo laughed.

'Then follow me.'

They were up in a second and round the revetment through the nearby gap, into the cool shadows of the highway's far-side walkway.

The nearest Blood Pact fire-team was crouching down, locking an RPG into their tube. They looked up in surprise.

That was about all they had time for. The six Imperial las-guns killed them all so fast they didn't even have time to rise. Bodies fell, crouched or squatting.

Ten metres behind them, the second ambush team had time to react. Las-fire chopped in the Ghosts' direction and Guthrie fell over with a moaning curse.

Milo and Chiria led the firefight, firing on auto. Milo shot the tube-gunner in the neck, and his ammo-man in the hand, shoulder and face. Chiria whooped as she aced the Pacter who had hit Guthrie, and wasted the man beside him.

The other two started to run for cover. Nehn crisped off a shot that hit one in the back of the head and dropped him flat on his face. Bonin got the other.

Corbec had knelt down beside Guthrie.

'You still with me, lad?'

'Yes… yes… feth, it hurts!'

A las-round had gone through Guthrie's left thigh. It had cauterised itself, but he'd lost a good chunk of meat and it was so clean-through you could see daylight from the other side.

Corbec took out his field dressings and started to patch Guthrie's leg, smacking a one-shot needle-vial of morphia into the flesh above his hip first.

'Colonel!' Corbec heard Milo cry out.

He started to turn. A las-round. In flight, at full velocity, passing so close beside his face that he felt its stinging heat. He smelt the sheath of ozone fuming off it.

If he hadn't turned his head at the sound of Milo's warning, it would have hit him squarely between ear and eye. The round exploded harmlessly against the roadwall.

'Feth me…' Corbec gasped.

There was a third Blood Pact fire-team, and it had gone into cover when the first two were attacked.

They had the very positive advantage of decent cover. There were six of them, counting by the muzzle flashes from the shadowed doorways and arches down the walkway. Las-shots smashed into the ground and wall around the pinned Imperials. Chiria threw Nehn flat and most probably saved his life.

Bonin started to fire back from the hip. Milo grabbed Guthrie and began to haul him towards the nearest cover... ten metres back down the walkway.

Corbec knew they would all be dead in seconds.

He grabbed the fallen Blood Pact rocket tube off the deck, swung it end over end like a baton to get it across his shoulder pointing the right way and yelled, 'Ease!'

Automatically, Nehn, Chiria, Bonin, Milo and even Guthrie, cried the same word aloud. The drilled answer-response meant their mouths would be open when the rocket fired, and therefore their eardrums wouldn't burst under the savagely unequal pressure.

The bulbous rocket flared down the walkway, passing over Bonin so close it scorched the fabric of his jacket's back. It entered the narrow angle of a doorway ten metres beyond and detonated. The flash was blinding, and the concussion wave brutal. Fragments of stone and pieces of enemy trooper flushed out in the firewash and pelted the inside face of the roadwall.

One surviving Blood Pact trooper, caught by the edges of the blast, stumbled out into the walkway, tearing off his helmet and iron visor, screaming. Bonin had been knocked flat by the concussion, but Milo got up fast and aimed his lasgun.

He saw the naked face of the tormented, wounded Blood Pact soldier. Hairless, pale, ear lobes and brows distended by the multiple piercings, the face brutally scarred from top to bottom with thick folds of rouched tissue. The blast had not done that. The Blood Pact's heinous initiation rituals had made those fearful, lifetime marks.

'Feth!' Milo gasped, and fired. The red-armoured figure buckled and fell. His screaming ceased.

'Colonel?' Chiria called anxiously, getting to her feet and pulling Nehn up after her.

Corbec was on his face on the walkway. His makeshift ploy with the launcher had ignored one crucial detail. The revetment had been right behind him when he fired and the huge exhaust kick of the tube had had nowhere to vent. The force had thrown Corbec forward five metres like a hammer blow. He'd made an even bigger balls-up of using a tread fether than Kazel had done a few hours before.

'Colm? Colm!' Bonin cried, running to him.

Bruised and battered, Corbec rolled over on to his back, giggling.

'Teach me to be fething spontaneous,' he sniggered.

There was a loud explosion from the other side of the revetment wall. Dragging Corbec to his feet and leaving Nehn to finish Guthrie's dressing, Milo, Bonin and Chiria hurried to the nearest gap.

The Vanquisher *Wild One* was dead. It was hard to tell what had done the work. The remaining Reavers and the AT83 were throttling back down the Principal, the stalk-tanks clattering away behind them.

Emboldened by the sight of a Leman Russ burning, the Brigand stirred forward again, and hammered a shot at the *Access Denied* that crushed its front bracings and fore-hull plating. By now, the roadway was punctured in dozens of places by deep shell craters.

'Feth all that,' Corbec declared, still woozy. 'Load me up, somebody.' He had picked up the Blood Pact rocket launcher again.

'Come on, now I know how the fething thing works...'

Chiria ran to the fallen satchel of shell spares and came back with one. With some discussion, the four of them figured out how to slot it into place, lock it in, prime it and arm the launcher.

This time, Corbec checked there was plenty of venting room behind him. 'Stand well back,' he told them. 'I've heard that's the smart move with these things.'

Bonin, Milo and Chiria backed right off, laughing despite the tension of the moment.

Corbec got down on one knee and rested the weight of the snout-heavy launcher on his right shoulder. The scope was an open sight, just a wire cross inside a metal bracket. He settled the centre of the sight against the junction between turret and hull on the AT83, then lowered this estimate by a few centimetres. Recent experience had taught him Blood Pact launchers pulled up like a fething bastard when fired.

'Ease!'

The RPG shot across the highway and hit the 83 in the side turret plates. The tank shook, but came no closer to death. It rapidly traversed its main gun towards Corbec's position.

'Not good…' Corbec admitted, starting to run.

But the distraction had given the *Demands* a good shot at the 83's throat. It fired, main-load AT, and took the big tread's turret off with the precision of a ceremonial guillotine.

The *Access* and the *Demands* stood their ground now on the ruined highway, whipping shells at the rapidly retreating Reavers and stalk-tanks. A pall of fuel-oil burn smoke and fyceline discharge hung over the area.

'One, this is two,' Corbec voxed.

'Two, you're clear.'

'The assault here is over, boss. We've turned them back and–'

Corbec broke off.

'Repeat, two. Repeat, two. Transmission interrupted.'

'Ibram? Corbec. I'm still here. Forget what I just said. The bastards just got serious.'

The reversing enemy tanks, now two hundred metres back down Principal III, were pulling over to the edges of the highway to allow something to pass. It came up monstrously fast, too fast, it seemed, for something so huge.

Access Denied and *Demands With Menaces* started to retreat rapidly, slamming into full reverse. A huge shell impact ripped the *Demands* apart catastrophically, spraying armour parts into the air on the hard tide of an expanding fireball.

Coming down the highway towards them was a Baneblade super-heavy war tank. All three hundred and sixteen tonnes of it were painted bright crimson, even the drive wheels and tracks, and foul symbols were inscribed along the massive hull.

Corbec dropped the empty launcher tube with a clatter. It had no purpose any more. This was an entirely different scale of feth.

'Oh my bollocks,' Corbec gasped.

JUST OFF LATINATE Street, Soric dropped to his knees, panting. He cursed himself for being too old for this gak, but it didn't take away the thumping of his heart and the lactic acid burning in his leg muscles.

They'd had to run. His platoon and Criid's and Raglon's and Meryn's. The lingering infantry fight had suddenly turned on its head, just when they thought they were gaining ground.

A couple of Reavers, and at least three N20 halftracks with flamer mounts in their pulpits, had come steaming into the street fight, driving the Imperials back. A squad of Herodian PDF had tried to counter strike, and had been cooked and boiled for their efforts.

Running had turned into the only viable option.

Soric had tried hailing Gaunt and tac logis to call up armour cover, but the blurting sheet-fire bursts of the enemy 'tracks seemed to be interfering with the signal.

He crawled into a doorway, sucking air. Men ran past. Vivvo stumbled up and collapsed next to him.

'All right, son?' Soric asked.

'I'm sorry, chief,' Vivvo replied.

'Sorry? Sorry for what?'

'For speaking about the… the thing. In front of the commissar like that.'

'Don't you worry, son. I can look after myself.'

'I should have thought, chief. I should have realised the commissar was there.'

Soric shrugged. 'Vivvo… can I ask you a question?'

'O-of course, chief!'

'How long have you known?'

'Known what, chief?' Vivvo asked honestly.

'About me. And the messages I get.'

Vivvo frowned. 'I've suspected it since Aexe, tell the truth. But I've known since we got here.'

'Known what?'

'That the message shell keeps coming back to you with stuff in it.'

'Stuff?'

'Data. Info. The gakking truth, chief.'

Soric nodded. 'You told anyone?'

'No! Well, yeah. Kazel, Venar. Maybe Hefron.'

'They all sound?'

'I think so. They wouldn't go shooting their mouths off about-'

'About what, son?'

'About you, sir. You and what you've got.'

Men from Meryn's platoon thundered past where they were hiding. Behind them, a hundred metres down the street, heavy flamers hissed.

'And what have I got, son?' Soric asked.

He was expecting all sorts of answers. The hidden eye. The oracle. The touch of the warp. The sixth sense. The psyk.

'The lucky charm,' Vivvo said. The honest simplicity of it almost brought a tear to Soric's eye. Milo had told him they'd called him that too. That was the truth of things. In this dark galaxy, superstitious soldiers didn't set up a hue and cry for the execution of their touched ones. They regarded them as lucky charms, touchstones, fate-wards against the entirely luck-free doom that awaited all of Imperial culture.

'You're not afraid of me, then?' Soric asked.

'Afraid of you? Why the gak would I be afraid of you?'

'Because of what's in me. Because of… of the warp. A commissar, an inquisitor… they'd have me for buttons because of what I can do.'

Vivvo blinked away dust and stared into Soric's lined features. 'Everything you do, everything that shell tells you… it's luck speaking to us, giving us the edge. Like with Kazel back there. I believe… really, sir… that it's the Emperor himself, speaking through you and looking out for us all. So long as you give us the good stuff, chief, I'll never question where it comes from.'

'They'll be on to me sooner or later, son. Best case, the black ships, worst… a bolt-round in the head. People like me, lucky charms or not… we're liabilities.'

'They come for you, they'll have to go through me first.'

Soric reached out a hand and grabbed Vivvo's tight. 'No. Promise me you won't get in the way when it comes. Promise me that.'

'I swear.'

'You don't want that kind of trouble,' Soric assured him. He let go of Vivvo's hand. Almost at once, Vivvo grabbed Soric's dust-caked fist.

'Promise *me* then, chief,' he said. 'Everything the shell tells you… share it. Act on it. If I ever find out you've been holding stuff back… I dunno. I can't threaten you, but you must know what I mean. All the while the things it tells you are fit for general consumption, then be our lucky charm. If it tells you shit you don't share... well, that's where we start running to the commissar.'

Soric swallowed. He nodded. 'Fair point. Beyond fair, son.'

'We better move, chief.' The sucking, rushing breath of the flamers was closer now. They could both hear the clanking of the N20 tracks.

'Go!' Soric said, and Vivvo ran off down the street.

Soric tugged the message shell from his pocket and opened it.

What about it, Agun? Vivvo's right... and very forgiving too. You want to see him shot? Him and Kazel and Hefron and everyone else who knows? Shot for harbouring a piece of warp-filth? You're not telling everything. You're betraying them. Be a man. Tell Gaunt. Tell Gaunt about the nine.

'Nine? What nine are you talking about?' Soric raised the empty shell-case and yelled the words into its hollow body.

'Nine what?'

But the N20 was too close now. Soric ran.

'MORE ARMOUR! I said we need more armour!' Gaunt yelled into the vox-horn, but nothing except static-chopped distortion caterwauled back.

'What's wrong with this thing?' he barked at Beltayn. The signals officer was trying to tune the dial of his voxcaster.

'Something's awry, sir,' he said, too busy concentrating on his job to form a proper reply.

'What?'

'Jamming, most like. Heavy-grade electroference.'

Gaunt had feared as much. The invaders were adding to their advantages by muzzling the Imperial comms and chain of command. They were probably fething up their own vox-links too, but no doubt the Blood Pact was relying on psykers to coordinate their forces.

'Pack that up and round up the platoon here,' Gaunt told Beltayn, and then ran off down the dusty street. The air was full of the sounds of combat from the thoroughfares all around. 'Rawne!' he yelled. 'Rawne!'

Rawne's platoon was holding the end of the narrow street where it joined Tesk Hill Square. The small-arms exchange was fierce. Gaunt saw Feygor in cover behind a garbage drum, snapping off shots. He came up behind him, head low.

'Feygor!'

Feygor glanced round. 'Little busy, sir.'

'Where's Rawne?'

Feygor shrugged. 'Micro-bead's down.'

'All vox is down. Where's Rawne?'

'Last I saw, up in that hab block. Third floor.'

Gaunt nodded and sprinted across the debris-littered road to the side door of the hab. A decent kick or two had taken it off its hinges. He went inside.

The unlit stairwell within led up to all nine of the hab's levels. There was a scrappy notice panel screwed to the wall facing the door that listed the names of the occupant families next to their hab module numbers.

Gaunt ran up the stairs two at a time, drawing his laspistol. Fething thing seemed lightweight and inconsequential next to the solid memory of his lost bolt pistol.

He didn't bother with the first two floors, and went into the third level through the spring-latched entry.

'Rawne?'

A long hallway stretched out before him, scattered with scraps of paper and discarded clothes. On either side, numbered doors identified the separate hab modules. Some were open, and despite the fact the phospha lamps were dead in their brackets, the hall was filled with thin daylight from the open rooms.

'Rawne?'

Nothing but the rattle and slam of fighting down below.

He stepped into one open module. It was a mess. Furniture was overturned, and shelves cleared. Tape had been put in an X over the main window in the vain hope that it would protect the glass from blast damage. Whoever lived here had left in a hurry. Gaunt hoped they were tucked up safely in a Civitas shelter now.

He crossed to the window, keeping out of sight, and took a look. Gunfire was being exchanged savagely across the open space of Tesk Hill Square below. There were shell holes in the paving, and a five storey building on the far side of the square was on fire. The massive atmosphere processor in the centre of the open space was dented and buckled by countless stray shots. Several bodies lay out in the open. Most, Gaunt noted with satisfaction, were clad in dirty red.

From his vantage point, Gaunt could see a good way west across the northern sectors of the Civitas. Huge banks of firesmoke were puffing up from the Ironhall sector. Last he'd heard, before the vox went to feth, was that Kaldenbach's line of defence was taking the worst of it. He hoped to Terra that Kaldenbach was following GAR 3 too. Kaldenbach, so cock-sure and confident of his own abilities, had strategic ideas of his own. It would be just like him to ignore Biagi's fine prep-work and choreograph his own fight.

If he did, they'd all pay.

Further off, in the smoggy distance, he saw that enemy lan-ders were still dipping in over the obsidaes. The downpour of drop-pods had all but ceased, but the landers still came on, ferrying men and munitions down, retreating empty, refu-elling and repeating the process.

Gaunt had, for obvious reasons, a basic faith in the Guard being the backbone of the Imperium's fighting power. He had a healthy respect for the Astartes, for the Titan Legions, for the armoured regiments and the Navy, but the basic fething infantry was, in his book, the four square basis of victory. That's the way he'd been taught, after all, by his father, by Oktar, by Slaydo... even by Dercius. But right then, like never before, he longed for a squadron of Furies, or Lightnings, or anything air-mobile with a good rate of climb and armour-penetrator ammunition. Those landers were so vulnerable. One well led squadron could extermi-nate a huge chunk of the enemy strength in transit before it had even made surface-touch. It would be like a gamebird shoot.

He left the module and tried the next few. 'Rawne?' he called as he went.

Most of the hab flats were like the first one he'd entered – abandoned and untidy. He tried one where the door was locked, and came into a module that was completely empty except for a console table placed oddly in the middle of the floor. There was a book on it. The walls of the room were stripped bare, and there was no carpet or matting, just bare

218 *Dan Abnett*

boards. Even the single phospha overhead was missing its shade.

He paused for a moment. It was very odd. There was a door – closed – off to the left. Why was this room so empty?

He took a step forward, and then heard the distinctive crack of a hot-shot load from nearby.

He hustled out into the hallway again, and went down five more doors into another scruffy module.

As he came through the doorway, Banda swung round from the window and aimed her long-las at him. The target light from her scope glowed on his solar plexus.

'Sir!' she said, putting up her weapon.

'Sorry to spook you, Banda. Where's Rawne?'

'Right here,' said Rawne, behind him.

Gaunt turned.

'Looking for me?'

'What are you doing up here?'

'Link's down, so I was trying to get a better picture of what was going on by eyeball. Bastards have us locked. I was looking for an opening.'

Gaunt nodded. 'There's bad feth going down at Principal III.'

'Corbec?'

'Something about a super-heavy tank. I think that's where the emphasis is switching. This...' Gaunt gestured towards the window and the fighting immediately outside. 'This is just a holding pattern.'

Rawne shrugged. 'Tell that to my Ghosts.'

'Look, I'm taking my squad, and Haller's and Raglon's, and we're going to head east to see if we can help Corbec. That means you're in charge of this area. Okay?'

'Of course.'

'You've got GAR 3?'

Rawne patted the data-slate in his jacket pocket.

'Use it, Elim. We've got no vox to communicate with, but we can hold this together if we're all singing from the same sheet. Here and Latinate are the hold points. Failing that, back to Armonsfahl Boulevard.'

'Latinate may already be gone. A runner came through from Soric. Hard push by flamer 'tracks.'

'Armonsfahl then. Send your own runner and get Soric back into the game. Get him to group the platoons with him and–'

Gaunt stopped.

'You know how to run a defence, don't you?'

Rawne shrugged slightly.

'I'm wasting my breath, aren't I?'

Rawne nodded.

'The Emperor protects,' Gaunt said, giving Rawne a quick salute and hurrying out and away down the hall.

'Gaunt?'

He paused at the sound of Rawne's voice, and turned. Rawne stood in the module's doorway, looking back at him.

'Yeah?'

'Good luck hunting that super-heavy. Give it feth. Give 'em all feth.'

Gaunt nodded, and hit the stairs.

THE SPRING DOOR banged shut after him. Rawne wandered back into the module. At the window, Banda was lining up her long-las

'What's–'

'Shhh,' she said. 'I'm working. Second floor window. Blood Pact officer with a rocket launcher. Thinks that noooo-body can see him…'

Her voice was just a soft hiss. Her breathing dropped to a very low rate. The long-las bucked hard as it fired.

'Got him?' Rawne asked.

She turned and smiled sardonically at him. 'What do you think?'

He leaned forward and kissed her mouth. It was a brief but hungry kiss.

'You know what I think,' he said, moving back. 'Kill something else for me.'

'Like what? I could run to a side window and get a decent angle on Gaunt as he ponces off.'

Rawne smiled, and shook his head. 'Thanks, but no. Either the archenemy gets him or I do. No favours.'

She shrugged, and slapped in a new clip.

'I appreciate the thought though,' Rawne added.

'Ah, I couldn't anyway. Gaunt's all right. I like him.'

She saw the look in his eyes and added sweetly, 'Not like I like you, naturally.'

'Naturally.'

'So,' Banda said, lining up and scoping for a new shot. 'You're in charge now. What's the plan?'

'We keep killing them until they're all dead… or we are. Or was that a trick question?'

'EVERYONE SET?' GAUNT asked. There was a general assent. 'Let's move,' he told them.

With his own platoon, and Haller's and Raglon's, Gaunt set off away from Tesk Hill, into the middle streets of the Masonae District. The scouts moved ahead – Caober, Mkeller and Preed. Preed was Suth's replacement in seventeen. An older Tanith, he'd steadfastly remained a regular trooper until Mkoll had urged him to specialise. In his previous life as a gamekeeper, he'd developed great woodcraft, but he'd not joined the scout fraternity because of a lack of confidence. He thought himself too old. Gaunt hoped Preed was not finding his true calling too late.

Half a kilometre east of Tesk Hill, they ran into trouble. A serious wedge of Blood Pact infantry was biting down around Hisson Street, trying to break through to Principal III. The platoons commanded by Skerral, Folore, Mkendrick and Burone – respectively nineteen, twenty-six, eighteen and seven – were packing a splendid but tight resistance to that attack. But the neighbourhood streets were no go.

'Suggestions?' Gaunt asked.

'We go through those buildings there,' Caober said firmly. Haller nodded. Caober consulted his data-slate chart. 'Cut through them and we should come out on Fancible Street, clear of this mess.'

The buildings were a manufactory and a hab block. They had been bolted tight and secure by their departing owners. Mkeller las-knifed the padlock on the manufactory's outer door.

'What?' Haller asked Gaunt.

'Let's go careful. If this is the way through, then you can bet the enemy will have thought of it too.'

'Coming the other way, you reckon?' asked the tall Verghast.

'I think so,' said Gaunt.

The interior of the manufactory was cold and dark. Generally, the air in the Masonae District had become increasingly stale, so much so that many of the Ghosts were wearing their rebreathers. Too many atmosphere processors knocked out of action, Gaunt thought.

The machine shops and assembly sheds were quiet. As they moved along, they checked every side door and storeroom, just in case.

They exited the manufactory and crossed via a covered walkway into the worker habitat. The procedure resumed. A careful checking of rooms to cover their backs as they crossed the hab's lower halls.

'This one's locked,' Caober said.

Gaunt approached, the Ghosts behind him down in cover, weapons raised. He turned the door handle.

'No, it's not.'

Caober furrowed his brow in surprise.

Gaunt threw the door open and they looked in, guns aimed. Another hab module, standard, except…

…this one was entirely bare. No carpet or rugs, no shade on the overhead lamp, walls stripped. A door to one side, closed. A console table drawn up in the centre of the floor, with a book on it.

'Clear!' said Caober. 'Move forward…'

'Wait!' Gaunt hissed. He had a terribly uneasy feeling. He walked into the bare room, and smelt its musty cool. What was going on? Some kind of coincidence?

He walked to the small table oddly set in the centre of the room, and reached out to the book lying there. It was old. So very old, it was falling apart and dissolving into dust.

He opened the cover and read the title page.

It was a first edition of *On The Use of Armies* by Marchese.

Gaunt had his own copy of this obscure work. Tactician Biota had given it to him just before he'd left Aexe Cardinal.

What the hell…? What gross coincidence was this? Gaunt felt a rising sense of panic and fear. Warp magic was around him. He looked at the closed side door. What was beyond that? What?

He stepped towards it, and turned the handle. The door opened gently. Gaunt smelled fresh, clean air. There were plants in the doorway. Climbers and shrubs. This side room was obviously some kind of indoor herbarium, an agri-room for–

'Hostiles!' Caober yelled from the doorway, and started to fire.

Gaunt slammed the door shut and ran to join him.

A Blood Pact platoon was coming to meet them down the hab hallway, using doorways for cover and firing their lasri-fles and solid-slug weapons.

It took ten minutes of brutal fighting to kill them.

By the time the fight was over, Gaunt was at the east exit of the hab. He thought for a second about going back to that strange, bare room, but it didn't seem to matter so much any more. His blood was up. He'd just impaled a Blood Pact offi-cer on his power sword. And by the time the three platoon group was out and into Fancible Street, he'd forgotten entirely about the old book and the bare room.

GOL KOLEA DROPPED down out of the hab window onto the slip-road beneath and ran forty metres, fast, towards the rear wall of the dingy store-barn facing him. Every black, glass-less window along the road staring down on him seemed to hold the threat of hidden shooters, but no fire came his way. He was breathing hard by the time he crunched against the gritty wall and slid down, but he could still hear the clattering rat-tle of a belt-fed weapon nearby.

DaFelbe was trying to raise him on the vox, demanding to know his position. The link was very bad, very chopped. Kolea could only just make DaFelbe out. Kolea flicked the mic of his comm-link twice in quick succession, the non-verbal acknowledgement, the *can't talk now*.

He crawled to the end of the store-barn's retaining wall and then quickly swung up over the low barrier, firing from the chest. Two Blood Pact troopers, their backs to him at the next wall line, toppled over, taken completely by surprise.

He ducked back down. More belt-fed rattling. Some shout-ing now. A couple of shots whined over him.

Chancing it, he took a dash towards the looming doorway of the barn and threw himself into cover. Renewed shouts, in a harsh language that made him cringe.

He worked his way down the inside wall in the gloom, up onto a loading dock, and across to a shell hole in the wall. The fractured puncture gave him a view out into the freight yard behind the barn. From there, he could see the two-man team with the belt-fed cannon, nestled behind a stack of pre-fab rockcrete sheets. He could see them, but the firing angle was lousy.

He needed to be higher…

A metal ladder, secured to the wall on brackets, led up from the loading dock to a first floor stowage platform. Slinging his lasgun over his shoulder, he went up the ladder.

He was just climbing off onto the stowage decking when he realised he wasn't alone. He threw himself forward as the fig-ure came for him out of the dark, and they tumbled over together, grunting and thrashing. His opponent was quick, and Kolea got a warning glimpse of a bared blade. A flash of steel in the dimness. Gak to that. Kolea put all his upper body strength into a hooking punch and slammed the figure away onto its back.

He darted forward to finish the business scratch-company style, with his bare hands, and pulled up.

It was Cuu.

Cuu was writhing on the deck, cursing and clutching his bloody mouth.

'You!' Cuu hissed.

Kolea shrugged. 'Didn't you recognise me?'

Cuu shook his head. 'Thought you were one of them…'

That, disturbingly, didn't ring true to Kolea at all. Cuu had been up on the platform before Kolea, so his eyes would have had longer to adjust to the gloom. Surely, he should have been able to tell…

Unless he'd chosen not to. A quick slash with a warknife, and who'd have known better?

Kolea shook himself. Lijah Cuu was a scumbag, but he wasn't that much of a scumbag…

'Get up,' said Kolea. As Cuu rose, oathing and hawking bloody phlegm, Kolea crossed to the ventilator window in the wall, levered open the metal louvres, and looked out. Down below, at a steeper but better angle, he saw the gun-nest. He slid the barrel of his lasrifle through the louvres and took aim, even though he was going to fire on auto.

His shots rained down over the gun-position. The gunner himself flopped back dead at once. His loader turned, twitched as he was winged, and walloped over onto his back.

'The cannon's dead. Way's clear,' Kolea voxed to DaFelbe, hoping that the essence of his message would get through the fierce interference.

He turned to Cuu. 'Come on,' he said.

The platoon was moving up through the freight yard when they got down.

'Did I do that?' Criid asked Cuu as she brushed past him, glancing at his bloodied nose and mouth.

'No, sarge.'

She shrugged. 'Must be losing my touch.' Criid clicked her fingers and pointed, and Hwlan took the point men forward.

'Nice work,' Criid told Kolea with a smile. He nodded. He was still getting used to the odd looks his old friends and comrades were giving him, but there was something particu-lar about Criid's manner. She'd been fine at first, but now there was a wary reserve. What was that about?

'Criid okay?' he asked Lubba.

Lubba was adjusting the feeder pipe of his flamer's P-tanks. 'Sure. Why?'

'Keeps looking at me.'

'Probably thinks your gonna get your rank back off her.'

Kolea shook his head. 'I told her…'

'She's gonna worry. That's all it is.'

'Flamer here!' Criid's order echoed down the concourse. They hurried to join her.

It was a false alarm. Varl's platoon was coming in from the next street over. Baen, Varl's scout, had picked up an enemy grouping at the nearby crossroads.

'About thirty of them,' Baen reported. 'And they seem to have a stalk-tank… but it's not active.'

'Not active?' Criid asked.

Baen hunched his shoulders in a 'what can I tell you?' gesture. 'Looks like they're guarding it.'

'We set up a holding fire here to keep 'em busy,' Varl proposed, 'then we could sneak a fire-team round the side. Through there–' he pointed.

'I'll take it,' said Kolea. Criid looked at him. Again, that strange tension.

'Fine by me,' Varl grinned. He'd missed his old sparring partner Kolea. 'So long as you don't feth it up.'

'Okay,' Criid said, reluctantly. 'Nessa, Hwlan, Baen… with Kolea.'

The four of them ran off to the left into the twilight of a narrow, tall sidestreet as the combined platoons laid in. Kolea could hear the crackle of las-arms and the hiss of flamers.

The scouts led the way, followed by Nessa with her long-las. Kolea brought up the back. There were worse places to be in the galaxy than directly behind Nessa Bourah when she ran, he considered.

A sort of realisation hit him. He felt – at a gentle, normal, human level – desire. Appreciation of a sexy female's well-made backside. Gak, but it had been a long, long time since he'd registered anything like that.

Since he'd registered anything like anything.

It really did feel like this was the first day of his life and he was seeing everything new. Like he'd woken up from a deep, numb slumber. How had he described it to Curth? Like surfacing from deep water.

I'm alive again, he thought. Thanks be the Beati.

Baen and Hwlan led them off the street, through the cluttered, ransacked ground floor classrooms of a hab-district scholam, and up onto the first floor of a Munitorum laundry. The air was stale and damp from the water stagnating in the big steel wash-presses. Vermin gnawed and scurried in the mounds of wet overalls. Soap crystals littered the floorboards and lint clogged the grilles of the overhead ducts.

They reached a row of windows that a shell fall had blown in. The stalk-tank was below them, crouching against the side wall of a suburban chapel. Baen had been right – the enemy troopers down there were holding the street as if defending the machine.

Nessa took a look through her scope.

Something's not right, she signed.

'May I?' Kolea asked. Nessa handed him her long-las.

He spotted down, letting the auto-settings of the scope adjust to his eyeball.

The stalk-tank wasn't standard. It was lacking weapon pods and fore-turrets. Instead, its underslung body compartments were fat and distended, like a swollen belly. Within the gross, glassteel bubble, Kolea could see a human figure in front of the driver. The figure was leaning back, twitching and spasming. Hundreds of plug-wires snaked from its body into the guts of the tank's body assembly.

'Psyker,' he said, handing the long-las back to Nessa.

'Psyk-weapon?' Hwlan asked.

'No,' said Kolea. 'I reckon it's that... and things like it... that are fething up our comm-links.'

Do the honours, Baen signed to Nessa.

She took aim, her breathing slowing. She fired.

The hot-shot round ruptured the belly-bubble and blew the psyker's head and shoulders into meat shrapnel. The stalk-tank itself shuddered and then started to burn. A non-verbal scream shrilled into the air and made them all recoil and gasp.

Kolea, Baen and Hwlan got back up to the window and began firing down on the rapidly breaking Blood Pact units. Criid and Varl took advantage of the confusion and pressed in.

In under five minutes, they had the street cleared.

THE CRIMSON BANEBLADE was a horrifying thing, terror made into physical form. Corbec doubted the fething Archon himself, Urlock wassissname, would have more presence in person.

The sound it made was enough. Not a growl, not a rumble, not a roar. A profoundly deep, almost infrasonic howl that vibrated the diaphragm and harrowed the soul. Someone – Daur maybe, or Ana Curth – had once told Corbec that infrasound noise, down around the 18Hz level, triggered a primaeval fear-response in humans. It was as old as caves and darkness and the first fire. The infrasonic rumble in the snarls of Old Terra hunter-felids made humans freeze with terror. It was a base response, inherited from the primates.

When it fired its main gun, or its hull-mounted Demolisher cannon, it was worse. The ground quaked. Shells seared away into the mid-city and fireballs bloomed up over the roofline. There was nothing he could do against that. Nothing any lone human could do.

'Come on! Come on!' Milo was dragging at his sleeve desperately. His assault team was ready to flee into the eastern streets. The Baneblade crunched over the mangled wreck of the *Demands With Menaces*.

'Okay!' Corbec started, and struggled to his feet.

'What the gak is that?' Chiria asked.

Corbec turned to look.

A figure was striding out onto the highway in front of the super-heavy tank. She was clad in golden armour and a sword glittered in her hand.

NINE
THE JOURNEY
INTO NIGHT

'Stand with me, for as long as you are able.
A day, a week, a year, a minute. Whatever you can give,
however long you can stand, I welcome that.'

— Sabbat, epistles

IT WAS HER.

'Oh, feth me! The Beati!' Corbec whispered.

Milo stared. He had not yet got over the shock of the pilgrim girl's death. He could see her still, in his mind's eye, running out in front of the tank, waving her arms to distract it. This seemed too much like history repeating itself.

'Brin!' Corbec yelled, but Milo was already running out of cover.

'You'll be the death of me, boy!' Corbec added, as he shook off Chiria's hands and went after him.

Milo ran out onto the highway. The Beati didn't seem to see him. God-Emperor, but she looked so beautiful in her gilded, engraved armour.

He cried out. A second later, Corbec crashed into him and brought him down with a flying tackle. They both bruised hard on the road surface.

The Baneblade's coaxial sub-weapons swung to target the golden figure ahead of it and blazed away, but the Saint was no longer there. The vacant stretch of roadway ripped up in a messy blitz.

With a single leap, she had come up onto the fore-hull of the huge vehicle, behind the squat Demolisher mount and beside the main weapon. Her sword scythed in her hand.

The massive main barrel severed, the cut length of it crashing onto the hull before rolling off onto the ground. The sliced edges of the barrel stump crackled with discharging blue energy.

'Dear God-Emperor…' Corbec stammered in disbelief.

The Beati swung her sword up, grabbed the hilt with both hands and plunged it down, blade-first, between her well-planted feet, deep into the body of the tank's main hull.

It slewed to a stop. She had pin-pointed and executed the driver.

The top-hatch popped and a crew commander scrambled up, grabbing the yokes of the pintle-mounted bolter. She leapt again, somersaulting, and landed on her feet on the turret-top behind his hatch. Her purring blade cut through neck and pintle mount alike.

'Corbec… Corbec, did you see…?' Milo gasped, watching.

'The Emperor surely protects, lad,' muttered Corbec.

The Beati unclasped a golden tube-charge from her belt, thumbed off the spring and dropped it down into the open hatch. Then she dived headlong off the top of the tank.

Milo and Corbec started running for cover.

The Baneblade did not explode, but fire gusted through its heart, and blew off several hatches. One crewman staggered out, burning, and fell onto the highway.

Sword hanging low from her right hand, the Beati walked towards them, gleaming in her armour, backlit by the burning tank.

Milo and Corbec turned to face her.

'Well met, brothers,' she said.

They both found themselves smiling.

'That was astonishing, Holiness,' Milo said.

'Holiness?' she admonished. 'Is that how you greet a friend? I am Sabbat. Call me that if you must call me anything.'

Corbec glanced at Milo. He was amazed. The boy really didn't see it. This was Sanian, a girl Milo had spent years dreaming about. But he didn't recognise her, face to face.

But, when he came to think of it, Corbec realised he wouldn't have recognised her either. He only knew it was Sanian because Gaunt had told him so. This woman, this creature, was nothing like the esholi he'd met on Hagia. Sanian had been quiet, modest, restrained. This female blazed with confidence, power and drive.

And, while Sanian had been a treat for the eyes, the woman before them was beautiful. So beautiful it hurt. She was luminous. Beyond sex, beyond desire. A divine incarnation of beauty.

And she'd just killed a super-heavy tank outright in single combat.

Corbec suddenly felt awkward and pathetic.

'Nothing like the feats of valour you've performed in your time, Colm,' she said to him, as if reading his thoughts.

'You're too kind,' he mumbled.

Milo started to say something and then brought his lasrifle up rapidly, aiming – so it appeared – right at her head.

He fired, and the shot went over her left shoulder. The Baneblade crewman, bolt pistol raised, was half-out of the dead tank's side hatch, his weapon levelled at the Beati's back. Milo's shot hit him in the throat and he fell down on his face, the gun clattering to the deck.

The Beati flinched and looked round. When she turned back to look at Milo, she was smiling broadly.

'You see?' she said. 'You see? Without you, I am nothing. The Emperor, blessed be His divine grace, has given me strength and speed and power beyond the scope of man. But I can't fight the enemy alone. Alone, I will be overwhelmed. To live, and to be victorious, I rely on you… on you, Milo, and you Colm, on the brave men and women of the Imperial Guard, on all my fellow warriors… a fact that Milo has just demonstrated very clearly.'

'We only serve, Beati,' mumbled Corbec.

'We all only serve, Colm,' she assured him, placing her hand on his forehead. A raging headache he had not even begun to acknowledge, the after-effects of the Baneblade's awful infrasound, faded and vanished. He felt good. Feth! He felt twenty-one again!

'All of us, together, on the journey into night. I may be something… something… I don't know what. A figurehead, at least. A rallying point. A leader. But I am nothing without you. A leader is nothing if she has no one to lead.'

She looked at them both.

'Do you understand? I feel like I'm rambling…'

'N-no!' Corbec assured her.

'We understand,' said Milo.

'This is not about me,' she said. 'This is about all of us. Imperial souls, banding together to see off the dark.'

'We understand,' Milo repeated. She turned to look at him and smiled again.

'I knew you would, Milo. It is set, as a fact, in the warp. You will stay with me now. Now, until this is done. You will protect me. Gaunt has promised as much.'

'I will, lady,' Milo said.

'You're not scared, are you?' she asked.

He shook his head.

'I would be,' she told him.

GAUNT AND HIS force arrived on Principal III a few minutes later. Gaunt stared in amazement at the ruined super-heavy.

'What happened?' he asked.

'The Beati happened,' Corbec said.

'Where is she now?'

'Advancing. Domor's platoon went with her. Milo too.'

'Milo?'

'Looked to me like he'd been seconded. As her personal sidekick.'

Gaunt frowned. 'You look tired,' he said to Corbec.

'Been a long day, sir.'

And it would be longer, and without end. The Imperials had barely held back the archenemy's first wave, and the second was coming hard on its heels. There would be no break in this fight. The enemy would assault the Civitas until it fell.

'I've called for reinforcements,' Gaunt told his colonel. 'I want set units to drop back and refresh. Make yours one of them.'

'We're fine, sir,' Corbec protested.

'I know. But retire anyway. Soric's falling back, Haller, Burone, Ewler, Scafond, Folore, Meryn. Join them, please. Get your wounds patched. It'll make a difference tomorrow if I can pull platoons like yours fresh out of the hat.'

'If there is a tomorrow,' Corbec sighed.

'There will be,' said Gaunt emphatically. 'Now round up your platoon and retire.'

CORBEC'S PLATOON MEANDERED back through empty streets towards the inner guard stations, sandbagged emplacements manned by Regiment Civitas and PDF along the Guild Slope.

They could all hear the fighting raging on at the city limits.

'Medic station,' said a PDF officer, pointing. Dorden and Curth had set up shop in a vacant livestock hall. Corbec sent his injured in that direction, but he was distracted.

He'd heard something. A sound from his past, nostalgic, eddying out of a hab across from the hall.

He walked over, and ducked into the hab. That noise! The shriek of a woodsaw. That dusty smell, that memory…

There was a stack of seasoned timber just inside the low door. Pale stuff with a fine bloom. Corbec ran his fingers along the grain. He'd forgotten how much the smell and feel of wood had been part of his life. A part of every Tanith's life.

'Help you, trooper?'

Corbec turned and peered into the dark interior of the building. An old man with sawdust flakes in his wiry hair was feeding planks into a table saw beneath the light of a single phospha lamp.

'Just… didn't expect to find a place like this here,' Corbec shrugged. The old man frowned as if he didn't know what to say to that, and hefted up another board in his gloved hands. The saw whined.

'Colm Corbec,' Corbec nodded to the old man, holding out his hand. The man finished his cut, then set the wood aside, and removed a glove to shake Corbec's hand.

'Guffrey Wyze. Sure I can't help you?'

Corbec scratched his head, looking around. 'I used to work in a place like this. My father ran a machine shop back home, but he did a lot of timber cutting too. It was timber country.'

Wyze nodded. 'Where was that?'

'Tanith.'

Wyze thought for a moment then said a single word that shocked Corbec. 'Nalwood.'

'You know it?'

'Of course,' said the old man. He hit the rubber-sleeved switch on the side of the table saw and powered it down so they could talk without raising their voices.

'You know it?' Corbec repeated.

'You see many forests here on Herodor? Plantations? Sustainable woodstocks? We import from all over. People like wood. It's reassuring. And it's versatile too. Furniture, frames, panels, whatever.'

He wiggled a finger at Corbec, beckoning him towards a side door between laden shelves of tools, pots and junk. Beyond was the wood store. A great mass of timber was seasoning there, in floor-to-ceiling open shelves, divided by aisle gangways. The air smelled of resin and heartwood.

'All imported,' said Wyze. 'Most of it's coloci and sap-maple and white toft from Khan, cheap stuff. Everyday. But I sometimes get shipments of choicer grades. There, that's half-cut supple pine from Estima. You ever see better?'

'It's nice,' agreed Corbec, stroking the velvet surface of the exposed pile top.

'And this is mature shiln from Brunce. I've got some genuine Helican spruce somewhere.'

Wyze walked down the nearest aisle and bent down to a low shelf. He tore some pulp-paper freight wrapping away from a small consignment of dark wood. It was dusty. It hadn't been touched in a while.

'Here you go. Thought I had some left. Only use it for special jobs.'

Corbec bent down beside him and knew immediately what he was looking at. He swallowed hard.

'Nalwood.'

'That's right. Beautiful stuff. Costs too.'

'I know it,' Corbec said. Quality timber had been Tanith's one major export. He'd worked the mills himself, years back, rough cutting wood for off-world shipment.

'Can't remember what I paid. Must be a while back now, but when I saw what the merchant had, I didn't argue about the price. This stuff is worth the outlay.'

Corbec reached down. The shipment's paper wrapper had the vestiges of a merchant's excise ticket pasted to it. He read off the fading shipping date. It was fifteen years old.

'I've been thinking about ordering some more,' Wyze said.

Corbec sighed. 'You can't get it any more,' he said. 'The supply's run out.'

'Well, that's a shame,' said the old man.

'Indeed it is.' Corbec could scarcely credit what he was seeing. He – and every other man of Tanith – had assumed that every last part of their world was dead, except for them and the stuff they'd taken off world with them. But here was a piece of Tanith that had survived, spared from the fires. How many other small relics remained, in woodshops and carpenter's stores across the sector?

And how fething right it seemed for it to have found its way here with them. Gaunt believed that fate had bound them to Herodor, that some great, invisible process of coincidence and cosmic synchronicity had tied them to this place and time. And here was the proof of it.

'I was wondering…' Corbec began.

'What?'

'I was wondering what you were doing here. I mean, with the invasion going on. The streets are cleaned out and everyone's pulled back to the hives. Why are you still at work?'

'Reserved occupation,' said Wyze. 'All part of the war effort.'

'Reserved? What's the work, then?'

'Making coffins,' said Wyze. 'We're going to need a lot of them.'

NIGHT WAS FALLING. The fierce fighting in the northern sectors of the Civitas did not abate. It lit the darkness with its flashes and beams. Deeper into the city heart, thousands of yellow fires flickered and glowed, the legacy of the shelling and the constant airstrikes. Every few minutes, Locusts loomed out of the closing darkness and streaked over the Civitas at low level, dropping payloads or firing cannons.

Beyond, in the obsidaes, the invasion force continued to land. The belly lamps of landers, frost white, burning in the air like flares. Rigs of phospha lamps had been built around makeshift drop points and, under their glare, as the cold night wind rose in the desert, armour columns assembled under marshals, and infantry brigades formed up. The glass fields were bright with circles of brilliance. Locust formations criss-crossed the area at speed. Massive transports came in, raising walls of dust, and shook the soil with their land fall. Iris valve belly hatches yawned open along their fat flanks and they gave birth to litters of stalk-tanks. Others landed, ramp mouths open like basking crocodilians, and lines of tracked armour, APCs, self-propelled guns and gref-carriers spewed from them onto the dusty plain.

Overhead, the low, baleful stars of the watching enemy warships shone.

SAUL, THE MARKSMAN, entered the city through the Glass-works sector. He spent most of the first day shadowing the frontline forces as they ploughed into the Civitas, street by street. Saul had no aversion to fighting, but assault scrapping was not his business here on Herodor, so he preferred not to get his hands dirty. He left the slog to the death-brigades and the armour. He spoke to no one, for he was preparing his mind for the task the Magister had set him, but he kept his helmet link open and listened throughout the day to the comm-traffic of his own forces.

Occasionally, he retuned to the enemy channel. It was meant to be encrypted, but their tech-mages had broken the Imperial cryptography in the first few hours of the assault. Saul spoke Low Gothic fluently. He found it useful to under-stand the chatter of the weak souls he preyed on. When, in the middle part of the day, his forces had launched their jam-ming weapons, he'd been frustrated to lose the Imperial signal.

It was back on again now. This pleased him, even though it meant the enemy must have taken out at least a few of the specialist psyker vehicles.

By nightfall, he had reached the junction of Principal VI and Brazen Street. He knew this from his chart-slate. The tech mages in the first wave had almost literally ripped detailed street plans and schematics from the Civitas's tac logis data banks, which were protected by laughably crude protection programs. The information flowed from the tech-mages on the surface back to the warships, where it was collated and transmitted back down to any one with the appropriate field gear. That meant officers, squad leaders, tank chiefs and Saul. A constantly updating, constantly refining picture of the city was made available to him on his hand-held.

The Imperials had fought well on that first day, to give them their credit. They'd held onto the Masonae and Ironhall districts, though it had cost them. By morning, Saul was certain, it would be a different picture.

In the Glassworks, the Imperials had been broken three times during the course of daylight, falling back on each occasion and redoubling their resistance. Monitoring the comm lines, Saul had learned that the Glassworks was defended in the main by local PDF and Regiment Civitas soldiers. Their area commander was a colonel called Vibreson.

This Vibreson was doing well in a bad situation. Nightfall had his forces stalling the Blood Pact push along Brazen Street and the Glass Road hab estates. The death-brigade units Saul had been shadowing all day were now dug in and stationary.

That didn't suit Saul at all. He needed to get on, deeper into the city, where his goal awaited him. He realised the time had come to make an opening for himself.

The Marksman sat down on a kerb beside a torched hab, just a few hundred metres from the fierce front of the fight, and took out his chart. He scrolled the specific map reference onto the little screen and studied it as he listened to the enemy's channel.

Blood Pact units moved up past him, and he ignored them. The night was coming down, and that was his hour, a time to capitalise on shadows and move forward. Night could get him within rifle-range of the target, and then he could simply wait, still and silent like just another corpse, until the moment came.

Saul switched channels and listened for a while to his own side's chatter. Officers, using the name of the Magister as a threat and a promise, were screaming for more armour to push up into the Brazen Street defences and crack them. Saul smiled. That was no good. The Imperials were too well established. Their line would hold for a good time yet.

It would hold against force, that was. Against physical attack.

But Saul had murderous experience of war. Their line would not hold against fear and confusion. Not for a moment. Fear and confusion would do in a minute what it would take a full motor division a day to accomplish.

He flicked back to the Imperial channel. He listened for the word 'Drumroll'. The Imperials – those poor fools – so loved their code names. They thought they were so clever. They never mentioned Vibreson in person, but that was what 'Drumroll' meant. Drumroll was needed at Casten Street. Drumroll was moving with twelve platoon up to Ravenor Crossing. Would Drumroll approve the repositioning of PDF eleven to the Sespre Aqueduct?

Idiots. It was like a child's game, trying to hide the truth from adults. That was always the Imperial failing. They regarded the armies of the warp as scum, so they also assumed they were stupid.

Where was Drumroll now?

'Drumroll, this is Sentry. Respond.'

'Sentry, go. Situation?'

'Taking heavy fire now, major fire. Junction of Brazen and Filipi. Request support.'

'Hang tight, Sentry. Switching rolling one and rolling two to your position in five. Got a shit-storm here on VI. Chapel of Kiodrus under heavy, sustained.'

'Read that, Drumroll. Can you deal?'

'Stand by.'

Saul looked at his slate. He took off his right glove and traced the line of Principal VI with a scar-disfigured middle finger. He kept his right index finger curled protectively against his palm. It was the only part of his hands that was not ritual-scarred. It was his trigger finger, after all.

The Chapel of Kiodrus. There it was. A temple raised to the memory of some half-arsed commander who had stood with the Saint in the early times. Apparently, that made him a big deal.

Saul got to his feet and tucked his slate in his thigh pouch. He put his glove back on and picked up his long-las.

It took him twenty minutes to skirt round the back of the habs, avoiding his own forces as much as the enemy, before he came out onto Principal VI.

He could see the chapel, a tall, dignified place raised from ashlar. Its facade was dented with shell holes. Las crossfire whipped across the roadway in front of it. Smoke hazed the early night air.

Saul crossed to a hab on the other side of the wide avenue, keeping low, and knocked the entry door off its hinges with a single kick. The building was dirty and stale. The stench of decomposing food wafted from the shared larders on each block level.

The Marksman went up five flights and broke into a hab apartment. A glance told him the window view wasn't quite right, so he went back out and up another floor.

Better.

He slid the window up and braced it with a leg he snapped off a chair.

Then he lined up.

Saul fired up his scope. It whirred and blinked, then the image resolved. In green and black, light-boosted, high res. He panned around. The front of the chapel. The side. The alley beside it. The barricades. Now he got winks of brilliant light. Las-fire. The muzzle flash of several cannons. He adjusted the scope's glare setting.

He saw figures. Imperials. Dark blobs. PDF and Regiment Civitas, manning the defences, invisible from the street behind the solid defences, but oh so vulnerable from this lofty viewpoint.

Where are you, Drumroll?

'Drumroll, this is Sentry. Respond, urgent!'

'I hear you, Sentry. Little busy just now.'

'They're pushing hard, Drumroll.'

'Dammit, I said wait!'

Saul panned around again. Figures. An ammo runner scrambling up to the barricade with pannier boxes. A medic, bent over a sprawled body. Three riflemen in cover, firing. A vox-officer on one knee, offering up a speaker horn.

Offering up a speaker horn to a man whose very body language told of frustrated anger.

'Hello, Drumroll,' Saul said softly in Low Gothic, sniggering to himself at the odd sound of it.

He'd taken off his right glove so his hand was bare, and settled it around the grip. His one perfect finger hooked gently against the trigger.

With his gloved left hand he pulled a kill-clip from his belt pouch and snapped it into the long-las's belly.

The weapon pinged and a little red light lit up.

Charged to power.

'In the name of the Beati, Drumroll! We're getting pasted here!'

'Shut up, Sentry! Keep it together. Rolling is inbound to you. Keep it together and no one will get killed.'

Not a promise you're really in any position to make, Saul thought.

He didn't slow his breathing for the shot. He didn't have to. His lungs had been replaced thirty years before by augmetic air-exchangers which did the work with no moving parts and therefore no body motion. He simply shut them off and went rigid, a flesh statue.

The long-las cracked.

Saul pulled the weapon in and sat back against the wall.

'Say again?'

'Down! He's down!'

'Say again, Drumroll!'

'He's dead! Vibreson's dead!'

So much for your silly code names, Saul thought.

FEAR AND CONFUSION. More devastating than a full motor division. The PDF around the chapel panicked when their beloved leader went down. In under fifteen minutes, that panic turned into a fatal flaw.

Rushed by death-brigades, the line broke. It broke at six other places along the Principal at roughly the same time. Headless, the Imperial defenders went into a mindless spiral and were slaughtered.

By midnight, the invaders had smashed their way into the Civitas as far as Loman Street, just a few blocks short of

Astronomer's Circle, deep in the western sectors of the city. Saul followed the tide, walking in its bloody wake through burning streets piled with PDF dead.

Just after midnight, alone and on foot, he pushed past the front-line of his own forces and slipped away into the dark streets of the mid-city and the Guild Slope. The rapidly retreating, badly organised Imperial defences were easy to avoid.

The target awaited him.

THE WAR GRUMBLED far above him like someone else's nightmare. Leg-mounts splashing through warm water, Karess advanced. Where the limestone chambers became too tight and encumbering, he used his cutting beams to burn them smooth and open. The reek of cooked stone and ash filled the air.

Karess couldn't smell it. He couldn't feel the heat. He felt nothing but the machine-induced pain of his being. He strode forward, metre by metre, into the belly of the Civitas.

'THE WEST HAS fallen,' said the life company aide.

Kaldenbach turned to face him, a harrowed look on his face.

'Fallen?'

'Broken, sir. Gone. Vibreson's dead. They're pouring in through the Glassworks now.'

The room, a small sub-chamber in the basement of an Ironhall manufactory, fell silent. The phospha lamps flickered. Vox officers looked up from the portable rigs and apparatus they'd set up in the makeshift command space.

Kaldenbach had been holding the Ironhall for nearly eighteen hours, and was excessively proud of that achievement. The Guard forces under Gaunt in the east had done well too, but Kaldenbach felt their efforts had been nothing compared to those of himself and his men. Two spearheads of the archenemy had struck at the Ironhall, and he'd fended them off.

If the Glassworks had gone, then his entire left flank was open suddenly.

Kaldenbach waved Captain Lamm over to the hololithic tactical display. 'We're down to the wire here, mister. I need you to mount a counter-guard. Here, here and here. Use Principal II as a line defence.'

'Gladly. What can you give me?'

'Nine units. Your own carriers. I'll signal the marshal and get him to send reinforcements up.'

'He needs to do more than that, sir,' said Captain Lamm. 'He needs to extend his forces along the Guild Slope, or we might as well give up now.'

Kaldenbach nodded. 'Get out there, Lamm,' he ordered. 'Vox officer… to me!'

THE NIGHT AIR was bitter and dry. Lamm moved his units forward through the emptied city streets towards the swell of fire light that marked the archenemy advance. They had all switched to rebreathers. Too many processors had been choked and destroyed in the invasion.

Fanning out, his overstretched forces reached Principal II and some of them engaged. Lamm broke into a hab unit and went up to the top floor with a vox man and three of his officers to get a good overview.

Lamm knelt at the sill of an upper floor window and swung his field glasses over the burning, dying Civitas below. Fires and explosions showed up as points of white light so bright they baffled the instrument's filters. 'There,' said Lamm. 'There on the walkway. Bring a unit in there now.'

The vox-man didn't reply.

Lamm looked round, blinking to adjust his sight to the gloomy room. There was no sign of Forbes, his vox-man. Or of his three fellow officers.

Lamm rose, bemused.

'What…?' he began.

He heard something stir in the apartment's adjoining bathroom.

'This is out of order, you idiots!' he barked, drawing his pistol all the same. 'Where the hell are you? Forbes? This is no time for a joke!'

'Respond!'

The crackly voice made Lamm jump. It came from the voxcaster. It was leaning against the wall, straps dangling. There was no sign of the vox-man who had been carrying it.

There was another noise from the bathroom. Lamm raised his pistol and fired at the door. The las-round punched a hole in the fibre-board. Light shone through it. With the snout of his pistol, he pushed the bathroom door open.

The overhead light was on, shade-less, bright, harsh.

Lamm found Forbes and his three officers. They were in the moulded plastic bathtub.

They had been stripped of their clothes and their skins and of all semblance of articulation. The tub was full to the brim with a thick, gleaming bouillabaisse of blood and meat and bones and organs. Blood trickled down the side onto the tiled floor.

Lamm gasped in disbelief then fell to his knees and vomited.

He heard a swish behind him, in the dark. It was the swish of a cloak. A cloak of wet, human skin.

Lamm rolled and fired, blasting shot after shot against the far wall of the room.

He stopped firing and rose, gun clenched in a shaking hand. His own breath rasped in his ears. He swung the gun round, left and right. Had he killed it? Had he?

Lamm's chest suddenly felt warm. He blinked and raised his hand. His chest was awash with thick, hot blood.

His hand went up to his throat and two of his fingers unexpectedly went in through a slit in the flesh that hadn't been there ten seconds before. His fingertips nudged his exposed larynx, neck tendons and oesophagus. His throat had been cut. He felt no real pain, just enormous surprise.

Skarwael finished his artistry. His boline, double-bladed, each edge mono-molecular sharp, punched into Lamm's teetering, choking form. He revealed the length of the spine while the man was still standing upright, and cut down through his kidneys and lumbar muscles.

Blood squirted out under pressure. Skarwael opened his mouth and stuck out his long, grey tongue as it spattered over him.

Lamm fell over onto his face.

Skarwael smeared the blood on his cheeks up and around his deep eye sockets. It made them seem even blacker and deeper against his stretched, white flesh.

He sighed. He would not be so patient and merciful with the Beati.

PATER SIN HUSHED his eyeless charges and cuddled them to his sides. They were walking down the middle of Principal I in the dark, fires around them, and the runt psykers were skittish. They were right in the middle of the wide highway.

Figures emerged from cover ahead of them. Imperial men. Their lasguns were raised. They shouted challenges, certain no enemy would approach so brazenly and out in the open. A shell-shocked pilgrim and his children, in desperate need of help, wandering blind... that's who they were...

Sin leant down and whispered into the ears of his runts and they trembled. They opened their wet, slit mouths wide. A deep buzzing filled the air.

The Imperial troopers came to a halt and turned to look at one another dimly. Then they opened fire. Within five seconds they were all dead, comrade killed by comrade.

The little malformed creatures closed their mouths and Sin used the hem of his silk robes to dab the spittle away from the corners of their mouths. Then he took them by the hands, one on each side, and led them on past the scattered bodies. The psykers stumbled, reluctant, like very young children. One began to open and close its mouth in a soft, agitated manner. The other had his free arm up and crooked, and was waving his hand back and forth next to his ear.

'We're almost there,' Sin crooned over and over to his runts. 'Almost there...'

VIKTOR HARK CREPT forward through the firelit rubble of the Masonae. His plasma pistol was drawn.

'Mkendrick?' he voxed impatiently. 'Mkendrick? Where the feth are you?'

There was no response from eighteen platoon. They had been holding the cross street at Armonsfahl Boulevard West, but they hadn't answered standard vox in fifteen minutes.

Hark didn't need this delay. His mind was on Soric. He wasn't sure how to break it to Gaunt, but his duty was clear. Soric had to die. He was a liability. A psyk-stain. He was a danger. Meryn had been right. Even Soric's own men, people like Vivvo, couldn't hide him any longer.

Hark felt sad about it. Soric was a good man and the Verghastite Ghosts loved him. But that didn't hide the truth that Soric was too lethal to live. Far, far too lethal. He needed a round in the head before it came to anything worse.

That was a commissar's job. In simple terms. In black and white. That was the duty. And Hark was nothing if not a slave to duty.

Hark tripped and fell flat on his face. His pistol bounced away into the street shadows. He cursed his stupid self and looked back at what he'd fallen over.

Hark froze.

He'd tripped over Mkendrick. The Tanith was dead, exploded, ripped apart. In the street around, Hark slowly resolved the other bodies in the darkness. Lentrim, Mkauley, Dill, Commo… all the men and women of eighteen platoon. All dead.

'Oh Holy Terra…' Hark mumbled and reached for his micro-bead. Then he froze again. Above the smell of soot and blood, he could suddenly detect a stink like crushed mint, and rancid milk.

He glanced up and saw them.

Sliding their clammy grey hides against one another, the triplets slithered down the street. Though three, they moved sinuously as one. Their weapon frames clacked as they reloaded.

Hark reached for his fallen plasma pistol, but it was too far away. Rolling, he wrenched out his back-up, a snub-nose Hostec Livery hard-slug revolver.

He fired it. The cut-nose round smacked into the greasy flank of one of the loxatl, and it began to hiss and whistle like a kettle on a burner ring.

Its two brethren fired their flechette cannons.

Hark rocked, as if caught in the slipstream of some large, fast-moving vehicle that had passed close by. But he did not fall, nor did he feel any pain. He looked round slowly. Three metres away from him, he saw his left arm, cleanly severed, lying in a widening pool of arterial blood. He couldn't see out of his left eye either.

With an angry, helpless cry, Hark slumped over onto his back and began the swift and involuntary job of bleeding to death.

TEN
THE SECOND DAY

*'Our high and mighty Lord General Lugo
says "victory or death!"
What gives him the idea we're being offered a choice?'*

— Rawne

A FEW MINUTES before sunrise on the second day, from his command post high in the hives, Lugo sent out the order to withdraw.

With the north-western suburbs of the Civitas wide open, the Ironhall district came under increasing pressure during the second half of the night, and Kaldenbach had finally, reluctantly, signalled that his forces could no longer hold onto it.

When the order reached Gaunt, he cursed even though he saw the sense of it. If Kaldenbach fell back, the Masonae would be left alone, a salient vulnerable to the pincer of the archenemy forces flowing in around it.

The northern Civitas sectors had to be given up.

Fortunately, Kaldenbach was a sound leader and a man of method. He did not simply throw his overstretched forces into flight. He knew the vital importance of a measured retreat, knew that ground must be given only for tactical consolidation. He coordinated with Gaunt so that the entire line could be withdrawn as cleanly as possible, supplying mutual cover and support.

It was a tough and bloody process, and it took five hours. On more than a dozen occasions, it nearly failed. Twice, PDF armour on the Glassworks flank retreated too fast, without provisioning cover for the infantry sections north of it, and created gaps that Kaldenbach managed to plug through the narrowest of luck. Then a charge of enemy AFVs against Kaldenbach's own command section almost managed a coup de grâce which was only held off by an improvised counterstrike by men of the Regiment Civitas. Gaunt's withdrawing sections were harried by airstrikes, three of which damaged the line badly and led to precarious moments of redeployment as invader units tried to capitalise on the weaknesses. Then Daur's units were sent east along Farkindle Street to take the pressure off a brace of platoons trying to withdraw under fire, but found their route impossibly blocked by a street-wide firestorm. Raglon's platoon, already backed into a certain measure of safety, extemporised courageously, and pushed forward again, in time to provide the cover Daur had been prevented from supplying.

Any one of these near-disasters might have cut a hole in the retreating Guard line, and that would have quickly ensured a miserable doom for every soldier in the withdrawing forces.

In the hour before noon, under a pale sky leaden with the smoke of the burning outer city, the last of Gaunt's and Kaldenbach's forces reached the defences of the Guild Slope and were absorbed into the second line. To their north, at their heels, the monstrous regiments of the archenemy surged down through the abandoned suburbs to begin the concentrated assault of the Guild Slope.

The second phase of the battle for the Civitas Beati had begun.

SHELLS AND OTHER ranged munitions were now falling on the inner city, and striking the hive towers too. The explosions dotting the vast faces of the soaring hives seemed like match-sparks on the slopes of mountains, but the damage was progressive. Heavier artillery was advanced from the obsidaes to positions inside the captured north up-city. The enemy's airpower also began to concentrate its attacks on the hive superstructures. Anti-fighter batteries on the roofs and upper levels of all four hive towers, most of them hastily erected during the previous days, set up brusque resistance. From the Guild Slope, the display was intense, even if smoke cover frequently obscured it: the attack craft, zipping and circling like flies through air striped and fretted with tracer and laser fire and the blossom of detonations.

Other sounds rolled in across the Civitas too: ghastly sounds. Filthy proclamations of warp-texts were flooding the vox channels, or being broadcast from the speakers of advancing armour at high volume.

The fallen prayer horn, Gorgonaught, was set back on its shot-up tower and directed at the hives. Through it, obscenity was blasted, often the amplified screams of Imperial troops, citizens or pilgrims captured during the first phase. The aural assault chilled and unsettled the already rattled and weary defenders. Life company commissars – the Keetle twins especially – were kept busy chastening, by execution, those soldiers whose mettle broke under the psychological torment.

For it became hard to think. It became hard to want to be alive. By the early afternoon, though the effects of the noise bombardment had yet to fully penetrate the interior of the hive towers, all those in the open Guild Slope and mid-city, including the bulk of the defenders, were sweating and sick. Nerves were frayed, stomachs acid and swilling. Even so, they had to fight on. The death-brigades assaulted the Guild Slope from north-east and north-west. At the barricades, defence lines and strong points, Imperial troopers fought and died with tears in their eyes, driven to anguish by the sputtering, hissing sounds of evil incarnate.

SORIC HAD STOPPED reading the message shell notes that came to him. The writing had become increasingly spidery and frantic, and where it was legible, it was simply abuse. He was a *weak fool*. He was a *coward*. He was *gakking scum*. The author, whatever it was, whatever part of him it might be, had become incoherent and desperate.

He rested his platoon for fifteen minutes between artillery barrages, and sat on his own in a doorway, hunched up, hands twitching, smoking a lho-stick. There was a taste of bile in his mouth that would not go away, and his eye kept watering. He kept looking for Hark. Hark knew.

Soric had been a brave man all his life. For all the sickness and fear he felt, now more than ever he knew Milo had been right. Soric just had to be brave enough now to do it the right way.

If it wasn't already too late.

'MOHR!' SORIC SHOUTED as he got up and squashed the stub underfoot. His unit's vox-officer ran up smartly.

'Find Gaunt for me, if you please.'

Mohr nodded, set his caster down, and started to speak into the horn as he adjusted the tuning dials.

'Heading for the field station on Tarif Street, chief.'

Soric checked his chart. Tarif Street was close.

'He's been summoned to see Commissar Hark, chief,' Mohr added.

Soric's face darkened. Too late, too late, too late...

'Vivvo!' he yelled.

'Chief?'

'You have platoon command here for the duration, lad. Listen to orders and make a good job of it.'

'Chief? Where are you going? Chief?'

But Soric was already thumping away down the street.

FILMY GREY SMOKE from tank shelling wafted down the narrow roadway in the Guild Slope. Ornate guild-owned warehouses stood on either side of the cobbled lane, and to the south, up the gentle incline, the colossal masses of the hive towers rose above the rooftops.

There was little, Varl considered, that distinguished this particular street from the one immediately north of it, or the one directly south. They were all part of the mid-city maze, all shell-pummelled and smoke-choked.

This street, however, marked the second line, the defensive ring around the mid-city to which all Imperial forces had withdrawn. More particularly, this street was the assigned part of the second line that was his platoon's duty to hold. A block away to the west was a company of PDF riflemen. A block to the east, Varl had it on good authority – well, tac logis at least – was a quartet of life company tanks. He hadn't seen them, but he trusted they were there.

Since noon, it had been quiet in his immediate neighbourhood, apart from the echoing torment of the archenemy's broadcasts and a single push-assault from a Blood Pact death-brigade that his men had discouraged with their excellently positioned enfilade.

Varl took a squint down the street where the men of number nine platoon were all in cover, waiting. He saw Baen, his platoon's scout, hurrying back to him from a foray down to the crossroads.

Pater Sin and his two charges were walking in step behind Baen.

Varl slid a lho-stick out of his jacket pocket and held it out to Brostin, in cover beside him. Brostin obligingly singed the tip of his sergeant's smoke with the hot-blue pilot light of his flamer.

Drawing deep and exhaling, Varl nodded to Baen as he drew close. The Pater and the psykers were virtually at Baen's heels.

'Anything?' Varl asked.

Baen shook his head. 'Not a fething sign. I checked the crossroads and just over. They're shelling Katz Street for all they're worth, poor PDF bastards. But nothing. Except–'

'Except what?'

Baen shrugged. Sin placed his massive hands firmly on the shoulders of his two runts and walked them forward. All three passed between Varl and Baen.

'Got this funny feeling we're being watched,' said Baen.

Varl smiled. 'It's nothing. Just edge. We all feel it.'

Sin paused, and kept his psykers huddled close to him as he stepped back and gazed into Varl's face. He recognised the man's uniform. Tanith. These men were Ghosts. The ones who had robbed him of his victory on Hagia. He'd come so close there, and had only escaped with his life thanks to a warning from his guide psykers. Very few of his breed had escaped Hagia alive.

Resentment and vengeance simmered inside him. Sin's lips curled back from his implanted steel fangs. These were the wretches who had denied him. This one, a sergeant by his markings, slovenly, casual, disfigured by an augmetic shoulder. A worthless little bastard who–

For a moment, Sin almost let the psyk-cloak drop so they could see him. He could kill them all, slaughter them, turning their own guns on them.

But patience and devotion to his sworn duty kept him true. He'd over-taxed his children already, and he wanted them strong and refreshed for the work ahead. They were tired, and that made them harder to control. One of them persisted in waving his hand. Masking was easier than goading, otherwise he'd have turned this street into a charnel place to make passage.

Besides, his revenge on the Tanith would be total when his work was complete. These men would all be dead soon. Better still, they would die stripped of all hope and faith.

He led his children away, up the climbing street. They crossed three more blocks, ignored by the Imperial defenders, and then turned directly south. Sin put his hands flat on the tops of his psykers' heads. They both winced and murmured.

Sin felt his way. He was close enough now.

He hurried the pair of them off the roadway into a covered market. The produce shops were all closed up and shuttered, and wooden screens had been partially raised to protect the glass roof.

He led the runts down the tiled walkway of one of the marketplace's aisles, and then crouched them down behind a buttonmaker's cart.

Sin soothed them with his low, sweet moaning, and lulled them into a calm, trance state by repeated use of their ritual command words.

They both became motionless. Even the waving stopped.

'Reach out,' he whispered. 'Find the instrument…'

His tattooed skin flushed and prickled as he felt their nightmarish minds seethe and boil. The low buzzing began. Slowly, a street at a time, they reached out, hunting.

Hunting for the flawed. The dangerous. The suitable.

There was one. No, too strong.

There! Another, weaker… but, no. Injured.

Another… and it recoiled, too fragile to be imprinted.

'More, more…' he soothed.

There…

RAWNE BLINKED. He put his hand to his mouth, coughed, and when he brought the hand away again, the palm was wet with aspirated blood.

'You all right?' Banda asked.

Rawne didn't answer her. He started to walk away towards the exit that led out from the hab into the street.

'Major?' Banda called, more urgently.

'Major Rawne?' Caffran said, getting up out of cover at a broken window to hurry after his platoon leader.

'As you were, trooper,' Rawne said sharply, and coughed again.

Outside, tank rounds from the latest wave of Blood Pact assault whizzed and thumped into the nearby manufactories. Small-arms fire rattled and cracked up the open street.

Leyr, three platoon's scout, was watching the door, head down, and looked in dismay as Rawne started to walk past him.

'Sir!'

'Get out of my way,' said Rawne.

'Sir!' Leyr cried, more insistently. 'You'll be dead in five seconds if you stick your head out of that d–'

He reached out a hand to grab Rawne's arm. Rawne lashed around, blood dripping from his nose. His fist caught Leyr around the side of the head and smacked the scout to the ground.

Feygor lunged, leaping over the sprawled Leyr and crashing into Rawne. He brought the major down hard in the doorway, nudging the wooden door open. Enemy fire, fierce and unabating, smashed into the door and its surround, filling the air with wood chips and dust.

Rawne had landed on his back. Prone, he lashed out a kick with both legs that propelled Feygor, doubled up, right across the room, and also flipped Rawne back onto his feet. Caffran came in fast from the side, throwing a punch that Rawne blocked with a raised forearm. Caffran rallied with another smash, and Rawne turned that away with a hard, open palm, sidestepping Caffran's third blow, and elbowed the trooper in the throat.

Caffran fell down on all fours, gasping. Leyr was up again by then, swinging a hook at the side of Rawne's head. Rawne grabbed the scout's wrist and twisted so hard it almost broke. Leyr cried out in pain, and fell to his knees. Feygor clubbed Rawne across the shoulders and neck with both fists locked together.

Rawne staggered, blood flying from his nose. He swung out with a side kick that threw Feygor back against the wall, and then turned and staggered towards the door.

Banda brought him down.

She rolled Rawne over under her, and pressed her straight silver to his neck. Desperate, she glared down into his face.

'Elim! Elim! What the gak are you trying to do?'

He looked up at her, and then went limp, his unfocused eyes refocusing.

'Feth…' he stammered.

She climbed off him, keeping her warknife raised, point towards him. Rawne got up as Caffran, Feygor and Leyr closed in again.

Rawne blinked at them all.

'Caff? Jessi? Murt? What the feth was I just doing…?'

No! Too STRONG. Too willful. Too beloved by other souls that anchored him and dragged him back.

The twins were upset. They started to howl and whimper, and the buzzing leaked out of their open mouths.

'Sssshhh!' Sin cooed at them. 'There'll be another. Find him. Find the instrument. Reach out.'

Calming, they sent out their minds again.

There was one… no, too agitated.

Another… useless, about to be killed by the Blood Pact.

'Find one, find one… find the one who will serve and mark him out. Imprint him. Brand him with the purpose. Make him the instrument…'

The twin minds stopped with a sudden jolt. For a moment, Sin thought he'd have to start again, but then he realised they had stopped because they had found exactly what they were looking for.

Without doubt.

Pater Sin smiled. Through his empathic rapport with the runts, he could taste the chosen instrument's mind. It was delicious. *Perfect.*

'Brand that one!' he hissed, and the imprinting began.

BRIN MILO BLINKED. His head hurt and he was beyond any fatigue he had ever known.

'You need to sleep,' she said.

Milo looked up. He wasn't sure if it had been an instruction or an assessment. He couldn't tell with her.

'I'm tired,' he said.

Sabbat smiled. 'We're all tired, Milo. But it won't be much longer now. Fate has made its decision. It's coming.'

He wondered if she meant the overwhelming assault that was falling on their position at the second line, but she seemed to be gazing at the sky for some reason.

Milo was caked in dust and cut in a dozen places from shrapnel. Most of Domor's platoon, moving with them, were the same. The Beati was unmarked and unblemished. If anything, her pale skin and golden armour seemed brighter and cleaner than ever.

'How will this end?' he asked.

'The way fate wishes it,' she replied.

'You seem to trust in fate,' he said. 'I thought you'd trust in the God-Emperor.'

'If there is any law, any justice to this cosmos, Milo, they're the same thing. I have found my way, and the way is set.'

Rocket grenades slammed into the buildings west of them, and in their wake came a ripple of mortar rounds. Milo heard Domor yelling for his platoon to fall back. Milo got up and led the Beati after them.

All around the vaunted second line, the Imperials were withdrawing now. Before nightfall, it would be street fighting right back through the Guild Slope towards the hives. They were losing.

Fighting hard, fighting well, but losing anyway.

Milo and Sabbat got into cover, hearing the clank of advancing enemy tanks and the crunch of broken walls driven over under churning treads.

'I knew someone once who said that,' Milo said.

'Said what?' she asked, wiping dust from her sword blade.

'That she was looking for her way. That she had found her way.'

'Had she?'

'I don't know. She said that she thought her way was in war… but I didn't believe her.'

Sabbat frowned. 'Why? Wasn't she telling the truth?'

Milo laughed and shook his head. 'Nothing like that. I just don't know if she realised what war means.'

'What was her name?'

'Sanian. Her name was Sanian. I knew her for a while on Hagia. We were protecting y–'

'I know what you were doing on Hagia, Milo.'

Milo shrugged. 'I think I was in love with her. She was very strong. Very beautiful. I would have stayed with her if I could.'

'What stopped you?' asked the Beati. She turned and waved Domor's .50 crew up to a spot where they could crossfire the advancing death-brigade push.

'Duty?' Milo suggested.

'Duty is its own reward,' she said.

'So they say,' he replied.

'Who am I?' she asked, leaning close to him.

'You are Sabbat. You are the Beati,' he answered.

She nodded. 'He'll soon be coming.'

'Who?'

'The reason I'm here and not elsewhere. The reason we're all here.'

'I don't understand.'

'You will,' she said. Another RPG fell close to them and blew in a wall ten paces from where they were concealed. Milo gasped.

'Are you hurt?' she asked.

'My head. I have the worst headache.'

The Beati nodded. She crawled back under the firing line and called to Domor.

'Shoggy!' She was delighted by the way his smile lit up when he heard her use his nickname.

'Pull them back to Saenz Crossing. Get them dug in. Armour support is coming.'

'How do you know that, Holiness?' Domor called back. 'The vox is down!'

'Trust me,' she said. 'Do it. I won't be long.'

SOMEHOW OBLIVIOUS TO – or invulnerable to – the shells and crossfire drumming around them, she led Milo through the devastated streets to a small Civitas chapel whose roof had been taken off by the recent efforts of the archenemy. The chapel had been dedicated to Faltornus.

The cracked rafters smouldered, and the floor was littered with chafstone tiles and broken pews. She beckoned him forward across the debris until they were standing in front of the aquila altarblock. Milo's head throbbed and rolled. He could hear how close to the bloody front of the fight they were. Why had she brought him here? She was so vital, so valuable. She was taking such a risk. This was crazy...

With gentle hands, she turned his dirty face towards the altar and pressed the middle three fingers of her right hand against his brow.

In a second, a single wonderful second of glass-cold clarity, his headache cleared and he saw everything.

Everything.

'You know it all now. Will you stand with me?'

'I would have done anyway.'

'I know. But I mean it. Gaunt does not understand. Will you stand with me, even in the face of his displeasure? I know you love him like a father.'

'This is too important, Sabbat. I will. And Gaunt will understand.'

Sabbat nodded. A golden glow seemed to back-light her eyes. 'Let us–'

'I think we should make observance first,' Milo said. 'I mean, this undertaking is so dangerous, we should offer a prayer to the God-Emperor... to fate... while we still have a chance.'

'You're right. You're here to remind me such things are right,' she said. They settled to their knees before the altar.

SAUL SUCKED IN his breath. The tagger points of his scope now blinked on empty space. Just a second before, he'd had a near-perfect shot. The broken lancet window looking into the Chapel of Faltornus, five hundred metres, negligible crosswind... no adjustment he couldn't make.

For a while, she'd been screened by the boy, the young Guard trooper, who'd kept getting in the line of sight. Saul was confident one of his custom rounds would penetrate the boy's body and waste the Beati too, but he didn't want to risk it. Neither did he want the impurity. He wanted a clean headshot. The Beati. In his sights. As the Magister would have wanted it. One shot.

But the bloody boy would not get out of the way. Not until the last minute, when he had disappeared suddenly below the level of the broken sill. Kneeling, presumably.

For one brief moment, the Beati was exposed, a clear shot through the broken lancet.

Then she too dropped from view beside the boy. What were they doing? Praying, he supposed. As if that would do any good now.

Saul slid his long-las back from the gap. The hab he was in was almost a kilometre long, bridging over six Guild Slope streets, and there were windows all along it. He could easily slip down to another firing position and get her on the way back up.

Saul started to gather his kit up and paused. He suddenly felt that rush only a sniper ever feels. He ducked.

SIX HUNDRED PLUS metres west, Hlaine Larkin raised his aim and sighed. He could have sworn he'd seen something at that hab window. A shooter lining up. Gone now.

Sliding quietly to one side, he touched his micro-bead.

'See him?'

A pause. 'No.'

'Keep her looking,' Larkin said. 'He's there. I swear.'

* * *

SAUL SNUGGLED UP against a window five arches down and took the scope off his gun. He peered out, using the device free, like a telescope. There was the chapel. Still no movement.

He waited. How long does a prayer last?

He couldn't shake off that feeling, that six sense *rush*.

Just to be safe, he dropped back to the next window.

He scoped again. This time, a movement. The briefest suggestion of heads.

He fitted his scope back onto his long-las and rolled over to the window's far corner, lining up.

The prayer finished, Milo and Sabbat rose back into view. He saw her nod to him and say something. Saul had his shot. Clean… no, the boy was in the way *again*. If he leant out further…

THERE HE WAS! Larkin tensed and then slumped back. He saw movement in the hab window, but a chimney stack was blocking direct shot from his position.

'Have you got it? Tell me you've got it!' he snarled into his vox-link.

SAUL'S UNSCARRED FINGER began to squeeze the trigger. There was a crack-whine, a distant echo, and for one glorious moment, Saul thought he'd fired.

But the counter on his lasgun still read full.

Exploded by a hot-shot round, Saul's head came away entirely. His corpse, smoking at the neck, fell back into the hab. The long-las clattered from his hands, unfired.

'SHE GOT HIM, Larks!' Jajjo voxed gleefully.

Kneeling beside him, in the shelter of the dorm window, Nessa Bourah raised her smoking long-las and grinned.

THE RECIRCULATED AIR in the Tarif Street triage was clammy, and stank of chemicals. A stream of trucks, driven by civilian volunteers, nosed into the yard, shifting the mobile wounded back to the infirmaries in the hives. Gaunt pushed his way in through the crowds of casualties. Screams and moans and frantic voices came at him from all sides.

'Where's Dorden?' Gaunt yelled.

Foskin, his smock spattered with blood, glanced up from a thrashing life company trooper on a stretcher and pointed down the hall.

'Doctor?'

Dorden appeared through a makeshift screen made from a plastic sheet nailed to a door frame. He too was soiled in blood, and his face was sunk with fatigue.

'In here,' he said.

Several orderlies were lifting Hark onto a trolley for evacuation to the hives. Gaunt could barely see the commissar under the plastic hood of the medicae respirator and the sterile packing wadded to his left side. Thick IV drips and other tubes snaked out of his body, hooked up to fluid packs hanging from a wire stand at the head of the gurney, and to a resuscitrex unit and a haemopump stowed underneath.

'Feth...' said Gaunt. He glanced at Dorden.

'Massive trauma to the left body. Lost his arm, his left eye, his ear, and a lot of bone mass and tissue. Grell's boys found him, got him back here. He'd almost bled out.'

'Will he make it?'

The floor shook.

'Will any of us?' Dorden asked darkly.

'You know what I mean!'

Dorden sighed. 'He's strong. Determined. He might. We're shipping him back for intensive. Ibram...'

'What?'

'When Grell found him, Hark was surrounded by the corpses of Mkendrick and his entire platoon.'

'All... all dead?'

'Yes. Grell said it was like a butcher's shop. Something really did a number on them.'

'The Blood Pact are–'

Dorden shook his head, and picked up a little stainless steel surgical dish. He held it out. Several objects lay in it, matted with blood. Gaunt reached in to take one, curious.

'Don't,' Dorden said. 'Unless you want to slice off your finger tips.'

'Are they what I think they are?'

Dorden nodded. 'Blade slivers from a loxatl flechette round. I dug them out of Hark's shoulder.'

'God-Emperor, they're throwing everything at us.'

'It's the only report I've had of loxatl injuries, but I thought you should know.'

'Thanks,' Gaunt said. 'I need to get back out there.'

'One more I want you to see,' said Dorden.

The ward room was reserved for the most seriously injured, including those that Dorden didn't dare move. The doctor led Gaunt over to a corner bunk where a Tanith trooper lay on vital support. It was Costin, the drunk whose carelessness had damaged Raglon's platoon so badly on Aexe.

'You heard what Raglon's platoon did this afternoon?' Dorden asked.

Gaunt nodded. He was proud of them. They'd improvised a cover action when Daur had been cut off, and in doing so had saved more than seventy men.

'Raglon brought Costin in. Gut-shot in the fight. Probably won't last the day. But Raglon wanted him cared for particularly. The cover action was Costin's work. Raglon told me this himself. Raglon got pinned down, so Costin took point and led the platoon in. Set up some fierce cover. Got all those men out. Raglon wants to recommend him for valour.'

Gaunt looked at Dorden. Weariness had robbed the medic of his usual subtlety.

'So if I'd had my way and executed Costin on Aexe, all these lives would have been forfeit. You're saying I should thank you for–'

'Don't be an arse, Gaunt!' Dorden snarled, turning away. 'I was just telling you how it was.'

'You're right,' said Gaunt. Dorden stopped. 'I'm a commissar, and you're a medic. There are always going to be times when our first duties clash... clash in the worst ways. Hard discipline and selfless care do not overlap comfortably. I suppose it's a problem two friends on either side of that divide have to live with.'

'I suppose it is.

'But now, here... I'm sorry. You were right.'

Dorden looked away, awkwardly. 'Okay, then. Haven't you got a war to win or something?'

GAUNT PUSHED HIS way back out through the screen and found himself facing Soric in the hallway.

'Chief? What are you doing here?'

Soric's face was set firmly. 'I'm sorry, sir. I hope you will believe me when I say I meant no harm. I was always loyal, despite what he might tell you.'

'Who? What is this?'

'Just do me one thing, sir. Hear me out and then make it quick.'

'Make what quick, Agun?'

'My execution, sir.'

'Soric? What the feth are you talking about?'

'I know Hark's told you everything, sir. I blame myself for not coming forward earlier.'

The plastic screen behind Gaunt wrenched back, and three orderlies emerged, wheeling Hark's gurney to the boarding ramp.

Soric's eyes widened as he saw the body roll past.

'I'm here because Hark's been hit bad, Soric. He's not been in a position to say anything to me. So... why don't you?'

Soric straightened up, pulling his ramshackle bulk to attention. 'Colonel-Commissar, sir. It is my duty and my shame to admit to you here that I... I have the touch of the warp in me. It's been in me since Phantine, and I have pretended for too long. The curse of the psyker corrupts my mind. I have been receiving messages, sir. Guidance, advice, warnings. All of them have been true. I am so sorry, sir.'

'Is this a joke, Soric?'

'No, sir. I wish it was.'

Gaunt was stunned. 'You realise I can take no chances, Sergeant? I have no choice. If there is any truth in this... if you are warp-touched, I must–'

'I know it, sir.'

'What are you going to do, Gaunt? Shoot him?' Dorden stood behind Gaunt. He'd overheard the whole exchange.

'I don't believe even selfless medics take chances with the warp, doctor.'

'This isn't some enemy warp-scum, Ibram,' Dorden said. 'It's fething Agun Soric!'

'Don't fight my corner, doc,' Soric said. 'Please, it's not right. You know yourself what's in me. Back on Phantine, with Corbec. I know it spooked you.'

Both Gaunt and Dorden remembered the incident well. It had indeed rattled them.

'It's been getting worse since then. A lot worse.' Soric seemed to be getting agitated, as if there was something alive in his pocket that was nagging at him.

'Standard practice says I should shoot you right here,' said Gaunt. 'But it's you, Agun, and I've never heard of a warp-freak turning himself in. Duty troopers?'

Three sentries from the Herodian PDF hurried over. 'Take this man's weapons, and his rank pins, and bind his limbs. Escort him to the hives and lock him down in the securest cell they have. If he tries anything, shoot him. And when you get to the hive, summon the local Guild Astropathicae to examine him.'

'Yes sir.'

'Sir, please. Before they take me. I have to warn you.'

'Agun, go. Before I change my mind.'

'Sir, please!' The troopers grabbed Soric, and pinned him hard. 'Please! For the good of us all! It told me nine are coming! Nine are coming! They will kill her and the blood will be on my hands! Please, sir! In the name of all that's holy! Please listen to me!'

Dragged by the troopers, shouting, Soric disappeared down the busy triage station hallway.

'Should you have listened?' Dorden asked.

Gaunt shook his head. 'Either he's snapped under pressure, in which case, I lament his passing, because he was a damn good soldier. Or... he's warp-touched like he says he is. I favour the former explanation. Whichever, he has nothing to say that I should trust. The rantings of a lunatic, or the perverse lies of the warp.'

'Because the warp never reveals truth to mankind?'

'Not to the untrained and the unsanctioned, doctor. No, it doesn't.'

* * *

'PSYKER TRICKS,' SAID Corbec. 'Sounds like it to me.'

'Fething psykers,' Feygor agreed.

'Felt like it had hold of my mind. I wasn't me any more. I...' Rawne's voice trailed off.

'What?' asked Corbec.

'If I hadn't shaken it off, Colm. Feth. I was going to kill her.'

'Who, Banda?'

'Feth, no! Her. The Beati.'

Feygor swore colourfully. It sounded, as always, curiously funny coming out of his flat-pitched augmetic voice box.

'Something got in your head and made you decide to kill the Saint?' Caffran asked.

Rawne shrugged. He couldn't tell them the truth. How would they ever trust him again?

Something had got into his head, all right. Something so soft and strong and seductive, he'd forgotten everything. Every loyalty, every friendship, every oath he'd ever sworn, even his startling intense affection for Jessi Banda.

All of it, forgotten. The only thing that had remained had been his ruthless streak of hate. His killer instinct. The part of his character that made others eternally wary of him, the part of his character that made sure Ibram Gaunt never quite turned his back.

The very, very worst part of him. It had swelled and grown and taken over his mind, body and soul completely. For that brief moment, he would have happily killed anything and anyone.

Then it had gone again, rushing out like a fast ebbing tide.

One terrible thought remained. If it had done that to him, what might it do to others? If it had cast him aside, where had it gone now?

MILO BLINKED AGAIN, his mind unsteady. He was so damn tired. The effects of the Beati's touch were fading, and the headache was returning. Voices seemed to be calling, as from a dream, as from the edge of sleep.

'You okay there, Brin?' Dremmond asked.

'Yeah, sure,' Milo said.

Twelve platoon was retreating carefully down a low alley in the Guild Slope, falling back towards the hives. The second

line hadn't broken so much as compressed. Shells sang overhead from the massed enemy batteries down in the suburbs.

The sun was setting. Already, it was out of sight behind the
rooftops. By nightfall, they would be into the hives, sealing
the hatches, making those massive towers the site of their last
stand.

Domor suddenly held up a hand, and the troopers in his
company dropped into cover positions.

All, except the Beati. Gleaming bright, she walked down
the alley to the head of the position, in open view.

'Get down!' Milo hissed.

'Get down, ma'am!' Domor added, urgently.

A death-brigade stormed the street. They came running,
howling, charging, weapons blasting. Stone flecks exploded
off the alley's side walls as they advanced.

Milo sighted up and fired. His shot brought down the closest of the iron-masked Blood Pact. The men around him
began to fire too.

Sabbat stood her ground, her power sword whirling, rico-
cheting las-rounds off in all directions. She gutted the first
two Blood Pacters who reached her, and decapitated the next
one.

'Into them! Into them! Straight silver!' Domor yelled, and
the platoon rose and charged, surging up around the defiant
Beati, meeting the enemy head on.

Milo ran forward, his head pounding. He lanced his rifle-
mounted warknife into the face of the nearest Blood Pact
trooper, twisting it to pull it free.

He saw her. She looked so vulnerable. Just one shot. One
last shot, and she'd be finished.

He threw himself against the enemy tide.

THE LAST DREGS of fading daylight filtered slantwise through the
partially shuttered glass hoarding of the covered market, and
gleamed off Pater Sin's steel teeth as he mouthed soothing
words to his twins. They had done their work. They were
linked to the instrument, and with each passing moment, they
were imprinting the task deeper and deeper into its mind.

The twins were the most potent psykers in the sector. They
were alpha level. Between them, their combined minds

packed more power than all the astropaths and psykers on Herodor, Imperial and foe alike.

His children. The children of Sin.

KARESS WAS SUBMERGED now, ten metres deep in chalybeate spring water that pushed at him, heavy with current. Beads of escaped gas twinkled along the seams of his adamite casing and around the perforated cowls of his heavy weapons. His auditory tracts rippled with the *swoosh* of aquatic pressure.

The rock base of the aquifer was soft, and Karess's massive hooves churned up silt and eyeless mote-creatures, bacterium and thermal scum.

Machine-pain thrummed through his superstructure. He checked his positioning systems.

True south, true south. There, he would rise and kill.

TLFEH WAS DEAD. The human's bullet had lodged deep inside it and killed it. Chto, who had brood command, ordered Reghh to let Tlfeh drop. The cold, rank body slipped to the ground. Chto and Reghh stood up on their heels and howled at the sky in mourning. There was no sound audible to human ears, just a deep, sickening throb that shook the air.

Wet and gleaming, the two remaining loxatl wound round each other and slithered away down the next street.

Their harness cannons were armed. Woe betide anything that met them now.

'ORDERS, SIR!' THE signals officer yelled. Major Landfreed ran over to him, ducking down below the parapet. Shrapnel fluttered through the air from the nearby bombardment.

Orders were for the life company elements under Landfreed to fall back to Old Hive.

Landfreed relayed the orders to his men. Since noon, he had lost sixty troopers to the Blood Pact death-brigades. He was determined that those who remained would stay alive. His men started to move out: two squads, tight order.

A hi-ex shell landed just the other side of the ruined wall and the blast shook the ground. Tiles rattled down from the remains of the rafters. Landfreed threw himself down hard.

When he got up again, he was surrounded by smoke. He couldn't see any of his men.

Blinking, his eyes watering, he peered around, and found himself face to face with a black-robed figure that appeared out of nowhere.

Landfreed froze. Terror locked up his limbs and his reflexes. He gazed up into a face materialising just twenty centimetres from his.

It was bald and white, and utterly hairless. Deep folds criss-crossed the skin, and made furrows around the smiling mouth and the dark eyes. A dried, brown residue soiled the eye-sockets. It was the face of death, the bogey man that Landfreed had been taught to fear.

The haunter of the dark.

Skarwael slowly slid the tip of his boline up Landfreed's tunic front, effortlessly slicing off every button in turn. The silver fastenings cascaded to the floor, bouncing and clattering.

Skarwael's boline stopped when it reached Landfreed's bare throat.

Skarwael smiled. The smile made furrows deepen. Predatory teeth, whiter than the pallid flesh that cased them, were distressingly revealed.

Landfreed tried to find a scream.

'Sir? Sir? Major Landfreed?' Some of his men – Sanchez, Grohowski, Landis, Boles – came blundering forward through the acrid shell-smoke looking for him, and drew to a halt, astonished by what they saw.

Landis yelled out, bringing his lasrifle up. He didn't know precisely what the cadaverous thing in black was, but his gut told him enough.

Skarwael wheeled, his leathery black robes swishing out and twisting vortices in the dust-thick air. Landis's shots rippled the dust patterns but struck nothing solid.

Like a shadow, thrown suddenly elsewhere by a switching light-source, Skarwael reappeared on the other side of them. A glinting splinter pistol came up from under his cloak of raw human hides, gripped by long, pale fingers. Energy-charged filaments of toxic crystal spat from the barrel, and Grohowski doubled over, explosively gutted. Landis fired again, and missed again.

'Move! Move!' Landfreed yelled, finding his voice at last. And his laspistol.

He opened fire on the monstrous shadow, but it had vanished. With a baffled gurgle, Landis fell on his back, shot apart by his commander's blasts.

Boles and Sanchez fired together, hosing the ruined brick wall in front of them with auto-fire. They had the shadow in their sights, but it moved like a black flicker up the wall, around their raking shots, and into the air. It turned for a moment in mid-flight, the ghastly black cape flowing out behind it like wings, then fell on Sanchez. The life company trooper struggled and yelled and came apart as the near invisible shadow mauled him and then threw him aside.

Backing away, Boles looked at Landfreed.

'Run,' Landfreed said simply.

Boles ran. Behind him, Landfreed turned to face the monster, raising his arm to shoot.

But there was no pistol. No hand. Just a cleanly severed wrist-stump.

Skarwael materialised in front of Landfreed and impaled him on his boline.

Boles threw himself forward through the smoke and rubble. He could hear his commander dying back there. In the back of his terrified mind, he wondered one thing. What could make a death scream last so long?

'WHAT'S AWRY?' GAUNT asked Beltayn, pre-empting his signals officer's usual remark.

'How about... everything?' Beltayn replied.

First platoon was dug down in Digre Street, a commercial block off Principal I in the Guild Slope, when Gaunt rejoined them from the triage station. The pull back from the second line was a mess compared with the one the Imperials had staged from the northern suburbs at first light. They hadn't held the second line for anything like as long as Gaunt had hoped. The archenemy was ploughing deep furrows up through the dense Guild Slope and was already threatening the agridomes to the west. The defenders were meant to be withdrawing to the hive towers for the last stand, a tactical move overseen by Biagi and Lugo. Landfreed had gone off line and his forces were in rout. Kaldenbach's retreat was fundamentally impaired too – it seemed from the vox-log that he'd somehow lost several of his key subordinates, including Lamm from the Regiment Civitas. Even the Ghosts were in disarray. Gaunt tried and failed to coordinate with Corbec and Rawne. Their actions had been delayed by incidents that the vox-log gave no details of.

The last contact from the Beati had been a report of a hellish firefight in the low Slope region.

On Digre Street, it was getting bloody. First, fourth and twentieth platoons were heads down under heavy bombardment. The archenemy had drawn up a serious wedge of self-propelled guns into the skirts of the Guild Slope below their position, and now they were pasting the area.

Bright green-yellow geysers of fire erupted from the buildings around them, showering roof tiles and slabs into the air, and cascading rivulets of fire down off the intact rooftops. The air smelled of burned brick dust, so earthy and intense, it made the nostrils close.

Gaunt knew they were right on the edge now. They had a very narrow hope of getting the withdrawal to work. If they fumbled it – and fate wasn't with them – they wouldn't even live long enough to stage a last stand at the hives. If the enemy kept this pressure up, the Imperial defence on Herodor would be annihilated before it even reached the hives.

Gaunt ran across a burning street with Beltayn, and joined with Mkoll and Ewler in the shelter of a half-tumbled wall.

'We need to get out now. Back to the hives.'

Mkoll nodded. 'It'll be tight.'

'Wish I could get Corbec or Rawne on the vox.'

'Too much interference,' said Mkoll. 'The shelling alone is scrambling basic signals.'

'If I put up a line here, can you start leading the men out south?' Gaunt asked.

Ewler nodded. Mkoll shrugged. 'We have to look for snipers.'

'This deep in?'

Mkoll looked at his commander darkly. 'I got a report earlier. Larks and Nessa aced a sniper right up in the Guild

Slopes. He'd almost drawn the Beati. They got him before he could take the shot.'

Mkoll showed Gaunt the location on the chart.

'Feth,' murmured Gaunt. 'Really, that far in?'

'Yes,' said Mkoll. 'I think they've got specialists deep into us now. Far, far deeper than their main front. And they're gunning for one thing.'

'Her,' said Gaunt.

Mkoll nodded.

Gaunt looked over at Beltayn. 'Bel… raise the Beati. Raise her or anyone with her. Tell her to fall back to the hives. My orders. She's what they're after.'

Beltayn flipped the dust-cover up off his caster-set. 'Do my best, sir,' he said.

'I just got Domor,' he said, a moment later. 'He says the Beati's with him. He'll urge her to withdraw.'

'Tell him to do more than urge, Bel. If she dies, it's all over.'

Beltayn nodded and turned back to his work.

Shells hammered down around them again. They all ducked.

'Right,' said Gaunt. 'Let's try and find a way out of this rat-trap. Ewler? Take the south side there. Mkoll, with me. You too, Bel.'

They ran from cover, dodging the sprays of debris and flame. Unsteady with his heavy vox-pack, Beltayn stumbled. Mkoll dragged him to his feet and pushed him into cover in a hab doorway beside Gaunt.

Gaunt's power sword took the lock off and they went inside, into a dark, drafty hallway where the air-rush of the shells outside ebbed and sucked like a giant respirator, fluttering paper scraps and dust back and forth.

It was pitch black. Mkoll kicked open a door and revealed an untidy hab module. Beltayn opened another, a blank room. Mkoll hurried on, and revealed another cluttered apartment with his boot.

'Mkoll!'

Mkoll backtracked and rejoined Gaunt and Beltayn at the door of the empty room Beltayn had opened.

There was nothing to see, an entirely bare hab module. No carpet or rugs, no shade on the overhead lamp, walls stripped. A door to one side, closed. A console table drawn up in the centre of the floor, with a book on it.

'What's the matter?' Mkoll said.

'Cover me,' Gaunt said, walking in. He had drawn his laspistol and sheathed his sword. Mkoll glanced at Beltayn, and Beltayn shrugged.

Gaunt walked to the small table oddly set in the centre of the room, and reached out to the book lying there. It was old. So very old it was falling apart and dissolving into dust.

He opened the cover and read the title page, knowing, with a sick feeling, what he would find there. It was another first edition of *On The Use of Armies* by Marchese.

He reached out towards it and the cover fell open, as if flipped by a strong wind. The pages fluttered and turned.

Gaunt stared down at the open book, and began to read:

When I speak of a body in this way, I mean the body as a figure for an armed force. To the leader, that force becomes his body...

He took a step back. He had been mindful of the things that had been shown to him, yet now they seemed to repeat with unsubtle reinforcement. Had he missed so much? Was he not being careful?

The closed door nearby rattled in its frame, as if shaken by a strong wind.

'Time's short, sir,' Mkoll cried out to him from the doorway.

Gaunt beckoned the two of them in to join him.

'What is this?' Beltayn asked.

'Sir?' said Mkoll.

'Do me this one service, my friends. Come with me and prove I'm not insane.'

Gaunt opened the door.

ELEVEN
THE CHAPEL AT NOWHERE

'Two dangers, one truly evil, one misunderstood.'
— Elinor Zaker, of the Herodian Commandery

It was a chapel, old and rundown, buried in the green twilight of the wood. Trailing ivy and fleece-flower clung to its walls. Bright green lichens gnawed the chafstone. Bemused, afraid, Mkoll and Beltayn followed Gaunt around the partially collapsed wall, in through the old gate, and up the path to the door. The scent was back, that flower scent. It was so strong it made Gaunt feel like sneezing. It was islumbine.

Gaunt pushed open the door and stepped into the cold gloom of the chapel. The interior was plain, but well-kept. At the end of the rows of hardwood pews, a taper burned at the Imperial altar. Gaunt walked down the aisle towards the graven image of the Emperor. In the stained glass of the lancet windows, he saw the image of Saint Sabbat amongst the worthies. Mkoll and Beltayn hung back.

'How could this be here?' Mkoll asked.

Beltayn didn't answer. He knew what this was and the thought of it made him too terrified to speak.

271

'Well,' murmured a voice from the darkness. 'There you are at last.'

SHE WAS AS she had been the last time: very old, and blind. A strip of black silk was wound around her head across her eyes. Her silver hair had been plaited tightly against the back of her skull. Age had hunched her, but standing erect she would have towered over Gaunt.

There was no mistaking her red and black robes.

'Sister Elinor,' Gaunt said. 'We meet again.'

'We do, Ibram.'

'This seems like the Chapel of the Holy Light Abundant, Veniq,' he said.

'It is.'

'Which I thought was on Aexe Cardinal, a great distance from here.'

'It was once,' said Elinor Zaker. 'It hasn't been for a long time, not even when you last visited it. It exists only as a memory now, a memory where I can dwell.'

Beltayn groaned quietly. Mkoll blinked fast.

'Someone is disheartened to hear that,' she said, cocking her head. 'You are not alone?'

'There are three of us this time. Myself, Beltayn and my chief scout.'

She sat down on one of the pews, feeling her way with one hand, leaning on her staff with the other. 'So… this is Herodor already?' she said. 'Has it really drawn so late?'

'Yes,' said Gaunt. 'And dangers press. Can you guide us?'

She settled herself against the stiff back of the pew. 'The divine powers allow me only to advise. But things have become more perilous since I last spoke to you. Forces and elements that the tarot did not foresee have entered the mechanism. To counterbalance this, I have been permitted to speak to you again.'

'You've been trying to make contact. I apologise for ignoring the signs. I've been busy.' He paused. 'Permitted by who?'

She turned her head towards him. It was the fluid neck-swivel of a human who had been habituated to helmet-display target sensors. Just like at their first meeting, Gaunt felt as if she was aiming at him.

'The divine powers. Their name may not be uttered for it is too bright.'

'So, speak, sister,' Gaunt said. 'The hour is on us. The Beati is with me, but she may yet die by the hand of the archenemy. No more riddles.'

Elinor Zaker started. 'She's with you?'

'Yes,' said Gaunt.

She smiled a little. 'Oh my God-Emperor, at last…'

'There is so little time…' Gaunt urged.

'The mechanism is delicate–'

'Shut up!' Gaunt snarled. The force of his voice made Beltayn jump. Mkoll stared in fascination through narrowed eyes. He had seen – and, more importantly, accepted – visions before.

'I've had enough of the vagueness and the enigmatic crap!' Gaunt snapped. 'Tell me! Just tell me! If you can help me win, help me win! If not, why the feth did you ever draw me into this nonsense in the first place?'

She didn't reply.

'Sister?'

She folded her hands in her lap. 'You drew yourself in when you served the Beati on Hagia. You drew yourself in when you spared Brin Milo from the flames of Tanith. You drew yourself in when you listened to Warmaster Slaydo retell the struggles of the Age of Sabbat and swore your blood oath to finish his work. You drew yourself in long before you were even born, before your ancestors were born, for you and your Ghosts are a small part of a manifest destiny so great in dimension that from here, even at this high point of it, we cannot see the beginning or the end.'

Gaunt swallowed. 'I see,' he stammered.

She nodded to him. 'I know you don't. This is all you need to understand to play your part. Milo, first. He is vital. Vital to what will come hereafter. But understand there will be no hereafter if you fail here.'

'Here? On Herodor?'

'On Herodor,' she echoed. "There is harm throughout, more than was originally anticipated. But still, the greatest harm is within. Within your body.'

'You use the word as DeMarchese used it. Body, meaning an armed force. My Ghosts?'

'Indeed. You've been studying since we last met.'

'Yes, sister,' said Gaunt.

'Well, then. For the last time. The harm is in two parts. Two dangers: one truly evil, one misunderstood. The latter holds the key. It's important you remember that, because you commissars are terribly trigger happy. That key is more important to you now than ever before. Lastly, let your sharpest eye show you the truth. That's it. There will be nine.'

'What did you say–?' Gaunt began.

Reality popped like a soap bubble.

Gaunt was beside Mkoll and Beltayn in a very empty, very ruined hab module.

'What in the name of feth just happened?' Mkoll asked.

Beltayn was quivering with fear and confusion.

'Nine…' Gaunt murmured. 'Bel. Get on the vox. Find out where Soric is.'

IN DARKNESS, THE spread of carnage through the Civitas was more visible. Whole sections of the outer skirts and slopes were ablaze, and fires clustered and spread around the north faces of hive towers one and two as well. Gaunt wasn't entirely sure when the city shield had failed, but it was long gone now, and winds from the north blew in across the Civitas basin and fanned the firestorms.

Imperial troop units and support crews fled south up the streets of the high Guild Slope, some on foot, some in roaring carriers and trucks. The second line had entirely broken.

Pressing hard at a trot, Gaunt's three platoon force got as far as the atmosphere processor in Fenzy Yard, and there managed to hop a ride on a quartet of PDF troop carriers that raced them up the last third of the Guild Slope to the keep in the high town district that served as main barracks for the Regiment Civitas.

The keep was largely intact. It had been hit by some long-range shelling, but its main structure, overlooking Principal I, had survived. Inside the assembly yard, hundreds of Herodian troopers were massing, loading spare ordnance into waiting transports.

Gaunt jumped down from his ride and looked around as Mkoll and Ewler did a head count. The night air was pungent with exhaust fumes, and ringing with the urgent shouts of men from all around. Gaunt looked up. The high town district was the base area of the hives, and their immense forms rose up above him, giddyingly tall and reassuringly massive. They weren't towers, they were vertical cities, and they were of cyclopean construction. Gaunt took a deep breath. He had forgotten how massive they were. They might hold, for a while at least.

'Gaunt!' He turned at the sound of his name and saw Biagi pushing through the crowds towards him. The marshal had clearly seen his own share of the combat. A hasty field dressing was taped across a wound to his hip.

Gaunt saluted. 'We look to the hives now, I suppose?' he said.

'Old Hive,' said Biagi. 'The lord general and the Civitas officiaries have withdrawn there. We will compose our defence around them.'

'Isn't Old Hive the most vulnerable?' Gaunt asked. 'It's ancient, and far less robust than the other towers.'

'Old Hive is the seat of Herodian culture,' Biagi said. 'It is our heart. The Holy Balneary is there, and the oldest shrines. If we concentrate anywhere, it must be there.'

The implication was grim. The other towers would be left unprotected. Their citizens would perish. It must have been a hard decision for Biagi to make.

Gaunt caught himself. No, the decision was easy. It was precisely the same one that he had made during the fall of Tanith. The whole could not be saved, and any attempt to do so would be doomed. The only course of action was to concentrate all combat efforts to save one part of it.

Biagi stared out at the rippling fireglow lighting the northern sky.

'To think I forbade your use of flamers, Gaunt. Look how my city burns.'

'Be thankful, sir, that I ignored your orders. But for my flamers, your city would have been burning far more, far sooner.'

Gaunt looked at Biagi. 'I sent a signal on my way up. Concerning a trooper of mine. Sergeant Soric?'

'Indeed. I've had him escorted down from the hives as you asked. What's so important about him?'

'Come with me and we may find out.'

ESCORTED BY BELTAYN, and Biagi's own signals officer Sires, Gaunt and the marshal strode into the Regiment Civitas keep. Emergency lighting was on, and the corridors were flushed with a dull green glow. Men hurried past them in teams, carrying boxes of supplies or pushing munitions on carts. The old fortress was being stripped bare of anything that might prove useful.

'Anything from Kaldenbach?' Gaunt asked.

'Brief signals. He's caught in a pocket to the west, but he has some armour left.'

'And the Beati herself?'

'We're having difficulty pinpointing her right now. I have implored her to retreat.'

'So have I. It's imperative. You understand this war is entirely symbolic?'

'The thought had crossed my mind,' said Biagi.

'Don't let it cross. Keep it centred. She's what this is all about. Herodor has no strategic importance. By coming here, she made this world a target. This invasion has one purpose. To find her and kill her. She's the lure. If we recognise that and use it, we might be in with a chance.'

'Does she recognise it?' Biagi said.

Gaunt glanced at him. 'I'm rather afraid that's why she came here in the first place, marshal.'

'I see,' said Biagi.

They came to a halt outside a security hatch, triple locked. Two PDF sentries stood aside for them, and beat a hasty retreat when Biagi dismissed them. The marshal fitted his authority key into the socket and the hatch whirred open. The chamber beyond was starkly lit by white phospha lamps. It was the keep's brig.

A group of armed Ghosts waited for them inside: Meryn and his unit, serving as guard detail.

'Sir!' said Meryn sharply.

'We can handle this, sergeant. Head for the evac transports. I'll see you in Old Hive.'

Meryn nodded. He looked angry. 'You should have shot him, sir,' he said.

'I beg your pardon, Meryn?'

'He's scum. Filth. I knew it. I told Commissar Hark. The bastard should have been executed long since.'

'That's your opinion, is it, Meryn?'

'Sir, every moment he lives, he brings shame on our regiment! I don't know why you didn't do your job as commissar and shoot the bastard thr–'

Gaunt's blow caught Meryn unawares and surprised everyone around them. Meryn sprawled on his back, clutching at his bloody mouth.

'Agun Soric has served the Ghosts with distinction, Meryn. He volunteered himself for detention, and he may yet prove to be something quite different from the bogey man you fear. As far as the bringing shame thing goes, you're doing fine all by yourself.'

Gaunt looked up at the men of Meryn's platoon. 'I am a commissar. It's my business to judge. But unlike the Keetles of this bloody cosmos, I will not be hasty in that judgment. Soric lives or dies by my word alone. Understood?'

There was a nervous growl of voices. Gaunt glanced down at Meryn. 'Get out of my sight, and pray I've forgotten your insolence the next time we meet.'

Fargher and Guheen dragged their sergeant to his feet, and fourteenth platoon left the chamber.

'I thought Meryn was one of your best?' Biagi said.

'He is, in a sound, unimaginative way.'

'What did he mean, then? About this Soric?'

'I need you to be patient, Biagi. Soric came to me earlier and confessed. He's a psyker.'

'He's in here,' said Dorden, showing the four soldiers to the door of the fifth cell. The Tanith doctor had taken it upon himself to escort Soric personally. A robed astropath and two bullish men in long grey leather coats stood by the cell door. The grey men, clutching power-goads, were officer-handlers from the life company's sanctioned psyker cadre. Wire-grilled augmetic damper units were sutured into their ears and eye-sockets.

'I heard what you said. To Meryn, just then,' said Dorden.

'Did you? I trust I'm starting to live up to your high standards, doctor?'

Dorden smiled sarcastically. 'One thing I don't get,' he said. 'Earlier, you told me you believed the warp never revealed truth to mankind, especially not to the untrained and the unsanctioned.'

'I changed my mind,' said Gaunt. 'I'm not trained or sanctioned but, as Zweil has freely pointed out, powers divine or otherwise have chosen to speak to me. Just this afternoon, in a little chapel, I–'

'What?'

'Never mind. This it?'

Dorden opened the cell hatch.

Soric was lying on the perforated metal cot, bathed in the hard light of the overhead phosphas. He had been badly beaten. Dorden had done his best to patch him up.

'Feth! What happened?'

'Meryn's platoon happened. They gave him hell on the transit down.'

'Bastards. Ignorant bastards…'

'What the hell is this?' Biagi muttered, bending down to collect up some of the hundreds of crumpled scraps of blue paper that littered the cell floor. Gaunt looked over his shoulder. The papers in the marshal's hands were covered in hasty, incomprehensible scrawl.

'I'd say that was torn from a standard Guard issue message pad,' Beltayn said.

'Did you give him paper? Writing tools?' Biagi asked the handlers.

'No sir,' one of them grunted, his voice a slabby monotone processed through an augmetic voicebox. 'We took all personal items from the prisoner. But they keep returning to him.'

'What the hell does that mean?' Biagi asked.

The handler crossed to Soric and searched him. Soric moaned at the touch. The handler produced a brass shell case from Soric's thigh pocket.

'I cannot count the number of times we've taken this off him. Every few seconds, it disappears from our evidence bag and reappears in his pocket.' The handler opened the message shell and shook out another fold of blue paper. 'And every time, there's another note in it.'

'Have you seen this before?' Gaunt asked.

'No, sir,' said the handler.

Gaunt knelt down beside Soric. 'Agun? Chief? You hear me?'

Soric's single eye opened, squeezed to a slit by the swollen flesh of his puffy face. The eye was bloodshot.

'Colonel-commissar, sir,' he sighed.

'There's not much time, chief. Tell me about the nine.'

'So tired... hurts so much...'

'Chief! You were desperate to tell me before! Tell me now!'

Soric nodded slowly, and, with Dorden's help, got himself up to a half-sitting position.

'Nine are coming,' he said.

'Nine?'

'Nine,' he repeated, swallowing pain. 'I'm so sorry, sir. I never meant to risk yo–'

'Save it for later, Agun. Tell me about the nine.'

'Nine. The shell told me there would be nine. Because nine is the sacred number of the Beati...'

'The nine holy wounds,' said Biagi solemnly.

'The nine holy wounds,' Soric nodded. 'I saw her. She was looking at me. Right at me. She knew...'

'Chief! Chief! Come on, stay with me!'

Soric had faded and slumped. Gaunt looked over at Dorden. 'Can't you do something?'

'That will help us? Of course. That will help him? No. Besides, if he's what you're afraid he is, a stimm-shot might not be a good idea.'

'I think we might have to take that chance,' said Gaunt. 'Agreed?'

Biagi nodded. The handlers charged their goads. The sharp stink of ozone filled the little cell.

Dorden thumped the one-dose derma-ject into Soric's arm and wiped the puncture with a swab loaded with rubbing alcohol. Soric trembled, shivered and convulsed.

Then he snapped awake, staring at Gaunt with his one good eye.

'Sir?'

'Tell me about the nine, chief.'

'Nine. That's what it said. It wouldn't shut up about it.' Soric raised his hand, and Gaunt saw it was holding the brass message shell. How the feth had it got back into his hand?

'Ever since Phantine, when I was hurt on Phantine, the thing has been there. Not speaking to me, you understand. Writing to me. All very civilised. I would open the shell and ooops! There's another message. Split left, split right, head down the wall there… all that shit. Combat shit. Just a word to the wise. I never worried about it. God-Emperor, I know I should have! I should have told you about it long ago!'

'Why didn't you worry about it?' asked Gaunt.

'Because it was in my handwriting. I like a drink or two, you know that, sir. I wondered… had I written it and forgotten…?'

'All these messages?'

'No. No! But at the start of it, a little. Then, when I realised it was more than that, I was too scared.'

'Of what?'

'Of men like you,' Soric said, pointing at Gaunt. 'Of men like them,' he added sourly, gesturing to the handlers.

'Milo told me what I should do,' said Soric. Gaunt glanced at Beltayn. 'He told me to be a man and fess up.'

'What… what is the shell telling you now, chief?'

'The shell always knows. It knew about Herodor long before we were marked up and shipped out. It knew. It just knows. Nine. Nine are coming.'

'Nine what?'

'Nine killers.'

'Coming to kill the Beati?'

Soric nodded.

'There is a vast army on Herodor trying to kill the Beati,' said Biagi.

'But the nine are special. They have been charged by the Magister. They are deep inside us. The shell says so. Deeper inside us than we dare realise.'

'What are they?' Gaunt asked.

'Wait,' said Soric. He put the message shell back into his pocket and then drew it out again. When he opened it, there was a flimsy sheet of blue paper folded up inside.

He flattened the sheet out to read it, and held it up close to his deformed eye.

'Nine. A marksman. Three psykers. Three reptiles. A phantom. A death-machine.'

OUTSIDE THE SIMPLE cell, Gaunt leaned heavily against the wall and wiped the rank sweat from his brow.

'Did you feel it in there?'

Biagi nodded.

'Like a swamp suddenly, so hot, so damp…'

'He's a psyker. He should burn.'

'Not while he's useful. Forget the invasion force, the archenemy has deployed specialist assassins into the Civitas. We have to find them fast.'

'But–'

'Think, Biagi! I told you this war was symbolic! All that matters, all that your world is worth, is the life or death of the Beati. We have to find these killers and kill them before they win this outright.'

Biagi shrugged. 'What do we know? He told us so little. A marksman…?'

'Dead already, I think,' said Gaunt. 'One down. The reptiles…'

'We know there are loxatl active,' said Dorden. Gaunt nodded.

'He mentioned a phantom,' said Biagi. 'I interviewed a life company trooper called Boles just thirty minutes ago. He told me how Landfreed and a whole fire-team were taken down by a ghost that came out of nowhere.'

'Ghost?' Dorden echoed.

Biagi smiled. 'Forgive me. A spectre. Boles is an experienced veteran. He was sure it was of the piratical devil-breed.'

Gaunt shuddered. Not since his days as a cadet, many years before Balhaut, had he been forced to deal with those vicious killers, the so-called dark eldar.

'What about the three psykers? And this… what did he call it? This death-machine?'

'We'll find them,' said Gaunt.

'How?' Biagi laughed.

'We'll find the Beati. They're all looking for her.'

* * *

'WHAT DID THE prophecy mean, sir?' Beltayn asked as he walked with Gaunt out through the exit hatches of the keep.

'Sister Elinor said there were two dangers: one truly evil, one misunderstood. I believe that misunderstood one is Soric. Remember, she told me to be wary, because commissars are trigger happy? That seems to fit. He's the key and I could have had him executed before I found that out.'

'What about the other?'

'Well, that's what we're looking for.'

'And what did she say at the end… "Let your sharpest eye show you the truth"?'

Gaunt nodded. 'Raise all sections still in the field. Tell them the Beati is at risk and they should locate her and safeguard her. And get me Mkoll on the link. He's my sharpest eye.'

Gaunt paused. 'And get me Larkin too.'

'HOLINESS! YOUR HOLINESS!' Domor ran across the yard to where the Beati stood. Milo was with her. She seemed to be staring at the sky.

Domor had to shout to make himself heard over the bombardment rippling through the nearby streets.

'Another vox-signal! From Marshal Biagi this time. He repeats Colonel-commissar Gaunt's instructions. We must make our way to Old Hive. It's imperative! Holiness?'

'I think she understands,' said Milo. The ground shook as a tank round demolished a commercial property not seventy metres away. 'We can't stay out here much longer anyway.'

Sabbat shivered, as if the night air was cold. In truth, it was sweltering hot from the raging firestorms.

'What is it?' Milo asked.

'He's coming. The endgame is on us.'

'Who is she talking about?' Domor asked Milo.

Milo shook his head. 'We have to go to Old Hive now, Sabbat,' Milo said. 'They're waiting for us. They need us.'

The Beati turned and looked at him with a half-smile. Sometimes, like now with the flame-light starkly side-lighting her features, she had a terrible, terrifying aspect.

'Soon,' she assured. 'One last venture. We must get to the agridomes.'

* * *

OUT ON THE bare wastes of the Great Western Obsidae, the night was a hard, dry sub-zero, cut by merciless winds from the outer zones. Phospha lamps glowed and swung in the wind, coldly illuminating the row upon row of empty landers and transport ships. Their mouth hatches were open, pointing south.

There, distantly, the Civitas lay, submerged in the murk and flash of war. The orange glow of the firestorms lit the low sky.

Thrusters whining and cycling hard a single lander, more massively armoured than the rest, came in low, sheeting up dust waves more fiercely than the desert winds. Its Locust escort turned and banked away. Burners flared blue. Hydraulic landing claws extended, and the battle transport settled like a giant mosquito.

The ramps opened. Light shone out. Crews of slave-carls spewed from the hatches, followed by a formal marching block of Retinue in full armour. The Retinue, five hundred strong, divided with parade ground precision, swung their weapons to shoulder in a perfectly synchronised movement, and formed two lines of honour guard.

Etrodai, his changeling blade skinned and hungry, strode down the ramp and He followed.

He was dressed for war in gleaming beetle-black armour. His face was masked by His antlered helmet. The Retinue murmured their moan of respect.

Enok Innokenti, Magister, Warlord, chosen disciple of the Archon, set foot on the dusty soil of Herodor. He raised His arms in salutation.

The Retinue screamed His name.

TWELVE
IN THE NAME
OF SABBAT

'As the Emperor protects, so must we.'

— Ibram Gaunt

SOME OF THE men in Corbec's platoon were getting vocal with their complaints, and Corbec could half understand why.

'When the feth do we get to fall back?' said Bewl.

'For feth's sake, why are we still out here?' said Cown.

'We have a job to do, boys,' Corbec assured them. Instructions had been simple. Find the Beati and get her back to Old Hive. And watch out in particular for the really bad things. Of which there were nine, apparently.

They weren't fighting any more. They were sneaking. Cloaked up, stealthy, using every shred of Tanith woodcraft to edge through the splintered ruins of Guild Slope. They dodged advancing Blood Pact units, and hid while crimson tanks grumbled past, lamps blazing. There was the odd fire-fight or three, when circumstances demanded, but then it was strictly hit and run.

They were working the shadows and staying alive.

Corbec was glad to have Mkvenner back with him. He'd lost count of the Blood Pact throats Ven had sliced that night as he led them at point. There was no getting away from the fact that they were all going to die here on Herodor, one way or another. That was the way the odds were stacked, and not even Varl or Feygor would have given better. But by feth, they were going to make a good account of themselves.

His camo-cloak pulled up around him like a hood, Corbec scuttled forward at a signal from Ven, passing Orrin, Cown, Cole and Irvinn in cover. He reached the street turn and used the shadows cast by a burning community hall to blend into the scenery. He raised a hand, made a signal of his own. Veddekin, Ponore, Sillo, Androby and Brown sprinted up on his heels and vanished into the shot-up print shop to his left. Then Surch and Loell moved up smartly, lugging the .50 and its panniers of ammo.

Corbec scurried over to fresh cover. He was quiet for a big man. Rerval and Roskil covered him, and then slipped in behind him.

The three of them were running, in file, down to the end of the block. A tank, or something similar, had flattened the building there and left nothing but ragged rockcrete sections, sprouting the broken strands of their internal metal reinforcement.

Mkvenner reappeared, jogging back to them, light on his feet.

'Some kind of covered market to the left there. The road to the right is blocked. We could carry on down the hill if we follow that side street.'

'Can we go through the market?' Corbec asked.

'I haven't scoped it.'

'Let's try.' Corbec rose, and flashed a finger signal back. Then he and Ven were running forward again, with Brown, Cole, Sillo and Roskil behind them.

The covered market had once had a glass roof, but the shockwaves from the shelling had brought it down. Some wooden screens remained. The produce shops and trader barrows inside were all locked up and shuttered.

'Doesn't look promising,' Ven said.

Corbec nodded, and turned to go back. Then he stopped.
He had smelt something. It was faint, very faint, almost
masked by the rich stink of smoke and burning fuel.

Something like cinnamon. He knew that smell, vividly.
That particular reek. From Hagia, the Doctrinopolis... what
was it now? Four years ago?

He'd never forget it. It was in his nightmares still. A
moment in his life no amount of good nights' sleep could
wear away. Him and the poor boy Yael. Prisoners of the
Infardi. And that thing, that monster in human form. The
one who'd butchered Yael just to hear him scream.

It couldn't be! That bastard was long dead...

Corbec breathed in again: cinnamon, sweat, decay. Faint,
but lingering.

'Cover me,' he said to Ven, and ignored the askance look
the scout gave him.

Corbec advanced into the market, lasrifle low and ready.
He took care with every step. The floor was covered in chips
of broken glass from the roof. On the edge of his nerves and
as fine as any Tanith scout, Corbec made no sound.

He prowled in, checking from side to side. Twice, he
jumped at shadows and almost discharged his weapon. The
smell grew stronger.

Corbec saw movement. Low down, under a trader's barrow.
He circled, switching his lasrifle to a single-handed grip as he
fished out a lamp-pack. He edged round the cart, and saw
there were two kids hiding between the wheels. Little,
hunched up kids. One of them was waving his hand beside
his head, as if he was trying to fan the close air. Corbec came
around further, and clicked on the pack. He lit the kids up
with a hard-light beam and they didn't flinch. He saw their
faces.

'Oh feth!' he growled.

Something hit him from behind, a heavy, powerful mass
that reeked of sweat and cinnamon. Corbec lurched forward
and crashed into the cart, overturning it.

The weight was on him. He felt a knifing pain in his left
shoulder.

Corbec yowled and smacked back with his elbow. The
weight reduced, and he rolled, groping for his rifle. He

blundered into the kids... though from his brief glimpse of them he knew they were not kids... and felt them grab at him.

'Colonel? Sir?' Corbec could hear Ven shouting. He heard men running forward over the glass litter. A lasrifle fired.

Mkvenner came charging in, with Brown and Cole beside him. Roskil and Sillo were close behind. Cole had already fired, shredding the shutters of a produce shop behind the shuffling twins. The twins seized each other and switched their sightless heads around in unison, looking at Cole. The concussive psi-wave hit him and broke every bone in his body. His limp, flopping form flew backwards into the air like a weighted sack, up and out through the market's roof, snapping a support truss with a sickening crunch.

Corbec leapt up, and switched around. He saw a flash of green silk and a glint of exposed fangs.

'Sin!' he screamed, and slammed out a fist that met Pater Sin in the face. The huge Infardi crumpled and crashed away, smashing over another two carts. Buttons and beads spilled across the floor.

'Pater Sin!' Corbec yelled again, and dived at the rolling bulk. The twins heard his cry and switched their heads towards him. The psi-shock caught him a glancing blow and tumbled him head over heels into the shutters of a shop on the far side of the aisle. He broke several slats, and fell onto the ground.

Mkvenner leapt onto Sin as he tried to get up. They grappled furiously, and the scout brought him down again. Sin slammed out a tattooed arm and smacked Mkvenner sideways.

The twins opened their mouths and the buzzing sound gushed out. Brown and Roskil skidded to a halt, and swayed, blood gushing from their nostrils and ears. Roskil raised his lasrifle and shot Brown between the eyes. Then he swung round drunkenly and aimed at Sillo, who was backing away in terror.

There was a blurt of las-fire on auto. Mkvenner was up on one knee, blasting. The twins slammed back against the wall together, and slid down, leaving sticky swipes of blood behind them. Roskil, brain-fried, collapsed as they died.

Howling, Pater Sin threw himself at Corbec. His lethal implants gnashed and bit at the Ghost's neck. Corbec fended Sin off with his left arm, groping with his right to find something to use against the maniac. Something. Anything.

He got his fingers around something metallic and hard. He hoped to feth it was his warknife. He pulled it and stabbed it into the side of Sin's skull. It didn't penetrate, but the blow cracked Sin back for a second.

It wasn't Corbec's straight silver at all. It was a tube-charge.

Corbec swore and flinched as Sin came in again. His massive body pinned Corbec, and his augmetic fangs opened to rip his enemy's throat out.

Corbec jammed the tube into the yawning mouth as Sin bit down. His razor teeth clamped solidly into the tube's metal casing. Sin tried to pull away. Corbec got his legs up under Sin's torso and kicked out, throwing the heretic backwards off him.

A torn strand of det tape remained between Corbec's fingers.

'That's for Yael, feth-face!' Corbec yelled as he threw himself flat.

The tube-charge anchored in Pater Sin's teeth detonated.

Spattered in Sin's vaporised remains, Corbec rose. He hurried over to Mkvenner, who'd been thrown flat by the blast.

'Got the bastard,' Corbec said.

CAFFRAN SUDDENLY REALISED what he was looking at. He'd taken point down a side street, and was hunched in cover as the Ghosts moved up behind him. The view ahead was dark and empty, heavily shadowed by the bulk of an aqueduct that ran overhead and down the slope into the lower city where the night was firelit orange.

Caffran was looking for movement at street level, but he was distracted by a motion up in the shadows of the aqueduct. Roosting birds, he thought, and then remembered that he'd not seen any bird life on Herodor.

He stared up. A pale shape seemed to be moving along the outside of the aqueduct, insubstantial as smoke.

'Stand by,' he voxed. 'There's something–'

And he realised what he was seeing. Two loxatl, sleek and fluid as fish in water, racing along the sheer brickwork, about to cross right over their position.

'Hostiles! Eleven o'clock!' he yelled and opened fire up into the shadows of the arch. The gunfire rolled in the echoing space and his shots, bright and furious, lit up the bricks beside creatures. One immediately disappeared up over the top of the aqueduct, and the other one came down the support pier at a stupendous rate, its long body undulating and glinting. About three metres from the street, it propelled itself over onto the facing wall of the hab opposite, its dewclaws allowing it to skitter up the vertical surface.

Caffran ran forward, firing again. Feygor, Leyr and Dunik were up beside him, but they hadn't seen what he had seen.

'Caff?'

'Loxatl! Feth, up there!'

Caffran shot at the front of the hab, though in truth he couldn't see the thing clearly any more. Dunik and Feygor blasted with him, blindly following his lead. The Ghosts had a particular revulsion for the loxatl kind.

The thing reappeared, lower than Caffran was estimating. Little augmetic servo-limbs in its weapons harness clacked its blaster round and it fired.

The first two flechette rounds hit the wall behind Feygor making deep holes haloed by hundreds of lesser micro-impacts. The third atomised Dunik's head and shoulders in a bloody vapour.

Caffran and Feygor threw themselves flat. Leyr, cut along the hand and arm by stray barbs, yelped and stumbled.

They dragged him into cover. 'Down! Stay the feth down!' Caffran yelled, seeing Rawne and a half dozen other Ghosts rushing up the street to assist them. The loxatl's cannon repeated its distinctive rattling cough and hailed splinters along the street wall at head height. Someone screamed.

Rawne was on his hands and knees behind an abandoned ground car and glanced up in horror at the huge, ragged holes the xenos weapon was punching in the wall above him. Each impact was actually a thousand razor barbs hitting simultaneously.

'Where the feth is it?' he yelled.

Caffran couldn't see. 'Facing us, about two floors up,' he voxed. 'There's another one gone over the top of the aqueduct. For feth's sake, someone cover that angle!'

Fifty metres back, Kolea and Criid heard his signal and glanced at each other. The whining cough of loxatl cannons had a particular resonance for them both. Ouranberg. Criid in trouble. Kolea effectively giving up his life to save her.

As if reading her thoughts, Kolea said, 'Not this time.'

They doubled back under the aqueduct, hunting for the second creature. On the far side, visibility was better. The street was well lit by the amber glow of the firestorms. Guns raised, twitchy, they fanned forward, trying to hug cover. Criid and Kolea first… Jajjo… Skeen, Pozetine… Kenfeld.

Jajjo saw firelight reflecting off inhuman eyes clouded by protective han lids. He dived forward as flechette rounds shattered the cobbles around him. Several barbs sliced into his calves and shins, but he managed to land and roll, and came up firing.

Jajjo's las-fire peppered the wall where the thing had been, but sharp dewclaws and chillingly nimble reflexes had propelled the thing ten metres up the front facade of the tenement and along under the edge of the roof.

Criid saw it go, and fired at it, Kenfeld joining in.

'Gak, it's so fething fast!' she wailed.

'I think–' Kenfeld began and then suddenly wasn't beside her any more. She flinched. Her face was sticky and wet. It was Kenfeld's blood. His mangled body had been thrown five metres backwards, as hard and fast as if a speeding truck had run into it.

Criid ducked into cover and started to recell her weapon with shaking hands. She heard las-shots, the answering cough of the blaster, and then footsteps running. Gol Kolea threw himself down beside her.

'Where is it?' she asked.

'Up to the left, but moving. You okay?'

She nodded. Her earpiece was ringing with calls and alerts from the rest of the squad, trying to move up but pinned down by the mercilessly switching fire.

Kolea made ready to run out again, but she grabbed his arm and pulled him back.

'No heroics now,' she said. 'We've only just got you back.'

'That an order?'

'Yes, and–'

'And what?'

'I want you alive when we're done. We need to talk about… about your children.'

He looked at her strangely. 'My kids died in the hive-war, Tona. My wife too. The only children we need to worry about these days are yours.'

'But–'

'Yours,' he said emphatically. 'The Emperor protects, and when he's busy, Tona Criid performs miracles for him. It's enough to know they're alive and loved. More than I could ever have hoped for.'

He embraced her, and held her tight for a second. Then he scooped up his weapon and ran. The cannon coughed and roared.

ON THE OTHER side of the aqueduct, Rawne was running too. Three more of his platoon were messily dead now, but the loxatl had stopped shooting for a moment. He figured it had gone up over the roof of the hab.

He ran right across the street and came up against the front wall of the tenement, pressing his back to it, edging along. The street was quiet. Thin wisps of smoke drifted down it. Across the road, he could see Ghosts creeping forward behind cover.

Rawne's nostrils were suddenly assailed by a rancid stink of milk. Milk and mint.

His shoulders pressed to the wall, he tilted his head back and looked straight up. The loxatl gazed down at him. It was directly above him, about three metres up the wall, head down, snuffling its wattled snout. Its augmetic harness clicked and aimed the cannon's barrel into his eyes.

'Well, shit,' said Rawne.

From across the street, Banda's hot-shot hit it in the base of the tail and blew it off the wall. It crashed down beside Rawne in a shower of shattered bricks, thrashing its sinuous body in agony. Fluid leaked out of its lipless mouth. Rawne pressed the muzzle of his lasrifle into the exposed folds of its throat and fired.

'Nice decoy work, baby,' Banda said, sauntering out of cover with her long-las over her shoulder.

'Ha fething ha,' said Rawne.

CHTO BROOD LEADER was dead. Reghh had heard his subsonic pain-wails. Anger-hunger swamped his mind, and his gleaming skin began to pulse with grief-codes. Iridescent patterns flashed along his snaking body. He scuttled down a wall, across a stretch of pavement, and then up a side wall into the next alley. These mammals were not the target. They were delaying him and making him waste shots.

Loxatl senses were dull tools. Out of water, their vision, hearing and smell were poor. Taste and vibration were their primary skills. Reghh could feel the mammal soldiers running up along the street he'd just left, looking for him. He could feel their footsteps, their mouth noises, their heartbeats and their lung-puffs. He could taste their fear-sweat and skin-scents.

He started to scurry back down the length of the wall, moving south, when pain slammed into his torso. White-cold, brutal pain. He staggered, double-lids blinking.

The mammal wrenched his rifle back and tugged the long, silver bayonet out. How had Reghh not tasted him or known he was there?

Reghh coiled round. The ground was awash with the life-fluid draining out of him. He dimly saw the mammal.

The mammal had no taste. No taste at all. As if he was somehow newborn: pure and as yet unsoured by the rank flavours accumulated in their filthy skins during their lives.

How could that be? The mammal was full grown.

Reghh tried to turn around enough to bring his harness weapon to bear. The pain in his belly was too great. The mammal-with-no-taste lunged again.

Gol Kolea rammed the bayonet into the thing's twitching body twice more to make sure it was dead. Loxatl blood dripped off the straight silver clamped to his rifle's barrel. Dark spirals of colour flashed up and down the animal's gleaming hide and then it went a dull white.

Breathing hard, Kolea tapped his micro-bead. 'Sarge?' he said. 'I got it.'

* * *

THE STRANGEST THING. In all his years of kill-hunts, he'd never had this feeling before. He was being hunted.

Skarwael shifted silently through the abandoned avenues of the Guild Slope, invisible to all. The Imperial city towers rose before him, but the neighbourhood was quiet and dead. The humans had fled, leaving ruin in their wake. Rumbling, like a sinister threat, the invading host was twenty minutes behind him.

Skarwael had preyed a few times on his approach to the hives, not because he had to but because he was thirsty for pain. Herodor was smashed. In less than a day, the hives would burn and the Magister would have his victory.

The task remained. She was elusive, this martyr. That made the hunt all the sweeter.

And this strange feeling. It made the whole enterprise rewarding. Skarwael had accepted the task on the basis of the price the Magister was offering – a fortune in territory and inner transition metals, and a tolerance treaty between his kabal and the Archon Gaur. But this thrill now was reward enough. The hunter was hunted.

He'd not felt like this since his bitter years as a novitiate, when Lord Kaah had hunted them all in the miserable vaults of the murderdromes to hone their skills.

What could it be out there? Certainly no human. No human could ever hope to best the stealth and guile of a mandrake.

Skarwael melted into shadow, and doubled back. Like a phantom, he flowed through the shadows of a burned-out hab and came out onto the street. Darkness swam about him, unnaturally extending his flesh-cloak, bonding him to the night.

Where are you, he wondered?

The street was empty. Patchy fires burned in several buildings. The stiff corpses of Imperial soldiers decorated the ground. A wounded man, a PDF private, ran past him up the street, terrified, hoping to reach the towers before the gate hatches locked. The human didn't even see Skarwael, even though he was standing in the middle of the thoroughfare. The oblivious human passed so close by Skarwael could have reached out with his boline and cut his throat.

Still that feeling.

Skarwael turned, became brick, became glass, became stone, shifting his visual form against the backdrop behind him. His unseen adversary was close by. He could feel it. His pallid skin prickled. Behind him? No! To the left…

He passed through shadow and firelight, bending light and sound around himself as he moved. His chameleon powers segued him into walls and doorways, like a spectre from the afterlife.

There! Skarwael turned and flowed back through the night. At last his peerless skills as a stalker had paid off. There was his adversary, huddled down behind a railing, trying to hide.

You were good, Skarwael conceded. *A pleasure to hunt, a pleasure to test my skill against. But you are no match for a mandrake. Don't move. I will honour you with a slow, delicious death.*

Skarwael lunged with his sacred knife. The boline stabbed between the railings and speared through lifeless cloth.

Surprised, Skarwael dragged the cloth through the bars and sniffed it. A cloak, an empty cloak, made of some camouflage material. He turned and saw the rifle aimed at him.

'You're good,' said Mkoll grudgingly.

The single las-round hit the mandrake between the eyes.

THIRTEEN
THE LAST HOURS

'Nine is still one.'

— message written in Soric's hand

CLOSURE REQUIRED THE gene-print of the first officiary. Leger was frightened, and had to be talked through the procedure, but Biagi was patient.

'Are they all in? Are they?' Leger mumbled.

Cannon teams guarded the slopes of the hive gate below. Gaunt had already checked in Criid's platoon, Rawne's and Obel's. 'Wait,' he said.

Rolling gunfire was hitting Old Hive's base level precincts. Waves of archenemy units, most of them motorised, stormed in towards the towers at ground level, and the air assault had redoubled.

It was close to dawn.

A string of shot-up carriers rumbled in under the gate, and thundered down the slip road into Old Hive's vast entry halls. As soon as they stopped, they popped their hatches. Domor's platoon scrambled out. The Beati and Milo were with them.

'Sabbat,' said Gaunt, bowing. 'We were fearful for your life.'

'I'm sorry for that, Ibram. But I'm here now. Your Ghosts have kept me safe.'

'Gaunt?' Biagi yelled from the walkway above. 'Now?'

Gaunt paused and consulted his data-slate. They were all inside Old Hive now, all the surviving Regiment Civitas, the PDF and life company. All that could be expected anyway.

On his own list, the Tanith list, one unit was missing. Sergeant Skerral's, number nineteen, last seen in a firefight with the death brigades on Neshion Street.

'Sir?' Corbec gazed at Gaunt. 'I think we have to draw the line now.'

Gaunt nodded.

'Seal the gates!' Biagi yelled. Leger placed his hand on the gene-reader plate and declared his authority. The massive blast shutters of the Old Hive gates clanged into place.

NINETEENTH PLATOON WERE about five hundred metres from Old Hive's north entrance when they saw the gates close.

Skerral stopped in his tracks, and pulled the men up. Half his unit were dead. He ejected a cell from his lasrifle and slammed in a new one.

'Come on,' he said, turning back to face down the slope at the waves of assault sweeping in. 'Let's see how many we can kill.'

The remnants of nineteenth lasted seventeen minutes from the time the gates closed. They accounted for one hundred and eighty-nine enemy casualties. No one witnessed their heroism.

OLD HIVE, AS massive as it was, throbbed under the attack hailing at it from outside. Many upper levels were on fire. The massed forces of the Magister slammed against the outer walls again and again.

Word came through that hive tower two had been taken. Innokenti himself was there, receiving civilian sacrifices.

The main gates of Old Hive fell at mid morning. The death brigades flowed in, fighting street by street and compartment by compartment to overrun the tower.

* * *

GAUNT WALKED DOWN the staircase into the Holy Balneary in the base of Old Hive. The thousands of electrocandles flickered and twinkled. Most of the notables were already assembled below at the poolside. Lugo, Biagi, Leger, Kilosh and the ayatanis, Kaldenbach, the chief astropaths, the senior ecclesiarchs.

The service had been the Beati's idea. A final blessing for her loyal forces before the end came.

Gaunt felt resigned to it all. They were just hours from death now. Ferocious hive fighting tore through the outer levels of the tower. Parts of the external superstructure were beginning to collapse under intense bombardment.

Even so, he'd allowed just a bare minimum of Ghosts to attend. Fighting the enemy took priority over any sacred blessing. The only Ghosts who he had permitted to accompany him marched in a double file down the steps behind him. The Tanith flame troopers. They carried their tanks and hoses proudly. Biagi had personally requested their attendance. He wanted to honour them, and recognise the vital role they'd played, despite the ancient Civitas laws.

Gaunt ushered them onto the poolside, and they formed up in neat ranks. Some of the city officiaries and life company officers regarded the dirty flame-troopers with disdain.

'Ignore them,' Gaunt said.

The Beati, encased in her golden armour, stood thigh deep in the pool, proclaiming the devotional of Kiodrus. Milo waited nearby, with the temple adepts, at the top of the bath steps. Sabbat's voice echoed through the warm, damp air. She praised the forces that had drawn about her on Herodor, and mentioned the officers and unit commanders by name. Seventy per cent of the names she spoke were the names of dead men.

Gaunt, standing to attention with his troopers, started to blank out her words. The air was warm, and he was filled with a sense of mortality. This was all just fine talk. Battle awaited them, above in the hive, and it would be their last. Gaunt found his attention drifting to a pulse of bubbles that rippled the water at the far end of the balneary pool from Sabbat. Some kind of vent.

More bubbles. Bigger, more violent. 'Beati–' Gaunt began, breaking rank to step forward.

Karess erupted from the balneary pool.

His hull was rank and filthy from his passage through the deep places under the Civitas. His weapon limbs swung up and started to fire. A heavy bolter cannon and a plasma gun.

Horrified panic seized the congregation in the Holy Balneary. Priests and soldiers scattered in all directions, some slipping on the wet stone. No one quite believed a Chaos dreadnought could suddenly reveal itself like this.

Karess strode forward through the swirling water of the pool, weapon-limbs firing, broadcasting obscenities. Basalt chips spattered out of the pool side. Bolter rounds slaughtered five temple adepts and three life company officers. Kilosh was incinerated by a plasma beam. Kaldenbach fell over, blood pouring from a gut-wound.

Karess advanced onto the pool steps, emerging more fully from the water. He traversed his hull to target the left side of the bathhouse. His heavy bolter slammed and roared and the side wall was plastered with blood and exploded tissue. First Officiary Leger and the civitas master astropath both ceased to exist in that salvo. Sabbat stumbled up the pool steps and Milo started to drag her towards the cover of one of the balneary's massive stone columns.

Biagi ran to help him, firing his service pistol into the pool. A bolt round hit him in the chest and threw his ruptured corpse back across the chamber, knocking several people over as they tried to flee.

One of them was Lord General Lugo.

Shrieking, Lugo tore himself clear of the fallen bodies and rose. The killing machine was now nearly at the top of the pool steps, setting its first massive claw-foot on the poolside proper. Milo had got the Beati behind a pillar and just about everybody else still alive in the room was in cover. Karess's sensor augmetics dialled and clicked as it swung its bulk around, hunting for targets.

Hunting for *the* target.

It saw Lugo, eyes wild in terror as he staggered backwards. Karess emitted another stream of strangled obscenity and aimed his bolter.

It didn't fire. A blow had rocked it. Spitting filth, it swung its massive iron torso round to locate the source and felt another strike at its flank.

Gaunt drew back the power blade of Heironymo Sondar and struck again. The war machine was monumental and vastly powerful, but it was slow and cumbersome. It fired, but Gaunt was behind it, splashing through the shallow water at the top of the steps. He lashed out with the sword again and split a deep gash right through Karess's rear hull casing.

Karess uttered an electronic squeal, and rocked around with a grinding clank of gears. The edge of his plasma cannon smashed into Gaunt and hurled him back into the pool.

The dreadnought turned back, screaming blasphemies, and located the pillar where the Beati was sheltering.

Clutching his terrible belly wound, Kaldenbach struggled to his knees. He was only a few metres from the killer. Gasping with pain, he pulled a stick grenade and rolled it across the flagstones. It came to rest between Karess's massive foot-claws.

The blast blew the upper part of the pool steps into fragments. It barely damaged Karess, but it pitched him off his feet. The brute machine crashed backwards into the pool, sheeting water up into the air.

Ghosts ran forward from cover to drag Gaunt up onto the pool's edge. Coughing, Gaunt gazed back at the seething frenzy of water where the infuriated Karess was attempting to right himself.

'Brostin! Lubba!' Gaunt spluttered. 'Boil the bastard!'

Five Tanith flame-troops ran to the edge of the pool and hosed the water with liquid fire. In the enclosed stone chamber, the heat was immense. Steam gouted up. They continued to hose… Brostin, Lubba, Dremmond, Lyse, Neskon… churning the water into a scalding, bubbling froth.

Karess's armoured hull was proof against just about anything, but Gaunt's sword had sliced a hole in it. Boiling water squirted in, into his casing, broiling the living vestige inside. Karess sank, his hull lights dimmed, and went out.

Brostin and his brethren ceased fire and raised their burner-guns. The air was sweltering hot and thick with steam and smoke. Blood coated almost every surface of the ancient chamber.

At terrible cost, the last of the nine had been stopped.

IN HIS CELL, much further up in Old Hive, Agun Soric felt a sudden rush of relief. He lay back on his cot, his heart pounding.

Then he felt something twitch in the pocket of his jacket.

'THERE WERE TIMES,' Sabbat said quietly, 'when I did not think we would get this far.'

He didn't know what to say. She seemed to be speaking as if there was some chance of victory remaining. 'Lugo has a ship,' he said. 'I doubt very much if it will survive an escape run, but he wants you aboard it.'

'Do you?'

Gaunt shook his head. 'I think there are few chances of you surviving this war, my Saint, and Lugo's ship is not one of them. Mkoll has suggested an escape on foot through the rear of the city basin, into the Southern Ramparts. It would be hard, but you and a small force might remain alive out there, hidden.'

'While you keep Innokenti busy with a final stand here?'

'No one else is going to do it. Biagi's dead, Kaldenbach as good as. Lugo's too far gone with fear.'

Gaunt and the Beati sat alone in a debate chamber of the Herodian Officiate, on the ninth level of Old Hive. Despite the monolithic build of the city tower around them, they could feel the vibration of warfare tearing through the lowest districts.

'Ibram?' she smiled. 'Did you suppose I had no purpose to play here?'

'If you have a purpose, Sabbat, it is beyond my grasp. I have never understood why you chose to come to Herodor. You're too valuable – to us and to the archenemy. You could have swept our forces to victory on Morlond. Here, you've trapped yourself, for no gain at all. The only ones you've served by coming here are the forces of Chaos. Your death will boost their morale for years to come.'

'You understand risk, Ibram. Tell me, is it better to risk a little for an easy victory, or everything for a great one?'

Gaunt laughed sadly. 'I can't see the p–'

'If I had gone to Morlond, Ibram, I would indeed have assured a fast victory there. But the Crusade would have been lost. Macaroth has overstretched himself. Innokenti's flank attack now bites deep into the Khan Group. The Warmaster and I would have achieved victory on Morlond, only to see the forces behind us destroyed by counter-attack. We would have been cut off, and exterminated.'

'So you go to the Khan Group instead? Without any significant forces?'

'How important is Herodor, Ibram?'

'Compared to the major Khan worlds, and the main population centres? It's worth is zero.'

'So why is the Magister himself… and such a large portion of his host… bothering with it?'

Gaunt shrugged. 'Because you're here.'

She nodded. 'Innokenti could have won the war outright for Chaos with one merciless thrust up through the Khan flank. We did not have the forces available to stop him. But it occurred to me we could distract him entirely and make him waste vital time on a pointless invasion of a worthless world.'

'You… you used yourself as bait?'

'You said yourself, I'm too valuable. To us and the archenemy. Innokenti could not ignore me.' She reached into her cloak and produced a data-slate. 'This was received via the astropaths a few minutes before we sealed the hive gates. I intended to announce it at the ceremony in the balneary, but we were interrupted.'

Gaunt took the slate and read it. The text had been deciphered from a very high level encryption. In a final, bloody push, Macaroth's forces had taken Morlond. Urlock Gaur was in frantic retreat. It would take time, but Imperial divisions could now be spared to bolster the defences of the Khan Group against Innokenti's attack.

An attack that, despite every advantage, had stalled at Herodor.

'By the Golden Throne…!' Gaunt sighed, astonished.

'We may yet die here, Ibram. But we will have died in the name of victory.'

'Thanks be to the Emperor,' he said.

She rose to her feet. 'And if I am to perish here, I would like to make it count for as much as possible. Milo?'

Milo had been waiting in the chamber's anteroom. He hurried in and bowed to her before saluting Gaunt.

'The time has come,' she said. 'My message?'

'I took it to tac logis command. They have it loaded into the Civitas public address system. Just say the word.'

'Now, Milo.'

He adjusted his micro-bead and sent a quick voice command.

THE PICT MESSAGE was brief. She had recorded it straight to camera, speaking quickly and clearly. Every operational public address screen, comm monitor and view plate in the Civitas broadcast it, and the vocal strand boomed out of all the vox horns and speakers still wired into the city systems. It lasted about fifty seconds. Tac logis set it to a looping repeat. For hours, it could be seen and heard throughout the Civitas Beati, by friend and foe alike.

The broadcast told of the great victory at Morlond. It defiantly declared that Innokenti's murderous gamble had failed. It dared him to flee before the wrath of the God-Emperor overtook him for the brutalities he had heaped upon Herodor. The final words were as follows:

'All living souls of men still in this city, all people of the Civitas left alive, know this. With overwhelming forces, the monster Innokenti has crushed us physically, but he cannot crush our spirit. Our sacrifice has ensured great victory. Do not die in fear and hiding. Make the price of your lives dear. The Emperor of Mankind has room for all in his Imperial army.'

THEY CAME FROM the agridomes at first. The archenemy's ground assault had ignored the western agri-sectors in its efforts to concentrate on the main hives. Blood Pact field observers on the invader's western flank suddenly saw figures pouring from the agridomes in their thousands.

Children of the Beati. The pilgrim mass.

Despite the losses they had suffered in the short but fero-cious war so far, they still numbered in their hundreds of thousands. The giant agridomes had offered them shelter when the city started to fall. They were men and women who had come to Herodor without really knowing why, except that the Beati had called them.

And now she called them again, directly, through the broadcast.

Some had captured enemy weapons, or PDF ordnance, some had horticultural implements or broken pipes or staves of wood. Some had nothing but their own bare hands.

Thousands of them died, miserably outclassed by the weapons and equipment of the enemy host. But they did not falter for a moment.

An hour after they first appeared to unleash their holy rage into the Magister's legions, similar tides began to flow from hive tower one and hive tower three, and from public shelters and basements through the Guild Slope and the low town.

The Civitas Beati, crushed almost to death by Enok Inno-kenti, turned like a mortally wounded animal in a trap and bit out at the hunter.

AGUN SORIC HAMMERED his fists against the door of his cell. His hands were bloody and swollen from his efforts, and left smears of blood on the steel.

'Please!' he yelled. 'Please! You have to let me out! I need to warn her! I need to warn her!'

No one answered. At this late hour, with the city falling, there was in truth no one left on duty in the detention block to hear him anyway.

He screamed and hammered again, tears coursing down his craggy face.

The open shell case, and its fold of blue paper, lay on the cot behind him.

FOURTEEN
SABBAT MARTYR

'Know him for what he truly is. A killer.'

— message written in Soric's hand

FOR THE FIRST hour or so of the fight, Anton Alphant had used a pistol looted from an enemy corpse, but then they'd found a PDF carrier abandoned at the side of one of the approach streets to hive tower one, and they'd recovered half a dozen lasrifles from it.

It had a wire stock instead of the pressed metal one he'd been used to in his Guard days, but apart from that it was shockingly familiar.

Night, wild with firestorms and a monumental roar of war, had engulfed the Civitas, and Alphant found himself caught up in the bloodiest fighting he had ever known, his former days of soldiering included. He did his best to try and make sense of the street combat, and to guide the pilgrim forces with him through.

There was no formal structure to the pilgrim army. It was essentially a gigantic mob. But the Beati had come to them in the agridomes, drawing men like Alphant out of the crowd, and telling the pilgrims to look to them for leadership. Most already did. Sabbat had unerringly picked on those people who had some military background, or on men or women who had already become the natural leaders of pilgrim bands.

They had no plan as such... except to throw themselves against the enemy. Alphant tried to rally his part of the zealot tide towards Old Hive, where the Beati was said to be under siege.

Her life was all that mattered.

ETRODAI HAD NEVER known Him so deranged by rage. The Magister's fury was so great that Etrodai even feared for his own life. Howling, a blinding sphere of crackling corposant around Him, Enok Innokenti drove the Retinue and three of the Blood Pact's veteran death-brigades into the bowels of Old Hive, through hallways and gallery levels shattered by fighting and littered with the bodies of the slain.

Hatchway by hatchway, hall by hall, they ground into the failing defences of the tower city. At the forefront, Etrodai swept his changeling blade through PDF troopers, Imperial Guardsmen and frantic civilian fighters.

Over a hundred thousand Blood Pact soldiers, along with armoured vehicles, were now inside Old Hive, spreading like wildfire through the lower levels. Hundreds of thousands more massed outside in the ruins of the high town as the city burned behind them.

There were reports of counter attacks to the flank, but Etrodai was sure they couldn't be right. There were no other Imperial forces here on Herodor to stage such attacks.

The saint's defiant broadcast had driven the Magister to His pitch of rage. He wanted her. He would kill her Himself.

Her life was all that mattered.

JUST BEFORE MIDNIGHT, a death brigade managed to mine two central power generators in the sub-ground levels of Old Hive, mainly in an effort to shut off the continued broadcasts of the saint's message, which so maddened their master. The blast tore out two hive levels, and caused a great internal collapse that killed thousands. Power was cut on eighteen city levels above. Where the slaughter raged in the lower levels, the halls and hive thoroughfares became like infernal caves, lit only by flames and the flash of weapons fire. Fires burned out of control with the suppression systems cut, and smoke collected in the uncirculating airspaces.

Innokenti and his vanguard swept through it all, lit by the glittering fires of his psyker malice and by the lethal ribbons of energy that were his blood-rage made manifest. The invaders surged in behind them.

IN THE CELL block high above, darkness fell. Soric, hoarse and exhausted, waited for the secondary systems to kick in, but none did.

He wedged his hands against the cell door and started to pull at it. If the power had comprehensively failed, then the mag-locks would have failed too.

The door refused to budge. He tried again, snorting with effort, and at last the steel plate began to slide back in its groove. Soric pulled until he could get his bloodied fingers into the gap and grab more purchase.

He slid the cell door open and staggered out. The cell dock was dark. Stumbling and groping, he made his way out and down into an assembly yard. The main gates of the detention unit were open. Outside, the hive thoroughfare was pitch black and abandoned. He felt a rumbling from below, distant. The air was stale and smelled of smoke. Through the big riser vents in the thoroughfare he could hear noises echoing upwards through the vast structure of the hive.

Sounds of carnage and destruction, sounds of death.

Soric limped down the empty hallway in search of a stairwell.

THE MAGISTER'S ARRIVAL on the Great Concourse, a vast public space on the ninth level of Old Hive, was announced by the stalk-tanks that came blasting up the three great ashlar staircases that ascended from the transit terminals and ornamental gardens below. Such was the scale of the staircases, the war machines were able to climb five or six abreast, with Retinue and Blood Pact troopers rushing on foot in their wake, firing up at the Imperials dug in around the ornate basalt rails of the concourse level. The vast space was three hive levels deep, and the massive glass pendant lights that hung from the arched roof had been dark since the power failure. Great windows thirty metres high overlooked the staircases and lit the concourse with the glow of the burning city outside.

Major Udol, now ranking commander of the planetary forces, had assembled the last of his armour on the concourse, and their guns met the stalk-tanks as they came up from the steps. Shell blasts tore across the pavements, hurling stone slabs and men into the air. Pulse-lasers spat their pumping streams through the hellish gloom, ripping open the fronts of the buildings lining the concourse and shattering the huge obsidian sculptures that hung down from the roof. Glass images of the aquila and other Imperial crests crashed down in avalanches of glass shards, exploding into fragments like falling ice.

The Magister's forces surged up onto the concourse.

Gaunt had drawn up half the Tanith regiment and the last of the life company behind the armour for this stand. All remaining forces were occupied on other levels, meeting other invasions, but this, Gaunt knew, was the key.

She had told him so. She had felt the wrath of Innokenti approaching.

Udol's armour rolled back slowly across the pavements, crunching over the vast heaps of broken glass, firing as it went. They took heavy losses, but not a single stalk-tank made it more than twenty metres from the head of the steps. Udol's gentle retreat was designed to lure a good portion of enemy infantry up onto the concourse, where there was no cover.

'In the Emperor's name... now!' Gaunt signalled, and his infantry strength emerged from around the sides of the huge public space, firing as it came. The first fifty seconds were a blistering massacre. The concourse lit up as bright as day with the las-weapon discharge. Hundreds of Blood Pact and Retinue troopers were cut down or blown apart. Then the archenemy rallied, and the firefight began in earnest. Still the Imperials punished them.

'Hold the line! Hold cover!' Gaunt ordered. His men had the full advantage of the buildings on either side of the pavements, and the still advancing enemy had nothing but open space.

Gaunt saw a ripple of light at the top of the steps. Unearthly, malevolent light, crackling like lightning. In horror, he realised that the Beati and the life company had broken cover formation and were charging onto the concourse towards it. The Beati herself was lit up in a halo of green fire.

Alone, despite that great power suffusing her, she would die.

'Ghosts of Tanith!' he yelled, raising his sword. 'Charge!'

Only on Balhaut, in that hell of war, had Gaunt known pitched fighting on such a great scale. Like seas clashing, the waves of soldiers tore into one another, stabbing and firing. Flamers roared. The force of the clash made the ancient concourse shake. Gaunt ran with his men, laspistol blasting in his left hand, power sword scything in his right. Within seconds, he had been hit twice, glancing shots to his body, and a half dozen tears had ripped through his clothes. The sword of Heironymo Sondar bit through Blood Pact veterans who lunged at him with fixed bayonets, and hacked open the dark blue armour of the Magister's elite troopers, savage brutes with bulbous insectoid goggles.

He tried to find the Saint. His face was wet with blood and his breath was rancid in his throat. The din around him was so immense he was deafened. Every second, every part of a second, he was striking and moving, dodging, stabbing, caught up at the heart of a combat melee so feral it seemed to be an echo from the barbaric wars of the past.

He saw Rawne and Caffran for a moment, blasting into the enemy as they ran forward. Feygor, kneeling over a fallen Ghost and firing on auto. Varl, Criid, Obel, Domor, Meryn, their men around them as they charged into the enemy mass. He saw Daur shoot a Blood Pact officer through the head. He saw Brostin spraying flamer-fire into a collapsing pack of Retinue troops. He saw straight silver and blood and courage.

He saw men he'd known for almost seven years fight and die.

The men and women of Verghast, true Ghosts all, stalwart and brave.

The men of Tanith, staunchest warriors he'd ever known, who so surely deserved to live forever.

Gaunt knew war was fickle, and seldom let a warrior choose his place of death. But this, this was enough. As good, as worthy, as honorable, as any he could have chosen.

The flare of unholy radiance was close to him, and he hacked through closing ranks of Retinue soldiers to reach it. His pistol had gone. Only the charged blade of his sword remained. A las-round creased his cheek but he ignored the burning pain and took the head off a member of the Retinue, leaping forward into the lightning.

Surrounded by the heaped dead, Innokenti stood before him. The Magister, more vile and wretched than anything Gaunt could have imagined, was locked sword to sword with the Beati.

Every blow they exchanged, every strike, crashed like thunder. Sparks flew. Shockwaves from the meeting blades threw men around them – friend and foe alike – off their feet. Hideous corposant writhed and seared around the Magister. Cold green fire, in the form of a great eagle with its wings unfurled, lit up the Saint.

Gaunt charged forward, his boots slipping on the blood-wet stone.

A daemon sprang at him, blocking his path. The beast was huge. It was cased in the blue-black armour of the Retinue, but its head was bare, the pink flesh grievously marked with ritual scars. Its mouth and nose were hidden behind an augmetic grille and its eyes were glowing yellow slits. It wielded a ghastly sword of serrated bone which grew out of its right fist. The flesh of that fist had peeled back, exposing grey finger bones that were fused into the long blade. It swung at Gaunt.

Blood saved him. His boot slipped and he fell. The bone-blade whistled over his head and Gaunt rolled before it could slice back. He jumped to his feet and parried the daemon's sword as it came at him, and then drove hard with a thrust that the beast turned aside.

They circled amid the whirling carnage, trading blows with all their strength. Gaunt could no longer see the Beati.

Only a greenish light in the air suggested she was still alive. Desperately, Gaunt lunged, but the daemon hooked the strike away, countering with a thrust that juddered Gaunt's power sword down.

His guard was open. The bone-blade came at his throat.

A las-round smacked into the side of the daemon's neck, and a second ripped open its shoulder guard. It stumbled away from Gaunt, turning.

Brin Milo charged forward, power-cell spent, and rammed his straight silver up to the hilt in the daemon's chest.

Eaten by the beast's acid blood, the blade snapped off. Milo staggered back. With a wordless scream, Gaunt swung around and put his power blade clean through the thing's neck.

Etrodai, life-ward of the Magister, fell dead, his changeling blade crumbling to dust.

Gaunt and Milo turned and ran towards the Beati. Living fire was sizzling around her, and pouring like burning oil out across the pavements of the concourse.

The fire was pouring from the disembowelled corpse of Enok Innokenti.

'Holy Terra…' Gaunt stammered.

Sabbat rose, the sightless, gaping head of the Magister dangling from her raised fist.

'In the name of the Emperor!' she yelled. The luminous aquila around her flared to three times its size, snapping and beating at the high roof.

The sound of her voice was so clear, so loud, it blew out the great windows of the concourse in a vast blizzard of glass.

To a man, every archenemy warrior on Herodor shrieked.

WHERE HE HAD been hard-pressed just a minute before, Corbec now found himself facing an empty hallway. Weary and nervous, he edged his forces forward, clearing through to the western gate of the hive.

Something had most definitely happened. The enemy forces had been all over them and now they were in flight.

'Rerval? What's the story, son?'

Rerval shook his head. A huge and devastating rush of psyk-noise had just burned out all the comm channels and fused every vox-set in the hive area.

'Could be a trick,' said Mkvenner.

Corbec nodded. 'Hold it here. The fethers don't give up that easily. We've got a breathing space at least.'

Mkvenner nodded. He rounded up the Ghosts and PDF in the immediate area and put them to work building barricades with the debris in the hall.

Haller ran up as the work began.

'Something's going on,' he told Corbec. 'Got no vox, but word of mouth says the enemy is falling back all over.'

Corbec scratched his head. 'Damned if I know what this is about.'

'Colm?'

Corbec looked round. Mkoll was approaching now. Some of his squad came up behind, battered and bleeding like the rest of them, escorting a figure.

It was Soric.

'He… he demands to talk to you,' said Mkoll.

'Agun's never had to ask for my ear in his life, Mkoll. He won't start now either.'

Corbec walked over to Soric. The old Verghastite was shaking and exhausted.

'You have to warn Gaunt.'

'Warn him?'

'It's not over.'

'I'll not argue with you, Agun. Something fishy's going on but I d–'

'No, Colm!' Soric pulled a brass message shell out of his pocket and opened it. 'The nine. The nine are not finished. The psykers–'

Corbec smiled. 'I killed the psykers, Agun. Pater Sin and his two freaks. I sent them to hell.'

Soric swallowed. 'I know you did. It told me.'

'What did?'

'Doesn't matter. Colm, they'd already imprinted their task. That's what they were for. Not to kill the Beati like the others, but to choose and direct a killer who would do it for them. Someone close to her. And he's still out there.'

Corbec's eyes widened. 'Feth… What? Who?'

'It showed me everything, Colm. It showed me what he was,' he said, holding out the ragged sheet of blue paper for Corbec to see.

MILO PUT HIS arm around the Beati's shoulders and led her across the concourse. She was shaking with exhaustion, and deep slashes from Innokenti's blade were bleeding freely.

'Medic! Medic here!' he called.

The enemy had gone, in rapid retreat, their morale broken as much by the death of their overlord as by the victory of the Beati. Even now, the fleeing enemy forces were engaging with the pilgrim army in the high town as they tried to break off.

It was not over. Indeed, the fight for Herodor was a long way from done. But for now, the looming defeat was postponed.

The ruined concourse, adrift with smoke and crackling fires, was littered with the dead of both sides. Men picked their way through the rubble, looking for the wounded, for fallen comrades. Where they found the enemy alive, they were merciless.

Dorden led a gaggle of medic teams out into the battlefield.

'Here!' Milo called, and Dorden came running over.

Gaunt and other officers stood warily by as Dorden treated the Beati's wounds. 'Can we get vox?' he asked Beltayn.

'It's all out, sir. The death scream of the enemy leader fried every circuit.'

Gaunt turned to the men around him. 'We've done a great thing this day. We've pulled back from a brink I was sure we would topple over. We have struck a great blow at the arch-enemy of mankind. Gather your units, see to the wounded, and spread this word, by mouth, to all you meet. The Beati is triumphant. Innokenti is dead. Make sure everyone knows it. Make sure every last damn citizen in the hives knows it.'

The officers nodded and spread out.

'I need to get her to an infirmary where there's power,' Dorden said. 'And I'll need a stretcher…'

'I can walk,' said Sabbat, rising.

'Then we'll walk with you,' said Gaunt. 'Honour guard, here!'

Milo stepped up, as well as Daur and Derin. Nessa also took a step forward. Gaunt nodded.

Larkin, sat wearily against a wall nearby, got to his feet.

'Me too, sir,' he said.

Gaunt looked at him. 'Any special reason, Larks?'

Larkin gestured at the Ghosts around the Beati. 'They were the honour guard. On Hagia. The ones she called.'

Gaunt looked and realised the old sniper was right. Dorden, Daur, Nessa, Milo and Derin had all been part of Corbec's inspired mission on the Shrineworld. Apart from Corbec himself, the only ones missing were the ones no longer alive. Greer, Vamberfeld and Bragg.

'Try would've wanted me to fill in for him,' Larkin said. 'It mattered to him. She mattered. I… I can see why now.'

'Carry on,' said Gaunt.

USING LAMP PACKS to light their way, and moving slowly, the escort left the Great Concourse and headed down the connective hallways towards the main stairwell. They walked through abandoned hive streets littered by warfare and looting. Terrified and stunned civilians huddled in the ruins and watched them pass by, bowing at the sight of the Saint.

Edgy, Gaunt walked with them, desperate for the vox to come back so he could get a picture of the situation. He'd have to trust Rawne and Udol to get things solid without him.

They were clearing another hallway, close to the access shafts, when Gaunt saw a flash of torchlight and heard a voice calling his name.

Panting hard, Corbec ran up, followed by Soric.

'What's he doing here?' Gaunt asked.

'His duty,' said Corbec. 'There's a killer out there still. One of the nine.'

'What?'

'The psyker's imprinted someone,' Corbec said. 'Someone suitable.' He held out the rag of blue paper to Gaunt.

'Get her in cover!' Gaunt yelled and raised his lamp to read the scrap as Dorden and the honour guard hurried the Beati towards shelter. Nessa and Larkin immediately raised their long-lases and started to scan for trouble through their scopes.

'No…' Gaunt said, reading the name on the paper. He swung round. 'Milo! Get h–'

A las-shot seared out of the darkness around them and hit the wall centimetres from the Beati's head.

Everyone dropped. Another two shots zapped at them. One hit Derin in the shoulder and threw him off his feet.

'I can't see him!' Larkin moaned, training his weapon.

Two more shots whined in. Nessa tried a return, and banged a hot-shot into the darkness. The killer's reply, a semi-auto flurry, hit Daur in the hip and slammed Dorden over against the wall.

'He's all over us!' Corbec yelled, down in cover beside Gaunt. 'Did you see Soric's note? Did you read what he did?'

Fury boiled through Ibram Gaunt. Soric's talent had not only identified the killer imprinted by Sin's psykers, it had exposed him for all he was. Soric had seen into the hateful mind of a stone killer and revealed all his crimes.

Lijah Cuu. Murderer. Rapist. Killer of Bragg. Killer of Sehra Muril.

Corbec held out his laspistol to Gaunt.

'On three?' he suggested.

Gaunt looked back at the beleaguered escort. Daur and Derin were both writhing in pain. Dorden was lying on the ground and looked like he was dead. Nessa was pumping his chest frantically. Milo and Larkin, weapons raised, were shielding the Beati with their bodies.

'Get ready to move her!' Gaunt yelled.

He and Corbec leapt up and charged, firing into the dark. The laspistol cracked in Gaunt's hand, spitting bars of light into the shadows. Corbec was beside him, spraying auto-fire from his lasrifle.

A flurry of shots burned back at them.

Gaunt leapt over a scatter of fallen wall stones and darted along the far wall. He fired into the shadows. 'Cuu! Cuu, you bastard! I will have you!'

A las-round hit Gaunt in the back and threw him hard onto his face. He felt the hot rush of blood leaking out of him. He tried to turn.

'You first, sure as sure, then the bitch Beati,' Cuu said, kneeling on Gaunt's back and making him yell with pain. 'I'll kill you all.'

The straight silver came down to Gaunt's throat.

The hot-shot was so loud the noise of it rolled up and back down the hallway. Gaunt felt Cuu's deadweight slam down across him. He struggled out from under Cuu's body. Larkin bent down and dragged him up.

Gaunt swayed. The wound in his back was agonising. He gazed down at Cuu's ruined corpse.

'Never did like him,' Larkin said.

'He killed Bragg.'

'I know, sir,' Larkin said.

'Good shot. In the dark like that.'

'I just fething wish I could have got a bead on him sooner,' said Larkin. His voice was low, as if strained by massive emotion.

'What do you mean?' Gaunt asked. He stirred up and looked back down the hall. Pain flared through his back, but what he saw hurt him so much more.

Twenty metres back down the hall, face down in a pool of blood, Colm Corbec lay dead.

EPILOGUE

THE BATTLE FOR Herodor lasted another six weeks. The vast
invasion force fell back after Innokenti's death, harried and
harassed by the militant pilgrim army. Two days later,
renewed and using its strengths to the full, it re-assaulted the
Civitas. Thousands of pilgrims perished in the resistance. The
Beati, limping from her wounds, led the counter push with
the remnants of the Imperial strength – Ghosts, Regiment
Civitas, PDF and the pilgrim host – and kept the massive
force at bay for a week.

Then the reinforcement fleet arrived, sent by the Warmaster. The initial fleet engagement lit up the night sky. A far
greater and more bloody combat than is recorded in this
account then took place. Over a period of weeks, the Magister's forces were driven out of the Civitas, and extinguished in
a final pitched land battle in the Stove Hills.

The Tanith Ghosts played no part in that.

NOR DID THEY play a part in the overall victory. Freed from
their obligations at Morlond and the front, large segments of
the Crusade force were loosed to defend the Khan flank. The

details of those actions is recorded in other works. It is sufficient to point out that had the Magister's warhost not been so detained with the business of Herodor, the entire Khan Group would most likely have fallen, and the Crusade efforts been lost.

The Beati's efforts had been emphatic. She had forced the flank attack to be stillborn, and furthermore she had killed one of Gaur's most senior lieutenants. The message sent to the enemy was devastating. As the Archon's forces tumbled back into the edge systems of the Sabbat Worlds, Macaroth prepared for the final, triumphant era of the Crusade.

As history records, it would not be easy. But for the while, the advantage was entirely his.

GAUNT TURNED HIS face away from the stinging dust as the lander came in. It settled on the roofpad of Old Hive, and the thrusters died.

He turned to face the Beati and knelt. She lifted him up again with both hands.

'Not to me,' she said. 'I should kneel to you.'

'Do you know where they're sending you?' Gaunt asked.

'The front line. Carcaradon. To Macaroth's side… as Lugo kept advising.'

Gaunt smiled. 'You knew better.'

'Now, he's right. I will not forget the service of the Ghosts, Ibram.'

'Just do me a favour and look after him.'

She smiled and nodded. 'His destiny awaits us, Ibram Gaunt. It is more than you could possibly imagine.'

She kissed Gaunt's forehead and walked away towards the open ramp of the lander. Gaunt looked at Milo. He seemed happy and terrified, all at once. He ran over to Gaunt as if to hug him and then, at the last minute, stopped and threw a hard salute.

Gaunt returned the salute. Then he drew his warknife and handed it to Milo.

'You lost yours. Take mine with you now.'

Milo looked at the straight silver in his hands for a moment and then ran to join Sabbat. The lander's ramp closed, and it lifted away into the colourless sky on a roar of jets.

'Goodbye, Brin,' Gaunt said, certain he would never see the boy again.

THE SHUTTLE FROM the black ship was waiting. Ominous men in long dark robes paced about the platform. He could smell the ozone stink of power-goads. His hands shook in their cuffs.

A black-robed figure strode down the landing ramp, glanced at a data-slate offered by a servitor, and walked towards him.

'Name?'

'Agun S–'

A power-goad lashed him into silence.

'His name is Agun Soric,' said the man standing beside him.

'Evaluation?'

'Psyker, level beta.'

The black robed figure nodded. 'Sign the release, please.'

Viktor Hark took hold of the data-slate with his newly implanted augmetic limb and studied it. He put his signature on the plate with the stylus and handed the slate back to the inquisitor.

'Where are you taking him?' Hark asked.

'Where he belongs. It's no concern of yours,' said the robed inquisitor. 'Advance him!' he yelled, and the handlers goaded the shackled Soric up the ramp.

Hark could hear Soric sobbing. He turned away, shutting it out.

A brass message shell sat on the deck grille at his feet. Hark leaned down and picked it up in his augmetic hand. He opened it and knocked out the paper.

Two words were written on the blue scrap.

Help me

Hark turned back and watched as the shuttle lifted off and swung up and away into the sky.

THE SAW WAS shrilling. The lovely whine of good wood splitting. The air was thick with aromatic dust.

Colm Corbec walked into the little woodshop off Guild Slope and watched for a while as the old man – what was his name again... Wyze? – worked the wood. Business had been brisk. Feth, yes! Coffins for the departed. God-Emperor, that was supply and demand!

Corbec stepped into the pungent, dry air of the woodshop, and ran his hand down a length of mature timber. Not nalwood, but good.

This Wyze. He was all on his own, without any assistance. Not the way Corbec's father would have run it. He needed a hand.

Corbec rolled up his sleeves. He knew this work. He liked it. He'd stay awhile and help out.

'No OTHER WOOD will do. You understand?'

'Yes, Mister Gaunt,' said Guffrey Wyze.

'That's Colonel-commissar–' Gaunt began and then shook his head. 'Nalwood. All of it.'

'It's your money, sir. Friend of yours, was it?'

'Friend. Brother. Ghost,' said Gaunt.

Wyze smiled. 'Plenty of them hereabouts.'

ABOUT THE AUTHOR

Dan Abnett lives and works in Maidstone, Kent, in England. Well known for his comics work, he has written everything from Mr Men to the X-Men in the last decade, and currently scripts *Legion of Superheroes* for DC Comics and *Sinister Dexter* and *Durham Red* for 2000 AD.

His work for the Black Library includes the popular strips *Lone Wolves* and *Darkblade*, the best-selling Gaunt's Ghosts novels, the acclaimed Inquisitor Eisenhorn trilogy and his fantasy novel *Riders of the Dead*.